Kia Lui Media, LLC

LOVE'S AWAKENING

A BILLIONAIRES OF MISSOURI ROMANCE

And Beyond

KIA LUI

This is a work of fiction. Names, characters, places, and incidents either are the product of the author's imagination or are used factiously. Any resemblance to actual persons, living or dead, events, or locales is entirely coincidental.

 Love's Awakening – Evolving
Copyright © 2023, Kia Lui
Self-published by Kia Lui Media, LLC
(cskialuimedia@outlook.com)

All rights reserved. No part of this publication may be reproduced, stored in a retrieval system, stored in a database and / or published in any form or by any means, electronic, mechanical, photocopying, recording or otherwise, without the prior written permission of the publisher.

ISBN: 978-1-73-331982-9
Cover design by Kia Lui
Cover images by Kia Lui
www.kialuimedia.com
Printed in the United States of America

-1-

Zion still can't believe the direction his life has taken in such a short time. Six months ago, he was single. Traveling. Partying. Living life as only a billionaire can. Everything and anything he wanted was at his fingertips. Then he met Lea Adams. Every thought of her, every mention of her name, makes him smile and giggle like a teenager. She's awakened so much in him he never knew existed. His life expectations have changed from finding a woman he could tolerate as a wife and wouldn't take him for every dime he's made, to planning a future with the love of his life. And becoming parents. Zion is going to be a father.

Fucking me a father. Yes, Lord thank you for all my blessings! With Lea as my partner, my world is fantastic.

Accepting this chance to be a father was like any other business opportunity that presented itself. Quickly work out the pros and cons, negotiate and either fully accept or reject.

It's time he ensures Lea understands she's included.

After his eye-opening lunch with Tom telling him Lea has her doubts about her place in his life, Zion rushes to her. He hasn't seen his kitten all week and his mind and body are calling for her. Calming and exciting him as only she can.

Arriving at her house, he sees her car is parked on the street.

Odd. Why is she parking on the street and not in the driveway?

Hearing a car, Lea looks out the window and see's Zion. Taking a deep breath to calm her nerves, she positions herself lying in the bed with her feet propped on the wall.

Zion uses his key to let himself in. Walking to her dining room table, he notices her computer is on and unlocked, displaying her company and personal email accounts. Both screens show her unopened emails side by side. He takes a sip of the wine from the glass sitting next to the empty wine bottle. He walks to the bedroom pausing in the doorway. The sight of her in one of his dress shirts arouses him knowing she's naked underneath. There's a soft glow coming from a diffuser lighting the room and emitting the scent of his cologne in the mist. Lea doesn't move but speaks over the music playing softly in the background.

"Hello, Bear."

He walks over to the bed, climbs in, and lays next to her, propped up on his elbow. "Hello, Kitten." He kisses her forehead, her temple, her cheek, and on the lips. "How was your week?" he asks her, hoping she'll open up to him. He caresses her temple, playing with the curls in her hair, watching them spring back into place after he pulls on one.

"Stressful," she whispers.

"Talk to me."

She frowns, "What's my role in your future with the boys?"

Hold it together, Lea. You can calmly discuss this without getting emotional.

"I've screwed up. I haven't made it clear you were going to adopt them and be their mother. I'm sorry about that. The second I said yes to Wendy, all I could think about is I was giving you a family, our family, and that we are going to be married and happy. Together."

"No, you never. You haven't even asked me. It was all about you and the boys."

"Lea, you're a part of this. Of my future."

"If that's true—."

"No ifs about it."

"As I was saying, if that's true, I need you to make me a promise. Well, three promises."

"Tell me."

"Promise me you won't marry Wendy, you'll never live with her, and you won't hide me from her."

"Lea, babe." Before Zion can say anymore, she cuts him off.

"No, don't 'Lea babe' me," she snaps. She takes a deep breath and blows it out. "Zion, I've accepted and done everything you've asked of me regarding Addison. We rarely go out in public. Few of my friends even know about you. Us. I am and will continue to support you during this adoption process. I'm ecstatic you're being given the opportunity to become a father. I wouldn't do anything to keep this from happening, but I need some things from you if we are to continue."

"What promises do you want?" *I can't deny her anything right now.*

"Promise you won't marry her. Promise you won't move in with her, and promise you won't hide me or us from her if we're to stay together. If I can't get that, we can go back to being business associates and friends, and as your friend, I'll continue to support you. But I'll have someone else work with you on your contract."

"Wait, what the fuck you mean, if we're to stay together? Lea."

"I don't know your plans."

"My plans are us, you and I, together. Period. No doubts in that."

"For now," she whispers.

"Not for now. I'm not letting you go and you're not leaving me. Lea, I promise you I won't marry Wendy, I promise you I won't live with Wendy, and I promise you I'll never hide you or deny you as a part of my life. Ever. To anyone, including Wendy. We'll always be more than business associates to each other. And you're not getting off this contract. So, stop with that threat."

"It's not a threat. I can get off it any time I want. If you try and cancel it, I'll sue your ass."

"Dammit woman, we're not going to fight about this contract. It stays as is. You and I will continue our relationship. Business and personal. It's time we stop hiding from the world. Let's go out to dinner tonight, maybe go to the movies, or listen to a live band. Meet up with Gordon and Lily."

"No, we can't," she states.

"Lea, come on, forget about Addison. She's given up. I don't think I'm ever going to hear from her again," he says, hoping this is true.

"You will. She's. She found me. She knows about us. She. Has. Threatened. Me." Lea says calmly, never even moving from her original position but turning her head away from him, attempting to hide the fear in her voice.

"What?" he sits up in the bed. "Lea, look at me. What's happened? And why is your car parked on the street in front of your house and not in your driveway?"

Her voice breaking, "I didn't wanna be blocked in. In case something happened. Go look at my computer. Work email is open for you to see. Look at my phone, you know the code," she whispers.

"What?"

"Zion. Go look at my computer."

He goes into the dining room and sits down at her computer, looking at her emails. There's a folder titled, 'Stalker Bitch'. There are over twenty-five hateful, threatening emails. All escalating in anger. There are pictures of Lea and him leaving his birthday party with Lea's face x'ed out. Zion looks at her phone. She has twenty text messages, telling her to get out of Zion's life, or she'll regret it.

He forwards the emails to Saul to let him know what's going on. Zion looks at her phone and notes the number the messages are coming from and blocks it. He returns to the bedroom. Lea hasn't moved from her spot.

"I know what you're going to say. You'll be putting a security detail on me. That's fine. Do whatever you need to do. I'll become a hermit. I'm not exiting your life. I love you too much to walk away and end this. If it ends, it'll be because you end it."

Instead of giving him an easy out by suggesting a breakup, Lea says what she can to ensure she stays and to make it clear to him she wants this. All of this.

Lea thinks, *I must be out of my fucking mind sticking around for this bullshit.*

WELL, I KNOW WHAT *A* PART OF YOU IS STICKING AROUND FOR.

Sex Diva, some days I hate it when you be so damn out front honest with me.

YEAH, WELL THAT'S LIFE.

Zion strips and crawls into bed with Lea.

"Kitten, come here."

She rolls over into his arms.

"I'm sorry, Lea, about everything. I'll make and keep any promise you ask of me." He embraces her, kissing and wiping away her tears.

"Lea, Kitten, don't cry."

"You're staying?" she asks, stunned. She figured he would balk at the promises. "You don't wanna leave? To handle things like you first did when you got the emails? Why?"

"I'm not repeating that hell again. It was selfish of me to think you would fall into line without asking you. Kitten, don't let me assume things are okay when they're not. We can only make it through this by communicating.

"I'm not going to walk away and leave you vulnerable and open to my crazy ex. I'm going to protect you as I'm going to protect my family with whatever I have to do or whatever it takes."

"Zion, you gonna have so much to deal with."

"Lea, keep telling me what you want and need. And I have enough people working for me, I can delegate tasks. You. You are my priority."

"I want to tell people about us."

"This won't last much longer. That sounds crude but it's the truth. You'll be able to subtly rub it in people faces like you do when you wanna tell people but not tell people."

"How do you know about me subtly telling people about me?"

"Kitten, I've watched you in action. It's a turn-on. Promise me you won't hide what you're thinking or feeling, Lea."

Lea realizes she has to accept the fact her relationship with Zion will remain private outside of their tight circle of family and friends. She likes and hates it.

"It's back to being the odd woman out if I get to hang out at all. I'll focus on what we have."

She wipes her hand across her eyes. "I promise to try and share with you what I'm thinking and feeling about what's going on without worrying you. How's that?"

"I don't like it. I'll accept it for now with the understanding this is a work-as-you-go process."

Lea lays her head on his chest, trying not to let him know she's crying again.

He feels the wetness. "Oh sweetheart, don't cry."

"Zion, I'm scared."

"Lea, I'm here, and I'll protect you," Zion murmurs into her head.

She caresses his chest hairs slowly, moving down to caress his pelvis and fuzz.

"Why is it you playing with my pubic hairs is soothing? It relaxes me."

"You don't look relaxed. You look up and ready to go. Wide awake," Lea climbs on top of Zion and presses his manhood against her pussy, ensuring she's wet and lubed to slide him in. She strokes him up and down, getting him harder.

"Hmmm, so good," he moans.

Lea needs to please him, to hear him in ecstasy wanting her, feeling her, being pleased by her. She leans over and kisses his neck, licking her tongue out, trailing it around his throat. She licks the skin below his ear lobe gently, and he presses her head into the crook of his neck.

"Oh baby, that feels so good." He brings her lips to his and kisses her deeply.

She breaks the kiss and trails more down his chin and onto his chest flicking her tongue over his nipples and lightly biting them. With each soft bite he lifts his chest pressing it into her face. She goes further down, licking his stomach, moving from side to side biting his waist. She lifts up and he slides inside her.

Every time Zion and Lea make love, that initial slide into her pussy is heaven to him. Home. He never gets tired of it. "God, Lea your pussy swallows my dick so good, shit baby, fuck me."

Lea slowly glides up and down on his dick. Zion grips her thighs, loving her, watching her fuck him. She adjusts her position slightly, moving back so she's almost positioned where he's pumping into her straight up and down. She places her legs under his thighs, locking them in place to ensure Zion doesn't slip out. Moving her hands to his wrist, she grips them. Making sure she has full control, she squeezes his dick, riding it faster.

"Oh, Lea. Yes, baby yes."

"Cum for me Bear. Come on Zion, cum for me, please, cum for me."

Shit her pleading drives me wild. I let go and enjoy myself. To enjoy my Lea fucking her dick and she feels so damn fucking good. I pump faster and harder and she squeezes my dick with every thrust. I can't hold back any longer.

"Dammit Lea, shit ooooooooooooo, fuck baby, yes, shit yes."

After cumming, my penis is sensitive, but she keeps going, fucking and squeezing my dick, causing me to cum again.

"Oh, baby damn."

I grip her waist as the orgasm racks my entire body. My cum is sliding out of her pussy onto my pubic hairs making the friction between Lea and me unbearable.

"Shit, Lea, fuck baby, yes, fuck me, damn baby," he flops around the pillows, riding the waves of ecstasy.

Zion finishes cumming the second time. Lea releases him, moving slowly to get off. "No, Lea. Don't move. Come here," he opens his arms to have her lay on his chest.

He lifts her head, kissing her. Lea grabs the towel sitting on the nightstand and puts it between them so she can unclench and let his sperm seep out.

"You planned your seduction of me?" He notices where she got the towel from.

"Yes, I wanted to be with you one last time. To hear you cum, to hear your moans and groans, calling my name, wanting me. When you walked away from me, I wanted these memories to sustain me. I wanted these memories to haunt you. So, you would never forget me."

"Baby, you've succeeded. You haunt my entire life," he says kissing her. "Lea, I'm not leaving you, and you're not leaving me. If we have to move to an island and it be us and the boys, we will. I won't let you go. Do you understand me? I'm not letting you out of my life."

"I do now."

She smiles as she lays back on his chest. *In all honesty, I don't believe him.*

HUMPFH, I KNOW I'M NOT GOING NO DAMN PLACE. Adonis murmurs in the Sex Diva's ear.

-2-

"Lea, I want to meet your parents. Don't you think it's time they met the man in your life?" Zion asks. They are lazily enjoying their time together. A great way to spend an afternoon. In bed.

"Parent, singular. She wants to meet you also now that she knows how I feel about you," she tells him.

"Parent? What about your father?" he asks her.

"Mom knew him, but he never wanted to know me. Single mom raised me with a village of aunts, uncles, cousins, family, and friends."

"Well, when do I get to meet her?"

"What are your plans for tomorrow?"

"Meeting your mother, wherever you need me."

"Okay, I'll call her now." Lea reaches over him for the phone.

I caress her, watching her every move. Sometimes I can't believe how lucky I am.

"Hey, Ma, where you at?" she says talking to her mother.

"Leaving the movies. Why?" Ms. Adams asks Lea.

"You still want to meet Zion? He's ready to meet you or has been ready." Lea watches Zion while talking to her mother to see if he's sure about this.

"Good. Cause I'm parked in front of your house. Mommy's here, hope you're dressed. Interrogation time," she informs Lea.

"Wait, what makes you think he's here and that I'm not dressed? And when were you going to tell me you were coming by?" Lea is getting out of bed and putting on clothes. She throws Zion's jeans and shirt at him, waving at him to put them on. From her side of the conversation, he realizes her mother is here.

"I wasn't. I had no plans on stopping, only driving by. There's a car parked in your driveway. Gordon drives a truck. And if you're in there with your man, I'm sure y'all messing up the bed sheets. So, stop and get dressed. I always do a drive-by when I'm in the mood. Now come open the door. Bye."

"Get dressed, she's coming to the door." He lays with his head propped on the pillow grinning at her. "Zion, move!"

He watches Lea finish dressing and running to open the door for her mother.

I love that woman.

He puts on clothes and walks into the living room right as Lea turns to introduce him. "Mom, this is Zion, Zion Landon. Zion, this is my mother, Sarah Adams."

Lea's mother is two inches shorter than her daughter. She steps across the threshold. She's wearing jeans, a black t-shirt with the wording, 'I'm not adulting today, so don't even ask', and red Converse sneakers. Her hair is in what he can only describe as a seventies Afro. It's shaped perfectly, not one strand out of place.

This lady goes to an old school barber. Her coif is lined up flawlessly.

After Lea closes the door, her mother takes her in her arms and hugs her back and forth. "How my child doing?"

Lea is being squeezed so hard, Zion barely hears her mumble, "Fine, mom."

Releasing Lea, Ms. Adams turns her attention to the tall burly figure in the hallway. She looks him up and down with a stern look, then breaks out into her perfect fake-meeting-a-stranger smile.

Zion crosses the room to introduce himself. "Ms. Adams, it's a pleasure to meet you." Zion holds out his hand to shake hers and ready to escort her to the couch.

Ms. Adams looks down at it, then quickly back up at him. *Now I know I don't look like I need help.* She thinks to herself. Not making a scene, she puts her hand in his, shakes it in greeting, then pulls away.

"Nice to finally meet you." Taking charge, Lea's mother tells him, "Sit. Let's talk." Then she walks to her favorite cushion to sit and get comfortable.

"Lea, get us some water," Ms. Adams instructs her.

"Yes, ma'am." Lea goes to get them each a drink.

Zion takes a seat across from Ms. Adams, moving over to make room for Lea to sit as she hands him his glass.

Ms. Adams looks at her pointedly, "Lea, don't you have something to do in the basement or outside?"

Knowing that look, Lea says, "Yes ma'am. Sorry Zion. You're on your own for this interview." Lea goes downstairs to be quiet and listen, but all she can think about is some other woman is giving Zion kids.

Something I'll never be able to do. She puts her hand on her flat stomach.

Nope, no baby will ever grow in here. Never Zion's baby. If this thing with Wendy hadn't come along, it would've never been an issue. Now it's a slap in the face of what I'm unable to give him and someone else can.

She wipes away a tear and heads for her closet.

Keep busy, Lea, keep busy.

Back upstairs in the living room, Lea's mother has started the interrogation. "Okay, young man, I know the basics, you're gainfully employed, obviously handsome, own your own place, fifty, no children, never been married and up until you met my daughter you were single. A ho to be exact. She also tells me you're in love with her and she you. You're the third man she's ever fought for in her life. The first one, he's like a son to me. The second one, well he's not around anymore, thank goodness, and now you. I want to know what about you that my daughter is fighting for?"

"Ms. Adams, you're as straight forward as your daughter. After college, I became a playa. I never ho'ed around, but I wasn't the type to settle down either. Your daughter wanted nothing to do with a temporary relationship, but I wanted to get to know her. She got me to see what being in a long-term relationship is about without telling me to change for her."

"Playa' huh. So, do you love her or is that just her wishful thinking?"

"Ma'am, I love your daughter very much?"

"You going to marry her?"

"Yes ma'am."

"You answered that pretty quickly. Like you all that. Lea says you're having issues with some things, and she doesn't think you guys are going to make it through them. What are they? Lea said they're not hers to tell. So, I'm asking you and I want the truth." She stares at him, daring him to lie to her.

"Yes, ma'am. First off, we're going to make it through them. I have an ex from college that has come back into my life to give me grief. It's to the point where I need to have security personnel to protect Lea, my family, myself, and my office and employees. I would like to include you on that list. I protect those I love and whom they love. The reason I don't have kids is because I'm sterile, but a former lover is pregnant and won't survive the birth of her kids. She has asked me to adopt them, and I have agreed. They will be born in about three months."

"How can you afford security on all these people. What kinda security?" her mother asks.

"Well, whenever you need to go somewhere, I'll have one of my security team drive you and protect you. I'm not simply gainfully employed, I'm a billionaire." Zion waits for the stunned expression he usually gets with that word, but Ms. Adams gives him a look of *so, big deal you a billionaire.*

"Billionaire. Well whoop de fucking doo, you have lots of money. You can still be an ass. Just an ass with money. A billionaire playa."

Ms. Adams can't believe she's sitting here talking to a black billionaire. A fine-looking black billionaire. Who lives in St. Louis. And her daughter is dating, no, in love with. And he with her. *Dang my daughter got it going on, like I always knew.* But Lea's mother shows nothing of what she's thinking visually to Zion.

"Well, I don't go out much and I can limit that to only going with Lea. I suppose she's accepted your security detail?" she asks.

"We have to work out the logistics, but yes. Ms. Adams, I've given up my billionaire playa status. Not because I'm going to be a father but because I want to be with your daughter. I have no interest in being with other women."

Another woman not impressed with my money. And she thinks I could be an ass. Okay I'll take that over the expected handout and neediness I usually get.

"Sure, sure. Now the babies. I'm sorry about the mother. Not ever seeing your child grow up, well, I don't want to even imagine that. You're a good man for taking them. With your resources, why wouldn't you? You asking my daughter to accept this is a stretch for me. I don't like that at all. Honestly, I would have her walk away, but like I said, she's fightin' for you. I don't dislike you. I'm just not ready to go all in and say you're the best man for my daughter. She loves you. I respect her choices as long as she's not being abused. You get points for being willing to adopt those kids. I give you props for wanting to protect her and myself."

Zion's heart swells two sizes hearing from her mother that Lea's fighting for him.

"Ms. Adams, will you give me permission to marry your daughter?" Zion doesn't need Ms. Adams permission, but he knows the right move is to have her approval.

If I have to kidnap Lea and we elope, I'll marry her.

"Mr. Landon, I want to be sure you really do love my daughter and will do everything in your power to protect her. I'll reserve my answer for now. She loves you very much. Don't hurt her. Or I'll hurt you."

Another person threatening to hurt me if I hurt Lea. My Kitten is extremely loved and protected. I feel privileged to be a part of that circle.

"Please call me Zion. And me hurting your daughter is not an option for me, ever. I want to do all I can to keep her safe and forever loving me. She's home for me. I'm never letting her go."

"We'll see. You have a lot to get through in the next few months. I wish you the best of luck. Now could you go get my daughter so the two of you can drive me home? I'm not keen on driving right now." she tells him. "Oh, one more thing Mr. Landon, my daughter loves to take off and go for long drives, to clear her head. I don't always agree when, where or how often she does this, but they re-energize her. If you limit those, she'll internalize her emotions and feelings. I hate it when she does that. She gets quiet, and it scares me. Then she blows up, and well, it ain't always pretty. I call it my-only-child-syndrome. You say you love her and want to protect her. If this becomes too much for her, I'll do everything in my power to get her away from you."

"Ma'am, thank you for the information. I'll never let your daughter go. Never." Zion says in that deadly calm voice that lets others know the discussion is over.

Ms. Adams challenges him back, "Whatever." Not taking her eyes off him. From that moment, Lea's mother earned Zion's respect and loyalty.

No woman outside my mother, sister and Crystal have stood up to me like that. Well Lea of course but that's different.

He goes downstairs to find her. She comes out of the closet smiling at him. "Your mom is ready to go." He wipes his face and takes a few deep breaths.

"You okay, baby? You've never met a woman's parents other than Addison's, have you?" Lea walks into his arms and he holds her.

"No, hell no!"

Lea pulls back and laughs at him.

"Come on, you can follow me to her house, then it's just us."

"Okay." He's still in shock. And a little scared. Lea's mother ain't no joke when it comes to the love she has for her daughter. That's for sure.

-3-

In the car, Lea's mother brings up the baby issues with Zion.

"Lea, why are you staying with this man? He's about to have kids with another woman. I don't get it. Clue me in."

"Ignoring the money and baby aspect, Zion is the closest I've come to a man having many of the qualities I want and need. And he wants me."

"He used to have sex with this woman? Have you thought about what this entails? He's going to be spending time with her. Doctors' appointments, talking, planning these kids' futures."

"With him being sterile, I can't tell him not to do this. I wouldn't to a woman who had this opportunity."

"How will you play into this?"

"I don't know. I assume we'll work it out."

"Work it out? You haven't given it any consideration, have you?"

"No, not really."

"Where's this woman living at if I may ask?"

"She has her own apartment."

"That Zion will be spending time at. With her. Where's it located?"

"Mom, why are you asking me this? I don't know where she lives. And I don't care."

"Well, you need to start caring."

"Why?"

"Because he's going to be spending time with her, going to her place. Where will you be? At your house? At his house waiting for him to come home?"

"My house or his place, I guess."

"What about when he gets tired and won't feel like driving home? What if they get so close, he starts going to her place to hang?

On the other side of town in the opposite direction of your house or his place? That leaves you where?"

"At home wondering what he's doing," Lea admits the truth out loud.

"Lea, do you love him that much?"

"Mom, I don't know."

"Think about the hard possibilities of what can happen, Lea. Put yourself in her place. What would you want? What would you really want? Don't tell me. It's your decision from this point on. Whatever you decide, I'll support you. You're my priority. Just think about it and what you're ready to accept and deal with."

Lea's quiet for the remainder of the ride to her mother's house. Thinking hard, she finally puts herself in Wendy's place. Into Wendy's mind.

Lea would want to move in with Zion, to marry Zion, to be introduced as the mother of Zion's kids. Lea would not want to be left alone to go through this. She would demand Zion's full commitment to her. Lea would make herself be the most important part of his life.

They've arrived at her mother's house and they're standing in her living room. "You okay, my child?" her mother asks her.

"No, not really."

"What're you thinking?"

"I love him and I'm going to fight for him. But not with my claws, or games, or being evil. I'll continue to support him. I'll even suggest things to help him get through this. I'll try to keep my fears and opinions to myself because he doesn't need that. This is his chance to be a father. With me or not, I'm not going to block that. But as long as he loves me and keeps telling me he loves me; I'm going to fight for him."

"I hope you don't pull another Jake. Waiting to be anything. I wish you would walk away from this. But I see that's a futile wish."

"Extremely futile. And Zion is so much more than Jake will ever be. I think I'm going to suggest Zion have her move into an apartment in his building."

"Wait. What? You pushing them together? How many times did you fall out the bed on your head when you was a kid? The damage has materialized."

"If she's living in his building, it cuts down on his driving time. I won't sit around while he goes and visits with her, but I can control some of their time together. Some of it."

"Lea Grace Adams, you're mental. Get out of this now. Let him do this on his own."

"Mom, I'm not doing that. If he walks away, fine, that's his choice." Lea hesitates before verbalizing the one thought that's planted itself in her mind. "Mom, Wendy is dying. I know this is going to sound mean as hell, but—. I have no qualms fighting her for Zion as long as he wants me, because in the end, I'll win. I'll have his love and the family I always wanted."

"Fine. I'm done talking against this. No more out of me. You better get out of here. I'm tired." Ms. Adams has dismissed the topic as she walks to the back of her house.

As far as I'm concerned, Zion is back to temporary status, and I don't want anything to do with him right now. He's put my daughter in a position I don't agree with but will accept because I've always taught my daughter to make logical decisions based on what she wants. And she wants him.

"Lea Adams, you need to get your head examined," Ms. Adams yells from her bedroom.

-4-

Zion followed the women to Lea's mother's house, rehashing in his mind the conversation he had with Ms. Adams. He smiles at the protective nature she has for her daughter and how Ms. Adams is not impressed by his money.

His phone rings, displaying Wendy's number. He connects the call, the smile lingering in his voice, "This is Zion."

"Hi Zion, how are you?" Wendy asks.

"Hey, I'm good. Everything okay?" Zion asks. He isn't sure how to handle speaking with her now that they've signed all the documentation with the lawyers yesterday.

"Oh, yes. I was calling to see what you were up to this evening. Maybe you would like to come by for dinner."

He promised Lea he would not hide her and here's his first opportunity to inform Wendy that she exists. "I'm sorry, Wendy I can't. I'm going out with my girlfriend. Is your nurse there?"

"Yes, she's here. I wasn't aware you're in a relationship now. You didn't mention anything about this when we signed the paperwork. Wow, you in a relationship. I never imagined that."

So, he finally confirms it.

"I didn't think it would matter. I'm not going to allow anyone around the kids I don't fully trust. Lea and I've been together since April."

Must be the heffa he was kissing the night of his birthday. I need to get rid of her.

"Oh, so it's still new and fresh then? No, it doesn't matter. I'll let you go."

What the heck is a name like LEA. EEEkkkk.

"How about I come by Sunday to see how you're doing?" Zion will let that first comment slide. He's informed her about Lea and how long they've been together.

Wendy doesn't need to know more as far as I'm concerned.

"Okay, that's fine, see you then."

"Goodnight, Wendy."

Parked now in Ms. Adams' driveway, Zion watches Lea come out of her mother's house. She looks dejected. Back to the Lea he found lying on her bed in the dark.

I wonder what was said between her and her mother. Shit. Damage control.

Zion meets her at the passenger door, lifting her chin to look at him. "Everything okay?"

"No. My mom's relegated you to temporary status in my life again. She doesn't agree with me being with you."

That revelation turns Zion's stomach. He understands Mrs. Adams reservations. "I'm sorry to hear that. And how do you feel?"

"This is my choice Zion. I'm not going anywhere. Unless you state you don't want me."

"Lea, I'll keep repeating though I shouldn't need to. We're not breaking up."

"Well, okay then. Now what?"

"How about a late dinner?" he suggests.

"Sure. If you really think it's safe." Lea gets in the car. After Zion positions himself in the driver's seat, he calls Porter's Steakhouse for a table.

"It's safe." He tells Lea about the added security plan. Some of it will involve him being driven. Some days, he will drive himself and will be tracked by Sam via GPS. Some days he will be followed. Tonight, Sam is tracking him.

At this point, he doesn't care about being safe. He just wants to have a night out with his girl. The drive to Porter's was relaxing with them discussing business instead of steering away from the subject as they normally do after business hours.

They get to the restaurant and are escorted to their table. The atmosphere is muted and dignified: subdued lighting, practically dark, quiet, with great food. This is a date night restaurant. After they're seated next to each other, Zion places the orders for both of them as he usually does after conferring with Lea what she would like. He likes to keep the interruptions down to a bare minimum with the wait staff by doing it this way. They turn toward each other in the booth.

"So, how did you enjoy meeting my mother?" Lea asks him.

"I'm still sweating bullets. You only told her I was gainfully employed. Why? Isn't that hiding or lying to her?"

"No. You are gainfully employed. Just because you can afford to do things others can't on a regular basis doesn't make any difference. What makes you the man you are is how you treat me, not the amount of money you have."

"Sometimes, I feel like I'm treating you as a cheap date. I lavished all the other women with trips, money, flowers and so on, the things a man in my position usually does. You want me and I want to give you more of me. Instead, I want to lavish you with more important things. Like taking you away again, but I don't think I'll be able to do that anytime soon. Wendy called while you were in your mother's house. I told her about us."

"Time is more important than things, Zion. How is Wendy doing? This week must have been long and stressful for her. What's her social circle like?" Lea is going to approach this as if it was one of her girlfriends who's pregnant. Offering helpful suggestions and ideas.

"I actually don't know. I'm going over there Sunday. Maybe have lunch and spend some time with her." He waits for Lea's reaction. On cue her leg starts its nervous twitch.

Mustering her courage and attempting to keep her voice level, she plows ahead with her idea. "Why don't you see if she would like to meet your family. It may give her some comfort to know the family her kids, sorry, *your* children will become a part of. You could even suggest they visit her," Lea states.

"Why are you suggesting that? What are you up to?" he asks nervously.

"I'm not up to anything," Lea lies. "I was thinking about the promise I asked you to make about living with her. When I think about this Addison crap, it may be better to have Wendy in a much safer environment." *God I can't believe I'm about to suggest this, but here goes.* "What about Wendy moving into an apartment in your building?" Her leg is twitching double time under the table.

I've just made myself sick to my stomach. I'm pushing him and Wendy together and probably edging myself out of the picture. Fuck, Lea, what have you done? I can't take it back now.

"I don't know what to say. Lea, you keep throwing curve balls at me. Baby, why?" He puts his hand on her leg, in a combined squeeze and caressing movement, attempting to calm her.

Lea lays her hand on top of his, "Look, if she doesn't have any friends coming to see her or helping her get through this, I can only imagine it's very lonely knowing she's giving birth and dying. Having her around your family could be a good thing. Perhaps it could even take some of the stress off you."

And I can get my time in if she's being entertained and watched by your family.

"Your time and energy are gonna be focused on her. I'm not stupid. Our time together will become limited as the birth gets closer."

Make sure he believes you're doing this for him even though this is killing you.

"I would be scared to death right now if I were her. Honestly, what I'm suggesting is scaring me to death, but I'm suggesting it anyway. As long as you keep your promise of not marrying her, not denying me, and not moving in with her in the same apartment, do what you have to do."

"Baby, I don't know about this. And our time together won't become limited." *I pray that it doesn't, I just don't know how I'll keep up with everything that's going on*, Zion thinks.

"Talk to your family about it. See what they say," Lea suggests.

"How about WE talk to my family about it and WE see what they say. You're a part of this. I want you to go shopping with me. WE have a nursery to design and things to buy, and I want your input. Especially as their mother," he says to her.

Lea twirls a curl around her finger. *As their mother he said. I'm going to be a mom. A mother to the kids of a woman he used to fuck.* Lea looks at Zion's ear and not into his eyes. Re-focusing on his brown gaze, peering into her, Lea let's her eyes say how much she loves him. Verbally she says, "Sure, I would like that."

Zion caresses her leg, "Lea, what if she wants to meet you? Would you be willing to meet Wendy?"

With this question, Lea stills her leg and has turned away from him. She's now twisting the napkin in her lap.

"Yes," she whispers, staring at her hands and not at him.

"Lea, look at me."

She shakes her head no and turns it toward the other diners. Her leg is twitching again. Zion gently turns her face to him. "Sweetheart, we have to have this conversation. If Wendy wants to meet the woman who will become the mother of her children after we're married, and yes, we're getting married and I'm going to have you be their mother, are you willing to meet with her, probably on multiple occasions?"

Lea wants to burst into tears.

Hold it together girl.

She responds hoarsely, "Yes."

OH MY GOD. ARE YOU SERIOUS. Lea unable to react to Zion's question as she'd like, the Sex Diva does so in her mind.

Stomping her feet, pacing back and forth, tugging on her hair, biting her lip and kicking at imaginary dust bunnies, the Sex Diva yells, WHY THE FUCK WE DOING THIS?

A tear slips from Lea's right eye. Zion catches it on his thumb. The tear tore at his heart. He's brought Lea to so many tears lately. It's obvious she's more upset about this situation than he imagined. "We need to get home." Zion signals the waiter, and the man hastens to their table.

"We have an emergency we have to leave for. Can you make that order to go?" Zion takes out his wallet and hands the waiter five one-hundred-dollar bills telling him to keep the change. The waiter carries the food out to Zion's car and puts it in the trunk. Zion and Lea get in the car and sit, Zion facing Lea and Lea not looking at him.

"Lea, you wanna tell me where in the hell all this is coming from? Moving Wendy into an apartment in my building. Having my family spend time with her. Baby I'm confused here. I feel like you're pushing Wendy and me together and you out of the picture. I'm not having that, no way in hell am I letting that happen."

"Zion, in three months, she'll be dead, and she may not even get to hold her babies. She shouldn't be alone in going through this. Unless you plan on moving your office into her apartment and working from there on a daily basis, she should have people around her." Tears are streaming down Lea's face. She takes out his handkerchief from her back pocket, using it to wipe away her tears. It's become a talisman for her since she found out about all of this.

Lea put herself in Wendy's shoes and is thinking from Wendy's standpoint. To be dying and only having to deal with a nurse and maybe the baby's father every now and then is so unfair.

"Oh, baby, don't cry. Please Lea." Zion pleads. He gets out of the car and goes to the passenger side, opening the door and pulls Lea out and into his arms.

"Zion, you said she has no family. She's going to need you more than you realize. If she's in your apartment building, you can see her on a daily basis without having to travel all over the city. If your family is involved, she'll have people to talk with. She'll need this. I'm sorry, I don't mean to cry like this, but, dammit, every time I think about what this woman is going through, it breaks my heart. I'm not going to get in the way of you becoming a father. I don't want to push you toward her, but that's what I'm doing. I know I am. I keep thinking how stupid my promises are. But you! God! You have to do this; you can't let her be alone. You have to make this as pleasant for her as you can. You have to."

Lea's bawling now and Zion can't get her to stop. He holds onto her letting the sobs rack her body, having her cry it all out.

Shit, what have I done to this wonderful happy woman I love. Putting her through all this turmoil? Fuck Zion, what the hell is wrong with you?

"Oh baby, don't worry, I will. I will. You're not pushing me toward her. I love you for supporting me in this. Any other woman would have left yet you're staying. Lea, stop crying. Please. Stop crying. I'll move her into my building. I won't allow her to go through this alone. I promise you. Please Lea, stop crying."

He holds her tighter as she calms down. She has her head buried in his chest and he's caressing her back. "Let's get you home. My place is closer than yours." He kisses away her remaining tears. "Oh Kitten, my sweet kitten. I love you so much."

Lea settles back into her seat and buckles herself in. She turns her face away from Zion trying to halt her silent misery. She thinks painfully, *oh well, it's done. Wendy will have a support system other than a nurse, doctors and Zion around her to get her through this. This is the right thing to do. No matter what happens, this is the right thing to do.* JUST KEEP TELLING YOURSELF THAT WHEN YOU'RE NOT SEEING ZION FOR WHO KNOWS HOW LONG.

The shaking in her leg is on overload and she's twisting her hair around her finger.

Lea falls asleep on the way to his apartment. She wakes up when she realizes the car has stopped and the engine is turned off.

Zion reaches over and lifts her face up so he can see her eyes. "Hey, sleepy head," he kisses her.

"Hey. Sorry about that display back at the restaurant."

"Lea, don't apologize. I'll get this all worked out. Let's go upstairs and get some rest."

He grabs the food and they step into the building. She pushes the button for the elevator.

"Come here." He opens his arms and she walks into them.

I can never get enough of his hugs, the smell of him, how strong and in control he is. How safe she feels with him.

They head into the apartment and Lea stops to look at the pictures. Soon, it will be Zion and the boys, maybe even Wendy. She stands with her arms folded, staring at them.

How long will my pictures remain displayed? How long before he takes them down replacing them with his new family? How long before I'm edged out of the picture altogether?

"Zion, you should take pictures of Wendy. Her boys, again sorry, your boys will want to know what their mom looked like. I'll get the wording correct I promise. Make sure they're pictures of her upbeat and smiling," she tells him.

"Where's all this coming from?" he asks her as they walk toward the kitchen.

"When they look in the mirror, they'll wonder whom they look like. If they have a picture of their mom, at least that's something," she says.

"Okay, I'll take pictures. Let's eat. Sit. I'll serve."

She sits watching him.

"Keep staring at me like that, and I'm going to eat you instead of this dinner. You taste better anyway," he says.

"Food please," she smiles at him.

"Good, you're smiling. I like your smiles."

They keep up the banter and playfulness the rest of the night.

-5-

Saturday morning, Zion calls his family to invite them over to discuss Lea's idea of more family involvement with Wendy.

He and Lea are lying on the couch lazily making out. "Kitten, everyone should be here in a few. Are you ready for this discussion?" he asks her.

"I don't know," Lea looks up at him, "I'll get ready."

The ding of the elevator announces the other's arrival. He presses the button on a remote granting access to the apartment. The girls come running down the hall ahead of their parents, Star and Garrett, with Zion's parents, Patty and Royal, not far behind.

Lea gets up from Zion's chest, attempting to move away from him, but he holds her in place. "Uhm, where you think you going?" He looks at her intently.

She stares back at him and says, "Nowhere. Adjust your jeans. You're awake. If you know what I mean."

He looks down. Pulling his pants away from his crotch he grins and leans over kissing her. "See what you do to me, beautiful."

The adults greet one another and take seats, with the girls running and hopping onto his and Lea's laps. Lea offers to get everyone drinks, but Zion halts her in her spot.

"What?" she asks, staring at him.

Zion whispers in her ear, "You sit. I'll get them. I know you want to make a beeline out of here, but I'm not going to allow it."

"Garrett, you want to help me out?" Zion asks, standing, ignoring the looks from his family.

"Sure bro." Garrett says, following Zion to the kitchen and getting glasses of lemonade for everyone.

The adults stare at Lea. "What?" she asks, uncomfortable with the attention.

Patty speaks up. "My son is getting lemonade. My son and son-in-law are getting us all lemonade. I'm a little shocked."

"Patty, it's not like you didn't bring him up with manners," Royal says.

"No. But. Well, never mind. Zion, what's up? Why the family meeting?" Patty asks. She turns to Zion, deciding to ignore this change in her son for the moment.

"Okay everyone, Lea suggested it would be a good idea to create a support system for Wendy. I must admit, it hadn't crossed my mind it would be just Wendy, me and the doctors. I would like you guys to be a part of this. I'm going to look into renting an apartment here in the building to make it easier on me to visit with her daily."

"Why rent an apartment? Just use the corporate apartment on the third floor," Star suggests.

"What corporate apartment?" he asks.

"You're a dunce sometimes. When you purchased this apartment, we were offered an additional two-bedroom apartment to use for corporate visitors. Or we're supposed to. We've all used it a number of times, for friends and visitors," Star informs him.

"Is it in use now?"

"Nope. Wanna go see it?" Star asks.

"Well yeah." Zion says. "I have a corporate apartment and don't know about it. How is that possible?"

Everyone gets up walking to the elevator. Lea gets on first, moving to the back corner listening to the conversation. Zion stands across from her.

Star continues with the explanation about the corporate apartment, "Zion, when you were working on moving back to St. Louis, this building had plenty of apartments to fill up. When you had signed the deal on yours, the management company was eager to negotiate a deal on another one. It's a part of Landon Enterprises real estate holdings."

"And you negotiated the deal?"

"No. Dad did."

"Dad, really?"

"Yep. I figured it would be good for game nights. No need to drive home."

"Well thanks, everyone," Zion says smiling.

"That's what families are for. We're here for each other and always will be," his father says.

Lea listens from the corner of the elevator. It's always been only her mother and herself. Watching this family unit makes her ache to be a part of it. To be included. But it may not be her. It'll probably end up being Wendy. She twirls the charm on her necklace in nervousness.

The elevator stops on the third floor. Zion and his family rush to get off with Lea slowly following behind them. They walk down the hall to the fifth door. Star pulls out a key, this one not being a security key card and unlocks and opens the door.

They enter the apartment. The balcony has a view of Ballpark Village. It's comfortable, homey, fully furnished, and ready to move in. It's stocked with linens, towels, and all the basic necessities. It's only missing food and humans.

Lea walks around looking into rooms and cupboards. Wendy could be happy here. She could have visitors and entertain friends. And with Zion in the building, he can come down at any time to visit with her.

ANY FRICKING TIME OF THE DAY OR NIGHT. GREAT IDEA, LEA, JUST A GREAT FRICKING IDEA YOU HAD THERE, MISSY. WENDY CAN BE EXTREMELY COMFORTABLE HERE. ONLY A FEW FLOORS DOWN FROM HER BABY DADDY. EVERY DAMN DAY. UGH. Lea and the Sex Diva go on the same silent tangent.

Zion's father speaks up. "So, this support system. Would Wendy be willing to meet us and have us visit her? I don't mind at all, but I don't want her feeling we're trying to bum rush her or anything like that. And how are you going to get her to agree to move in here?"

"I'm having lunch with her tomorrow. Legally, I have control over her living arrangements. I'll explain to her how I don't want her to be alone in her apartment, how it's best to have her in my building. In her own apartment. She'll still have her privacy. I'll also explain to her about meeting the family she's allowing her sons to be a part of. Maybe meeting their cousins if that's okay with Star and Garrett."

The girls are running around the apartment playing a tickling game every time they pass Lea. Zion watches them, his pride in Lea showing.

"And Lea, you're okay with this?" Zion's mother asks her.

Everyone turns and looks at her. The girls catch her, and she holds onto them so they don't knock her over. "Yes. Whatever it takes within reason to make this as manageable a situation for Zion, I'm okay with. Within reason," Lea stresses looking directly at Zion. She keeps her expression neutral. He stares at her with complete understanding.

Lea can speak volumes to Zion with a look and not a single word. Something that astounds him every time she does it. Now her look is saying 'don't forget about those promises'.

I hear you babe, loud and clear.

Star comes over to her. "Did you really suggest this to him? I've been wanting to contact you and see how you're doing, how you're coping with all this."

"Yes. I want this to work out for him. That's all that matters right now," Lea stares at her, willing her not to ask anything else. Star doesn't.

"Well, okay then, I guess it's just a matter of getting her moved in here and you introducing us to her. Why don't you bring her to dinner to the house?" his mother suggests.

"Are you fricking kidding me?" The words were out of Lea's mouth before she could even stop them.

"What?" Patty asks Lea, stunned at her response.

"Nothing. Nothing at all. Please continue on with your plans. Of Wendy—having dinner with the Landon clan," Lea says.

"Well, she's going to be a part of the family in a way, and entertaining is what I do best."

Patty not realizing what she's saying or not saying, is about to rattle on with plans about inviting Wendy to dinner before Zion speaks up.

"Why don't we all get out of here," he suggests.

Lea hangs back a second looking into the apartment listening to Sex Diva. GREAT LEA. JUST GREAT. YOUR MAN'S BABY MAMA'S CRIB IN THE SAME BUILDING AS HIS. ANY WAY IN HELL THIS CAN POSSIBLY GET WORSE, BRING IT ON. SHE GETS A FRICKING INVITE TO THE PARENT'S HOUSE AND YOU DON'T GET JACK SHIT. YOU DON'T EVEN GET ASKED DO YOU WANT TO BE A PART OF THIS FUCKING DREAM FAMILY.

Zion walks up behind her and gives her a hug. "Lea, come on. I love you. Remember that."

She nods in resignation, and they leave the corporate apartment.

Everyone heads back up to his place to finish discussing getting to know Wendy and setting up a positive support system for her. Zion shows them to the bedroom he's planning to convert into the nursery. His sister suggests the two of them go shopping and that she'll look at all the stuff she can bring over that she's no longer using for the girls. Zion keeps Lea at his side making sure she hears and sees everything that's discussed.

His phone rings and he glance at it with a strained look on his face. It's Wendy. Lea walks off toward the window turning her back on him. "Hi Wendy, how are you?" he answers. "No, it's okay, call any time you need me." He doesn't take his eyes off Lea during the phone conversation, and his family quietly watch the two of them. "How are you feeling? That's good. I was just talking about you with my family. Yes, they're excited. They would all like to meet you if that's okay? No, we can talk about it tomorrow when I get there. A salad would be great for lunch; I'll see you around one o'clock. Okay bye."

Turning around, Lea breaks the eerie silence. "Why's everyone so quiet? You were talking about decorating the nursery. You hiring a professional or doing it yourself?" The girls are chanting juice, juice, juice. "I'll take them downstairs. Y'all keep talking. Gotta make plans for that family get-together at the parent's house. Don't need an outsider listening in on THAT conversation."

Lea escapes with the girls before anyone can rebuttal. Downstairs, they're sitting in the kitchen drinking juice. Hers just happened to be spiked with vodka. In between the numerous questions from the girls about dolls, puppies, and kittens, Lea was having a conversation with her conscience.

Lea, it's okay, you can do this. I know it's going to be hard to be happy. He loves you and wants you as their mom. No, he hasn't fully proposed; he wants this over with first, but it could still happen. Look, you get to help decorate a nursery. Maybe pick out names, get with it. Girl. Be happy for him. You're able to be happy for your girlfriends when they're having babies and planning futures. Just do the same for him. Be happy.

HAPPY, MY ASS.

While Lea and the young girls are gone, Zion and his family discuss her.

"What the heck was the outsider comment about?" Patty asks.

Zion explains, "Mom, you suggested inviting Wendy to dinner to your house. You've never suggested inviting the woman I love. Lea. I'm including Lea on everything."

"Oh. Well, we figured you were handling things with Lea," Patty says.

"Patty, handling things with Lea? Is that how you see things with Zion and Lea?" Royal asks her.

Before Patty can respond Garrett asks, "Zion, is Lea really okay with all of this? She couldn't get outta here fast enough."

"She's supportive. I keep waiting for her to break up with me. The thought of losing her is as scary as me making the decision about adopting these boys. But I want her and all of this."

"You scared of a woman breaking up with you?" his mother asks. "I wanted you to fall in love and get married and stop screwing around. But I never thought you would be so far gone you would be scared of losing a woman. I'm not sure I like hearing that, Zion."

"Mom, this is new for me. Being in love. But it feels hella fantastic. Would you prefer me be the hard ass I was, not giving a care about women's feelings? I coulda been in a loveless marriage by now with a woman I hate. Probably with a divorce behind me."

"Zion, no. Your mother doesn't prefer that. Seeing you happy and finally in love is a shock to us all. We have let you live your life without much interference. Doesn't mean we haven't worried and won't continue to worry. Lea has been good for you. If you truly love her and don't wanna lose her, don't lose sight of her feelings in this."

"I won't. And neither should any of you. No invites to Wendy to the house. All visits will take place downstairs in the apartment. Let's get out of here."

Zion and his family arrive back downstairs to find the girls and Lea sitting on the couch. He hasn't taken his eyes off Lea while descending the stairs. He's willing her to look at him. She looks up with sadness in her eyes. He walks directly over to her, sitting down giving her a kiss on the temple. It's a tough situation he's put her in and he has to reassure her she's a part of this.

His family leaves, saying goodbye, with Royal telling Zion to let them know when he would like for them to meet Wendy at the apartment after she moves in.

After they're gone and the elevators are locked, Zion returns to the couch joining Lea. "I enjoy seeing you with the girls. They like you, and our sons will like you also. They will love you." She jerks her head around and looks at him at the words 'our sons'. "What baby?"

"Nothing," she says.

"You're lying. Talk to me."

"I'm proud of you. Becoming a father at your age."

"Thank you. Now tell me what you're really thinking."

"I wish we had met years ago."

"I'm ecstatic we met at all. I look forward to our future together."

"Wendy chose well."

"Lea, you chose well when you wouldn't allow yourself to be a temporary fuck. This is going to get rough. I'm going to do whatever I can to make sure we get through this."

-6-

I haven't seen the bitch in days. Where the hell is she?

The individual stomps around his house throwing items. A plate hits the wall. A glass hits the top of the fireplace and shatters. An empty bottle of Svedka is kicked across the room.

The person sitting on the couch watches the tantrum.

"Fucker I am not cleaning that shit up."

"You will do as I tell you."

"Now we know that ain't gonna happen. My baby will protect me from you."

Individual one pulls out a gun and points it at the person sitting at the kitchen table. A shot is fired past their head into the microwave oven.

"Bitch, you wanna keep him alive, you will NEVER tell me what will and won't happen."

He leaves, slamming the door on a mission to find her.

Sunday dawns bright and shiny for Zion and Lea. It's his first day of spending time with Wendy. Lea has to meet Ryan at her house to discuss how security issues will be handled with her.

Lea, Zion, and Ryan arrive at Lea's house around ten. Ryan walks the perimeter of the house, checking windows, access points, and doors. Inside, he checks the locks and asks about the alarm system and who has keys and codes. She's sitting on the couch answering questions as if she has a spotlight on her.

This is so damn ridiculous.

They arrange times for him to pick her up and drive her around daily. If she has any appointments to be out of the office, she's to set up meeting invites with Ryan and Zion so they'll know where she is at all times, whether at doctors' appointments, events with friends, *like that will ever happen again,* anything that will take her out of the house. She's beginning to think staying at home locked away is the better option.

Zion sits down at the dining room table and reviews Lea's emails, looking for anything from Addison. He finds ten more emails threatening Lea. He forwards them to his email account and deletes them from hers, making sure she can't read them. There haven't been any new text messages or calls because he's blocked the number they were coming from. He considers getting her a new phone, one he can control.

"Seriously. Y'all tracking my schedule like this? So, I get no privacy? This is fucking ridiculous, heavy-handed, and stupid. What happened to me being asked what I'm doing, how I'm doing, where am I going? Where is the trust in this fucking relationship? I've taken care of myself for years and now I have to report every fucking move I do. This is bullshit."

Lea's pacing her living room, walking from the dining room to the kitchen taking her frustration and anger out on them both.

"Lea, I do trust you. This has nothing to do with trust. It's only about safety."

"No, you don't trust me. That's fine. Fuck it." Lea sits back down on the couch her head down, using the tips of her fingers to massage her scalp in an attempt to soothe the oncoming headache, not looking at either of them.

Ryan leaves, letting her know he'll be there tomorrow at seven to pick her up. He and Zion give each other a silent understanding look.

She catches the look between them.

Fucking jackasses. Zion's leaving and I'm going to do what? Not sit in this fucking house.

He takes a seat next to her running his fingers up and down her back. "I know you hate all this."

"Zion, you don't know the half of it."

"When I get to work tomorrow, I'll be meeting with a friend of mine on the police force to see what he suggests. I trust you, Lea. This is about your safety. That's all."

Lea turns to him. She's sitting ramrod straight, staring at him, not looking away, "You better get going."

"Lea, what are you thinking?"

"Rainbows and Unicorns."

"Lea."

"What?"

"Don't do anything risky."

"What makes you think I would?"

"I'm asking you not to do anything risky. I'll be back later," he assures her.

"Why? I'm fine. Don't come back on my account."

"Lea," he says, staring at her, trying to gauge what she could be thinking. Lea blinks, then stands up, walks to the door, opening it.

"You'll be late, Zion."

He stands, walking to the door, closing it, and pinning her against it kissing her. "I love you, Kitten. I'll be back in a few hours. I promise."

"I love you, too, Bear."

He won't allow her to accompany him to his car. He makes sure she closes and locks the door before driving off.

Lea walks into her bedroom.

Fuck! I need to scream.

She grabs a pillow off the bed and screams into it until she's hoarse. Her man just left her to go have lunch with another woman and she let him. She bursts into tears.

Zion makes it to Wendy's house with five minutes to spare. When he pulls up, it hits him, Lea didn't assure him she would not do anything risky. It's too late for him to do anything about that now. He looks at his phone.

Well, she's still home. That's good.

Out of respect, he doesn't let himself into Wendy's place, and knocks. The nurse answers the door. "Hello Becky. How are you today?" he asks her as he steps in.

"I'm doing fine, Mr. Landon. Ms. Wendy is in the living room." She directs him there.

He walks in and sees Wendy surrounded by boxes. "Hello, Wendy. How are you? What are you up to?"

Wendy looks up at Zion and literally loses her breath. *Why the fuck can't I be having your biological children? Damn man, you fine. I got to sex you and didn't lock your ass down. Whew, I must've been out of my fricking mind. Well, that's okay. I got you now. Yesssss, baby. I got you now.*

"Hello, Zion. I'm getting rid of stuff. I've already sold or given away most of my things. Now, I'm packing up personal stuff. Things I would like you to share with the boys when they're older. Letters, pictures, things I liked. Over there is a box of baby items I purchased. I hope you'll use them. Or not, it's up to you. How you been?"

Zion looks around. "Okay. Can I help? Lifting, moving? Anything at all? What about this place, what's going on with it?"

Maybe this is how he can broach the subject of her moving into the corporate apartment without it offending her.

"The landlord is looking forward to getting it vacated as soon as he can. I really hate men," she says.

"How about I provide you with an alternative living arrangement? My company has a corporate apartment in my building. You can move in there. It's on the third floor. You and your nurse. You don't have to worry about me being too far away should anything happen. And you can get out from under this landlord's thumb."

"Would you prefer I move into the corporate apartment or live here?" she asks.

Wendy has been thinking about what Zion said to her all-damn night long. Hearing he has a fucking girlfriend is throwing off her plans exponentially. *He's a fucking career bachelor. Five fricking months they been together. How the hell am I supposed to stop this shit? She was supposed to be a temporary fuck like all the rest.*

"I would prefer you move into the corporate apartment," he tells her.

"When do you want me to move?" *Maybe with me physically closer to him and seeing me on a daily basis, he'll decide to drop that girlfriend, like I know he should.*

"By August nineteenth. Wendy, I'm not trying to isolate you from anyone. Any and all of your friends can come visit you. My family would like to meet you also. I want you to be as comfortable as possible. I'll have a driver available for all your appointments and anywhere else you would like to go. I would prefer you closer to me," he says hoping to comfort her with the idea.

"Zion, you don't have to convince me of anything. I'll move wherever you want me to. I look forward to meeting your family. Only a few of my friends know about my situation. They'll be happy to visit me there. Thank you for suggesting I be closer to you. I like that idea," she says smiling. *See witch, whoever you are. He prefers me closer to him.*

"Ms. Wendy, Mr. Landon, lunch is ready. Shall I serve it in here?" the nurse asks.

"Becky, remember we have a deal. As long as I'm mobile, I'll stay mobile. Lunch at the table please. Thank you," Wendy smiles at Nurse Becky and she smiles back. "Yes ma'am."

"And stop calling me ma'am. We can stop being so formal. Zion won't mind." Wendy walks to the dining table and Zion follows, listening to the fun banter between her and Becky. It's refreshing, considering everything.

They sit down and enjoy lunch and talking. Zion thinks if he and Wendy hadn't let themselves get into a temporary fuck situation, maybe they could have been more. Then he thinks about Lea, and he feels so much more for her than he felt for Wendy. Wendy and he could have been close friends. Lea is the love of his life.

Returning to the banter between Wendy and Becky, Zion shares details about his family.

He and Wendy have come to an agreement to move her into the corporate apartment by the following Friday. Zion will hire movers to pack up and move the items she wants to keep to the apartment or into storage and deliver whatever items have been purchased by friends, to their homes. What isn't being sold or being kept for the babies will be donated per Wendy's request.

They even discuss what will happen after her death. Wendy has decided on cremation, with her remains being interred in Hotchkiss Chapel at Bellefontaine Cemetery. She has explicit instructions about not coming to visit her every year as some kind of morbid ritual. She wants to be remembered in a positive way. She's even agreed to Zion taking pictures of her. He can tell she's tired, and at seven o'clock he insists she goes to bed.

"I'll call you tomorrow. We have a doctor's appointment Tuesday. If you need anything, call me. Either of you," he tells them. "We'll discuss the move more on Tuesday if you aren't too tired."

"No problem. See you Tuesday," Wendy says as she and Becky walk up the steps to her bedroom. Zion lets himself out and locks the door behind him ensuring they're safe.

He drives straight to Lea's place. He'd only planned on being away a couple of hours. It's been close to five and she's probably pissed. He covertly checked his phone to be sure she was home. That helped to ease his conscience about staying longer than he expected. But now, he just needs to get to his Lea.

-7-

After her crying and screaming spell that morning, Lea decided to have one last excursion of freedom. She went shoe, purse, and grocery shopping. Her mall purchases resulted in five pairs of new shoes and three purses. Coming out of the last store she ran into Martin, the former electrician she was working with on Zion's remodel, almost knocking him over, dropping one of her bags.

"Lea. Hi. You, okay?" he asks, bending over, picking up the bag.

"Hello, Martin. Yeah fine." Lea grabs the bag, moving away from him. She gives him a closer look. He looks haggard and worn out. "You, okay?"

"Yeah. Good. It's nice seeing you. How are things at the job site?" he asks, hoping to detain her, maybe get her to have lunch with him.

"Sorry, Martin. I can't discuss that with you. Look, I gotta go. You take care. Get some rest or a vacation or something. You look tired. Bye." Lea walks off.

"Bye, Lea." Martin says, staring after her. He decides to follow behind at a safe distance. She stops at a jewelry store looking at wedding ring sets.

Lea has never looked at wedding rings, especially diamonds. Her eyes widen at how the larger ones catch the lights and reflection of the multi-colored prisms on the glass cases.

"Now why would she be looking at wedding rings?" Martin mumbles to himself. He continues to follow her to the garage toward her car. He watches her put the bags in the trunk. "I can do it now," again mumbling in a low voice.

"Excuse you?" A security guard standing a few steps away from Martin, asks him.

"Huh? Oh, nothing man. Was just thinking out loud about shit is all." Martin says, turning away and walking in the opposite direction of Lea and the security guard. *Fucking nosy people.*

Lea next, heads to the supermarket to finish her grocery shopping and gets back home around five. Sitting in her car, she wonders why she hasn't even heard from Zion. Reaching for her purse, she digs around in it searching for her phone. She realizes she left the house without it. Four hours of shopping, being away from home and she didn't even have her phone. Checking it when she gets in the house, she has no missed calls or texts.

GUESS LUNCH MUST BE GOING GREAT. JUSSSSTTT GREAT.

At seven-thirty, she's sitting on the couch, in a tank top and boy shorts, putting on baby oil. She leans back onto the cushions, flicking through channels on the TV, wondering if she'll hear from Zion. As she's about to text him, the lock on her door turns, and Zion walks in.

GODDAMN THIS MAN IS FINE AND OURS. Sex Diva murmurs in the back of Lea's mind. Lea devours him, excitement coursing through her veins. Her nipples harden. Her clit swells and she feel moisture. She pushes the vibrator out of his view.

NAW, WE NOT GONE NEED THAT TONIGHT.

"I thought you were going home?" she says to him, feeling better that he's there, but still angry about earlier.

"Baby, I'm home wherever you're at," he walks over to her and sits down. "Hi beautiful," he says before kissing her.

"Hi," she says.

His eyes zero in on the bags from her shopping excursion.

"You went shopping?"

"Yes."

"Lea, come on. Why? You promised me you wouldn't do anything risky. Your phone never said you left the house. And you talk about trust. I trusted you—."

"You trusted me not to do anything risky. I didn't do anything risky. I forgot the phone and didn't realize it. I'm not that big of a slave to my phone. Talk about trust. How many times you kept looking at yours? Should I be flattered or pissed? I needed to get out of this house before your security detail kicks in and I become your prisoner. I needed to do some grocery shopping, and I wanted to spend some money to make me feel better. But I'm having buyer's remorse, so I'll return everything tomorrow. I'll be sure to add THAT to the calendar. And I'll strap my phone around my neck. That okay with you?"

He stares at her with a determined look. "You've been angry all day. Normally, I would walk away from this display, but I get it. I understand where this is coming from and what it's about. Lea, we gotta find some common ground between us. Promise me you will not take any chances like this again? Please? No more taking off."

"No."

"Lea."

"I can't make that promise, Zion. I hear what you're saying. Tomorrow I'll have Ryan take me to the mall to return everything and follow me around like a guard dog. No more risky excursions. I'm sorry. You have every right to walk away. Save you a headache at least with me out of the picture. One less worry."

"You don't believe that, do you? I'd go crazy without you. No. That's not happening. Not walking away. Why are you having buyer's remorse?" He goes over to look at her purchases. Pulling out a pair of forest green lace four-inch heels, Zion whistles. Thinking about what Lea's legs can look in these heels turns him on.

"I spent way too much money out of frustration. No big deal. My credit card doesn't need the hit and I'm not going out, so there's no need for new stuff. I'll window shop on the Internet. It's safer for both of us that way. I'm not out in public where cray-cray can get to me and looking on the net will save me money. I can talk myself out of a purchase before clicking on that final link."

At this point, Zion doesn't know what to say. Her going out without his security detail makes him angry. Her having to or wanting to return purchases because she can't afford them or feels she doesn't really need them is stupid. He'll fix this. All of this. He walks back over to the couch and sits down.

"Keep it all. I want to see you in every pair." For now, he leaves it at that. He needs to think things through on how to handle her frustration and how to ease it.

He moves closer to her on the couch and sits on the WeVibe Touch vibrator. Sitting back, he looks down and pulls it out. Lea watches him. He looks at her for an explanation.

"Lea?"

"What now?" she asks him.

"Explain please."

"What's to explain, it's self-explanatory."

"We agreed to none of this unless it was more than two weeks and because we could not get to each other. It hasn't been twenty-four hours, and I'm a phone call away. Explain. Or shall I administer a punishment. Your orgasms are for me. All mine," he tells her. "Maybe I need to spank your clit as well as your ass? Teach you a lesson. Is that what you need? An ass spanking? A clit spanking? A tongue lashing? My dick throbbing inside you? My Kitten."

"Yes. Z. Please." Sex diva is stripping naked screaming, HELL TO THE MUTHERFUCKING YES, LET'S GET IT ON BABY.

You feeling better now.

YES. ALL THAT BABY, EX TRAMP CRAP, JUST DON'T SIT RIGHT WITH ME. I WANNA BE THE FOCUS OF ATTENTION.

Zion stands up and undresses, throwing his clothes onto the other couch. He bends down and lifts her chin, kissing her.

"Scoot to the edge of the couch and get my dick hard." he instructs her. "My Kitten."

She scoots to the edge. He stands, straddling her legs placing his hands on her shoulders anticipating the first touch of her hot tongue on his penis. She puts his dick in her mouth, sucking on him. Lea closes her legs so she can bring him in closer. "Oh fuck. Yes. My Kitten. Suck me."

He moves in and out of her mouth slowly, controlling the pace. She sucks him until he's standing straight up, rock-hard. He pulls out and pulls her up. He then sits down and bends her over his lap. "Now how many times shall I spank you for not taking the phone? My Kitten. How many licks will make your ass red? How many licks? My Kitten. Pick a number," he tells her.

"Six," she says. "Will you rub it after each smack?"

"Do you want me to rub your ass after each smack?"

"Yes, please."

Zion smacks her ass lightly the first time. "Count. My Kitten."

"One."

He smacks harder than the last time and rubs the ass cheek he just smacked.

"Two."

He smacks both cheeks harder, and rubs both.

"Three."

He smacks, then rubs.

"Four." She presses her pelvis into his lap in an attempt to bring herself off.

He smacks her hard, then rubs.

"Five." She breathes, trying to lift up. His dick is twitching to get inside her. He smacks her again and rubs and squeezes her ass cheeks.

"Six."

He bends over and blows on her ass. He can see the handprint of his last smack.

Lea is rubbing her pelvis against his leg lightly. He flips her up and makes her stand in front of him, spreading her legs. He presses his nose into her crotch and takes a deep breath, loving the smell of her, baby oil and sex. He sticks out his tongue and licks her right thigh. She grips his shoulders to maintain her balance. He moves over and bites her other thigh. She moans at the bite. He moves to her pussy lips, licking up and down the sides of them.

"My Kitten. How does your ass feel, are you too sore?" He loves spanking her and big hands can be heavy handed.

"No, not sore," she says gripping his shoulders, reassuring him to continue. He buries his tongue between the folds of her pussy and latches onto her clit, licking and sucking. He inserts two fingers into her pussy, rubbing her g-spot. Right as she moves, attempting to fuck his face he stops and pulls back. "Shit. Z. Don't stop."

"I don't want you to fall over. Sit down," he smiles. She sits down on the couch, and he crouches in front of her, opening her legs wide, watching her juices stretch across her pussy lips. He dives into her pussy, eating like there will never be another chance. He sucks and licks her clit, pressing her into the couch as she moves her pelvis in motion fucking his face. She wraps her hands around his head and presses him further into her pussy.

"Oh yes. Suck it, suck my clit. Fuck, bring me off. Make me cum," she pleads. "Shit yes. Yes, eat my pussy, fuck you, eat my pussy. So good baby. Yes, eat it," Lea can't get enough of the way he eats her out.

OH, DAMN HIS TONGUE IS SO FUCKING GOOD.

Lea can feel the orgasm building to that moment, and she fucks his face harder and trying to move back at the same time. He holds onto her waist and keeps sucking on her clit.

God my baby tastes so damn good.

One more flick of his tongue and Lea cums, squirting in Zion's mouth bucking up and down. He catches all her juices, leaving her just wet enough so he can slide in. He sits up, opens her legs and presses into her, pounding into her pussy. He buries his face into her neck as she grips his ass, spreading her legs. This allows him to slip in deeper with each thrust.

Oh shit, she feels so good.

Zion cums fast and hard. "Oooooooooooooooo fuck." He keeps pumping into her until he feels as if he's drained. They stay in this position until his dick goes limp and slips out of her.

"Baby, I'm always here for all your orgasms. And your punishments. Don't make me have to lock up your toy box," he laughs.

"Yes, sir. But if it causes me to be punished like this, I just may have to break that rule again."

They kiss.

-8-

While sitting down to a late dinner, Zion tells Lea about his visit with Wendy and how by the end of next week, she and the nurse will be moved into the corporate apartment.

"What do Crystal and Tom know about what's going on? I would like to know what I should be telling them if anything."

"Tom knows everything. I had lunch with him Friday. I'm sure he's told Crystal. Be truthful. Only with them though. Not the entire office," he says.

"Well, of course not the entire office. Duh. What do you think I am? A gossip? Trust me I have no desire to go blabbing this," Lea hears the bitterness in her tone.

"I know you're not a gossip." Zion caught it also. "Don't be so flippant. What are you planning on telling your circle of friends about us? How will you drop the bomb about becoming a mom and wife in less than a year?"

"When this is over with and we can fully be open and honest, I'll introduce you as the sexy, gorgeous colleague I fell in love with. As for the boys, I'll cross that bridge when I need to. Or let people think I'm walking into a ready-made family. No matter what I say, I'll come off looking bad."

Lea walks out of the kitchen going into the bedroom with Zion following behind her. She flops on the bed. He stops at the end, grinning.

Running a finger up and down her leg, he says, "I don't know what to say. You think I'm sexy and gorgeous. I'm so flattered. Wow and I thought you wanted me for my body. But you think I'm sexy. Oh, my. Thank heaven!" He catches the pillow Lea throws at him. "Lea, it bothers you what others will be saying, no need to deny it. You want people to know you're dating me, especially before we get married and you adopt the boys. Soon baby, real soon. I want all men to know you're off the market. I hate not having to be able to show them that. I keep thinking if I don't visually stake my claim, you'll still be viewed as available. I don't like that at all," he admits, displaying some jealousy.

"Look, unless they specifically ask, I'll deal with it by ignoring it. Now, can we sleep? We have early mornings and busy weeks."

"Stop ignoring the subject of us getting married," he says crawling into bed with her.

"Why shouldn't I ignore the subject. You keep talking marriage and me adopting the boys, but you haven't asked me to marry you. And you have yet to ask me if I want to adopt the boys or be a mother. I don't know how to respond or what I should be saying when you say things like before we get married, after we're married, our family, our kids. I was perfectly fine growing old, childless and even single. You can make an instant decision to adopt the kids of a former fuck buddy without even discussing it with me first."

"Kitten, I don't want your proposal and us announcing our engagement and marriage overshadowed by Addison, Wendy or the birth of the boys. But to make you understand I want to marry you…" Zion gets out of bed, pulls Lea to the side and in all the glory of their nakedness, he gets down on one knee. With his hands placed on either side of her waist he pops the question. "Lea, will you marry me?"

She bursts out laughing at the spectacle of him proposing to her in the nude with his face at her boobs.

"Naw. I want my big special proposal. But you do look cute down there."

"Oh, so now you rejecting me. How dare you. I plan this in five split seconds, and you reject me. I think I'm kinda hurt." He says grinning that grin that melts her heart every time she sees it.

"Lea, I'm not going to stop talking about us being married. Your over-the-top memorable proposal, will be when everything is set in place for us without any obstacles. I enjoy thinking about our future and living happily ever after. I'm speaking our future into existence. I apologize for not discussing the adoption with you before deciding. Things were happening so fast."

"I was the last to know Zion."

"No, you weren't. But I get it. If you are so important in my life, you should have been the second to know. Lea, you supporting me, I assumed you wanted this also. Am I wrong?"

"Zion, I don't know what I want for me right now. I do know that I will not do anything to keep you from becoming a father. You loving and wanting to marry me, the thought of it. Well, I'm scared to think that way. I do love you. But with everything that's going on, I'm scared to believe in it."

"Sweetheart, I'm all yours." He leans in kissing her. They climb back into bed cuddling, leaving the discussion of their future for another day.

They wake up the next morning and dress for work. "Zion, it's impossible for me to get dressed if you keep trying to take off what I put on. We have to go to work." She tries to dodge a kiss from him, but he pins her against the wall for the umpteenth time pressing his pelvis into hers.

Between sentences, he kisses her, "We don't have to go to work. Let's work from here. Or from my apartment. In the nude having sex between breaks in meetings, phone calls, and stuff." He nibbles her neck loving the smell of her. "Baby come on, let's stay home today. I can have Sam pick up my computer and bring it here." He grabs a breast, squeezing her nipple under her bra.

"Zion, remember, Ryan. You're having me shadowed. Ready to cancel it before it even gets started? Fuck that feels so good. Look I don't want to say it, but I will." She looks at him.

"No, not forgetting about Ryan. No need to safe word me." He kisses her one last time and pulls back. "Are you meeting with male clients today?" *Damn she looks good in that dress and heels.* "Don't you have like jeans, an oversized sweatshirt, or a burlap sack? How about a muumuu?"

"Hey, I'll wear a muumuu when you agree to wear a robe that covers you from head to toe and a mask to hide your face. And you promise to use a chalk board to talk. Have you looked in the mirror? Shit, I know I couldn't work with you on a daily basis."

"Working with you daily. That's a thought," he murmurs.

"No, it's not. Zion Landon, get that out of your head. Now! I'm not working for you."

"Who said anything about for me. I'm thinking with me. I can have my office extended to include you. You can be in the same room."

Lea flashes him her cleavage. "Waiting is much more enticing than having these at the drop of a hat, don't you think?"

Laughing out loud he says, "Yes and no, but I get your point."

Ryan arrives at seven. Lea reaches for the bags of purchases she made yesterday, ready to return them. Zion halts her. "Kitten, leave them here. I look forward to seeing you in those shoes."

"Zion, that's almost three-grand. I told you my credit card doesn't need the hit."

"Then I'll pay off the damn credit card. If you return any of it, I'll send Ryan back to purchase every last item and add on clothes to go with it."

"Ha, buying me clothes is not a threat. But I won't argue with you. I'll think about the credit card bill later."

"Good."

Leaving the house Zion ensures the alarm is set and the alarm on Lea's car is armed, having moved it back into the driveway. She's being driven to work in Zion's Cadillac CT6. He walks her to the car, opening the back door for her to get in. Lea hesitates. How many times in life has she dreamed about being chauffeured around and now that it's happening, she's dreading it.

Zion hugs her from behind. "Kitten, I'll call you later. Have a good day."

"You, too, Zion." Lea gets in. She tries to get comfortable but she's uneasy. *I wanna go back home.*

Arriving at her office, Ryan parks in front of the building and escorts Lea up to the office, retreating after he has handed over her computer bag. Crystal gazes at him waiting for him to get on the elevator. Once it closes, she pounces. "Okay missy. Your office. Now. I need to talk to you."

Once the door to Lea's office is closed, Crystal starts in. "Okay what's going on. Tom tells me Zion is going to be a father in about three months. Who is the guy that just walked you into the office? Is that an Addison thing?"

"Crystal, Zion is adopting the twins of a former lover. She's dying, not going to live through the birth of the kids. He wants to be a father and isn't passing up this opportunity, and I'm fully supporting him no matter what happens between us."

"Well, this is some freaking weird shit," Crystal says.

"Look, I love Zion. Even if we don't end up being with each other, I'm not going to allow my feelings and emotions about being replaced by another woman who can give him kids, affect him in any way. He wants this. As for the guy who escorted me into the office, his name is Ryan. Addison has been threatening me in emails and on my phone. Ryan will be driving me, or as I've come to accept it in my mind, shadowing me outside the office. Zion and I won't be going out in public as much. I can't tell anyone about our relationship, but I don't have to deny it if asked. Now, can we get back to work and live and just keep the subject of Zion and his situation to ourselves?"

"Sure, but tell me how you really doing. Lea Adams don't go into your inner world and shut me or Gordon out. Talk to me," Crystal demands.

"I'm scared out of my mind that I could lose him over this. He has an opportunity to have everything with Wendy. He can look at her and say, I need to marry this woman, give my kids my name legally and I could be left out in the cold with my heart in shreds. I'm not regretting I met him, but I hate everything about what's going on. Addison, I can deal with. I can fight her for him and win. But this thing with Wendy and the babies is different. There's nothing I can do but support him. I just want to work and keep busy," she says trying not to cry.

"Okay sweetheart. But that doesn't mean shutting people out or holding your tongue. I'll let you get to work." Crystal leaves Lea's office. *Oh God! What have we done by hooking these two up.*

When Zion arrives at his office, his friend, Greg Chouteau, a detective on the St. Louis City police force, is there waiting for him. "Hey Greg, what up man?" They shake hands and enter Zion's office with Morgan closing the door behind them.

Zion and Greg met in college. Greg is a six-foot black man, trim and wiry, well under two hundred pounds, with a pepper gray goatee. Dressed in his police patrol uniform surprises Zion.

Greg loves the St. Louis streets almost as much as Zion loves St. Louis. When he was promoted and was offered the opportunity to stay behind the desk, everyone was surprised when he accepted it.

He and Zion have kept in touch, getting together about twice a year. Zion envied Greg's relationship with his wife. Greg was a college senior and married when they met Zion in his junior year. They would hang out in the library studying with Greg's wife. Zion used this time to escape Addison. Discovering Greg was a St. Louis implant cemented their friendship. When Zion and Greg met, the relationship with Addison was imploding. Back then Zion was too humiliated to discuss it with anyone. So, Greg never got to meet or hear about her. All he knew was Zion was an angry, brooding black man who simply wanted to get through college.

"Why are you in your street uniform?" Zion asks him.

"I came directly here from the Matthews Dickey Boy's and Girl's Club for a 'Meet Your Police Officer' event. Uniform required so they could ask questions about the attire. Without the gun of course. You wanna tell me what's going on with you and your stalker issue? All those emails and messages I've listened to and you're just now calling me or involving the police? Seriously man, this woman can flip out at any time."

"Greg, you've told me, until a person has physically done something the authorities could do nothing. I've heard the lectures about the restraining orders, keeping away from stalkers, not goading them, and not escalating things. I haven't been out with my girlfriend in weeks because of this. She doesn't hang out with her friends like she used to. I have ensured she and I have not been seen together to avoid setting Addison off, hoping she would keep her focus on me. But the birthday party. I didn't end up in any major magazines when I was partying with my celebrity clients but these small St. Louis magazines and business journals have taken photos of me and posted them twice already. I'm like, seriously. Now I'm about to be a father. I'm adopting two boys. I need to protect everyone I love. Tell me what I should do?"

"I'm going to need all the information you have on Addison Raymond. Do you know where she is? Have you seen her around lately? I can run some checks on her, but I need to know if you want this to be an official report? I'm giving you an option before informing you I'm going to make this an official investigation, which takes away your option of saying no. It's what I do, give you an option then make you do what I say," Greg says laughing.

"Do whatever you need to do. I had a trace on her for about two months. Then she disappeared. I thought she had moved on and left me alone, so I cancelled the person who was following her. Then she started back up after my birthday. Not with me but with my girlfriend. I've hired extra security to include her and her mother. I've told you everything I know so far."

"Okay, well, I'll go do some checking and get back to you." He stands up to leave.

"Thanks, man." Zion says as he escorts Greg out of his office. "Morgan, I'll be down with Star if you need me," Zion informs his assistant as he walks off. While walking through the office, things are flowing along well with the preparations for the move. Right as he's about to enter the corridor to Star's office, he sees his mom and dad coming from the opposite direction.

"What are you guys doing here?" he asks them, giving his mom a hug.

"Your mother is helping out with the move. Her compliance skills have kicked in and she's determined to make sure client paper and electronic files are handled properly. She's been cataloging hard drives removed from old computers, old smartphones and has been doing employee desk audits all week. Her team is making sure this move is completed confidentially. I'm here to do the staff and client meetings you're unable to attend. It's great getting back into things again. I didn't realize how much I missed work."

"Have I been missing that many meetings? Shit. It's only been a couple of weeks since this all began. Let's go to Star's office, I need to update you guys anyway."

When they arrive, Star is on the phone talking with someone about Zion and some rumors. She's saying, "Well I'm glad you called before you ran some crazy article like that. Hey that's all I ask. And I promise, once we have firmed up the dates, you'll have exclusive rights to the event. No problem. Thanks, Meredith. Goodbye."

"What was that about?" Royal asks Star.

"Meredith with the St. Louis American was following up on a rumor of Zion going to Mexico to marry his pregnant girlfriend and wanted to know how this would affect the opening of his new headquarters and who was the lucky girl? I informed her you were not getting married at this time, your girlfriend is not pregnant, and we should be moving into the new building in about three months. I gave her exclusive rights to the grand ceremony event for the entertainment section of the paper," Star says smiling.

"Thanks, Star," Zion says. "Wendy has agreed to relocate into the apartment. She should be moved in by the nineteenth. It's not much left. She's been getting rid of things for a while now. I was wondering, when did you guys want to meet her? Not all at the same time of course."

"Let's do lunch at the apartment that Sunday after she's moved in," his mother says. "Your father and I can come, and she can meet Star and Garrett some time the following week after she's settled in."

"Works for me," Star says.

"Okay," Zion replies, "I'll let Wendy know tomorrow. We have a doctor's appointment. It's our first ultrasound together. I'll get to see the boys." He's seen the printed ultrasound pictures as Wendy has been having one every month to make sure the babies are okay.

This is our first one together. I'm excited but anxious.

"What's wrong?" his father asks. "You just went pale on us."

"I'm going to see the babies for the first time. Lea won't be there. It hit me how much I want her there. How many other firsts will we miss out on?" Zion whispers.

"Oh, sweetie, you can't keep thinking like that. Focus on the firsts you two will have together," his mother says.

Star says, "I was thinking about hanging out with Lea after work on Wednesday. Happy hour and dinner, she and I. You cool with that bro?"

"Yeah, that would be great." Zion loves his family for helping him to get through this. "Thanks guys, I never thought about all the ins and outs of this. I was thinking I could do it all."

"That's what families are for," his father tells him.

They leave Star's office. Zion looks over the details and the quotes Morgan has given him for packing and moving Wendy. He circles the one he wants to use and spends the rest of the day talking with clients, following up with issues with his employees, and making arrangements with Mrs. Vance who has agreed to help with Wendy and Becky. Zion told her there was no need, but she insisted. He increased her salary. He's beyond grateful to everyone who is helping him probably will never be able to thank them enough.

-9-

Lea has been in and out of meetings all day Monday after her talk with Crystal. She makes sure her focus is work, work, work and more work. If anyone needed help, she volunteered.

She sends Zion a text message after lunch not having heard from him all day, saying hello and that she missed him. He responded back an hour later telling her that he loved her and was on his way into a meeting and he would call her later. Ryan picks her up at four-thirty and drives her straight home. No more detours to shop, visit friends, or go for a walk in the park. After a light dinner she lays on the couch watching TV, drifting into a restless sleep. Her abandonment dream returned, only this time, it includes two babies running from her telling her she's not their mother, never will be, and they'll never love her.

She wakes up and checks her phone. No calls or messages from Zion. She calls him and it goes straight to voicemail, so she leaves a message telling him goodnight and that she'll talk to him tomorrow. But tomorrow is the doctor's appointment day, so she probably won't. To avoid having another dream, she decides to do some house cleaning. One can survive on a couple hours of sleep. It's called coffee, coffee, coffee.

On Tuesday, her day goes pretty much the same as Monday minus the morning banter she had with Zion. She hasn't heard from him since his meeting text yesterday. She has a lunch meeting with a client, so Ryan picks her up at eleven forty-five and returns to get her at one-thirty.

"Ryan, drive out to the Landon Enterprises site," she tells him. Yesterday, after their first day of driving together, Lea decides to make a few changes. The first change is she will ride in the front seat. The second is she has control of the radio and all things music. Third is when she required a coffee, hot chocolate, French vanilla cappuccino with whip cream run, she didn't want any arguments, or she would drive herself and make Ryan ride in the back seat. They're still butting heads about unscheduled detours.

"Sure, Miss Adams, I just need to make Mr. Landon and Sam aware of the change in plans."

Lea stares at him, wanting to cuss him out. "Never mind, just go back to the office."

This bullshit is already wearing very thin.

"You sure?" he asks her.

"Yes, I'm sure. We need to do something about this going straight to one place and back. This is not how I work," she stares out the window, pissed.

On the way back to the office, Lea gets a call from Star inviting her for drinks and dinner on Wednesday. She accepts and sends the meeting invite to Zion and Ryan. Even a business meeting like this one is a chance to escape the house.

Lea's no longer communicating directly with Zion regarding issues for the new headquarters. All communications regarding the project have been with Sam, Saul, Star, and his father. That's not unusual, considering the items she's working on involve areas of IT, security, and marketing. Whenever she calls the office, she's questioned about why she's calling. If she says it's anything regarding the project, she gets transferred to one of the others. She elects to contact Zion via his cell when it's personal. Now she emails everyone updates and status reports and carbon copies Zion on all the details.

I hate working this way.

Lea makes it through the day and has Ryan drop her off at her mom's house. No need to give her entire life over to Zion's locking her away and having her escorted everywhere. She finally receives a text from him.

> *Zion:* Hey Kitten, sorry I haven't gotten back to you
> sooner. I miss and love you so much. I'll call
> you tonight, I have a business meeting with a
> client that flew in today.
>
> *Lea:* Have a good meeting.

On Wednesday, when Lea arrives for what she thought was a business dinner with Star, she's shocked and amazed Star wants to have a girls' night out. Lea hadn't expected this or dressed for it. She's in business mode for thirty seconds then relaxes. She greets Star with a warm hug. Their shadows are sitting at another table in full view of them.

"Lea, how are you? Finally, we get to hang out. No business talk. Please no more business today," Star begs.

"I'm good. How's everyone? I miss the girls. How is football season for Garrett?"

"Garrett is busy and stressed, but they've won the last six games they've played. The team this year is fantastic. The girls are getting into everything. They're with a baby-sitter tonight. I want to apologize about us not getting together like this sooner," Star says. "How've you been with all of this?"

Lea is wary about talking Zion and his baby mama-drama. This is Zion's sister; her loyalty lies with him, not her.

"Okay, keeping busy," she says.

"You don't want to vent or scream? I would understand. Well, the screaming anyway. I don't have a clue about what you could be feeling going through this."

"Star, what do you expect me to say to you? You're his sister. I don't want you going back to him telling him my feelings. He has enough to worry about," Lea admits to her.

"I'm not here to get a report about you for my brother. Honestly, I'm not. We're having dinner and that's all. I'm not going to tell our parents about how this went. It's really just between us. I promise you that," Star says.

"I'm jealous, frustrated, envious, sad, depressed, happy, bored, and have a strong desire to punch someone in the back of their head and push them down a flight of stairs. But this too shall pass," Lea says. "You look shocked. Was I supposed to sugar coat it and lie? You did ask after all."

"No, I'm, well I didn't expect all that."

"Okay, let's back up and start over. I'm wonderful, everything is sunshine and roses. No, not roses, Calla lilies. I don't like roses. Too damn typical for my tastes. There, you can tell Zion and your parents I said that. It'll make everyone feel better."

"Lea, I'm good with the honesty. I prefer it. I wish we would have become closer before all this. But here we are."

"Yep. Here we are. So now what?" Lea asks. She wants to see where Star is going with this.

"Lea, I'm not here on my brother's behalf the way you think. Let's eat, drink, and enjoy ourselves. I don't get out as much without the girls being the center of the meetup. You down?"

Lea bursts out laughing at Star's code switch and goes with it, "Girl I am so down."

Lea and Star talk about shopping, shoes, purses, malls, everything. Star tells her about the places she's traveled, her education. Star has Bachelor's and Master's degrees in Marketing and Communications. She even goes into details about how she and Garrett met, dated, and describes what loving a football coach is like and the life they have with twin girls.

Like her brother, Star keeps her friends' circle tight. She's been burned more in friendships than Zion has because of her trusting nature, but she says she's learned a lot about the evilness of money and the good it can do.

Star has plans to convince Zion of opening a small satellite office away from his Chesterfield digs, but hasn't thought it was a good idea to bring it up with this Addison crap going on. Up until now, it has been easy to keep the conversation off Lea as Star loves talking. All Lea has to do is ask Star leading questions and she's off and running.

"You've kept me talking. Now you. I want details, all the details," she says.

"What's there to tell? I'm an only child, spoiled rotten by my family. My circle of friends is also tight, but that has nothing to do with money. More to do with me being an introvert and I like to avoid drama. Bachelor's and Master's, you already know my hobby is photography. What else would you like to know?"

"This may be a hard one to answer, but do you have any regrets about meeting my brother?"

Lea thinks for a second, "Yes, I wish I had met him in my thirties. But when I think back to how I was then, I could have given him a run for his no attachment relationship persona. Don't get me wrong, I've never slept around, but I've been that fuck'em without emotions girl. We would've driven each other crazy. Good sex but emotionally detached."

"Oh my, my, my. No wonder he fell for you so hard. A kindred spirit in some ways and a balance to him in so many others. So, is it going to be a big or small wedding?" Star asks.

Lea chokes on her drink. "Why does everyone skip over the fucking question of has he asked me and go straight to after? Look, I want him to get beyond the birth and, sorry to say, the funeral. I want to be happy, but I feel an overwhelming amount of guilt and jealousy. It's not about me, it's about him and the adoption. I'm the low woman on the totem pole if I'm really on it at all." Now Lea is getting pissed. That subject keeps her agitated.

Star reaches over to touch Lea's hand, "Lea, you're on it. He lights up when he talks about you. Don't ever think you're not on his mind. I'm sure of it. Lea, my brother loves you. Very much. I know it's hard to believe or trust with what's going on, but he does love you."

"Thanks Star. I think it's time we called it a night. No offense to Ryan, but I need a break from him."

On the drive home Lea gets antsy. It's a wonderful balmy night at eight-thirty and she's about to go home and lock herself away behind closed doors. Before she had her shadow, going out for a late-night drive when Zion was out of town was fun. Now all that's over. Maybe soon she can try it, just for a couple of hours.

"Miss Adams. Miss Adams are you okay?" They're sitting in her driveway and Ryan is calling her name. She hadn't realized they had arrived at her house. She looks at him standing there holding the door open.

"Yes, I'm fine. Thanks Ryan." She gets out of the car and enters the house.

Ryan decides to sit for a bit. His instincts are telling him that something is wrong. He calls Zion.

"Ryan, what's up?" Zion answers his phone wondering why he could be getting a call from Ryan this late. He checked his phone to be sure that Lea was home. Star called him and told him how much they enjoyed themselves but wouldn't say anything else.

What's the point of the dinner if she's not going to tell me more about what was said.

"Sir, it's Miss Adams. She hasn't said anything, but she's distracted and jittery," Ryan tells Zion.

"Thanks Ryan. Where are you now?"

"Sitting outside her house. Just thought I would hang out here for a bit." Ryan has been instructed that after he drops Lea off at home, he's to make sure she's safely inside and not to hang around to give her some semblance of autonomy, but tonight is different. He feels the need to sit and watch.

"Okay. Let me know if she leaves. She's taken off once already before we had you in place. She likes going for drives. Don't stop her, but be sure to have someone follow her," Zion tells him.

-10-

Yesterday, Zion and Wendy had their first doctor's appointment together. She was on cloud three-million and fifty introducing Zion as the father of her sons to the nurses and doctors. Zion was out of his element, with the introductions and the whole ultrasound experience. When a nurse addressed him as Mr. Noelin, Zion instantly checked her, stated his full name, stressed he was the adoptive father and he and Wendy were not married.

Wendy eased the tensions, clarifying Zion's presence and they were escorted into the exam room. She walked him through what was happening and what he was seeing. After calming down, Zion focused on the experience.

God, it was wonderful. My sons, my boys are healthy and strong. I even got a video of it to share with Lea. It's strange how I've already, in such a short time taken ownership of them.

Getting back to the office on a high note, Zion walks to his desk phone to call Lea and tell her about the doctor's appointment, wanting her to share in his excitement. But before he could complete the call, one of his junior financial professionals, Anita, arrives with the news she has landed a million-dollar company in Arizona, her hometown, for Landon Enterprises to manage the employee's company investments. The owner of the company wanted to know if representatives from Landon Enterprises could meet with them in person to get everyone signed up. It's only a ten-employee company, but they have questions and concerns and wanted to talk to someone in person.

Switching gears, Zion instructs Morgan to get reservations made for hotel and meetings in Arizona, find out how fast the plane can be ready for departure, and have Anita pull forms, brochures, and all necessary paperwork required for enrolling employees in new investment plans. Realizing the scope and magnitude of what will be taking place over the next few days, Zion enlists two other junior financial professionals to give them some experience. He was at the office past midnight. Getting home he sees that Mrs. Vance has his luggage packed. Walking to his office, Zion clears up some calls with a couple of overseas clients. He barely gets in a couple of hours of sleep when his alarm wakes him.

Checking his phone, he sees that he had a message from Lea. He smiles while getting dressed making a mental note to call her when he gets on the plane. But that phone call gets delayed. He spends the plane ride explaining what Anita and the other two financial professionals will be doing, and why he asked them to come even though they would not be getting paid a commission.

"Gentlemen, Anita did all the work to find and negotiate with this client. This is essentially her deal. I'm here as the face of Landon Enterprises and to answer questions they may have. You two are here to listen, help and learn. Neither of you have managed to bring in a five-figure client in the year you've worked for me. I've given you plenty of opportunity and training. Now I want you to put that training to work and I want to see you in action to see where your training is lacking and how to improve it. Any questions?"

"No," they both responded.

"Good." They continue with their discussions; Zion having put any calls to Lea he wanted to make out of his mind.

From his hotel room in Arizona, Zion calls her. He thinks it's about to go to voicemail but she answers. "Hello Zion," her voice sounds flat.

"Hi Kitten. How are you? How was dinner with Star?" He feels the need to get her talking.

"It was good. A change. I thought she wanted to discuss business, but she said it was a girls' night out, so I allowed myself to relax and enjoy. Why are you in Arizona and how long will you be there?"

He didn't inform me he was leaving town and never returned any of my calls or messages yesterday. Good thing "find my friends" is setup on our phones.

"Sorry I didn't tell you about it before I left. It really came up at the last minute. One of my employees received a call from a client she's been attempting to get to invest with us."

"I thought your company only handled individual investments and not group plans?"

That's right Lea keep up the small talk.

"My company usually only handles individual plans. I've been targeting successful small businesses lately that don't have employee investment plans. I've been structuring and training my junior financial professionals for this and Anita is the first to succeed. No one has to sign up for anything but if they want to, we're here to help them out. I should be back sometime Saturday."

"You're with a woman?" Lea bites out.

"Lea, I'm traveling with employees. I've done this before. Not since we've been together, but it does happen. I'm locked away in my room talking with you. Want me to prove it?"

"No."

That single word 'no' speaks volumes. Lea is straining not to speak from emotion because she knows she'll wind up in tears.

"Sweetheart, what's wrong? Talk to me." Zion gently prods her.

"Zion, I'm tired of sitting in this house. I can't take it. I want to go to a show. I wanna go to happy hour with my friends. I wanna be able to do my job, checking on the status of my projects in person. That's how I keep things on track and earn the respect of my contractors. I'm not a hands-off, send-me-email-updates kinda person. That's probably why shit slipped through the cracks with Martin. You get to fly off at a minute's notice. You get to be out of the office meeting clients, having dinner. You get to keep doing your job. You're keeping me from living my life. I know I don't go out that much or often but to have the option taken away from me is getting on my damn nerves. What the hell is going on with Addison? I need updates. If this shit doesn't get handled quickly, I'll do my own investigation and take the shit to her. She's brought it to me via emails after all. I have every right to find her and tag her ass myself," Lea sniffs, wiping her nose on the back of her sleeve. When she gets pissed and angry, she gets teary.

Ryan was right. Lea has cabin fever. "Lea, please don't go after Addison. I—a. Geez, I'm sorry. It wasn't supposed to be like this. I didn't think. Look, I'll talk with Ryan. We'll have to adjust and allow you to get back to being you. Baby just promise me you won't do anything about Addison. Please sweetheart?" he asks her.

"Zion, I can't promise you that. I'll promise you I won't go looking for a fight. I'll promise you I won't start anything. BUT if I run into her and she threatens me, I'll do all in my power to take the witch out," she tells him, taking back some of her life.

"Dammit, baby. I—a."

Lea cuts him off. "Zion, my life will resume the way I want it to," she tells him. "Hell, as a matter of fact I'm going for a drive. You can tell Ryan he can go home now."

"I won't send Ryan home. If you leave your house, he has instructions not to stop you but only to follow you."

"What? Are you fucking kidding me? Ugh." She plops down on the sofa in defeat.

"Kitten, promise me you'll let me handle Addison. I'll adjust. I love you babe. Sleep tight. I'll talk with you tomorrow. Please don't go for a drive this late. I don't want you falling asleep behind the wheel."

"Gotta be sleepy for that to happen. Good night, Zion." She disconnects the call before he can say anything else. She turns off all the lights and opens the blinds watching Ryan sitting in his car. He keeps texting someone.

Lea calls him.

"Yes, Miss Adams."

"Go home, Ryan."

"But Mr. Landon-."

"Screw what Mr. Landon said. I'm telling you to go home. I'm not going anywhere. Go home and enjoy your life. You're not a prisoner." Lea cuts him off before he can disagree. He starts the car and drives off. She sits in the dark hoping to catch a quick nap.

The next morning she's still there. She gets up to be ready for work when Ryan arrives. Makeup to hide the status of not sleeping and coffee, to function. Maybe an espresso, triple.

-11-

Zion arrives back in St. Louis late Saturday night. Pulling into his building's garage, he calculates in his mind how much time it will take him to change and check on Wendy before he can get to Lea. As Sam drops him off, they see that Lea's car is parked across from his other cars. Without even saying goodbye to Sam, Zion speeds to the elevator punching the button until it arrives. Sam smiles and drives away after ensuring Zion is safely inside the elevator. He figures he can drop the bags off tomorrow giving Mr. Landon time to enjoy this unexpected home coming.

Zion can't get to his apartment fast enough. He enters and sees that Lea is laying on his couch sound asleep. He walks over to her and bends down, stroking her face, kissing her.

"Kitten, wake up," he says quietly not wanting to scare her. She opens her eyes, unfocused and sits up. "Hi, Lea."

"Zion," she stares at him.

She doesn't say anything else, just stares. Then she reaches out and gives him a hug, wrapping her legs around his waist drawing him into her. "Hi, Bear," she says, burying her face in his neck.

"I've missed you and am so glad you're here."

"You don't mind? I called to ask first but I guess your phone was turned off. It went straight to voice mail." She continues hugging him, smelling him, happy she can feel him.

Lea wasn't sleeping well at her place, so she decided to come here. When she sat down on his couch to watch some TV, she was surprised to be falling off to sleep. She figured a quick nap would be okay. That was four hours ago.

"No babe, of course I don't mind. It's wonderful coming home to you." He leans back and pulls out his phone. "Yep, it's still turned off." When he turns it back on, four messages come in. One from Lea and two from Wendy's nurse and the last one a hang-up. "You can come here at any time, whether I'm here or not," he says as he moves to sit on the couch next to her.

"Go ahead," she says, releasing him, "Return them."

"This will only take a second, and then it's just us." He calls Becky. Wendy was having a bad day and wanted to hear a friendly voice.

He asks Becky to put Wendy on the phone.

Lea gets up and goes to the kitchen, washing the glass she had, to give him some privacy.

Zion has a fifteen-minute conversation with Wendy, explaining he was out of town on a last-minute business trip. During his conversation he continues to keep his gaze on Lea. She looks worn out. Her shoulders are slumped. This woman is not his confident, blossoming, fun Lea. He doesn't like this Lea.

"No, Wendy, I'm sorry I can't make it tonight. I'll be there tomorrow and we can talk then. It's no problem. I turned my phone off to meet with a client and didn't turn it back on until a few minutes ago. Okay, get some rest and I'll see you tomorrow. Good night."

Lea moves to get her phone, keys, and wallet. "You can go if you need to. I can go home. It's no problem, really. We can talk more later."

He stands and pulls everything out of her hands. "Like I told Wendy, I'll see her tomorrow. Right now, it's about us."

Lea and Zion undress and shower together. He massages her shoulders, soaping her body in soothing rubs and circles.

"Zion, I should be giving you a massage," Lea murmurs, enjoying the feel of his hands on the middle of her back.

"Naw, not tonight, Babe. I wanna rub on you. This relaxes me."

"Good. I like hearing that. Something all for me."

Zion yawns. "Yep, all for you."

"Sleepy Bear, let's go to bed." Lea grabs towels, and they dry each other off. Zion climbs into bed first, opening his arms for Lea. She crawls in and lies down on his chest. He soon falls off to sleep. She makes an attempt to move out of Zion's arms, but he moves his hand down to her clit.

"Zion, no. I thought you were tired."

"Lea, yes. I may be tired, but my libido is wide awake. I'm not about to put it to sleep before—, well you know," he whispers.

HELLLLLLOOO, GIRL I'M IN CONTROL. WE NEED THIS. WE WANT THIS. ALWAYS. ANY TIME. ANY PLACE. YES LORD. ALWAYS. AS MARVIN GAYE SANG "LET'S GET IT ON."

"Baby, turn over and press your ass against me," Zion tells her, helping her to turn over. With her butt placed directly pressed against his dick, Lea arches her back into his warm body, opening her legs and closing her eyes, giving in to his expert ways of getting her hot and wet. She moans from the pleasurable feelings of it, never wanting it to stop. He kisses her neck, nibbling and licking the nape of her neck, knowing this will set her off.

Shit, it feels so good. Okay, Sex Diva. You right. Let's get it on.

Zion and Lea allow their bodies to do the talking. He positions her leg over his, opening her wide and slipping into her from behind. He exhales and groans with the feel of her pussy tightening around him. He sits up and flexes his dick inside of her. She slowly moves, fucking him, drawing out the pleasure, wanting it to last, needing it to never end. She covers his hand as it continues to stroke her clit, in movement to her fucking his dick. She sits up a little so she can get a better position of having him in her. He pulls her in close.

Oh fuck, this is so damn good.

Zion lets the feel of his dick adjust to the hotness of her pussy, while massaging her clit. She places her hand over his and presses into her slowly, agonizingly fucking him.

Oh shit, baby, yes. Zion thinks.

Lea adjusts her body to where her ass is pressing into his pelvis with each stroke of her pussy.

Shit, a slow fuck with my Lea is wonderful.

They continue the slow grinding movements, with him caressing her clit.

I could do this all day.

Zion feels her coming. Jerking in orgasm. It sends him over the edge. He groans into the back of her neck, holding onto her waist, not wanting her to move.

Shit, this feels so good I managed to have two orgasms in a row emptying myself into her.

"Oh, Lea." Zion drifts off to sleep, his dick still in Lea's pussy. He murmurs, "It's gonna be so amazing coming home to you and this every day."

Lea says nothing, relaxes and smiles drifting off to sleep. At some point during the night her nightmare begins.

-12-

Zion and the boys are at the zoo, getting ready to board the train. They all like the train. She's standing outside of the train taking pictures of them. A woman walks into the frame. She can't see her face, but Zion turns, looks, and kisses her. The boys scream "mommy, mommy," and reach up for a hug. The woman bends down and hugs them all. Lea stops taking pictures and watches them. Then the train moves. It's riding into the clouds with the family of four and she's being left behind. Again. Alone.

She wakes up and watches Zion next to her.

He's gonna leave you, Lea.

She moves to get out of bed, going into the bathroom. He adjusts slightly but goes back to sleep. She sits on the side of the tub, looking at herself in the mirror.

It will be just him and the boys and you'll be left in the wind. He will find someone else. Someone more to his liking. Someone more in line with his lifestyle. You're not up to the task of being his wife and the mother of his sons. You don't have what it takes.

All these things start going through her head.

OKAY YOU NEED TO STOP THIS SHITTY THINKING. I'M NOT HAVING THIS. SHE NOT GETTIN OUR MAN. NAW! AIN'T GONNA HAPPEN. NO SIR.

Lea silently cries into a towel, muffling the sounds, giving herself a headache.

Sex Diva, we have a fight on our hands.

Zion reaches for Lea in his sleep. Upon finding nothing, he wakes sitting straight up, looking around the room. He hears her in the bathroom crying. He gets up, goes to her, and bends at eye level, raising her head to look at him. "Bad dream?" he asks. She nods her head yes.

"Baby, don't cry," he takes a wet towel, wiping away her tears.

She wraps her arms and legs around him, and he carries her back to bed.

Sunday morning, they're still in bed with Lea wrapped in his arms. She hasn't slept much after her crying jag in the bathroom. Every time she moved; Zion moved.

Zion lightly trails his fingers up and down Lea's thigh, enjoying watching how her thigh muscles react to the movement. "Kitten, why did you say no to me?"

"You were supposed to be sleeping."

"I heard you. But I didn't want you thinking I forced myself on you by saying yes and continuing on. It's not always about our safe words."

"Oh, Zion. I know you would never do that." Lea links their fingers. "Baby, I'm just rather emotional. You're my wonderful sexy, sex fiend, and my body always reacts to your loving touch. You know my non-verbal cues. We've learned so much about each other that way since delving into BDSM."

"Your safety is my priority, Lea. Even from me."

"Bear, I know that. And you didn't force yourself on me. I wanted you to get some rest, and I didn't articulate that well with your hands and lips doing they thang."

"Good. That would have worried me all day. I love you." He hugs her tight.

"I love you, too. Let's get up and have breakfast, then I can get out of here."

"I guess," Zion murmurs.

They are sitting at the dining room table, with Lea straddling Zion's lap. He's caressing her back, trailing the tips of his fingers up and down her spine.

"Kitten, you keep grinding on me and kissing my neck, you're never getting out of here."

She stops and looks into his penetrating brown eyes. "Is that a bad thing?"

"No. But I don't want you using sex, thinking you have to compete for my attention with Wendy. Don't devalue our love and relationship like that."

"What makes you think I would do that, Zion?" Lea had thought of it. Or wanted to test out if he would delay his visit with Wendy and chose to spend more time with her.

"I've been with women that have turned to using sex to get their way. I'm aware of the signs. We're in a hellish situation and it's not going to get easier. I've walked away from women who thought they could use sex to control me."

"So, now you comparing me to other women?" Lea asks testily.

"I'm looking at the situation. Get angry with me. I don't care. I prefer you angry and communicating than quiet and using sex games. We not kids, Lea."

She's silent. It hadn't been a far-fetched idea her wanting to use sex to hold onto him.

"Smart ass."

"Sex Kitten. No games. Okay?"

"No games. I'm human, Zion. An imperfect human."

"We both are."

Lea gets off his lap, moving to clean up the kitchen. "Well, I'm going home. Go ahead and call Ryan to let him know I'm ready to be followed."

Zion reaches for his phone to text Ryan. "Lea, this is for your safety. Ryan is available to drive you at any time. Even on the spur of the moment when you wanna come here."

"Zion, I won't do that to him. I texted him I wanted to come here, and I was driving. I gave him time to get to my place and he followed me. I'm surprised he didn't tell you."

They're on the elevator riding down to the garage. "Lea, we're working on giving you some privacy. He made sure you were inside and safe, and he left. If you need to make a detour to the grocery store, or wherever today, do it. Or not. Your choice."

"And worry you? No thanks. I'm going home. Have a nice visit with Wendy. Talk to you later." She kisses him and gets in her car driving straight home.

-13-

Zion starts his week ensuring the arrangements to get Wendy and the nurse moved into the corporate apartment are in place. At the apartment, he meets with Sam and Saul to discuss a piece of business he doesn't want anyone else to know about.

"Sam, are the cameras installed?" Zion asks, while walking around surveying the new furniture and checking the entry and access points.

Sam responds, "Yes, Sir. The cameras at the front and back doors are installed in the hall lighting and the three-hundred-and-sixty-degree camera is installed in the ceiling, hidden as part of the new light fixture."

Zion looks up scrutinizing it. The fixture has eight globes stretching out in different directions with six lights. He tests it with the remote control turning it on and off. Looking at the feed from the camera on his phone, he maneuvers it around surveying the apartment.

Watching him Saul asks, "Sir, are you sure you want surveillance in here?"

Addressing Saul, Zion says, "I know what you're thinking. I will be in a shit load of trouble if anyone finds out about this one." He points to it with the remote turning it off. "I'll tell Wendy and the nurse about the ones for the door but this inside camera is for me and my viewing only. I'll setup a password for it. I need this for my own peace of mind." Zion says, daring Sam or Saul to argue with him.

"Well, the boss has spoken." Saul says, trying to ease the tension in the room. "As stated, the inside camera is only viewable by Zion. It's not connected to any of the company's security. Sir, it's motion-activated. Once the ladies move out, I'll go in and remove it. Unless needed for legal purposes, all evidence of the camera and recordings will be destroyed as agreed upon. Correct?" Saul asks.

"Correct." Zion responds. "Gentlemen, let's get out of here. Thanks for all your assistance on this."

Both gentlemen say "You're welcome" and leave without further discussion.

Checking his schedule on Thursday, Zion sees he has a walk-through inspection at the new headquarters with representatives from G-TEE and Landon Enterprises. And that Lea will be there. They haven't seen one another since Sunday. Excited about all the news he has to share with her, he gives her a call.

"Hi, this is Lea," she answers on the first ring.

My sexy, beautiful Lea. "Hi Kitten, good morning."

"Zion. How are you? Good morning, Bear," she breathes into the phone.

I can feel the smile in her voice.

"Missing you and looking forward to seeing you today for the inspection."

"Baby, I miss you too, but I won't be joining you. You'll be doing that with Tom."

"Say what? Your schedule says you're there today." He sits up straighter in his desk chair, looking at his calendar for confirmation.

"Yes, I'm here now, making sure things are ready. I'm working on some phone issues with the phone tech. He's checking some defective lines. And you no longer take meetings or work with your project lead. Remember. I've been pushed off to everyone else."

"He, he who? What he? Where's Ryan?" *What man is she there with in that office? There is no staff there and even the contractors have been given the day off so the walk-through inspection can take place without any distractions.*

"Oh, stop getting into pissing-contest mode. You know I work with a majority of men. That isn't going to change because we're dating."

"I'll think about it. I was and am looking forward to seeing you today. Just make sure you stick around."

"Maybe. I hadn't planned on it. We shall see. It's seven-thirty, and you're not scheduled to be here until ten. I may be done by then. So, how are you? Everything going well?"

"I'm good. I saw the babies Tuesday during the doctor's appointment. Wendy had an ultra-sound. Lea, it was wonderful. They were moving around, flashing the camera. I have a video I want to show you. Lea, you have to see them."

"Zion, I'm so happy for you. You know you can send me the video," she says. That way when she views it, she can cry in peace.

"No, I want us to watch it together. I love you, sweetheart. Don't leave before I get there. Please Kitten. I'll see you in a bit."

"I love you too," Lea ends the call. *Fuck, another first experienced without me. That, he, we, ugh forget it.*

At ten o'clock everyone scheduled for the first inspection arrives, Tom, Neal, Sam, Saul, Star and Zion. Lea stands at a window watching them get out of their cars.

Shit, watching Zion walk toward the building is hypnotizing.
AND HE OUR MAN. LORD HA MERCY.

Lea can't take her eyes off him. He stops in his tracks and looks up at the windows. Zion can't see anyone, but he smiles, feeling Lea's gaze on him behind the mirrored windows from somewhere.

Ryan buzzes Zion and everyone into the building.

To do her job, Lea made Ryan back off and stay in the lobby. He wanted to follow her floor by floor, but she nixed that by telling him she'd put her foot up his ass if he didn't stop hovering. Ryan backed off quickly. He elected to sit at the building security desk with the other security guards, monitoring the cameras and watching Lea from there. Having had the phone tech, Michael Stone, thoroughly investigated, Ryan was confident he could leave him and Lea alone to work.

"Ryan, where's Lea, why aren't you with her?" Zion asks him upon entering the building.

"I didn't want a foot up my ass, Sir," he answers.

"What?" Zion questioningly looks at him.

Tom walks up to the desk, laughing behind Zion. "Smart man, Ryan. Smart man. Zion, she has to do her job without her shadow. You may want to ease up on that before she flips the fuck out. Trust me. That's not a good sight. I saw it once. Or the end of it. I ran like a scared rabbit."

Zion stares Tom down, then turns back to Ryan. "Where is she? Find her and let me know. Let's get this over with," he says to the others and they walk off.

And I've eased up on her.

The inspection will take everyone onto each floor, checking offices, conference rooms, cubicles, break areas, computer/server room and the security office. They're scheduled to end on the top floor in Zion's new office. Lea, Sam, and Saul have tested all the equipment and upgraded security features of his office, the privacy walls and windows, the monitors for the security cameras, phones, computer, and desk. Zion could move in tomorrow if he wanted to.

Zion points out things he likes, don't like, wants replaced, and fixed. He listens to suggestions on furniture, art, and plants. He changes the paint in three of the conference rooms, along with the art. He only wants art from local black artists in the St. Louis area, none of these cheap, cheesy, and typical mass-produced pictures he sees on the walls. Its presence pisses him off.

The group has moved to the security room, looking at the cameras. Landon Enterprises has camera views of door, stair, floor access, and common areas displayed on the wall monitors. On one of the cameras, he sees Lea standing in a cube testing a phone and a man standing next to her. Too damn close for Zion's tastes. "Where is that?" he asks Sam.

"Third floor south Sir," he responds.

Zion makes a move to leave, thinking he can get to Lea, but she and the guy walk toward the elevators, pushing the Up button.

"It looks like she's headed to the executive floor, possibly to your office. Shall we meet her there?" Tom says smiling.

"Who's that with her?" Zion asks.

"Michael Stone, phone technician," Tom offers.

They leave and head for the elevators. Lea and Michael are in Zion's office testing his conference phone. They have tested all the other conference room phones in the building and are ready to call it a day.

"Michael, this has gone perfectly. Only four defective phones out of the entire bunch. Get those fixed for me and back in the conference rooms. Check and make sure all the ports are working once more and get that last one completed for the second-floor all-in-one copier. It keeps losing connection."

"Will do. You okay, Lea? You aren't your normal all-over-the-place self. It's unnerving. I expected to be running all over this building, going nuts," Michael asks. "Would you like to talk about it? Over dinner and drinks maybe?" Michael has been trying to get a date out of Lea since he met her a year ago. All his attempts have been shot down for one reason or another. Maybe it's time he pushed harder.

"It shows that much?" Lea says as two are walking toward the elevators. "I have some things going on. Rather distracted." They stand, waiting for its arrival after Lea punched the down button, going over more potential issues.

Lea thinks about what to do after she gets back to the lobby. *I can go sit in the lobby and wait for the inspection to be completed or have Ryan drive me back to the office. Escaping seeing Zion. Nope. Dare I admit, I need to see Zion. Yep. If only for a few minutes.*

"Thanks for the offer of dinner and drinks, but I'm seeing someone."

The elevator doors open and out comes everyone, Zion being last. He looks at Michael, then at Lea. She had moved back so they could get off and she could greet them, then get on with Michael. If looks could kill, poor Michael would be dead on the spot. He steps on the elevator.

"Hello everyone. Lea, I'll give you a call later to see if there is anything else that comes up from today's inspection. He's a lucky man," Michael states.

"Thanks Michael, talk to you later."

The door closes and Zion turns to her. "Miss Adams. What does he mean he's a lucky man?"

"Mr. Landon. The man that I'm involved with," she says staring into his eyes ensuring he fully understands that she was turning down a date from another man.

"You damn right he is. Everyone, if you'll excuse us a moment, I need a word with my Project Lead."

"Oh, so now you want a word with your Project Lead. How fascinating. I'm wanted again." Lea snaps out as Zion pulls her behind him toward the kitchen area.

He closes the door, takes her in his arms, and presses her against him, kissing her.

"I've missed you. And do I need to fire that phone company technician to make him understand you're not available to date him?"

Lea pulls away and steps out of his embrace. "You have an inspection to finish." She wipes her lipstick off his lips. "I'll be downstairs. And there's no need to fire anyone." She walks out, leaving him standing there.

Before she can step onto the elevator, he's behind her, directing her toward his office.

"Oh no you don't, Kitten." He pats her on her behind. "And that's for that smart ass remark, we'll discuss more later," he whispers in her ear.

Upon entering everyone turns around and stares at them. Lea walks to the other side of the room away from Zion not making eye contact with anyone.

"Okay, shall we proceed."

Zion listens to and watches the demo of how the cameras, phone, and security access work from his desk. There's a touch screen built into the surface of the desk, something like Tron. He has a monitor that pops up when desired. This office is the ultimate geek's electronic dream. Attempting to pay attention, Zion can't take his eyes completely off Lea standing to the side, ramrod straight with her hands folded in front of her, staring out the window.

"Lea, do you have any suggestions, ideas, or questions. I may be missing something," he attempts to engage her. "Lea?" *Baby look at me, what's wrong?*

"What?" She snaps back at him staring. "Oh, no, nothing. No suggestions. Sorry." She answers, but she's thinking, *Why the fuck are you asking me? Shit. This isn't my office. Can I fucking leave now? Just keep it together, Lea.* The others continue talking and she turns back toward the window.

Hell, how can I've been so self-involved and clueless to men being attracted to me? How many of these men have I let get away thinking they're just work colleagues without any kind of desire for me. I could've been dating Michael or any of the men I've come into contact with, but no, I end up with Zion. Sexy ass, billionaire, man who can fuck me into a coma, Zion. And now I'm being stalked by a crazy nut case crack-head, and my boyfriend is adopting the children of a former fuck buddy. What the fucking hell.

Lea is overthinking as usual about all the what ifs in life, giving herself a headache. She takes a deep breath and rolls her shoulders and neck for some relief, pinching the bridge of her nose, trying not to scream or cry. When she opens her eyes, she can see Zion watching her in the reflection of the window. She turns away.

Lea is jarred back to reality as all the others move around her, leaving the office.

Great. Time to go back into the cage. See what happens when you blindly agree to do something.

She turns around and follows them out with Zion behind her attempting to touch her. As they get to the elevator, Zion grabs her and moves her away from the others.

"You all go ahead, we'll be down in a few," Zion tells them.

As the elevator doors close, he turns to Lea, pinning her with his gaze then his body against the wall. They don't say anything, just stand with bodies pressed against each other. Zion caresses her neck. Lea puts her head on his chest taking in his scent.

"I'm glad you stuck around, Lea," Zion says. Holding her is comforting. His mind and body stop their frantic racing. He calms down and relaxes. All because he's holding Lea.

"I'm glad I got to see you today," she says unbuttoning his shirt and kissing his chest.

"Sweetheart, you keep that up we gonna break in my office. I don't have time for that."

Lea pulls back, buttons his shirt and straightens his tie.

THIS REJECTION SHIT BLOWS.

"Don't look at me like that. It's not a no, just a pause for later."

"Then safe word me."

"No. I want you. I want inside you."

The elevator dings and the doors open. They get on and Zion pushes the button stopping it mid-descent.

"Elevators are for making out." He kisses her.

Lea hits the button for the elevator to start back up and for the remainder of the ride down he continues kissing her, nibbling her neck when she turns her face, silencing her with his lips when she attempts to speak.

"Zion. Ocean."

"Dammit," he says, stepping back adjusting himself in his pants.

Lea pulls her top away from her chest, adjusting her breasts. They're feeling rather swollen at the moment. Zion stares at her, grinning. They arrive at the lobby, exiting the elevator flustered.

"Lea, ride with me. I want to show you the video before you go back to work. Sam and I'll drive you back to the office."

"Can you drive me home? I've been here since seven, so I'm officially off work now," Lea says, thinking quickly.

Tom comes over. "Lea, I'll get the changes to you Zion has requested. They're easy fixes. See you in the office tomorrow. Zion, take it easy and remember what I told you."

"See you in the morning, Tom. Ryan, can you pick me up around six-thirty?" Lea asks, wondering what Tom has said to Zion.

"Sure, Miss Adams. I'll see you in the morning. Good night, Mr. Landon." He exchanges a pointed look with Zion thinking Lea didn't catch him.

Who the hell do these men think they are fooling? The looks, the warnings. Well fuck all of them. Keep talking about me. Idiots.

"Y'all can stop with the sly looks at each other. I'm not fucking blind or oblivious to what y'all are doing. Assholes. Ryan, give me the keys to the car. I'll drive myself home," Lea snaps at them.

"Ryan will see you in the morning, Lea," Zion says. "You're not driving yourself home."

"Screw you all. I'll walk." Lea grabs her purse and marches outside. She knows what she said doesn't make sense. She's out in a field near Chesterfield Airport, thirty miles away from home, for heaven's sake.

Walk home. Yeah right.

"Star, ride with Ryan." Zion shouts over his shoulder as he takes off after Lea.

Tom yells at Zion's retreating back, "See told you. Freak the fuck out. Have a nice ride."

"Sure thing, big brother. Wow, I do enjoy seeing him like this. Ain't love grand y'all. Come on, Ryan, so I can see this." Star says rushing to get outside.

Lea has stopped at the SUV.

The others have filed out of the building moving to their vehicles. Lea stares at her reflection in the window of the SUV watching Zion approach her. He runs his hand over his face and turns to talk to Sam.

"Sam, get in, give us a second." Zion moves to stand in front of Lea staring down at her. She focuses on his tie.

"Assholes huh?" Zion asks. "Maybe we are a bunch of assholes. You're angry. What can I do to make this up to you?"

"Nothing. Can we just go? I'm tired."

"Of course, anything you want."

"You mean almost anything I want. What I want is out of my reach. Forever." It hit Lea in a nightmare last night. She'll never see the pride and happiness in his eyes from seeing his child growing inside of her. Wendy gets all of that. Even if it's not his biological child.

"Lea, look at me. Now. What do you mean almost?"

"Zion, I'll never see that look of admiration from you of me carrying your child and it irks me. God, verbalizing it sounds ridiculous. Without Wendy, there was no guarantee I coulda given you a child artificially. I know all that. But knowing you'll look at her, look at another woman, giving you what I can't, is bugging me. Even if they're not biologically yours, it still bugs me. I want to be the woman in your life that gives you everything. I don't want another woman giving you something I can't. She's crossing a personal line into our relationship, and I can't do anything about it. And don't you dare have second thoughts about any of this or change your mind in any way. I'll deck you if you do."

Lea gets in, leaving Zion standing outside the truck, stunned speechless.

What the hell do I say to that if anything? Shit, what do I fucking do now? I need to think. I can't ... how do I fucking fix this for my Lea?

He climbs in, ready to discuss this further, but before he opens his mouth, she asks him about the doctor's visit. He launches into the details, putting their discussion on hold, grateful for the change in subject.

"I was nervous about the ultrasound, praying the boys were okay. Watching them move around was an exciting experience. I can't believe how proud and anxious I am even though they're not biologically mine. It's like that part of the equation doesn't even matter. Once I made the decision to adopt them and be their father, biological or not, I felt connected. It's such a great feeling. Baby, I wish you can experience this," Zion says. He's rambling.

Proud, connection, what the hell is that? Hell, of all the things to hear, yep that one cut deep. I keep reminding myself about what Gordon said. 'Whatever you have to say and do to get him through this, do it.'

"Wendy's tumor is growing but not at a fast enough pace that she needs to be put on heavy pain medication. She's determined to make it through her seventh month. Second to agreeing to a long-term relationship with you, this has been the best decision I've made. It's crazy being this busy and it not having to do with work. By now, I thought all I would be worried about was getting into the new headquarters, not all this. Addison, Wendy, falling in love with you. It amazes me. I've started on the design of the nursery. I can't wait to show you." He trails off, clenching her hand in his.

Sam and Lea make eye contact a couple of times in the rearview mirror. Amazing how she recognizes the pity in his eyes for her. She's now the sad pathetic joke in this, whatever this is. She presses the button to raise the privacy window for the remainder of the drive. Zion says nothing, thinking she wants to make out. Instead, Lea keeps the conversation going, discussing details about the changes he wants at Landon Enterprises.

"Well, here we are at my place. Are you going back to work?" Lea asks him, keeping him away from talk of her confession or is it jealousy? *Maybe it's humiliation, yeah that's it, humiliation.*

"No, we're going to Wendy's and picking her and the nurse up. She's moving into the apartment tonight, and I wanted to help them get settled. I'll be at her place tomorrow with the movers, getting everything else moved, delivered, or put into storage. I'm free Saturday, why don't we spend the day together?"

"Sure, I would love that," she tells him. As they get out of the car, she notices the gate to her backyard is open. She never leaves it open. She freezes and stares at it, biting her lip.

"Lea, what's wrong?" Zion asks, not noticing the gate being opened, but only her hesitation. Sam noticed her reaction and went on alert.

"My gate is open. I didn't leave it open, and the wind can't blow it open," she whispers.

Sam pulls out his gun. Zion pushes her back into the SUV and grabs his own gun. "Stay here. Sam and I'll check it out." They walk off, locking her safely in.

Lea looks down at the impression of the gun in the opening of the area from below the glove box, accessible via his handprint.

A gun hidden in a secret area of his SUV. What the hell?

She looks back out the window towards the gate leading to the backyard.

Zion and Sam come back, giving her the all-clear to get out after making sure things are secure. Everything is intact, nothing looks like it has been tampered with, nothing is missing, nothing is different with the car, it has the same dust on it as yesterday, no fingerprints or smudge marks. Sam checks the inside of the house, again, nothing out of place.

Zion follows Lea in. She walks the house, checking her own security booby traps with Zion following. He doesn't say anything but watches her closely.

If anyone was to actually get into Lea's house and back out again without setting off her alarm, she would know it. This woman amazes him every day.

"You never told me about your own extras. Why not?"

"They're for my own peace of mind. I set them up the day I got the emails. I needed this for me. Now you know." They're back in her living room.

Sam goes to the SUV to make some calls.

"We didn't find anything out of the ordinary, but I want you at my place tonight. It may be nothing, but Sam is calling my detective friend and giving him a heads-up about the gate just in case."

"Then why do I need to stay at your place? Why can't I stay here?"

"Because I don't want you here alone," he snaps at her in frustration, unable to believe she would ask that. "I can and will send Ryan back here if you don't come with me."

"Great, so let's just change the layout and color of the four walls I have to be locked behind. At least it's in a tower. Maybe I'll bend over the balcony and let down my hair for people to come visit me. Oh, sorry, can't do that."

"Lea, stop being a smart-ass. I can't leave you here knowing someone may have been in your backyard scoping out the place. And I can't stay. I have to get to Wendy and get them moved in tonight.

Don't do this. Don't make me choose between you and her. Please? You just told me not to have second thoughts and change my mind about all this. If I leave you here, the second-guess monster will be in my ear the entire time. Is that what you want?"

Low blow, Zion. Real low blow, but I need her safe and myself focused. I'll say and do whatever it takes to accomplish both.

Lea freezes, staring at Zion. *Don't make him choose between us. That says it all. Don't make him choose between her and me.* "Fine, let's go," Lea walks out the house, and Zion locks up behind her, then follows her to the SUV.

They drive to his place in silence. Zion turns his body toward Lea, accepting she has folded her arms across her chest preventing him from holding her hand.

Don't make him choose. He told me, "Don't make me choose". Dammit, you did choose. And I get to go sit and wait while he moves her into the apartment. Lea, look at the big picture and don't focus on the parts that are hurting you.

FUCK THE DAMNED BIG PICTURE, HE CHOSE HER OVER US.

When the car arrives at the elevator in the garage to go up to his apartment, Lea hops out, grabbing her purse and computer bag. Zion moves to get out, but she looks at him and stops him with the word "Ocean".

He freezes, looking into her watery eyes, not allowing her to turn away from him. "Lea," he whispers. "Dammit, fuck the safe word. Not right now." He gets out and goes around to her side of the truck. Taking her in his arms, he holds her, practically squeezing the breath out of her. "Baby, I won't be long. I promise I'll get this taken care of and be back to you as fast as I can. Please, give me some time? Okay?" he asks, kissing her.

Lea pulls away attempting to get control of her emotions. "Go to Wendy. No second thoughts. I'll be fine." She walks toward the elevator with her head held high, not giving him reason to come after her.

Where the hell is the elevator?

She slams her hand on the button. Finally, it arrives and she gets on. Once the door closes, she sinks back to the wall and cries.

Her phone vibrates*: Baby, I love you. Don't cry. Please.*

She texts back*: Zion, just go. I love you, too.*

Standing in his living room, she surveys' her surroundings. She didn't even get to see the video, which was the entire point of the drive.

Hell, I don't wanna see what I'll never be able to give him.

"Are you fucking kidding me. You went to her house. What the fuck is wrong with you? We have already made one false move with the emails that caused her to get a fucking watch dog twenty-four-seven. Now this. I eased up hoping the security detail would back off, so I could finish this, and now you fucking go to her house. Did you get in, did you touch anything, and do you know if anyone could have seen you?"

The individual responds meekly, "I just looked around the outside of the house. I didn't even touch the dusty car. They won't notice anything. Oh wait, I did have to open the gate to go into the backyard, but I closed it."

"What? You touched the gate? That means fingerprints, you dumbass. I should blow your fucking brains out right now." A gun is pointed toward the temple of the individual and the sound of a cocking hammer echoes in the silence.

"Stop playing with your fucking guns. You ain't gonna shoot nobody."

The individual holding the gun, turns toward the voice. He points the gun. They stare one another down. He lowers his arm and leaves the house, slamming the door.

"Lil bitch ass. Come sweetie. Let's fuck. I needs my real man."

The remaining two strip and fuck.

-14-

Getting Wendy and the nurse moved into the corporate apartment was simple but annoying because all Zion could think about were the tears in Lea's eyes. It tore him apart when she said, "Ocean". He wanted to cancel this move and be with her. But practicalities won out. He had to go to Wendy, and he had to leave Lea alone. When he arrived at Wendy's apartment, she and the nurse were ready to go. His body was there helping and directing, but his mind was with Lea.

Wendy noticed how distracted Zion was and asked him numerous times if he was okay, did he want to talk about what was bothering him, and could she help in anyway. He assured her he was just distracted. When he got them to the apartment, they ordered in from a local deli, and he sat and talked with her and the nurse. All he wanted to do was to get to Lea and apologize, to make this up to her. Finally, Wendy drifted off to sleep. Zion rushed upstairs to Lea, taking the steps two at a time, not having the patience for the elevator.

Lea is sitting on his balcony, listening to the sounds of nightlife happening down in the streets around her, not able to enjoy any of it as she used to when she and Zion had dinner out here. She's been sitting, waiting, and regretting.

Waiting to hear from her man because he was fully involved in moving Wendy into his building; into an apartment his company owns. Yeah, she suggested it. So what? Doesn't mean she has to like it. Just goes to show you that until you know the full story behind a couple's relationship, you never know what they're going through to stay together and make things work. What other woman would still be in this? None. They would have walked away at the beginning, and Zion would have been alone. Lea regrets blurting out her frustrations, knowing he doesn't need that right now. He needs her support, not to have to deal with her neurotic emotions.

This is where Zion finds her, and he sits down on the lounger next to her. She sits up, crossing her legs, spinning her phone, avoiding making eye contact with him.

"Lea. I can't think straight knowing you're not safe and I know keeping you locked up is driving you up the wall. We've spent so much time alone not going out, I didn't think this would be different."

"Key word. We. Now I'm spending time alone, without you. Zion, I'm okay. Or I will be," she says. Lie to help him get through this, Lea, Gordon told her when she called him to vent. He had to talk her down from her freak-out moment she was having after Zion dropped her off. She was ready to break things.

"I wish I can believe that, but we know this is a fucked-up situation." He reaches over and caresses her arm. "Baby, talk to me, yell at me, tell me when I'm neglecting you."

"I'm not a priority for you anymore. I'm an afterthought. We don't talk anymore. Your focus is where it needs to be. I'll find a coping mechanism." Lea doesn't look at him. She keeps staring at her spinning phone, needing to get this all out.

"I've avoided emotional attachments and drama for years. I thought there would be none with you and here I am in the side chick position hoping I get to see my man. It's crazy," she admits.

"Don't ever call yourself the side chick. We knew this going in. What do you expect me to do?" he asks her, looking for direction, any suggestions to please her. Before she can answer, his phone buzzes.

Looking down at it pains him. This is not the time for this call.

"Shit. Don't get mad, Lea, but its Wendy's nurse. I should take this."

"Go ahead." She gets up and walks into the kitchen, bending over the sink, splashing cold water on her face. Her puffy, ugly face. She still hasn't looked at him. She's looked past him, above him, and away from him.

"How is she? Did the move go okay?" Lea asks him for something to break the silence after he ends the call.

"Things are fine with Wendy. Her nurse was calling to remind me about a specific box Wendy wanted brought back to the apartment tomorrow and not put in storage. It's a box of memories she's creating for the boys." Zion stares at Lea from across the room. "Look at me. You didn't answer my question. What do you expect of me, Lea?"

She stares him down. "You know what Zion. That's a fucked-up question to be asking me. I expect you to do what you need to do to get through this. It doesn't mean I have to like any of what is happening. I said I'll support you. As your friend, business colleague, or girlfriend. But don't think ima be this happy-go-lucky-everything-is-okay-little-miss-sunshine. I have feelings and being relegated to the bottom of the list ain't all that grand."

"First off, I'm not relegating you to the bottom of any list. The question is not a fucked-up question. I need to know what I can do to keep you happy. What you expect of me. Remember this relationship thing is new to me. Add the fact I'm agreeing to adopt kids, be a father at fifty. Hell, I'm stepping, no jumping, into territory I know nothing about. Being an uncle, no way prepared me for this. I don't wanna lose you or exclude you. Tell me Lea, what do you expect of me in this?"

"Zion, I don't know how to answer that. I wanted you to have all the answers. I wanted you to automatically make this right and make me feel better."

He closes the space between them, walking into the kitchen. "Kitten I'm doing my best, to ensure you feel needed and wanted by me. Please believe me. Okay?"

"Okay Zion. Let's move on. Shall we?"

"Lea, I'm going to worry about you. I love you." He takes her in his arms.

Pulling back away from him, Lea decides to broach a subject with him that has been bothering her. "Can I ask you a question?"

"Of course."

"You may not think that after you hear the question."

"Try me."

Lea takes a deep breath and plunges ahead. "How, ugh."

"Lea, go ahead," he says.

"Michael asked me out on a date, and before you jump to any conclusions let me finish."

"Okay," he deadpans.

"As many men I've worked with in the course of my job, you're the one to get me. You're the one I had a strong attraction for, allowed to get close to me, the one I fell in love with, and you're the one I see a future with."

"I'm glad to hear that. Where are you going with this conversation?"

"I have doubts going through my head, fucking with me and I don't know what to think or how to feel. Did you ever think I was undatable or someone you should run away from? Why did you stick around? I know you had plenty of opportunities before me. Wendy was right there."

"Lea, I can't and won't speak for other men. I'll just speak for me. You scaring the hell outta me right now."

Lea attempts to interrupt, but Zion cuts her off.

"No, let me finish. I didn't interrupt you so don't interrupt me. Forget the billionaire status. I saw you and wanted you, and I hate to admit this but I wanted you as a new temporary fuck. I'd been thinking about settling down for a couple of years. I just never pushed the issue with myself because the women I met never pushed the issue with me after I told them about being sterile. You, out the gate stated, nope, no temporary fucking. I don't know if I wanted you then because you said no, and I wanted to prove you wrong or because I wanted you for you. I still don't to this day know why. I do know I'm glad you said no and told me what you wanted. It made me think long and hard and I have no regrets. I'm not about to worry about the opportunities you could have had with other men. The thought of meeting you and you being with someone else pisses me the fuck off.

"If you were meant to be with any other man you had met over the years, you would be with him. I have no doubt about that. Whether you were happy with him or not. For me and this moment in time, I'm fucking ecstatic for our future that you didn't end up with another man and that you're mine. All mine. As I am yours. All yours. I only care about now and our future. The past, fuck it. It's done. No more looking back on the what ifs.

"Regarding other opportunities including Wendy. Well Wendy had her specific ideas regarding her future. The second she told me it included kids; she went into my "to be fucked category" and never made it out. Once a woman got there, I didn't take them out. Does any of what I just said help?"

"I guess. Fuck the past and no more looking back. I'm sorry I brought it up."

"Don't be. I would rather you tell me about what you're thinking then assuming and blowing it up in your head to be more than it should. Always remember that. Good, bad, or ugly, I would rather discuss it, yell about it, fight about it than ignore it. Deal?"

"Deal."

"Our first fight. I hate the way we've been with each other lately. I've gotten accustomed to the fun, the laughter, the good times, all that new relationship stuff we're supposed to be enjoying. I'd like to bring some of that back if you don't mind."

"Are we getting old and stale in our relationship already?"

"No, not old and stale. Distracted and allowing too much outside shit to encroach."

"Zion, I don't think we can avoid any of it now."

"No, we can't. But we won't be losing ourselves either. I'm not going to let that happen."

Zion pulls her into his arms, caressing her shoulders. Without a word Lea looks down and reaches to release him from his pants. The sound of his belt unbuckling and the zipper unzipping is a symphony to their ears.

Seductively Zion asks, "Kitten, is this Z and My Kitten or is this Zion and Lea?"

As his pants drop to the floor, Lea hooks her thumbs into his underwear sliding her fingers between his skin and elastic. She trails her fingers around his waist, scraping his skin with her fingernails. Zion moans.

"It's me staking my claim. It's me giving and taking pleasure. It's me wanting to hear you. Your moans, groans, saying my name."

Zion lifts her face and gazes into her eyes, "Woman I love it when you stake your claim." He gives her a bruising open mouthed, tonguing. He steps out of his pants along with his shoes and takes off his underwear. He strips from his suit jacket, shirt and tie, tossing them across the room. Still kissing Lea.

When he is finally naked, he bends down, releasing Lea from her shirt, bra, and jeans. He buries his face in her underwear clad vagina and he rips them off.

"Must you always do that?"

"Yes, as often as I can. Don't worry, I'll have a hundred more pairs, delivered tomorrow."

He is about to suck on her clit when Lea says, "Ocean."

"Lea, what the hell?"

"Zion, tonight you're mine."

"Okay. With everything that's going on, I can't be in dom/sub mode. Let's leave that behind for a while."

"I agree. Kinda. I want you to stand up and take me from behind. Fucking me, your pussy, squeezing my ass. I wanna feel your nut sack slapping against me."

"Fuck baby, I don't know where all this is coming from, but ima do that and fucking more."

He stands and turns her around, bending her over the kitchen counter, fingering her, making sure she's wet enough for his first thrust. He presses his dick between her legs, rubbing it up and down on her pussy, increasing her wetness.

"Baby, spread your legs. Oh yes, that's it. Nice. Fucking real nice." Zion bends over and slides his dick into Lea's hot and ready pussy. She presses back to receive him fully and comfortably.

Shit, she knows how to suck in my dick so fucking good.

Zion grabs onto her hips, slowly fucking her, making sure to hit her g-spot with every thrust in. Each time he hits it she whimpers and pushes back into his pelvis. He slowly fucks her, making it blissful agony for both of them.

A fucking good agony. Shit, her pussy is so tight and moist.

He continues the tormenting pleasure for another few strokes, then fully pulls out.

"Zion, fuck me harder. Please," she begs.

Zion moves his leg between Lea's and spreads hers open more. He leans over her back, stretching his arms across the counter top.

"Baby hold onto my arms, brace yourself," he tells her.

Lea grips one of his forearms. Zion bends slightly and slides back in, pounding into her pussy. Lea lifts one leg, using her free hand to hold it up. Zion reaches for it holding on, still fucking her deeply.

"Oh fucking dammit baby," Zion murmurs.

The sounds of their love making in the apartment is loud. They are sliding on the granite counter top, trying not to fall. Zion braces himself and shoots. His entire body trembling from his orgasm. Lea screams cumming.

He pulls out of her and moves them over to the couch. They lie down, catching their breaths. "Come here woman," Zion says, holding his arms open. Lea allows him to embrace her in his bear hug. She lifts her face, kissing him. Still aroused.

Recognizing she needs to cum again, Zion deepens the kiss. "You want more baby? You want another one?"

"Yes, please more."

Zion turns them to have Lea pressed up against the back of the couch. He slides his leg in between hers and maneuvers her to have her pussy and clit to rub against his penis. He knows even if he isn't hard, placed in the right position, he can stimulate Lea into an explosive orgasm with rubbing their pelvis together.

Once he gets her into place, he starts gyrating. Lea grips him under his arms, holding onto his ass. Pressing him into her. Between kisses on her neck, mouth, and face, he encourages her to cum.

"That's it Kitten, press your pussy against your dick. Yes, baby yes. Fuck you so wet. Cum for me baby."

Zion and Lea are humping so feverishly on the couch, he can barely keep them from falling. Seconds later Lea halts and cums.

"Oh, fucking hell yes." She kisses him holding on.

Caressing her as she calms down, he lays back onto a pillow, propping him up. Lea moves off him, sitting at the end of the couch. He wipes his face, grinning at her. Lea smiles back.

She watches him drift off to sleep. Lea gets up, puts a throw over him, and goes to the bathroom to take a shower. She needs a little quiet time before she wakes him and puts him to bed.

He steps into the shower behind her. "I thought you were asleep."

"I reached for you and you weren't there. Come here." She walks into his arms. "Now tell me what can I do to keep you smiling and staking your claim. Cause damn girl, that was fire." He nibbles her ear.

"Keep doing that, more and more of that, and remember I love you and need to know you haven't forgot about the low woman on the totem pole in your life right now."

"You're not a low priority for me." He smacks her ass.

"Yes, I am, Zion. I come after Wendy, after the boys, after your family, after work. I don't like it but I get it. It will be hard, but I get it. Don't ever move into that apartment, Zion. Ever. I don't care what's going on. Don't you ever move into that apartment. Do we understand each other on that point?"

"I won't sweetheart. I promise you. I won't." Zion strokes Lea to wetness again. He lifts her up and slips inside of her. "I need you again. Baby, your pussy be so hot and wet. The way you moan and groan for me begging me to make you cum. I be in a meeting thinking about it. You know that scarf you put in my bag is still in my desk drawer. Sometimes I want to wrap it around my dick and jack off but I don't want to lose your scent. Oh Lea, baby, your pussy is heaven."

This time around Lea doesn't orgasm. She relishes the feeling of Zion inside of her, watching his ecstasy. He kisses her and pounds into her until he cums.

"I adore watching you. It gives me a high."

He looks down at her, smiling that smile she loves. Zion moves them under the water to clean up again. He turns off the water and they get into bed.

"Zion, do you think we only connect on a sexual level? I don't want our lives to just be about sex. I think that's one of the reasons I've been so jittery. I want to be sure we have more to sustain us."

"Of course, we do. Business, music, hobbies. We can talk and it's not about superficial things is a major way we connected. Before you, I never wanted to talk about my business with a woman I was sexing. I had business associates for that and my father. A woman would only meet my family by accident. And don't discount the sex. I don't know about you, but I've never enjoyed it with any woman as much as I'm enjoying it with you. We get to leisurely and openly take pleasure in each other. It's not about getting fucked for a release and then going home after. I feel like a fucking teenager when it comes to our sex life. I look forward to more dom/sub play."

"That's wonderful to hear. How did a woman meet your family by accident? What do you mean?"

"The easier I could seduce a woman into bed, the less chance she had of meeting my family. If she wanted to be seen, it would be the typical restaurants and events a man with my money would be expected to attend. Some of those events I would run into Star and Garrett. Women wanted the money effect, so I would give it to them. Limousine, high class, high value dining, maybe attend events with a few celebrities in attendance."

"Okay, got it," Lea laughs. "So, because we know we're connecting on more than sex, my wanting to sex you as much as we want to is a good thing and I can give into it?"

"Be sure to give into your sexual desires as much as possible please. I like the sound of both, your laughter and the sex part. When you met Star and Garrett at the Humane Society Ball, that was an accidental meeting. But I was excited about you meeting them, and we hadn't even had a date yet. Odd that popped into my head. Star and I were talking about you at our table, and she knew instantly I was interested and attracted to you and wanted more even before I did."

Lea asks, "How are things at the office, other than the project?"

"Amazing. Dad has stepped in and is handling a lot of the business right now. Mom has even taken on more duties with the move. When I first started Landon Enterprises, they were heavily involved. Once I got it up and running and everything in place, they decided to be silent partners, board members and staff. Star heads the Marketing and Communications department so well; I'm thinking about making it a separate entity where she can work with other companies."

"She would love that. She's been wanting to talk to you about opening a smaller office here in the city for your clients who can't make it out to the headquarters, but didn't want to bring it up just yet. Landon Enterprises, Marketing and Communications. She would love to hear this. When are you going to tell her about it?"

"Well, I'm not sure. I have to find a location and bounce ideas around to see what she has in mind. And that keeps you working with me even longer because of course G-TEE would get the contract to setup technology in the new office."

"Uh yeah, I expect to. I have an inside track. Besides, that's bonus money to pay off my student loans and maybe even get a new car. I've been looking at the Nissan Maxima's. So, loving that car right now."

"Lea, I can pay off your student loans and get you a car with one swipe of my signature. Don't give me that look. I know you don't see me for my bank account, and you want to work and make your own money. I'm not saying this to insult you. When we get married, you'll be the wife of a billionaire and money available at your fingertips. It's time you let me spend on you as I want to. I won't go overboard because you're not a flashy person. What I bought you in Chicago and Charleston was nothing compared to what I want to buy you."

"Have you been working on the pre-nup? I can only assume with us getting married there will be some kind of pre-nup I'll have to sign. And what about a will and protections for the boys."

"I trust you; I'm not having you sign a pre-nup. You're not a money hungry individual. If something where to happen to either of us, I have faith that you would step in and take care of business for the benefit of us all and not rip me off."

"Zion, I love and adore you for having such faith in me, but let's not be stupid. You're a billionaire and that involves a lot. I'm not offended about signing a pre-nup. That's just good business and common sense for a man in your position. Don't shortchange either of us on this matter. Get into business mode and get one drawn up. I'll review it and have my own opinions, of course. I have my mom to take care of. I don't expect you to take on that responsibility."

"Lea, your mom will become as much a priority to me as you are. Got that, babe?"

"Got it."

"And one more thing."

"Yes, and that is?"

"Don't ever safe word me when you're hurting because I won't listen. Don't give me that innocent look. You safe worded me down in the garage when you got out of the truck. There's no way in hell I will ever listen to that word when you're crying, hurting, and needing me to comfort you. Not gonna happen sweetheart. You can safe word me during sex all you want and I will stop or back off but when it comes to you hurting like before, Ocean and Halo mean nothing to me. Understand?"

"Okay, understood." When Zion chastises Lea, she hates it. She has this thing about wanting to be perfect for him and not make any mistakes. Especially now.

"Good."

-15-

Upon waking the next morning, Lea is in an improved frame of mind about her relationship with Zion and the Wendy situation. It's time she looks forward to the future with the man she loves.

THAT'S GONNA INCLUDE THE KIDS WE NEVER WANTED TO CARRY ANYWAY.

Well, there was a time we wanted to carry a man's children.

NOT IN THE LAST DECADE WE HAVEN'T. LET'S FACE IT. WE MAY HAVE BEEN JEALOUS OF THE ATTENTION PREGNANT WOMEN GOT, BUT WE SURE AS HELL DIDN'T WANNA GO THROUGH IT.

Well. Whatever. Every relationship has its trials and tribulations. This one happens to be ours.

Sam drives them to Lea's office and Zion escorts her upstairs. They arrived early enough for an uninterrupted make-out session because Lea may not be seeing him tonight. "I'm going out with my girlfriends. We'll be meeting up at Club Déjà Vu for drinks," Lea informs him. "This was planned before my shadow came into the picture. I'm not cancelling. I need girl time."

"Sweetheart, fine with me. But Ryan will be driving you. He'll hang out in the background. Lea, something has been bothering me," he says with her pinned up against the wall.

"And that is?" she asks him, kissing his chest.

"Baby, why didn't you say anything about Sam and me grabbing guns out of secret compartments of the SUV? Why haven't you brought that up?"

"I'm a silent observer. I've observed a lot about you without saying anything. I ask about what I want to know about and keep my mouth shut about what I know is your private business. I know your SUV is not your typical SUV. You probably bullet proofed it. I know

Sam is not your typical head of security. He reminds me of one of those extreme spy guys. He has a commanding presence about him. I'm not clueless or stupid. All the fucking sly looks from you and your security are getting on my nerves. I think it's better to observe. Closed mouth and open eyes work better than open mouth and closed mind."

"Woman, I never thought you were stupid or clueless. No one knows anything about my SUV but Sam, Ryan and me. What else have you observed that you're not telling me?" he asks. "Sam probably would shit a brick knowing what you think about him."

"None of your business. Don't worry, I'm not going to say anything."

"Enjoy yourself tonight. I hate you going without me. This shit with Addison. I want you free of concern. I want us to enjoy life to the fullest. We can't do that by constantly worrying about who can hurt us. Go have fun with your friends. I may meet you there later. Actually, that's one of Star and Garrett's hangouts, so you might run into them. I'll text you and let you know if I'll meet you there or back at your place. We have a day of shopping tomorrow." He keeps pressing his pelvis and dick against her pussy trying to make her cum.

"Zion, stop it," she says not really wanting him to.

"If you want me to stop, use our safe word otherwise I'm going to bring you off," he says while kissing her neck.

Zion makes sure the door to her office is locked and he keeps rubbing his dick into her pussy, pinning her against the wall. He hasn't done clothes burning since grade school, and here he is, his second time with Lea and it's just as fulfilling as if his dick was inside of her.

"I know what brings you off just like you know what brings me off. Cum for me Lea. Come on baby. Yesssss. Like you did last night. Let me here you." He kisses her rubbing his dick against her pussy. He grips her ass really grinding into her and she into him. He can tell she's about to cum, so he keeps kissing her to smother the sounds of her ecstasy, tonguing her deeply. She cums, whimpering.

"Oh Zion," she whispers. "Bear what about you?" She unzips his pants and bends down taking him into her mouth.

As soon as she latchets on, he grips the side of her face, holding on and fucks her in the mouth, keeping as quiet as he can but shit it feels so damn good. "Oh Lea, fuck I'm about to cum. Baby yes. Suck me, shit suck me. Dammmit baby." He cums shooting down her throat. "Yes, baby you so damn good."

They straighten themselves up and after a few minutes, they open her office door, listening for others. Not hearing anyone they leave her office parting at the elevators with Lea going to the bathroom to brush her teeth and fix her makeup.

SHIT DAILY QUICKIES LIKE THAT CAN BECOME A HABIT.

Zion gets to Wendy's old apartment just as the movers are finishing up. They had everything packed and moved into storage in about four hours. Zion officially closes the apartment and transfers the keys to the landlord. He goes back to his office for the meeting with Detective Greg Chouteau.

"Hey Greg, what up man? You find out anything?" he asks him while closing the door to his office. Sam is joining them for this meeting.

"Man, this chick is a nut case. Where you find her crazy ass at?" Greg starts in.

"We hooked up in college. What do you mean crazy? What have you found?" Zion is nervous. Sam takes mental notes, his curiosity piqued.

"This the woman who messed you up in college? You never told me much about her. Okay, she has been fixated on a number of men in her life, to see which one would fall for her love of pain. She finally found one who fell for it about fifteen years ago and married him. Guy named Martin Jones. He started his own electrical installation business and was doing pretty damn good, up until about five years ago. Making money, nice clientele. The wifey decided to get into crack cocaine. Didn't work well with the meds she was taking. She been in and out of hospitals and rehabs during the course of the marriage. He would deny her existence when she was locked away or disappeared by her own decision, hanging out in some crack house."

"Wait. You said Martin Jones, electrical installation. Sam, is that—?" Zion asks him with a knot in his throat and gut.

"Yes sir, the one and only," Sam says.

Greg continues, "Ah, I see you two have put it together, only it wasn't planned. It was or is like a freak of nature and big-time coincidence. The planets aligned and have thrown all y'all together to fuck with your lives, right? Well, the fact that Martin is an electrician that your girlfriend has been working with for years is a coincidence. He was really good at his job. Then Mrs. Jones came back into the picture and bled the poor guy dry. She got fixated back on you after seeing you in the *Business Journal*. Actually, the husband had been reading the paper because he was looking for business opportunities and Mrs. Jones saw you in it.

"Well, Mrs. Jones got put away in rehab again after she had her little meeting with you. She can't stand rejection and you rejecting her threw her into a sex and drug fueled, kick my ass binge. The husband couldn't take it, so he had her locked up for his own good. Yes, I said for *his* own good. We haven't been able to determine how she was able to send your girlfriend the emails.

"She ditched the hospital with her drug pal about a month ago and hasn't been seen since. We have no clue who the guy is or what he looks like. The husband, Mr. Jones, has stated if she comes back to him, no one will have to worry about her hurting anyone ever again because he will put a bullet in her brain and then kill himself. The guy does not give a fuck that he threatened his wife in front of a policeman. He's completely done and broken. I feel sorry for the wife. They don't have any kids together, so it's not like he couldn't walk away, disappear, and abandon the marriage. But he wants her dead."

"Can't you do anything about the husband threatening her? You have no idea where she's at? What about following the husband?" Zion asks him. "What am I supposed to do to keep my family safe from her?"

"We have APB's out and we're looking for her because the hospital has reported her as a dangerous and unstable person. You have your own security detail on your family, so I would say increase it if that's possible. Off the record, I would pray the husband finds her before you do. He would not tell us anything about what he was doing to locate her. But I got a strange feeling he's out hunting for her. Other than the email threats, the police can't do anything about locking her up. If we find her, we have to legally take her back to the hospital. I would recommend you not hanging out in large crowded uncontrolled situations. Hell, if you could leave town, I would suggest that, but I know about the baby situation. Yes, I know. I'm good at my job. Don't worry. That isn't part of the report because it doesn't apply," Greg informs Zion.

"Detective, Greg, man, thanks so much for all the info. I'm fucking stunned. I need to go see Lea. She's going to kill me. She was supposed to be going out tonight, but I can't let her do that. Sam, get with your security you have hired and update them about all this. I'll drive myself over to Lea's office and pick her up. Maybe she can give me more information on Martin to help us out."

"If she has anything that would be great. I need to get back to the precinct. Other cases to work on as you know. Let's keep each other posted on anything out of the ordinary, any little thing. You never know with this crazy chick. Remember, her finding you now is a coincidence, a real fucked-up, crazy one. As nutty as she is, she would have found you anyway."

The detective leaves and Sam stands looking at Zion. "Sir, you need to call Miss Adams before she leaves for the day. Ms. Noelin and the nurse are safe in the apartment. We can get the extra security added in no time. Miss Adams will hate this. You have to make her believe her association with Martin Jones did not cause this."

"Get going. I'll be at Lea's," Zion instructs Sam and leaves the office. He gets back to Lea's office in twenty minutes.

-16-

When Zion walks into the lobby of G-TEE's office building, he sees Lea coming out of the café carrying her lunch. Forgetting for a moment why he's there, he smiles at her beauty, her walk, her sexiness. He looks around at people, looking for Addison or anyone watching Lea other than him. He notices nothing. She spots him.

"Hey you. What's up, everything okay?" *Why in the hell is Zion back here?*

"Everything's fine. I wanted to talk to you. You're eating late." He kisses her on the cheek, grabs her lunch to carry it and gently escorts her toward the elevators.

"Zion, what's going on?" she asks him quietly.

"Let's get upstairs," he answers.

They're quiet on the ride up.

She nervously plays with her necklace. Zion looks over at her and they make eye contact. She smiles. He stares at her and slowly looks away.

What the fucking hell? The smile on Lea's face disappears quickly. *I feel like a fool.*

They step off the elevator, and Crystal and Tom are standing in the lobby waiting for them. Crystal is holding a folder. Zion had called Tom to warn him about his visit, about Martin, and to see what information they have regarding Martin and his dealings with G-TEE and Lea.

"Okay, enough." Lea, bites out, jerking away from Zion. "What the hell is going on?"

"Lea, let's go down to Tom's office to talk," Zion says, moving her in that direction. It never bothered her before when Zion would guide her through doors, around obstacles, or out of the way of groups of people.

Now it's really getting on my fucking nerves.

She pulls away from him, his touch no longer being comforting and safe, mentally daring him to say something.

Once in Tom's office, they all sit down with Zion pulling a chair close to Lea. He takes a deep breath. "Lea, I want you to understand one thing before I go into this explanation. None of this is your fault and it would have happened anyway," Zion begins with saying this, hoping to calm her down, but it looks like he's making it worse.

He explains everything Detective Greg told him. She doesn't say a word. "Lea, I need to ask you some questions about Martin."

She doesn't respond, only gives him an expressionless look.

He waits for her consent.

"Go ahead."

"How did you and Martin meet?"

In a flat monotone, Lea responds to his questions. "He was a vendor at one of the Home and Garden shows. He was working for AmerenUE at the time and doing electrical installation work on the side. We had a couple of dates, but it didn't go anywhere. We kept in touch for business reasons."

The part about the dates irks Zion, but he continues. "Did he tell you he was married or ever mention anything about getting married?"

"No. I thought the dates were business dinners until a month later when he informed me, they had nothing to do with business. He never discussed his personal life, and it didn't seem important. He was good at what he did."

"Did he ever seem stressed out or in trouble with finances?"

"No. Nothing before being awarded the contract on your project." Lea takes a deep breath. Her patience is running very thin.

"Baby, just a few more questions, okay?" Zion leans toward her. Lea moves away from him. "Lea—." Zion starts to say something to comfort her, but she cuts him off.

"Zion, get this over with. Now." She tells him, again in that monotone voice.

Crystal recognizes this as Lea distancing herself from everyone in the room and retreating into her private space. She looks over at Tom, attempting to get his attention.

Zion continues with his questions. "Did Martin ever mention anything about knowing me or being aware of me and my company?"

"No, all our solicitations are blind proposals and submissions. Bidders sometimes get proposals for five different projects we're working on, and depending on pricing and availability, they can be awarded one, some, or all five. They don't find out who they're working for until they sign the contract, and even then, the project may be called something that has nothing to do with the original company or owner. Your project was submitted as a G-TEE project only. The reason you got to meet Martin and the new electrician was because of what happened and what you overheard," Lea snaps back on him.

He takes the hit with her attitude. He prefers her angry and in fighting mode instead of dead calm. "Lea. Addison being married to Martin and finding me has nothing to do with you. She would've found me eventually. She was going through her list of exes trying to see who would bite and take the bait of getting back with her. I don't want you thinking you're the cause of this. Do you understand me?" Zion looks at her, doing everything he can to reassure her this is not in any way her fault and only the fault of his sick-ass ex-girlfriend.

"So, what now?" she asks looking around at all of them. Crystal and Tom don't make eye contact with her. "I assume I can't go out tonight or any night until she's found."

No, Addison didn't find Zion because of me, but fuck, it sure doesn't feel all that great to be in her crosshairs.

"Well, the detective is trying to locate Addison. Even though Martin has threatened to kill his wife, the cops can't do anything. They're hoping he'll lead them to Addison. The detective thinks she's hiding away in some crack house waiting to strike out at you or me.

I'm adding additional security to Wendy, you, myself, and my family, which means, no, it would be to our benefit if you didn't go out tonight. I'm sorry sweetheart." He reaches over to touch her but she pulls away. "Lea," he whispers.

"I'm sorry, I just don't. I can't be touched right now," she says looking away from him.

"Baby, please, don't. Just give me time. Give us time. I promise this won't last much longer. We will find Addison, and we can go back to being us, to living," he says, attempting to reassure them both even though he has no idea how long it will take to find Addison or what will happen from this point. He knows he can't have Lea pulling away from him, avoiding his touch. He won't have that.

"No problem, Zion," she says, in that monotone voice again. "This bitch needs to be found. Tom, I'll work from home to keep all this mess away from the office. I don't want anyone to get hurt because of it, and I don't want your business to suffer."

"Lea, don't worry about the business," Tom replied. "I want to make sure you're safe. And that means whether you come into the office or not. I don't want you thinking you need to stay home. Do not give Addison that power over you. We don't have any scheduled new projects going on and it's winding down to the end of the year. Remember, us getting the contract with Zion has us set," Tom assures her, finally looking at Crystal over her head. *Shit, they have really fucked this up.*

"How about I come into the office for staff meetings and weekly status updates," she offers.

"How about you come to work every day, keep to your regular routine and not give some stupid-ass, crazy bitch control over what you do?" Crystal says, channeling her anger and fear toward the situation and not at anyone in the room. "Pardon my French, but I'm tired of this sick bitch controlling this situation. Why the hell does Lea have to stay locked up and not go anywhere? This is a bunch of bullshit. Zion. You claim to love her and want to protect her, but all you're doing is shutting her away from family, friends, and her life. I'm beginning to think G-TEE taking on your project was our biggest mistake ever, among other things," Crystal rushes out.

"Crystal, hey!" Tom yells, keeping her from admitting their role in introducing Zion and Lea. He doesn't think Lea can handle hearing how many more people have been pulling puppet strings in her life right now.

She looks over at Tom, "No! Don't 'Crystal' me. She shouldn't be shut away while we get to come and go as we please. Hell, even Zion gets to come and go as he pleases. But Lea has to be escorted everywhere, waiting until someone becomes available. Shit! When was the last time you been out to take pictures? When was the last time you met your girlfriends for anything at all?"

Lea mumbles, "I was supposed to go tonight."

But Crystal is on a roll and talks over her. Zion heard what Lea said, loud, and clear, and it's tearing him apart.

"If she's not fed up and pissed, I'll be fed up and pissed for her. Lea, I'm sorry. I'm sorry you're in this position more than you can ever imagine right now. I wish something completely different for you. If you decide to work from home, I'll be right there next to you working by your side. You want to hang out and disappear for a few hours, call me. I'll pick you up and take you away. I'm not going to allow you to be a hermit. I'll be there for you and make this up to you. I promise you that," Crystal gets up and hugs her.

Lea buries her face into Crystal shoulders, holding onto her tightly. Crystal pulls away, brushing her cheek against Lea's whispering, "Call me anytime. No matter when."

"Zion, I'll get you the copies of this file you need. There isn't much in here that you can't find out in your own documentation. Don't know why the fuck I got to give you copies." Crystal mumbles something under her breath the others are unable to hear as she storms out of Tom's office.

Lea stands up, turning away from Tom and Zion, not wanting them to see her cry. The angry tears are right there waiting. Tears of frustration and the need to punch someone. "I'll go get my computer and some things. I think it's time for me to go home. Zion, I assume you'll be taking me home or Ryan or whoever. I'll meet you in the front in about thirty minutes." Lea stands up and grabs her lunch and dumps it in the trash. Suddenly, she has lost her appetite.

"Lea, wait." Zion stands to go after her. They get to her office, and he closes and locks the door. Lea walks over to her desk, kicks the trash can across the room, then stands there unable to think straight about what else to do. It just misses hitting Zion.

"Got dammit, fuck my miserable life," she yells in frustration.

Zion says nothing, empathetic to what Lea is feeling.

The anger is boiling inside of Lea. She plops down in her chair, slamming her desk draw shut. She then turns in her chair and takes off her shoe, rubbing her aching toes. Having yet to look at Zion and his look of reproach for her display, she picks up her phone to text her girlfriend, letting her know she won't make it tonight; an emergency has come up.

Some emergency.

She would love to text saying she's being locked away and to please come rescue her from the hell that's now her life. Her hands are shaking so much she can barely type, but she gets the message sent. She tosses her phone onto her desk, burying her face in her hands. Before she can stop them, the tears fall silently.

Zion walks over to her, but she turns her chair away from him. "Don't. Don't touch me right now," she tells him.

"Baby, don't reject me, don't reject us." He bends down. Zion places his hands on her chair and gently turns it toward him. He takes her foot in his hand to rub it, taking out his handkerchief wiping away her tears. In the process, he wipes away her makeup and reveals the dark shadows under her eyes, the sunken cheeks.

Oh, my lovely Lea. What have I done to you?

"I'm not rejecting you. I'm pissed someone is controlling my movements and it isn't me. My choice to do anything is gone. We're going to leave here, and we'll go back to your or my place, and what, hang out all weekend staying in?"

Lea is balling pieces of paper from her desk, in her left hand and digging her fingernails into the air of the chair with her right. Zion continues rubbing her feet attempting to release the tension in her body. He doesn't interrupt her.

"Zion, that was wonderful in the beginning, but we had choices if we wanted to do something at any time. I don't have that anymore, and I'm really pissed and want to find her and KICK HER ASS," she says crying.

He wipes the tears from her cheeks, speaking softly, "Lea, you can go anywhere you want at any time. With or without me. Crystal was right, you shouldn't have to stop living because of this and I won't let you."

Lea continues to cry silently. "Everything I like doing, going for walks in the park, visiting the museum, going to the movies at rush hour, walking the mall window shopping, it's all gone because of one person. And I'm ready to beat the shit outta her." She looks up at Zion.

Zion takes her hands in his, bringing them to his lips to kiss them. The trembling from Lea breaks his heart. "Kitten, let's go away for the weekend. Down to the Lake of the Ozarks. We can leave right now. We don't have to go back to either of our places. Hell, we can fly out of town. Go to the airport and hop on my plane to anywhere. If our dates consist of getting out of town then we will. Baby, I love you and I don't want you to feel like you can't live freely by being with me."

Why was he the one? Why did I fall so hard for him? I can end this and get my life back right now.

BUT WE WON'T END IT. The Sex Diva screams in the back of Lea's mind.

'Cause truth is I don't want to end this.

Lea gets control of her emotions. She takes out a pack of make-up removers and cleans her face, wiping it clean. Zion watches, loving his cleaned faced Lea. When finished she turned to him and says, "Okay."

Zion watched the change and recognizes it as Lea internalizing her feelings as her mother said she would if she gets overwhelmed. *And right now, my Kitten is fucking stressed.*

"I need to stop by my house and pick up some clothes," she says, turning her head away from him, staring out the window watching other people going about their lives knowing she can't.

"Nope, no clothes. I'll buy what we need when we get there. Kitten, look at me."

Lea stares into his brown eyes.

"Baby, I'm not going to restrict your movements any longer," Zion says, trying to convince her.

I have to fix this. Lea can tell me to get out of her life, saying she can't deal, but I can't let that happen. I won't lose her. I need to get us away from St. Louis and get back to us.

Lea's phone vibrates with an incoming call. It's her mom. She takes the call hiding the tears in her voice. Zion lightly caresses her legs, listening to the conversation. "Hey Mom, what's up? Just finishing up at work. You need anything? Nope, I got time I can do that, what do you want? Okay I'll pick it up and bring it by before I leave town for the weekend. Yes, Zion and I are going to the Lake of the Ozarks." Lea turns to him looking for confirmation. He nods his head yes.

"We'll be back Sunday. He's having dinner with his family and Wendy. I know. I should be there within the hour. Okay, bye."

Before Lea can say anything, someone is knocking at her door. Zion goes over and unlocks it.

It's Crystal. "Here." She thrusts the folder at him and walks away.

"Well, she's pissed. What does your mother need? You're so quiet. You're scaring me; will you be blowing up at me later?" he asks her.

"Probably, I don't know. I just want. My head hurts. Let's get out of here. If we really are going to the Lake I want to drive by my house and make sure it's still standing," she tells him while shutting down her computer and grabbing files, her note pad, her tablet, and stuffing it in her computer bag.

"Lea, you won't need all that, you'll be back to work on Monday."

"Zion, stop telling me what I will and won't need. Dammit, don't you get it? I'm slowly losing control over my life. I can't go anywhere. I can barely do my fucking job as it is without having you and your damn security goons tracking my every move. Back off me right now. I don't need to hear this shit."

Zion stares at Lea. This time he loses the staring contest. She's right. He needs to let her take control of parts of her life and he needs to accept it. The last thing he wants to do is cause her to lose her fighting spirit and she reverts to being an extreme introvert, afraid of the smallest thing. He walks over and grabs the bag. "Ready, Kitten?"

"What?" Lea was itching for a fight. Something to take her anger out on. Him giving in flattened her.

"If you're ready, I am."

"You not going to correct me or tell me or instruct me——."

"Nope. I just wanna get out of town with you."

"Mom wants dinner. I can place the order from my phone."

"Okay, we'll get her dinner."

"Why—." Before she can finish her sentence, he kisses her.

"Lea, not to be instructing you, but the longer we stand here, the more time we lose of our weekend getaway. Let's go."

As they get to the reception area, Crystal is closing the office up for the night. "Lea, you call me when you get back to town, so we can go to the movies or do some museum hopping," she says after Lea informs her, she and Zion are going out of town in an attempt to calm her rising anger.

"Will do, Crystal," she tells her, smiling, hoping to reassure her she's okay when she's not sure she is.

"Crystal, I'm not going to lock her away. I'm sorry you thought that. You can stop throwing daggers at me. I love Lea as much as you do. Okay? I won't keep her from living," he tells her.

"Sure, Zion, sure. As I said, if I have to kidnap her myself and take her out and we do things, I will, and you'll have to deal with it. Good night you two and have a good weekend. See you Sunday Lea." Crystal leaves, walking toward the stairs.

They pick up the food for her mother. During the drive, Lea listens to Zion talking with Sam and Ryan about the plans for their weekend. When they arrive, Zion goes in to speak to Ms. Adams. Lea knows this is his sly way of scoping out the inside of her house to ensure she is safe.

"So, you taking my daughter out of town for the weekend?" Ms. Adams watches Zion closely. Something about this trip not sitting right with her. "About time she did something other than staying in the house. Have fun you two and don't worry about me. I'll lock up." Ms. Adams is giving Lea a hug while Zion goes outside to give them some privacy. Lea knows it's because he wants to look around.

"You want to go to the movies with Crystal and me on Sunday when I get back?" Lea asks her.

"Of course. Just let me know what time to be ready. Hell, I'm not driving. See ya Sunday."

Outside, Zion walks around the house, ensuring the windows are secure, and checking the doors to see if they have been tampered with. While doing this, he calls Morgan, "Morgan, I will not be back into the office today. Cancel any appointments I have. I'm taking Lea to the Lake of the Ozarks. Find romantic accommodations for two nights for Lea and I and a room for Sam. Send the details to Sam and I."

"Yes Sir. I'll get right on it," Morgan responds.

Zion then calls Star and asks her to go check on Wendy for him this weekend and to inform her he had to go out of town and would see her Sunday at dinner.

They drive to Lea's house. Pulling up, Zion parks in front of the neighbor's house because a gray New York Edition Chrysler 300 Limousine is parked in front of Lea's house. Sam and Ryan step out with Ryan approaching Zion's car. Zion hands his car keys over to Ryan, walks Lea to the limo and helps her in. He turns to talk with Ryan and Sam, informing them the reason for the trip and what he needs of Ryan while they are away.

"Zion, what did you tell them, and did you get my laptop bag out of your car?" she asks him after he takes the seat next to her in the limo.

"Yes, I grabbed it. I told Ryan to be sure to check on your mother and your house multiple times this weekend. He'll also make sure no one has tampered with your car and have a tracking device put on it. I gave him your car key. Every vehicle I own has a tracking device. Until you give me the go-ahead to get you a new car, your car will have one. I'll show you the app you can download on your phone to track all of mine as well as yours," he tells her.

She glares at him, flexing her fingers. "You putting a tracking device on my car? Are you for real? How is that a good thing for me? How is that not controlling my life? Could you have at least asked me first? Again, with the doing and not asking. Will you please stop that shit."

He brings her hand to his lips to kiss it. Talking softly, "Kitten, I'm not taking away control of your life. This is just an extra security precaution. I swear, Lea. It's just a precaution."

"But isn't the Find My app enough?"

Relinquishing this battle, Zion cancels having the device put on her car.

"You're right. The Find My app is enough. May I at least have Ryan get it checked to be sure it hasn't been tampered with?" Zion feels asking her permission is the right step.

She puts her hand in her hair, massaging her scalp, in an attempt to soothe away the nagging pain of what all has happened today. "Sure." She turns away and looks out at the scenery slipping by.

"What, baby? Talk to me?"

"You wanting to put a tracking device on my car. Security for my mom and myself. I can't imagine a man doing all this for a temporary fuck."

"I would have ghosted a temporary long before this point."

Lea glances at the car's interior, admiring the luxury of it. Tinted windows, beverage station, a small cooler with snacks. It can seat at least four to six people comfortably. If memory serves her right, this is the same car that Zion stepped into the night of the Humane Society ball after they kissed.

Zion watches her in silence. Every time he splurges on Lea, that wide-eyed scrutiny she displays, makes him beam. "Mrs. Vance packed us some clothes from my apartment, considering we may be getting to the lake too late to go shopping," he says, turning her attention back to him. Her interest in the car fades, and she looks downcast again.

"Lea, don't look like that. I know what you're thinking. Again, somebody else taking control. Look, a lot of lines are blurred right now. I'll straighten out as many as I can. We'll need clean clothes for tomorrow. Mrs. Vance is being thoughtful. With all that you've heard in the last few hours that's hard to see, but she is.

"The tracking device on your car, okay, I was being heavy-handed and stepped into my see-a-problem-solve-it persona. Us leaving town at a moment's notice. I'm taking you away to spoil you, to show you I love you and to get away from this mess."

"It's hard, Zion. I see my independence slipping away. I'm frustrated."

"Lea, you'll get your independence back. I promise. And giving up some of it ain't all bad. Especially giving it to me. Trust me with it okay? Please?"

"It's scary."

Before Zion can respond, his phone rings. By the ringtone, Lea can tell it's Wendy calling. Zion set up a different alert tone for her and the nurse.

Lea tells him to answer it, "You know you have to."

"Hello," he says into the phone.

"Hi, Zion."

"Hello, Wendy."

Lea turns her head toward the window again, looking out. She's turning her class ring on her finger. Zion stares at his shoes continuing the call.

Wendy mentions Star calling about him being out of town. She wanted to see if everything was okay and why he didn't call and tell her himself.

"Wendy, this is what I do. This has always been my life since the day you met me. No, I won't be able to call you. It's why I asked my sister to get in touch. I'll be unavailable for the next forty-eight hours. I'll see you Sunday. You can call Star or my assistant. They'll be able to reach me if it's an emergency. How are you feeling? Any pain? Do you need anything?" Zion is silent as he listens to Wendy talk.

Lea hears the words, "I need you to inform me when you're leaving town".

Zion responds back, "Wendy, if there's something I feel you need to know, you'll be informed. I take steps to insure you have what you need and will continue to do so. If you're not satisfied with the situation, I can change it."

Lea turns from gazing out the window and looks at him, uneasy by his tone and words. Maybe Wendy didn't catch on, but Lea sure as hell did. When Zion says, "I can change it", Lea knows he means he can let Wendy fend for herself. She grabs his hand, squeezing it making him look at her. She mouths, "Chill, Zion".

"Wendy, I gotta go. We'll talk about this more Sunday. And in the future if I have any trips, you'll be informed by my assistant. Okay? I'll see you Sunday." Zion disconnects the call and puts his phone on silence.

"Lea, I'm learning, okay. I didn't like her tone. I switch back and forth from this being a business deal and Wendy being the woman that's giving me the opportunity to be a father. I want this, but I'm not about to be treated like a doormat."

"Bear, I know. But you gotta be careful with how you speak and treat her. Please. For me."

"Anything for you," he whispers. "Come here, you're too far away." She scoots close to him and lays her head on his shoulder, taking off her shoes and putting her feet up on the seat.

They don't talk for a while, sitting in silence and holding hands. Lea absentmindedly strokes his fingers, his ring finger staring at it, hoping someday he'll be wearing a ring she picks out.

"Do you plan on wearing a wedding band when you're married?" She doesn't say we, leaving it open ended.

"Yes, whatever you pick out. I hope we discuss the design first. I noticed you didn't say us or we. I look forward to wearing the wedding ring you've chosen for me," he tells her, kissing her temple.

"How's your headache? We can stop and pickup painkillers if we need to."

"It's just a dull ache, it'll go away. And I have Tylenol in my purse. For emergencies."

His chest rumbles with a laugh. They're thinking about Chicago.

"I love it when you kiss me that way. It makes me feel special to you."

"Baby, you'll always be special to me," he squeezes her hand. He sits back more into the seat, taking off his shoes.

"Zion, are you tired?"

"No, not really. Why?"

"You seem to be getting comfortable, like you're about to take a nap."

"I'll probably doze a little, it's a three-hour drive."

"Will Sam be okay to drive that long?"

"Yes, he'll be fine. And you can doze in comfort if you like. In my arms the whole way there."

"I'm not sleepy, just yet. Have you ever had sex in a limo?"

"Yes," he says, caressing her hand.

"Oh. How many times, or was that the standard with the women you dated?"

"I don't consider what I was doing dating. I was hooking up, killing time, fucking to release some tension. Limo sex for them was a fantasy they wanted to live out. To me it was a way of getting off without the, "my place or yours" dilemma."

"You wanted to make out with me the night of the ball in your limo. Would that have been a hook up, killing time, or fucking to release tension?"

"At that time, so soon in our relationship, probably all of the above. You standing your ground, saying no and going home was a good thing. I still would have chased you down and made you my Lea. It would have taken more to convince you that you were more than a fuck to me, which you are and have been since the day I met you. Baby, why all the questions?"

"Wanting to talk about something other than what we're running away from."

"Making love to you in a limo has been my fantasy since that kiss. Wanting to slowly sex you during a long drive. Sounds like heaven to me. What about you?" he asks her.

"Having you make love to me is always heaven," she tells him, caressing his leg.

"Miss Adams, are you trying to get me to sex you in a limo? It's not like it wasn't my plan anyway, it's just nice to hear you wanting that also," he says, twisting the curls in her hair.

"Maybe. What about Sam?" Lea asks looking at the closed privacy window.

"Baby, its mirror tinted on his side. We can see him; he can't see us. He's listening to a book via his phone. And I have the music playing. If I need him, I hit the button and lower the window. We have plenty of privacy. Now, what I have in mind is not sex. But you giving me one of your delectable hand jobs. A little bit of edging."

"Edging huh?"

"Yes. I want to participate in some edging with you. We have the time."

"Zion, you know I'm all in." Lea sits up and slips off her dress. She unsnaps her bra from behind, pulling it off her shoulders.

"Lord woman I never get tired of seeing you do that."

Lea giggles. Before she can slip out of her underwear Zion stops her.

"Kitten, please allow me to assist you with that." He grips them by the side and rips them off.

"Zion, the strength you have in your hands is amazing. Are you buying me cheap panties so you can rip them?"

"I can't explain it, but when I get the urge to rip, the strength comes from within."

Zion removes his suit jacket and tie, unbuttoning his shirt and rolling up his sleeves to his elbows. He assists Lea with taking off his pants and shoes. "Now I want you to lay across me. You facing front with my dick right at your tits. I want to feel you rub me across them, to suck me and to stroke me."

"And what about me, Bear?"

"You'll be in the perfect spot for me to put my fingers in you and stroke your clit. Feeling your slick pussy lips."

"Wow, you have thoroughly thought this out. I'm aroused and highly impressed."

Lea crawls onto his lap as he instructed. Laying across his lap, she ensures his dick is at tit-and-eye level. He has her open her legs and he uses three fingers to open the lips of her vagina. He slides up and down the sides. Lea strokes his penis up and down, licking it to get it wet. Tasting pre-cum, she rolls her tongue around the tip, squeezing the shaft.

Zion concentrates on stroking Lea's clit, sliding two fingers inside to put pressure on her g-spot. She starts moving with his strokes. They get into a rhythm of bringing each other close to coming and stopping. Every time Lea gets close, she squeezes Zion hand between her thighs and he stops. Each time he gets close, he touches her on the back of her head, and she stops not moving.

They carry on this way for a good hour. Finally, Zion can't take it any longer. "Dammit Lea. I need inside you. NOW."

"No, Zion." Instead, Lea aggressively sucks him off. "Finger me, Zion. Don't stop fingering me." After she says this Zion leans further into her mouth and opens her legs wider. He inserts four fingers and keeps his thumb on her clit. He uses his other hand to keep her in place on his lap. Lea grips the shaft of his penis above his nut sack and squeezes, keeping the tip in her mouth. She's about to cum. He's about to squirt. Faster and faster, they pleasure each other. To the beat of 'Anytime, Anyplace' by Janet Jackson, they stroke, suck and lick. Lea cums, soaking Zion's fingers. But she doesn't stop sucking him off. She latches onto the tip of his penis and circles it with her tongue.

"Shit," Zion growls. He trembles and jerks, then cums. He wants to scream, *Oh fucking hell*. He rides through his orgasm, shooting down Lea's throat. "Oh, Baby. Oh, Shit. Oh, yes," he hisses.

They lay in this position a few minutes more. Lea stretches from her position, sitting up on the limo seat. Zion sits up staring at her smiling. "Do you feel dirty, sexy, and guilty?" she asks him.

"Dirty, sexy, guilty and like a teenager getting caught by their parents. For no penetration that was fucking outstanding."

"Yeah. Yes, it was. I think we need to get dressed and well, kinda cleanup." Lea looks at her chest, Zion's fingers, and his crotch. "How the fuck are we going to clean up?"

Zion opens a slide slot in the back of the limo. He pulls out bottles of water, wipes, and a plastic bag. "We'll do our best," he says.

WHAT THE FUCKING HELL DID I JUST EXPERIENCE?

The Sex Diva hears that deep male voice again.

I DON'T KNOW BUT DAMMIT I WANNA DO THAT SHIT AGAIN.

The Sex Diva jumps. ADONIS? She asks softly.

He mumbles, *YES, SEX DIVA.*

FUCK, IT'S GETTING CROWDED UP IN HERE.

-17-

It's after nine that evening when Sam pulls up to The Inn at Harbour Ridge, a bed and breakfast, situated in the woods overlooking the lake. Lea and Zion are taken to their room, called the Love Nest. It has a fireplace, a seating area, and private balcony. Zion places her laptop bag on the living room table. He's determined to keep Lea so busy this weekend, she won't even touch it.

Sam will be staying in a nearby hotel. Lea wonders if she should feel guilty about him being left out.

"Let's shower, change, and go out to dinner," Zion says. In the overnight bag is a dress from the clothes Zion purchased when they were in Chicago. There are jeans and casual shirts and shoes for tomorrow. Zion is wearing the slacks, white shirt, and suit jacket that Mrs. Vance included. They'll dine at J. Bruner's Restaurant with Sam joining them.

The conversation is about the new office, which Lea doesn't mind at all. Sam and Zion talk about next week's working and travel schedule. Zion will be traveling out of town, Thursday and Friday, being in Charleston to close on the property then to meet with some clients in California. Ryan will be her shadow again, and she's not to work from home. A couple of days is allowed but Zion pleaded with her to go into the office, keeping to as normal a routine as possible. He wants her to have some of her independence back.

Being out with him and having dinner is a welcome change. "Having a date night without having to worry if we're going to be attacked is nice. How can we make her go away and have more of this?" Lea asks no one in particular.

"The police are looking for her, so soon we'll be free. I enjoyed this. You'll be okay next week with me out of town, right? I don't want you to worry about if you can or can't go out. If you do go anywhere, let Ryan know and he'll make sure you and your friends are safe and protected."

After dinner, Sam drops them off and returns to his hotel.

"I'll be fine. How about we get some sleep? There's a Carter's baby store in the outlet mall. I think you're going to enjoy it," Lea says while looking at the mall's brochure.

"Uhm, *we* will enjoy it very much," Zion corrects her. He looks over her shoulder. "Get used to saying, 'we', 'us', and 'ours'. Practice in the mirror if you have to. Come to bed sexy. We must sleep."

Lea climbs in lying across his chest. "Love you, Zion."

"Love you, Lea. Why are you grinning at me like that?"

"Thinking about the drive here."

"Baby, it was a very, very nice drive," he says through a yawn. "You know, since I've met you, I fall off to sleep faster. It used to take me hours to wind down. Another benefit to being with you. Love it."

Lea watches him drift off to sleep. She's wide awake with the Sex Diva sitting on her shoulder egging her on.

SUCK HIM OFF, WAKE HIM UP, Y'ALL CAN SLEEP TOMORROW.

No. Didn't we get enough in the car?

YES. BUT WE WANT MORE.

No.

YES.

No.

DAMMIT, I SAID YES, THIS IS YOUR FUCKING WEEKEND, HE GOES BACK TO HER AND THEN OUT OF TOWN, YOU GET AS MUCH DICK AS YOU CAN. NOW DO IT.

YES, PLEASE DO IT NOW.

After about an hour of arguing with herself, Lea goes for the dick. He's sprawled out with one arm on his chest and his other arm reaching out for her, caressing her leg in his sleep. She slowly eases under the covers, crawling in between his legs, trying not to touch him. Even in sleep his dick is slightly hard. Lea licks his inner thigh lightly.

Zion was so tired and worn out, he couldn't keep his eyes open. He had planned on picking up where he and Lea left off in the limo but dream land overtook him. In his dreams, naked Lea meets him. He feels her everywhere, sees her everywhere, can taste her, smell her. He can even feel her tongue on his balls, licking them, sucking on them. Shit, he's about to have a wet dream if he doesn't wake up. But damn, her tongue feels so good. "Oh baby". In his dream state, he's enjoying what he thinks is Lea giving him a ball lashing and he'll have to wake alone, hard and unfulfilled. Then he feels a kiss on his stomach. He wakes looking down at Lea's head under the sheet.

OH, FUCK WHAT A WAY TO WAKE UP.

"Lea, that tickles. Ocean."

She stops and throws the covers off of them, coming up for air and wrapping the sheet around herself. She sits back on her haunches, in between his legs watching him come back down to earth his penis getting less hard than it was. Instead of looking at him, she stares at his dick, wanting him. But he said "Ocean".

He sits up and looks at her covered up. "I didn't mean 'Ocean' for you to cover up," he says as he unwraps her and lays her down on the bed. "I need your legs wrapped around me pressing me into you. Open up babe. We gotta finish what we started on the way here."

Lea lays down, spreading her legs open allowing him to position himself to slip inside of her. With one gentle push, he's in, feeling her envelope him, her heat spreads throughout his entire body. He props himself on his elbows, looking at her, watching her adjust to him and waiting for him to move.

"Did you know people are most vulnerable during sex, which is why they close their eyes, not looking at each other?" he asks while moving slowly inside her.

"Maybe they close their eyes to concentrate on what's happening, to focus on what they're feeling, to really get into the moment," she says biting her lip in an attempt to keep from cumming too soon. "Oh, fuck this feels so good."

"Lea, look at me." She looks at him and smiles. "Hi pretty eyes." He continues moving inside her, slowly pulling out to the tip and slowly pushing back in.

She wraps her legs around him, moving in sync, pressing him into her pelvis. She reaches up to kiss him. His chest hairs are scraping against her nipples, making them hard and sensitive. He moves faster, pushing them both to cum. She can feel his penis hitting the inside of her vaginal walls, rubbing against them. In and out he moves, loving the feel of her vagina walls massaging his dick. He grinds against her clit with each movement in, making her whimper.

"Oh baby, yes," he says, unable to keep quiet, praising her for such a good feeling pussy. Finally, they explode together. Groaning their release.

OH, SHIT YES. The Sex Diva screams.
OH, FUCKING SHIT YES. Adonis growls.
SO, I DID HEAR YOU EARLIER?
UUUUHHHHHMMM, YES YOU FUCKING DID.
WHY ARE YOU HERE?
BECAUSE I LIKE YOU.
I'M GONNA GO TAKE A BREAK.
I'LL COME WITH.

-18-

Zion pulls out and lifts himself off of Lea, lying down next to her. They're drenched in sweat and breathing hard. As their breathing slows, they drift off to sleep.

The vibration from his phone wakes them. Lea is on the side of the bed next to the phone. He slides up against her grabbing it off the nightstand, kissing her on her shoulder.

"Hello," he growls into the phone. "Good morning, Becky. What's up?" Zion sits up. Lea sits up along with him. "Is everything okay?" he asks her. "Sure, put her on," he says as he looks at Lea and throws his leg over hers.

"Good morning, Wendy. How are you?" Remembering his conversation with Lea, he takes the call. "Tired huh? Are you having any pain? Good. No, you don't have to cook anything, it's being catered."

Zion's becoming irritated. "Wendy, I need to end this call, if you're okay and there's nothing pressing, I'll see you tomorrow. Okay bye," Zion hangs up the phone and looks at Lea. "You okay, Kitten?"

"Yes. Let's get something to eat and go shopping. We must do some damage to your bank account," she says, heading for the bathroom.

After breakfast, they head to the mall. "It's an outlet mall. Shouldn't I be looking at furniture first?" he asks.

"I never shop in order. I have shoes in my closet without an outfit. I have outfits without shoes. You have a room, you have closets. Shopping. Sam, we're going to Carter's."

"Yes, Miss Adams." He opens the door for them, and they get in.

They get to the store, and Zion's eyes gets big as saucers. He's gonna blow his credit card up. The sales lady walks over to them, "Hello. How are you? I'm Shay. Can I be of assistance?"

"We're shopping for twin boys. Show me everything you have," Zion excitedly tells her.

"Oh, how wonderful. How far along are you? You don't even look pregnant," the sales lady states while walking them to the boys' section.

Okay, here we go. I'd been thinking about how to respond to this, and I think I've come up with something logical and won't allow any more probing.

Lea tells her, "We're using a surrogate. The babies are due in three months."

Zion puts his arms around her. "Good girl, see how easy it is to say we and us. I love you," he whispers in her ear.

"How wonderful. Have you chosen names yet?"

Shit! I hadn't planned on that.

"Yes, Royal and Isaac," Zion chirps in. "Okay, we need everything. We may be buying out the store today." He walks around picking up anything he can get his hands on.

Royal and Isaac. His father's name and Zion's middle name. He's been thinking about them and getting used to them being a family. Royal and Isaac. Nice.

"Zion, how about buying, but having it shipped? You can do that can't you?" Lea asks the sales lady as Zion is picking up bibs, rompers, blankets, socks, hats, booties. He has sets, sleep-n-play's, bodysuits, cloth diapers, and pajamas. He's moving his way toward the clothes, picking up complete outfit sets in multiple colors. After about two hours, Lea finally gets him to stop and breathe.

"I don't want to have it shipped but I guess I have no choice. All this will never get into the car. Can all this be shipped?" he asks Shay, forgetting Lea suggested this.

"Yes sir. Let's set this up as an online order, get all your information, and ring it up." They spend another hour with the sales lady, placing the order.

By the time all is said and done, Zion has spent five grand in this store for the boys. *Geez, five fucking thousand dollars and he hasn't even shopped for the furniture yet.* The sales lady thanks them profusely. *I don't know if she makes any extra money on this, but I hope so.* Zion insists on taking some of the clothes that weren't available online with them.

"Well, did you enjoy that?" Lea asks him.

"Yes, it was exciting. I can't wait to go shopping for the furniture, car seats and strollers, and wow, there's so much more stuff we have to get. Lea, we're going to be parents. Can you believe it? In three months, there will be four of us. Yes, baby four of us." He kisses her.

"Zion, if we're going out tonight, I need something to wear. And something to wear home tomorrow," she tells him as they're walking the mall. Next, they go clothes shopping.

Lea was looking at one dress, shoes, and a pair of jeans, shirt, and underwear. By the time Zion is finished, he has purchased ten dresses, five pairs of shoes, five pair of jeans, four tops and underwear for a week. Not to mention purses.

"Thank you, baby, for all this. You've just fed my shoe and purse addiction. Now I have to figure out what I'm going to be getting rid of to keep all this."

"Why do you have to get rid of anything? It's all going to be at my apartment anyway. And when we move into a new and bigger house, I'll make sure you have a closet large enough that can hold everything," he tells her.

"It's a habit of mine. Something comes in, something must go out. I don't think I'll ever get beyond that. Consider it a quirk of mine." They get back to their room and attempt to change into dinner clothes, but of course they can't keep their hands off each other. Lea is standing in the shower when he joins her. He caresses her ass, squeezing it. "Bear, we're supposed to be getting ready for dinner," she moans at his touch.

"Then you shouldn't have come in the shower. Besides, we always have time for sex. Always. I need to be inside you, Lea," he says as he presses her up against the shower wall.

He lifts her, wrapping her legs around his waist. He slips inside, pounding into her. His moans of pleasure are music to her ears, reveling in the knowledge she's making him feel this good and he's taking pleasure in her and not someone else. He buries his face in her neck kissing her, telling her how good it feels; how he can't get enough of her.

"Zion, I'm cumming. Yes." She explodes into orgasm and he follows, groaning, shooting inside of her.

He attempts to pull out, but she keeps him pressed against her, not allowing him to move or get soft.

"Don't, don't pull out. Please don't stop."

"Oh, baby don't beg like that, shit," he tells her, needing to please her over and over when she begs. "Oh Lea, fuck," he says breathlessly as he thrusts in and out, not believing he can fuck her again so damn soon. She squeezes him tight, shaking with her second orgasm and he comes. "Oh shit," he groans into her mouth kissing her, tonguing her. "Fuck baby, you feel so damn good." This time he slips out limp.

"Woman, you're dangerous and you're truly making up for two years of not getting any," he tells her, holding her against him.

"Zion, our amazing sex life has nothing to do with my two-year hiatus. It has everything to do with how we connect with each other. Think about all the women you had one nut with and got up and left."

"Let's get dressed, then we can talk more."

Tonight, it's just Zion and Lea dining together. Sam is back at the hotel getting everything packed up for tomorrow's departure. With regret, Lea thinks, *yes, tomorrow back to reality. Zion will be having dinner with his family and Wendy. I'll be having a movie night with Crystal and my mom.*

"Have lunch with me Monday. I want to see you every day before I go out of town," he whispers in her ear. Dinner is in the gazebo of the Inn. They're surrounded by candles, being catered to in the most romantic setting one could imagine.

"Of course. How did you plan all this? It's amazing."

"I wanted the best romantic dinner they could provide. I want to do this for you every day, give you romance, flowers, jewelry, me, my love, and my heart and soul. Whatever you need and want I'm going to provide for you," Zion says.

"This is hard for me, not just accepting things from a man, but all this. Everything is so unreal at times. Being on the receiving end of all this has been heaven. I don't want it to stop, but I need you to believe I'm not with you for your money. Tell me, no matter what happens or is said or done, you believe that."

"Baby, I know. What are you getting at?" he asks, nibbling her neck.

"What I'm getting at, if you'll let me think straight and get it out, is that I want to travel with you, I want the beautiful house and kids with you, I want it all with you, I want a loving family, great job, great career, but I need you to know that even if you weren't a billionaire and we were living paycheck to paycheck, trying to pay off debt, I would still want all that with you. You understand what I'm saying, right? All this is wonderful and great, but even if all this wasn't you, I would still want you."

"Lea, I know you're not with me for my money. I saw the hesitation and shock in your eyes when I was spending for the boys. I wanted to spend more on you. We should've been hitting up a jewelry store but we didn't. I'm okay with that, for now. I'll just have to ease you into the fact you're marrying a rich man who wants to do nothing more than to take care of you. However, you let him. And we'll be doing a lot of traveling. Just as soon as you decide about your career. I know you love your job, and I know Tom would hate to lose you, so I'm not going to say anything about you quitting when the boys are born. But we have to figure out about you moving in with us and all that. Once they're born, we'll be under the same roof. Either at your house or my apartment is fine, but, considering how small your house is, the logical place is my apartment until we find a house. I figure a year in the apartment. It'll take us that long to combine both households."

"Well, you've planned this out, haven't you?"

"Oh, and you haven't? You can't tell me you haven't been thinking about combining households. The purging, organizing, getting rid of stuff," he smirks at her.

"Okay, I was doing that way before you came along. I accelerated it a bit. I haven't even considered what to do with my house. Sell it or rent it?" Lea smiles at him. "Oh, stop looking at me with such a smart-ass look. Okay, I've been thinking and planning. Is that so bad?"

"No, it's wonderful. Finally, you're coming over to my side of things. Now I know this is going to be difficult over the next few months, but, as long as we know where we stand and where we're headed, we'll get through it. So, tell me, does this mean I get to buy you a ring when we get back? I won't go overboard; I promise to keep it at twenty-five grand. Not too big of a caret and no imperfections. Your mother told me you don't like diamonds so I was thinking we could go look at rings. You find at least five you could picture yourself wearing and I make the final selection. What do you think?"

"Twenty-five grand." Lea looks at her fingers, flexing them. "A ring worth more than my car on my finger. That's ridiculous."

"Lea!" He says, having her focus on what he's about to say, "It's what I want to do."

"Okay, I'll research rings."

"And your proposal has to be special. Not hastily put together."

Lea stares at him. She wants all the bells and whistles of a man proposing to her. If Zion has a plan/idea/whatever it can be with his money and resources, she's gonna wait to get it.

"Again, I give in to what you want."

"I promise, you won't regret it. Any of it."

Lea puts her head on his shoulder, hiding her face from him. She was kinda hoping for a proposal.

-19-

Lea, Zion, and Sam leave early Sunday morning, being sure to return to St. Louis before noon so that Lea and Zion can have the afternoon to themselves. Lea's house is still intact, safe and sound. She sends Ryan a silent thank you, knowing he probably stayed parked outside much of the time they were gone. Zion's car was left parked in her driveway, so Sam can leave and return the limo, drop off the purchases at Zion's apartment and have the rest of the evening with his wife.

During the drive home, Lea made arrangements with Crystal and her mom for dinner and a movie. They'll be meeting up around three, courtesy of Ryan being their driver. That leaves Zion and Lea two hours together before they part.

Zion called Wendy to see how she was doing on the way back to St. Louis. After ending the call, he tells Lea that Wendy sounded tired but excited about dinner tonight.

"That's good, you should take the camera, get some pictures. All memories are good memories. Or use your phone."

"You don't seem to be bothered by this as you were before we went out of town. I hoped this weekend alone helped to solidify how much you are to me." They're lying on her couch making out.

"Sex fiend, chill. Yes, it did. I'm not as bothered as before but some things will still irk me. I'm determined to look at the full meaning behind this before letting my emotions take over. Or I'll be trying my best to."

"Sex fiend? Me? I know not what you're talking about. Just because I can't keep my hands and lips off you does not make me a sex fiend. It makes me yours. We'll focus on the future ahead. Have a good time with your mom and Crystal." Zion says in between kisses. "I'll call you later tonight."

"This isn't bothering you? Me going out?"

"Yes. But I'll get over it. You'll be with security. I can't and won't lock you away. I'll worry when we're not together. Geez what a change in my life."

"What do you mean?"

"Lea, I'm worrying about you. I've never given thought or worried about anyone outside of my close circle of family and friends. Definitely not a woman. It still shocks me. I'm worried about you and can't stop thinking about you. I love it."

"It's a great feeling on my end. To be thought of by a man."

"I'm going to take off before I extend this further and be late." He stands, pulling her up with him from the couch. "Have fun," he says taking one more hug and kiss.

"I will. Enjoy your dinner." Lea closes the door behind him.

Lea, Crystal and her mom enjoy the movie, Hidden Figures. As they're leaving the theatre, with Ryan following behind them, they walk to the car, arguing about what to eat for dinner. The decision was seafood at Bristol Seafood Grill. When they get to the restaurant they're seated and enjoy themselves talking, joking, and having fun. Maybe Lea will allow Crystal to kidnap her after all.

"Crystal, are you still pissed at Zion?" Lea asks her.

"No, not as much as I was before. He does have your safety in mind, but I still won't allow you to work from home and I'll kidnap you to get you out."

"Okay, what am I missing?" her mom asks.

"The nutcase can't be located. They're searching for her and she will return to the looney bin or her husband will take her out. None of us knows which scenario will happen first. We just know we want her out of our lives," Lea says, answering her mom's question, hoping to keep her calm and not worry her.

"Well, let's drink to Zion keeping us safe. I pretty much like being escorted around. My shadow is rather cute." Ms. Adams says, looking over at Ryan sitting at his table enjoying his dinner keeping a close eye on them. She raises her glass to him in a toast. He nods.

"Mom, seriously. You flirting with your shadow?" Lea asks her.

"No, I'm not flirting with him. I said he's cute. It don't hurt to be seen with a cute young man once in a while. Does my ego good. Where's our lovely young man this evening and how did your weekend go?"

"He's having dinner with his parents and Wendy tonight. Our weekend was good. Saturday, we spent the day shopping for the boys. We shopped at Carter's, then he took me shopping for dresses, shoes, and purses. We stayed at this bed and breakfast overlooking the lake."

"He's having dinner with his family and her tonight. You shopped 'til you dropped." Her mom says. "Having dinner with HIS family and her. Geez."

"Yes, Mom. This will be happening often. There's nothing I can do to change that. Crystal, you're pretty silent. Let's hear it," Lea demands.

Silently, Crystal is now regretting putting Lea and Zion in a position to meet. *He's having dinner with his parents and the mother of the kids he's going to adopt. And Lea is pushed to the side. What have we done Tom?* She asks herself. To Lea she tries to show an upbeat mood. "Be happy, Lea. I'm sorry for the pain and heartache you'll probably be experiencing, but I'm very happy for you. I really am. To Zion and Lea. I love you both dearly and want the very best," she says raising her glass.

They all do so, knowing the road ahead will be difficult.

-20-

When Zion gets back to his apartment on Sunday, he sees all of Lea's new things have been unpacked and put away in his closet by Mrs. Vance. Everything for the boys, have been put in the second bedroom still in their bags, because the nursery is still in the planning stages. He refuses to move on any further construction until Lea has given her input. During lunch tomorrow, instead of sexing in his office they'll be going over those plans. *And kissing. Well maybe a fast quickie. Shit, dick, calm down. The thought of that woman arouses me.*

"Oh hello, Mr. Landon. How are you today?" Mrs. Vance asks, coming out of the home office.

"I'm wonderful. Has the caterer delivered the food yet for dinner tonight down to Wendy's?"

"Yes sir, and your parents are there. They're awaiting your arrival. She's a sweet girl. I'll be done with the cleaning in a bit and will see you tomorrow. Call if you need anything."

"Thanks, Mrs. Vance." Everyone he knows has taken a liking to Wendy. Well, almost. He really doesn't know how Lea feels about her, whether she likes her, hates her, despises her or what. He wonders what could have been between Wendy and him. Then Lea pops into his mind and all thoughts of any kind of future with Wendy vanish.

When Zion arrives downstairs, he knocks out of respect. Just because he's paying the bills and has all access to the apartment doesn't mean Wendy doesn't deserve her privacy. His mother lets him in.

"Hi mom, how are you?" He gives her a hug upon entering.

"I'm wonderful. How's my boy? We've been here awhile. Wendy's been enjoying listening to stories about you and Star growing up. The food is hot and ready, the table is set, and we can all sit and eat." She ushers him into the apartment.

"Hi everyone. Wendy, how are you?" Zion is still awkward with greeting her. If this was Lea pregnant, he knows he would be glued to her side, touching her, caressing her belly, wanting to feel the babies move. With Wendy, he doesn't know what to do. He always makes sure he sits down next to her, turning to her, listening to her intently. There've been a couple of bad nights when he was here late that he carried her to bed, helping Becky because Wendy was in too much pain to move. Even with that, he felt he was betraying Lea.

"Zion, hi, welcome home. I'm enjoying myself immensely," she answers, looking up at him, her face glowing.

Home? This is not my home. My home is upstairs or where Lea is. Man, put on a smile and say nothing.

"How was your trip?" Royal asks him.

"It was good. Made a lot of purchases for the boys. Hope to start on the construction of the nursery next week."

His father gets up from the other sofa and moves to the dining room table with Patty and Zion sits on the cushion next to Wendy.

"Zion, I have something to share with you. Sit here." Wendy pats the cushion next to her for him to sit closer.

"Give me your hand."

Zion looks at her questioningly, unsure of what's about to happen.

"Oh, come on, give me your hand." Wendy takes his hand and places it on her stomach. As if on cue he feels a kick. A hard kick. Then another one. He even feels a hand move across her stomach. Amazing, the boys are kicking him.

"Your sons are saying hello. They've been moving for the last two hours." She looks at him, and he looks at her then glances away quickly. He's happy and elated but he feels an overwhelming disappointment and doesn't want her to see it.

I want to be touching Lea's stomach and watching the boys grow inside of her. Not Wendy. Man, you gotta stop this thinking. Wendy deserves some elation.

"Wendy, this is wonderful. You're comfortable, right? The boys aren't causing you any discomfort by moving like this are they?" He can't take his hand away; they keep moving it would seem at the sound of his voice. Unaware of the movement, he caresses her stomach, reacting to the kicks.

"No, I'm not feeling any discomfort. Happy you got to feel them move." She puts her hand over his and squeezes it. He looks at her again and pulls away. "Did you guys get to feel them move?" He asks his parents, wanting to change the direction of the mood. The look Wendy gave him was one of desire.

Sorry Wendy, but that part of our past will stay in the past, he says to himself silently.

"Yes, we have," his mother tells him. "Come on everyone, let's eat." She sees the discomfort in Zion and moves to distract Wendy away from noticing it.

Zion helps Wendy to the dining room table. She's gotten bigger since he last saw her, a few days ago. He must get it together. He needs to talk with Lea about his reactions to Wendy. This confusion of betrayal is sitting poorly with him.

Dinner is a calming and happy affair. They talk about the nursery, the clothes he bought yesterday, and his upcoming trip to California and Charleston. Things are going well when following the cleanup, Wendy drops a bombshell subject.

"Zion, when are you going to introduce me to your girlfriend? Or if this is not the woman that will be helping you to raise the boys, maybe we shouldn't meet." Everyone pauses and there's a strained silence. His mother and father are still at the dining room table, and Zion and Wendy are back on the couch. He sits up, readying himself for a fight.

"You want to meet Lea? I wasn't going to push an introduction between the two of you."

"Well, are you going to marry her? Will she be adopting the boys?" she asks looking at him intently.

At this point, he might as well tell her the truth.

"Yes, I'll be marrying her. After we get married, I do have plans for her to adopt the boys." He's not going to even ask her if that's okay. This is what he wants, and that's how it will be. He can see the excited look from his mother out the corner of his eye. Zion keeps from looking at her directly.

"Well, I think she and I should meet. I would like to meet the woman you have selected to help you raise our sons." Wendy stares at him. "Maybe even hang out and get to know her better."

Zion drags his hand across his face.

Holy shit. Hanging out with Lea. Lea and Wendy, hanging. His intuition is telling him Wendy has staked that claim Lea mentioned and there's nothing he can do about it. *Shit how's he going to do this.*

"I'll talk to her. If Lea agrees, how about Wednesday evening?"

"Why wouldn't she agree? If it's something you want, I would think the last thing she would do is disagree."

"Wendy, maybe you shouldn't think about what Lea would or wouldn't do," Zion deadpans.

His mother and father recognize the tone in Zion's voice. Thinking a disagreement may be brewing, Royal readies himself to intervene.

Wendy realizes she may have crossed a line and adjusts her attitude. "Wednesday would be great. I look forward to it." *I'll have my say Wednesday.* She attempts to hide a yawn, but she is worn out from this visit. Everyone gets up and prepares to leave saying good night to her and Becky.

Zion informs them he may stop by tomorrow, but at this point, he's kinda pissed that Wendy used the words, "our sons", and doesn't want to be bothered with visiting her right now. Yes, they're Wendy and his sons, but Wendy and Zion won't be raising them.

I'm being an ass and I know it, but fuck, it should be Zion and Lea.

As he and his parent's step into the elevator to go up to his apartment, they remain silent. When they're in the safety and privacy of his home, he wants to voice what he's feeling, but catches himself.

He walks over to the bar to pour himself and his parents drinks. They follow, grabbing glasses, and return to the living room sofas. "Mom, Dad. Am I wrong to be angry right now, or am I being a selfish bastard because hearing her say 'our sons' did not sit well with me? I didn't like hearing that."

"No, you're right to feel how you're feeling. As much as we would like to keep picturing the future of you and Lea and the boys as a family, Wendy is the starting point of this journey," his father says.

"How you going to bring up to Lea about them meeting?" his mother asks.

"Lea knows it could be a possibility. I don't know how this is going to affect her. I sure as hell don't want her to freak out. And neither of us mentioned hanging out with Wendy. It wasn't something I even considered. Hell, Lea was the one to bring up the idea of you guys visiting with Wendy as you recall."

Royal mimics the movement Zion made downstairs by rubbing his hand across his chin, scratching at his pepper gray beard, "Well, Lea seems like a pretty tough woman. She knows you love and want her, and this is a trying time for you guys to get through. Keep loving and reassuring her. The road to fatherhood you picked is one hell of a path. These few months have been, well, out of the norm for you. After all the calm you had in life and now all this. Way to go son, way to go."

"Shut up will you, Dad?" Zion smiles at him. Yep, he has chosen one heck of a road to fatherhood.

Listening to Royal and Zion talk, Patty begins to have doubts about Lea. Why is she in this? Why hasn't she been more argumentative about my son adopting kids from an ex-lover? She focuses on the nursery instead of speaking up, "Can I see what you have bought for the boys?"

"Sure Mom."

They go upstairs with Patty deciding she needs to figure a time to ask Lea why she's staying with her son.

-21-

Zion calls Lea after his parents left to say good night.

"Hey Bear," she says answering the phone, "How did dinner go?"

He decides to leave the discussion about her meeting Wendy until their lunch tomorrow. "It was good. Mom and Dad were telling her stories about Star and me as kids. She enjoyed the company. How did your dinner and movie go? Has Crystal forgiven me yet?" Not that he really cares.

"Does it really matter?"

"No. You know I don't care what others think about my life. Lea, I wanna discuss something with you."

"Okay, what's up?"

"How do you feel about Wendy? Truthfully. How do you feel about her?" He may regret asking Lea this question, but it's best he knows before he puts them in a room together.

"Zion, of all the questions to ask, why that one?"

Shit, he directly asked me. Do I lie or tell the truth?

"Because I need to know. I want to know."

"I don't want to answer that."

"Sweetheart, tell me."

"I hate her. I'm jealous of her. I envy her. I'm proud of her. She has your undivided attention, and I hate having to take a backseat to her. I pray you don't fall in love with her or start thinking about what ifs."

Why can't I keep this to myself? Why can't I lie? Because I really want to say this out loud. That's why.

"I want to fight her for you. She's usurped my place in your life Zion. I'm supposed to be number one. THE one. I wish she had never come back. I want you to have told her no, you didn't want her kids. I keep having nightmares about all of you rejecting me, being left out in the cold. Zion, I'm so happy for you and that you're getting this chance to be a father. You're going to be a great father. It's truly a wonderful blessing that this is happening to and for you."

She takes a deep shaky breath.

Zion hasn't said a word, because he's in shock.

"Don't hate me for what I'm thinking and feeling. I would never act on any of this, and I'll never hurt any of you. These are just my crazy thoughts. You asked to hear how I feel. You wanted to know." After Lea says all this, she disconnects the call and turns off her phone.

Shit, I went there. Even Gordon didn't know all this. But Zion asked. Why the fuck did he ask? Why the fuck did I not lie?

She goes into the bathroom and sits on the end of the tub wondering what to do now. Turn on her phone and call him back or let it slide until tomorrow.

Fuck, Lea you just screwed up royally. He'll never look at you the same again. Or he won't ever trust you around the boys.

Zion could not believe what he was hearing from Lea. It was as if he was listening to one of his temporary fucks with their nasty attitudes. Normally, this would be his cue to ghost the woman and cut off all communications. But not Lea. When attempting to call her back, her phone keeps going to voicemail.

Oh, hell naw baby.

He throws on some sweats and drives to her house. Going in, he sees her standing in the dim hallway. Her hands are balled into fists. She's bracing herself for his anger, disappointment, and eventual words to end this relationship.

"I would take it all back if I could. But you asked."

"You're right. I asked. It was a shock to hear, but I don't feel any differently about you than I did before I asked the question." He walks to her and embraces her. "Baby, I'm glad you finally admitted to me what you feel about Wendy. Hate that I had to ask to hear it, but I'm glad you told me. Shit, woman, stop bottling up your emotions from me. I need to know this. I love you. I also hate that I'll never see my child growing in you, watching your stomach get big. Among many other things I hate about this situation, I'm as grateful to be going through it with you. Becoming a father is wonderful. Marrying the woman I love, is even better."

They stand in the hall holding onto each other, not saying much of anything else. Finally, Zion speaks up. "Don't ever turn your phone off again. I didn't like that. Not at all. It scares me having it go straight to voicemail."

"I didn't want to have you calling me back, berating me for what I said. I figured I could wait and hear what you had to say tomorrow or never. Especially if you were thinking about ending it."

"Good, bad, or ugly. Lea, we gotta be able to say what we feel without fear. Now I'm going to go home and you're going to go to bed. Remember lunch tomorrow, at least two hours. Actually, make it a late lunch and you can work from my office," he suggests.

"Lunch indeed. I do have to be at your office to discuss some things with Saul about the computers. I should be there around noon and am scheduled to meet with Saul at two. So, you get me for two hours max."

"Hmmmmm, I'm sure we can come up with something to entertain ourselves. Wear a skirt."

"I'm glad that you came by. Now go home. You have a call in a few hours with Germany, right?"

"Yes, I do. See you tomorrow at noon. I'll have lunch ready. And food, too. Love you babe. Turn your phone back on."

"Love you too, Bear." Lea turns on her phone and sends him a text. A picture of koala bears hugging. He responds back with a picture of himself laughing.

-22-

Lea goes back to work, making sure everyone is acting normally and not treating her with kid gloves. Crystal is happy to see her, as is Tom. He calls her into his office to discuss what happened last week. "Hey, Lady, how are you doing?"

"It's only been the weekend. I'm sticking to a plan and a schedule. Thanks for asking."

"We don't want you stressed, so whatever you need to do, let me know. We need to keep you safe."

"I will. I have the meeting with Saul at Landon Enterprises at two, but I was going to go a couple hours early to have lunch with Zion."

"That's perfect. Is this about the computer image and transfers? Is he needing to hire any people to help him with that? I'm sure we can get temps if need be."

"They're doing it in-house. Saul is particular about his network. He's hired someone to help him with the transition. A company called Normalcy Assistance. He won't tell me anything other than that. I'm surprised he's even letting me see and go over what he's wanting to talk about today."

"Good. Well as usual keep me posted. It says in the calendar appointment you'll be there until four. Go home from there and we'll see you in the morning. Be safe, Lea, please. No disappearing jaunts."

"Geez, Addison needs to get locked up, fast. She's messing with my lifestyle," she says smiling, hoping to ease his mind a little.

"I hear ya. I hear ya. Let me know if you need anything or if there are any changes. I do have a question."

"Go ahead."

"Will we be losing you here? Twin sons, marriage, getting settled. Will I be losing my best project lead?"

"Honestly, Tom, I don't want to stop working, but like you said, twins, marriage. I don't want to miss out on bonding. Usually that happens during pregnancy, and breast feeding. I won't have that chance, so I can only do it by being around them twenty-four/seven. I love my job. Would you be willing to work something out part-time, me working from home, or maybe another type of arrangement? I know we can discuss this later, but just think about it. You know me and how I think ahead."

"Lea, both ideas are perfect and doable. I don't want to lose you either. We're a great team here. We can absolutely consider working something out. I'm glad I brought this up. I wasn't going to at first but now that we have, well, we'll make it happen."

"Thanks Tom, I appreciate it. I'll get back to work. Did you know we're getting a second proposal from Landon Enterprises? For a small satellite office run by Star."

"Hell naw. Yes, girl, go get that money."

"Tom, I only met Zion five, six months ago and we're sitting here talking about my marriage, babies, combining households. Am I rushing into this? Am I moving too fast? Should I slow down? I'm asking from a father's viewpoint. Would you want your daughter to be in this situation?"

"Lea, how do you feel? Seriously, when you think about Zion and being with him versus being away from him, how do you feel?"

"Like I'm exactly where I should be and everything is going as planned," she says.

"That's the answer to all your previous questions. And if I didn't think Zion was the one for you, you would have never met him." Tom says this knowing if he and the cupids wanted to keep them apart, they would have.

"Uh, thanks." Lea goes back to her office and grabs her things. She calls Ryan to meet her downstairs as soon as he can, anxious to head over to Zion's office. "I'm downstairs in the car waiting now, Miss Adams."

"Great, I'll be right down." She gets on the elevator with some other co-workers and rides down, fidgeting, needing to see him, having this urgent need to be around him. It only takes them twenty-five minutes to get to his office building. She checks his calendar on her phone, and it doesn't say he's currently unavailable but even if he is, she can visit with Star or sit in his office or conference room until he becomes available.

"Hi, Morgan. Is Zion available? I know I'm not due here until noon."

"He's here, finishing up a meeting, but you're more than welcome to go into his office and wait. I'm making sure lunch is ready."

"Great, don't tell him I'm here. I can hang and get some work done. Thanks again." Lea goes into Zion's office and sits down on his couch to wait. After about twenty-five minutes, she hears his voice outside his office, talking to Morgan.

"When Lea gets here, show her in and no interruptions unless it's an emergency. I think I've put out all the fires."

He walks into his office, striding straight for his desk then freezes. He turns around and looks at her.

"Hi, Zion," Lea says.

After slipping in and placing their lunch on the table, Morgan leaves, closing the door. Zion leans over hitting the button to lock it.

"Hi, Lea. How long have you been here, and do I need to fire my assistant for not informing me of your arrival?" he says, leaning up against his desk.

"Why are you itching to fire someone? I asked Morgan not to tell you I was here because I arrived early. I took the time to catch up on some emails. So, Mr. Landon, how is your day going?"

He walks over to the couch and sits down next to her. "Hello, Miss Adams. It's lovely to see you today. I've been thinking about you all morning." He kisses her neck and nibbles on her earlobes with each word. He looks at her, closely.

"What?" she asks him, "What are you thinking?"

"Lea, I'm glad I waited so long to settle down. Good things do come to those who wait. How did you sleep after I left? Just a little I hope."

"About an hour's worth. Zion, do you ever think we're moving too fast? We've only known each other, for what, a few months, and we're talking about marriage. Doesn't this scare you?"

He turns her toward him and stretches her legs over his lap, caressing them. "Truthfully, sometimes I wake up in a cold sweat, not believing my luck. I've had more confidence in my business deals. This with you, not including the boys, terrifies me. Then I look at your picture. I think about all the conversations we've had, how we've connected, and I grin. Overwhelmed with happiness. I'm sure others are thinking we're moving too fast, but we're not teenagers. We've dated, we've lived, and we've matured. I don't care about the time frame. Baby, I could have married you that morning in Chicago. That's how sure I was that I needed you as a part of my life for the rest of my life. So, yes, I think about the timing, but if it means slowing down and letting you go, that ain't happening. I get over it. Why? Are you wanting to slow things down?"

"No. Tom and I were discussing my work schedule after the boys are born. About me taking some time off and bonding with them and it hit me that it's only been five months and I'm talking about maternity leave. Working part-time or maybe not even going back to work."

Zion gives her a sly glance.

"Don't look at me like that. I still want to work. I love my job. But I want to bond with you and the boys even more." His sly look changes to a look of anger.

"What's wrong?" Lea asks.

"Wendy had me touch her stomach last night. I was angry and elated at the same time. Angry because it wasn't your stomach I was touching, that they were not our biological kids moving in your belly, that I hadn't gotten you pregnant. But I was elated to feel them move. Then she said "our" boys, she and I. Technically, right now they're Wendy and my boys, but I so wanted them to be Lea and Zion's boys at that moment. Am I wrong for feeling that way?"

"No, you're not. It's called being human. You know about my horrible thoughts. Why didn't you tell me this last night?"

"I didn't want to add to your misery. What other horrible thoughts have you had? Don't worry, this is between us. I won't think any less of you. I trust you too much for that."

"I'm sometimes angry with you. She gets to share things with you I'll never share. The babies moving in her stomach, the ultrasounds, and even though they're not your kids biologically you're bonding with her and them every second you spend with them. I hate that I can't spend the night with you because I know I'll be jealous and angry if you have to leave me to go to her or I'm sitting waiting in your apartment while you're visiting her. But I want to be back in your bed with you. I don't want you visiting her when I'm there. I hate it when you have to drop everything and go running to her to see how she's doing when you get a call, but if you don't, I'll feel guilty if something happens and you weren't there. See how unfair that sounds?"

"It's okay, babe, I get it. I understand. So, it's good for me to respond positively toward Wendy and the boys without worrying I'm disloyal to you?"

"Zion, of course I want you to respond positively. I imagine there are going to be emotions and displays of affection between the two of you. She's the biological mother. I don't want you treating her negatively. Understand? Don't be cold, don't be business Zion."

"I needed to hear you say that," he says looking at her intently. "The subject of meeting you came up. Wendy asked about it Sunday."

Lea thumbs her fingertips on his arm. "Of course, she does. Set it up."

"Lea, I want you to spend some time getting to know her. I know this sounds crazy. It's not right the two of you not meeting. It's another of those things I hadn't given much thought to. You said you would be willing," he reminds her.

"Zion, I'm not disagreeing with you. I'm not going to make this difficult. I'll meet Wendy, visit with her. Understand, I won't allow either of you to treat me like shit."

Zion stares at her, speechless. "Lea, no one is going to treat you like shit. Especially me. Don't you know that by now?"

"You're about to have two women who have a claim on you in the same room together. Doesn't matter that she's dying. You're accustomed to walking away. That's no longer an option. So, brace yourself," Lea warns him.

He stares at her not believing what she said. Did he need to hear Lea say that? Probably.

"I was thinking Wednesday, before I leave, I can introduce you to her. And I wanted you to stay with me and drive to the airport with me. Or come with me."

"I can't. I have to be here. I'm close to finishing your project," she says kissing him on his neck and licking the under skin of his ear.

Lea pulls back and checks the time on one of his wall clocks. "Bear, we need to eat lunch; we've been talking so long we missed out on our quickie."

He checks his watch, forty-five minutes left. "Damn, and I can't extend this either. I have a conference call at two, with clients in Australia. Okay, let's eat." He stands and they walk over to his conference table. Zion uncovers their food, laying the covers to the side. He glances at her computer, noticing its opened to her emails. "Have you received any threats lately?" he asks as they sit down.

"Nope, none. Is there something I should be aware of?" They're eating salads with grilled chicken, fresh fruit for dessert and drinking strawberry lemonade tea.

"No, she's still off the radar. I gave the information you and Crystal provided me Friday to the police. Are you sure you don't want to come work here at Landon Enterprises? This, today, has been great. We can do lunch together in the office every day. Especially with the boys in the day care."

"Day care, what day care?"

"I'm having a day care added into the new building. The bottom floor is for other offices to lease out and I'm turning one of them into a day care. If our sons end up going to a day care, I want them either close by me or you and because your office building does not have that, mine will."

"My, you do think of everything don't you?"

"I try, I try. Ring shopping next week." He looks at her hand, staring at her college class ring. "I want to have one designed instead of a jewelry store purchase."

"You're going to have one designed for me? I never thought of that."

"Your mother told me don't do typical, so I'm not doing typical. Ideas, please," he says, holding onto her hand, twisting the ring on her finger.

"Well, not a diamond solitaire. Nothing huge that sticks out and snags onto everything or that I can call part of a brass knuckle. My favorite symbol is the infinity symbol. And you know cobalt blue is my favorite color. How about that for a start? And what did that conversation with my mother involve? She gave you information I didn't think she would ever give a man about me. She must kinda like you."

"I'm not telling. Hell, I've said too much as it is. This will give me something to think about. I'll call my jeweler later in the week and have him work on a design."

"You'll be telling me what kind of wedding band you want to wear, right? I mean, I have a slight idea of what I want, but I would like your input also. Wait, will you still be wearing a wedding band? You haven't changed your mind, have you?"

"Oh, hell yes, I'll be wearing a wedding band. I should get myself an engagement ring. All I know is that it has to have four stones representing you, me, and the boys. Not birth stones, that would be too colorful. I, on the other hand, like diamonds and your ring will be incorporating a diamond solitaire somehow, but I get you liking the blue stones."

Zion and Lea continue talking about their future plans and their confusing feelings about the situation with Wendy. He wants Lea to come home with him tonight, but she says no, knowing he'll be visiting Wendy. Lea isn't ready to sit around his place waiting for her turn. He'll make arrangements for them to meet on Wednesday, and she'll stay with him, then ride to the airport to see him off. That's her compromise.

"To think I wanted to sex you for a couple years and here we are talking about engagement rings." She kisses him lovingly, putting all her emotions and love into that kiss.

"And I wanted to make you my new temporary fuck. My how things change when you allow yourself to experience something new and different in life. Now go meet Saul and come back up here when you're done. We can make out in the car on the way home."

"Later, Bear," she says, walking out of his office.

"Later, Kitten," he says watching her leave.

Lea's meeting with Saul goes as planned. They've tested the image for the new machines on five different computers, making sure they work without losing data. The smartphones have been issued to the staff and are in use. The servers are setup in the new office and working as planned. The move will be around mid-September and should be fully done by the end of the month. If all works out, Landon Enterprises will have the grand opening celebration for family, friends, and clients in October.

She gets back upstairs to Zion's office as he's finishing up a meeting with Sam and Morgan about his trip this week. Both will be traveling with Zion. Watching him work is such a turn-on. Lea sits down at his conference room table and types an email to Tom, updating him on the meeting with Saul and how G-TEE could be done and close out the contract for Landon Enterprises by the end of September. They qualify for the bonus at this point.

"No more working. It's time for making out. Shut your computer down, missy."

"Yes sir. Are you having dinner with Wendy tonight?"

"Nope. I'll be stopping by her place when I get home, after our date."

"Ooh. A date. Am I dressed appropriately?"

"Well, you're wearing too many clothes for what I want to do with you because its only dinner, you're dressed perfectly."

Before they can get to his car, he gets a phone call from Becky. Seems that Wendy is having a headache and is wanting to see him. So, that means dinner for them tonight is off. Just the ride home. "Baby, I'm sorry," he says.

"Zion, don't apologize. Drop me off, then go. I'll talk to you later," she tells him. "We'll deal with everything as it happens. Now let's go make out. It's a short drive to my house."

-23-

Zion stops off at Wendy's apartment to check on her. This time he rings the bell and lets himself in. He calls out looking for her and the nurse.

"Wendy? Becky? Are you guys, okay?" Becky comes out of Wendy's bedroom smiling but looking tired. "Is she okay, what's wrong?" he questions her.

"One of her friends from the Smoking Lounge came by for a visit. Lil witch and I don't mean witch. She started going on about how things are so horrible for Wendy and how Wendy will never see her kids grow up and how Wendy will die and how the state will get Wendy's kids and split them up. After that, I told her she had to go and not come back. Wendy needs support, not negativity. Then the witch lit into me calling me a hired hand, waiting for my meal ticket to die so I can rip her off. I wanted to punch her into next week. Well, Wendy stressed herself out and got a headache. Usually, she does some meditation to calm herself down and make it go away but this time she couldn't. She's been asking for pain meds. A lot of them. I would only give her one and have been sitting and reading to her. She finally relaxed, but I figured you would want to know. I put the witch's name on the list of blocked visitors. I hope that was, okay?"

Listening to this story makes Zion's blood boil to the point he wants to go and the Smoking Lounge to find the witch. "You did everything right, Becky. Is she up, can I go see her?"

"Sure. I was about to bring her dinner. Can I get you the same? Soup and a sandwich?" she ask him.

"That would be great."

He walks into Wendy's bedroom and sees that she's propped up in bed, with a teacup sitting on her stomach. She stares at it wobbling back and forth, recording it on her phone. The boys are active.

"Hi Zion. Look, our babies are awake. They must have heard your voice and got excited like I did that you're here. Come sit down."

Again, the wording she chooses is the truth but, it still bugs him. He remembers what Lea told him. Do not be business Zion.

When I think about the boys asking me about my relationship with Wendy, I want my answers to be truthful.

He relaxes and walks toward her smiling. A natural smile but not the smiles he gives Lea.

"So, your visitor. Didn't go well, huh? How are you feeling?" he takes a seat in the chair on the side of the bed, watching the teacup move back and forth. He looks at her and catches her watching him.

"Yes, she was a total bitch. It didn't surprise me. She's been jealous of our relationship since it started years ago. She had eyes for you the second you stepped into the lounge. I figured you were going to be fucking her that night. Lucky you that you didn't. Imagine having to put up with that cattiness all these years."

"She drove you to take pain meds. Are you okay with that? I don't think I've heard anything about you taking any," he asks. He studies her closely gauging her mood on meds so he can report this to the doctor Tuesday.

"I don't want to take them; I've been using meditation to help me deal. But this, today, I couldn't get calm enough to deal with the pain. I took one. I may be drifting off to sleep so don't get offended."

"Well, let's get some food into your system before that happens," Becky says while rolling a cart into the bedroom.

Zion and Wendy talk more over dinner about the boys and what people she doesn't want around them.

"Zion, may I see what the nursery is going to look like?" Wendy asks him.

"Sure, I have some pictures of the different stages of redecorating if you like?" He moves to take out his phone.

"No, I would like to see the actual nursery. Please. To see where the boys will be growing up." Wendy has been thinking about a way to get to see Zion's place since the day she moved into the corporate apartment. *Then my snotty ass friend pointed out how I have never even been to Zion's home. So, this is my chance. Maybe to get invited up even more. Maybe even move in.*

"Okay, we can go up, if you're not too tired that is."

Shit, shit, shit. Okay Zion, she's not moving in. She's just going to see the nursery. A quick visit in and out and back downstairs.

"Great, and no, I'm not tired. I'm excited." *And even if I was, I would fake it.*

They exit the apartment and take the elevator up to his place. Walking through the entry way, she studies the paintings displayed. There are numerous pictures of Lea and Zion, and ones of he and Star growing up. There are many of his family in general. Wendy scrutinizes the ones of Lea alone but doesn't say anything. He switches on the lights as they walk into the living room area. He's now glad Lea decided to go home.

Geez, if they would have walked in unannounced, oh fucking hell. Nope that would not have been good.

"Where's your girlfriend?" Wendy asks. Another reason she wanted to unexpectedly come to Zion's place was to catch her waiting for him. *So I could see the tramp that's trying to steal my potential husband.*

"She's at home. You'll meet her Wednesday. Before I leave town."

"Yes. Morgan informed me of your schedule today." Wendy walks in looking around, making comments here and there saying how nice his place was and how good it is to get to finally see it.

"Thanks. The nursery is upstairs, we can head up there."

"Sure." Wendy walks to the bottom of the steps, looking up.

"Don't worry, I'm right behind you. Take your time." Wendy slowly walks up the steps with Zion behind her. Stepping onto the landing, Zion touches her shoulder and directs her toward the boy's bedroom.

I have decided I'm gonna to take every opportunity I can to get Zion to touch me, love me and even maybe make love to me. Anything to get him to drop the tramp.

Zion has Mrs. Vance close his bedroom door as a habit but leaves the other bedroom doors open. Wendy sees the purchases in bags laid out in the second bedroom. The door to the nursery is partially closed. Zion opens it allowing her to walk in first. It's currently painted. There isn't much to see. She walks around the room, looking at the closets, the bathroom, commenting on the colors.

"No blue for boys?" she asks him.

"I like the muted, earth tones." He refuses to mention how Lea vetoed powdered blue. 'Stop being standard and do something different', he remembers her saying, smiling at the conversation.

"You're smiling, what's so funny?" Wendy inquires. She never got to see these kinda smiles from Zion when they were fucking. Her heart swells.

"Nothing, just a random thought. Ready to go? There isn't much else to see. I haven't decided on furniture yet and other than some clothes, nothing else has been purchased." He keeps trying to put Wendy in places in his home. In places that Lea has been, and it just doesn't compute in his brain.

"Zion, thank you for sharing this with me. Our boys will have a happy life here. Is this a permanent place for you guys?"

"At least for the first two years. Lea and I want to focus on bonding with them instead of looking for a house. I haven't decided on whether or not I would want to sell this place or keep it after we move. I enjoy living downtown." He notices she looked away at the mention of Lea and bonding with the boys.

Well, I'm not going to deny it or hide it from her.

"So, you're going to have her raise them with you. That's good. Well, I'm ready now, I'm getting a little tired."

"Okay, let's get you back to your place." Zion holds her hand while they're walking down the stairs. He releases it on the walk to the elevator. Wendy stops again staring at the pictures of Lea and him. Especially the one he had blown up of him standing in front of the water fountain.

"I remember this night. We had dinner."

"Yes, that picture was taken by Lea that night."

"Zion, you could've been a model. Very handsome."

"Thanks Wendy," he says, wanting to cut this short.

Wendy is thinking about how much she hates Lea at this moment. *Zion was supposed to be mine. If I hadn't waited. If I'd told him everything that night in March, he would've been mine, along with all of this.*

"Wendy are you okay?" Zion asks her, not liking the way she's staring at the picture.

"I'm fine," she says turning to him.

They get back down to her apartment and discuss Lea coming for a visit. "Are you up for this?"

"Yes, I'm looking forward to it. Well, the boys have calmed down and are sleeping. I think I will, too. I'm glad you stopped by. I love seeing you." She scoots down into the bed and Zion covers her up. She grabs his hand, and he sits back down, figuring he'll wait until she's sound asleep. "I love you Zion," she says while drifting off.

Stunned, Zion says, "Goodnight, Wendy."

-24-

On Wednesday, Lea arrives at Zion's office mentally prepared to meet Wendy. She sits in the car with Sam, waiting for Zion to join them. He told her about Wendy's visit with an old friend Monday and how it went. Their appointment at the doctor's the next day revealed unexpected bad news. The tumor has increased in size by a quarter of a centimeter. Her having to take pain meds wasn't a good sign. It affected the boys. They were not moving as much and it bothered everyone. Wendy is at week thirty into the pregnancy, the further she gets into the third trimester the better chance they have at a healthy birth.

Getting dressed this morning, Lea couldn't decide on understated, casual, business or sexy. Listening to Sex Diva, she decided on business sexy. She's wearing her colors of confidence; black slacks, a cobalt blue blouse and black heels. She put on the chocolate diamond earrings Zion gave her and added a necklace she purchased to match. Lea glides on Zion's favorite scent behind her ears and between her breasts. Her spiral curls are popping, freshly washed and twisted last night. Lea sends up a silent prayer for a smooth conversation.

Zion comes striding out of the building looking hella sexy.

Shit, this man commands looks from everyone and all he's doing is walking toward the damn car. Well, I'm wet and aroused. Calm down Lea, calm down.

He's stopped by a woman, and they chat. She's coming on to him hard and he's backing away, keeping her at bay. He finally shakes his head, turns his back on the woman and walks toward the car.

"Don't say a word." He gets in, giving Lea a soul touching kiss. "Not a single word."

"Not even, hi sexy and that flake better stay away from my man?" She laughs.

"Don't make me put you over my knee and spank you. We don't have time. Carmen is always sitting outside the building whenever she sees one of my cars waiting. Even before I met you, I kept telling her no, I don't want to go to dinner, lunch, breakfast, or coffee. This time, I got to say sorry, I'm engaged, and my fiancée is waiting. The look on her face was priceless. Hey you," he gives her another kiss. "I've missed you."

"I've missed you, too. Now let's get this over with. I can feel my anxiety kicking in."

"Sam, drop us off in the garage at the regular elevators," Zion tells him. "We'll see you and Ryan in the morning around six."

"Yes, Sir."

"Lea, before we get there, I have a confession to make," Zion knows he has to tell her about taking Wendy up to his apartment to see the nursery.

"What?" She asks, getting nervous.

"Wendy wanted to see the nursery. I had pictures to show her, but she wanted to see the real deal. So, I took her up to the apartment." Zion can see Lea shutting down.

"Baby, look at me," he tells her.

"I'm looking at you."

"No, you're not, you're looking past me. Look at me, now." He gently moves her head by her chin, bringing her eyes to look directly at his. "Hello pretty eyes."

Lea smiles at his 'pretty eyes' reference then focuses on him and what he's saying.

"I don't want you to be surprised should this come up during this visit. We walked in, she stopped and looked at the pictures. I assisted her up and down the stairs, she looked around the nursery, then we left."

Lea's now biting her lip, but she's still focused on him and what he's saying.

"The visit was maybe about twenty minutes total. Lea, what're you thinking?"

"I don't know. Maybe I'm not thinking at all. I get it, Zion, some shit can't be avoided. Thanks for telling me."

"Lea—." Zion starts.

She puts her hand on his cheek and he kisses the palm of her hand. "Hey, I get it."

They ride in silence, not having anything else to say about what's to come of this visit. They want it to be over. Lea gives her purse and computer bag to Sam to take to Zion's along with his things, and they go to Wendy's apartment.

"It'll be okay; I won't leave you alone," Zion reassures her.

Lea leans into him, gathering some of his strength. "Thanks."

They knock and the nurse lets them in. "Hi Becky. This is Lea, Lea this is Wendy's nurse, Becky."

Lea and Becky shake hands. "Hi Becky. How are you?"

"I'm fine, Miss Lea. Come in, Wendy's waiting."

After closing the door and following them into the apartment, Becky walks toward the balcony and steps onto it. After closing the doors, she takes a seat and picks up her book and starts reading. Becky and Wendy discussed that Becky would stay close by if needed but would not listen in on the conversation.

Zion closes the door and, he and Lea walk into the apartment, approaching Wendy, who is sitting on the bigger couch waiting for them. She has her hair blown out flowing down to her shoulders. She has put on a white lace maternity dress. There is a large bouquet of red and white roses on the dining room table behind her. She's fully made up.

LOOKING LIKE A FUCKING BRIDE. UUUUGGGGGHHHH.

SHE DOESN'T LOOK BAD.

LOOK ADONIS, IF YOU CAN'T KEEP IN LINE AND UNDERSTAND THIS IS ABOUT ME AND MAYBE YOU, YOU CAN GET OUT.

ME SHUTTING UP NOW.

Wendy greets Zion with an excited, "Zion, hi. How are you?" while dismissing Lea.

Lea says nothing but places her hand on Zion's back, lightly applying pressure. Zion takes in Wendy and the flowers but says nothing out loud. He's never seen Wendy look so dolled up before. The flowers behind her almost make her look angelic. He brings Lea around to stand in front of him to make the introductions.

"Hello Wendy. I'm doing good." He responds to her question not displaying the closeness he has with Wendy in front of Lea. He makes the introductions, "Wendy, meet Lea. Lea, Wendy." Lea and Wendy exchange greetings and Lea sits down on the couch across from her. Wendy scoots over and pats the seat next to her for Zion.

"I'll sit at the dining room table, giving the two of you some freedom to talk."

If he would have sat next to Wendy, Lea would have chopped him into pieces. Wendy is seriously trying to stake a claim that Lea can do nothing about.

"So, you're the woman Zion has chosen to help him raise our boys. I'm glad to finally meet you," *I hate you more than you can imagine*, Wendy is thinking to herself.

See, I knew she was going to go there; I just knew it. Lea thinks to herself, ready to stake her own claim.

"Yes, I am. You've made him a happy and lucky man to raise your sons." Lea is not about to say their son's even if it's true. "He's grateful to you for that."

"I saw you the night you first met. Zion and I had finished having dinner and I was driving through the Central West End and I saw you two sitting on a bench talking. That was only in March. That's not long of a relationship, is it?"

Okay, she's breaking out the fangs.

"No, it isn't. And that wasn't the first time we'd met. So, how are you?"

Yes, I bared my own fangs. So what?

Wendy stares at Lea, wanting to snap off a smart remark but holds back.

"I'm doing the best that can be expected considering I'm dying and bringing two babies into the world. Have you ever been pregnant? It's crazy all the things that are happening to my body. Did Zion tell you he felt our babies kick? It was sooo wonderful." *There, let that sink in, Zion felt OUR babies move.*

"Yes, he did. He was excited and amazed. Wendy, why did you really want to meet me?" Lea is getting annoyed at this conversation. Everything Wendy is saying is on purpose to hurt her and make her feel excluded.

I get it. You and Zion have a connection. So, damn what.

"To be honest with you, I'm happy that Zion is going to have someone to help him raise our boys. I would have preferred it to be his family and not some temporary liaison he thinks he likes. Did you know all his sexual escapades have been temporary? I was his longest," she says.

Lea glances at Zion. He hasn't moved but she can tell he's becoming irritated. His facial expression, to others would be described as unreadable. But Lea knows this means he's preparing himself for the moment he will strike back and take control of a situation. When Lea first saw this happen, she was amazed.

Lea responds back to Wendy with unexpected confidence, "You WERE his longest temporary. Emphasis on temporary. And his last temporary. I'm his permanent, and his future and there will be no one after me. I'm the girlfriend and soon to-be-wife." Lea stares at Wendy daring her to contradict her.

Wendy looks at Lea as if she's ready to strike out at her physically. She probably would if she could move fast enough.

Zion's posture changed from relaxed to rigid back in the chair he's sitting in. *So, this is what it's like to see two women fighting for me,* he thinks to himself.

"Lea. I'm the one giving Zion this opportunity. It's me, I'm the reason this is taking place. Without you in the picture, Zion and I can be a true family. I wanted to meet you to ask you to step back and go away so we could." *There I said it. Without her, Zion and I could be a family. He would even marry me.*

"That's not going to happen! Zion is mine!" Lea uses the tone on Wendy that Ms. Adams uses with Lea when she steps out of line.

Zion stands up from the dining room table, moving to get in between the women. "Wendy! What the hell?" He's pissed. "Really? This is why you wanted to meet Lea? I'm not happy with the direction of this conversation." He takes a seat on the couch next to Lea.

Rushing over her words to get them out, Wendy says, "Zion, if you hadn't met her, and we had finished our dinner, I would've told you then about the babies and we would be married and a true family as I had planned. But with her in the picture," Wendy gestures toward a silent Lea, "there's no chance of that. She'll get you after I'm dead. So why can't she back off until then? We could be married and our boys will be born with your name. I don't see what the big deal is." Wendy spits at him. "If it's the sex you think you'll be missing, I can give you that. We always had it good when it came to that. There's no reason for HER to be in the picture while I'm alive."

"Wendy, I've never lied to you about my feelings for Lea. I plan on marrying one woman in my lifetime and she's it. I don't appreciate you talking to her the way you are and saying the things you're saying. If you would've told me, you were pregnant that night, I would've walked away from you and wished you the best of luck."

Lea sits still and lets him finish.

"It's because of Lea I'm at a place to even consider adopting them. I don't mean to hurt you or cause you any pain or grief about this, but I'm not going to marry you, nor am I going to break up with Lea to go back to her after you've given birth. I'm definitely not going to be having sex with you. I wanted you to get to know the woman I love and who will be the mother to your sons. To show you that I'm with someone you can have peace in knowing your boys will be loved and taken care of. I didn't bring her here for you to take out your anger and frustration on."

"Come on, Zion. The marriage is to give our sons your name legally. It's all I ask. Just get rid of her for a few weeks." Wendy turns her anger toward Lea asking, "Why are you sticking around anyway? Any other woman would have run away from him and this situation. Zion was supposed to be mine. Forever."

Lea turns to Zion, skoots away from him and opens her hands as if presenting Zion to Wendy for the first time. "Wendy, look at him. Are you serious? The man is a numbers wizard with the ability to calculate as second nature. He's a financial and investment savant. He's achieved wealth at a young age outside of the sports, entertainment, and food industry that for a black man doesn't often happen. He has a collective knowledge of music, and random history that astounds everyone that talks to him. And I haven't even mentioned looks. Again. Look. At. Him. The man is fine as fuck. You had your chance, and you did nothing with it. I'm not blowing mine. I'm the woman he's chosen. I'm in love with Zion. As long as he loves and wants me, I'm not going anywhere. Girl, you got me fucked up." Lea bites her bottom lip on that last sentence but she doesn't take it back.

It's difficult for Zion not to respond to what Lea just said. He knew Lea loved him, is in love with him and he makes her happy. But to hear all this. What she really thinks about him. He wants to hug her and twirl her around this room screaming 'hell fuck yeah, I got me a good one here'. But he holds all emotions and reactions in and refocuses on Wendy.

Wendy turns to Zion with her anguish on full display, "Zion you want me. The way you look at me. I know you do. She's a temporary. Get rid of her, and we can be together. Please. I beg of you. Or maybe you don't want our sons."

Before Zion can speak up Lea jumps in, "Wendy, I AM NOT A TEMPORARY. You the one who allowed herself to get into that roll."

Zion is awestruck at the words Wendy is throwing at him and Lea and Lea is throwing back at Wendy. He has to get control of this situation. "Wendy, if you're threatening me about the adoption, knock it off." Zion has switched to business Zion with a deadly calm in his voice, and stiff posture. He leans toward Wendy, with his right hand on his knee, flexing his fingers. "Don't ever try me like that. I can easily change this setup."

Lea touches him, trying to get him to step back from business Zion. He puts his left hand over hers, squeezing it and takes a deep breath.

Seeing the change in Zion after Lea touched him breaks Wendy's heart.

Zion looks down at Lea's hand, then continues in a much softer tone, "Wendy I'm not going to get rid of Lea and be with you. That's not going to happen. I'm not saying this to hurt you. If me marrying you is a condition on adopting your sons, say it now. Is my marrying you a condition for adopting your sons?"

Wendy stares at Lea instead of looking at Zion. "No, Zion. Marrying me is not a condition for adopting our sons." Wendy grinds her teeth on the words 'our sons'. She doesn't take her eyes from Lea, holding Zion's hand.

"Wendy, I'm extremely grateful to you for giving me the opportunity to adopt your sons." After Wendy's outburst Zion unconsciously refers to them as her sons and not our boys. Slightly distancing himself.

"I thank you for that. But I'm in love with only one woman and she's Lea. I'll only marry one woman and she's Lea. Wendy, look at me."

Wendy looks from Lea to Zion, heartbroken and devastated. She's in love with him. Head over heels unable to see past her love for him. She wants him to love her and hearing that he doesn't is hurting her. "I'm sorry, Zion. I'm tired, why don't you both leave now."

"Wendy are—," Zion starts but she cuts him off, staring at Lea. Hating her.

"I'll be fine. It's not. I'm not in pain, just tired. I'll get some rest. I'll see you tomorrow," Wendy says, attempting to get in a last dig to Lea, letting her know, Zion is coming to see her.

"I'll be flying out in the morning and won't be back 'til Saturday. I'll call you when I can and will stop by Sunday. In the mean time you have Becky call me if you need me. And Star and Garrett will be by Friday with the girls to visit. Is that okay with you? Wendy, look at me." Zion moves to sit on the couch next to Wendy, forcing her to focus on him, "Is that okay with you?" he prods.

Fuck, I forgot about this trip. Well at least SHE won't be with him either. "Yes, that's fine. I'll see you Sunday. Goodnight, Zion. I'm sorry for what I said. I was out of line," she says lovingly looking at Zion now that he's sitting next to her. Wendy's silently thinking, *bitch die. Zion could be mine.*

"Apologize to Lea, not to me," Zion tells her.

Wendy turns to Lea, "I'm sorry, Lea."

Wendy's apology doesn't reach her eyes, but Lea accepts it. "Apology accepted. And if at any time you want to get to know me as the mother to your children and not the woman that's taking away the love of your life, I'll be more than happy to come back, visit, and talk." Lea knows exactly where Wendy's anger is coming from.

Wendy is thinking, *Heffa I'm never meeting you again. I can't marry him but I'll get the illusion of my family before I die. Don't need your ass messing that up.* "Goodnight," she says.

Zion stands looking down at Wendy, "Do you want me to help you to bed?"

"No. I'm fine. Becky will help me. I'll talk to you tomorrow." Wendy looks up at Zion, "Goodnight Zion. Have a safe trip."

"Thank you, Wendy."

She watches them leave, hating Lea even more when Zion places his hand in the small of Lea's back.

No, Lea Adams. You'll not fuck with my family vision. Zion will love me. Zion will always love me. Zion will always be mine. Always.

After Zion and Lea leave, Becky comes back into the apartment and sits across from Wendy on the other couch.

Wendy glares at the door. "I hate her." Referring to Lea.

"Why?"

"Why?!!! Are you kidding me. She's with the man that's supposed to be my husband."

"From what I've read about Zion Landon and Landon Enterprises, he was never gonna be your husband."

"I've never shared anything about him with you. So, how the hell you come to that conclusion? I coulda had him if she wasn't in the picture."

"No Wendy, you would've never had him. Before you get upset and start ranting and raving, let me explain." Becky sits next to Wendy taking her vitals. "The day you interviewed me for this job I went home and researched you. During our interview, you mentioned marrying Zion Landon."

"I never mentioned him."

"Yes, you did. It was during one of your, what I call, stepping out of character moments. The doctor said you would have them because of the location of the tumor. Anyway, I went home and researched you. And him. From what I could find out, the man is or shall we now say, was a career bachelor. Forty-nine, never married, rarely linked to a woman for more than a month and no kids. A black billionaire never having a paternity suit filed against him. I was shocked you managed to gain his attention."

"Becky, you think I'm some kind of pathetic woman. I attracted plenty of men."

"Yep, you sure did. None of them wanted to marry you. And you stated they were not father material."

"I need to keep my mouth shut."

"Wendy, I'm sorry to say this, but you can't control what slips out any longer. Honey, you don't know it when you're doing it. Look, I get paid what I get paid because I listen, I do my job, and I keep my mouth shut. What you say when I'm with you, whether you're aware of it or not, will stay between us. And will die with me.

"Now back to Mr. Landon marrying you. Watching him around you and Miss Lea, the difference is astonishing. He may love you for giving him the opportunity to be a father, but he's IN love with Lea Adams. And he not letting her slip away. My advice to you is take the little you can get and focus on these little guys." Becky touches her stomach feeling the boys move and kick.

"My goal was for Zion and my boys, for us to be a family. I hate that I'm dying. I hate that I won't see my babies grow up. I hate it even more that Zion isn't mine."

Becky comforts Wendy, helping her to release these emotions. Knowing that Wendy only remembers bits and pieces of what's going on, Becky takes the step to have Wendy focus on what parts of Zion she'll have for the remainder of her pregnancy and sorry to say it, but life.

"Wendy, Zion loves you for giving him the chance to be a father. You're providing him with two healthy boys. Lea Adams isn't. Zion spends his evenings with you. He cares about you. You aren't alone in this. Your babies will be loved. Isn't that a good thing?"

"Yes Becky, it is. You right. Zion does love me. And we're a family. No one can take that away. He's the love of my life and our sons are gonna adore him. I did good selecting him as their father."

Becky realizes Wendy is having one of her out of character moments. "Yes Wendy, he's the love of your life and he's gonna be a great father."

Wendy deserves this dream. It'll get her through, Becky thinks as Wendy drifts off to sleep.

-25-

After Zion and Lea steps onto the elevator, he pushes the button for his floor then takes Lea into his arms and kisses her. He has her pressed against him, one hand on the back of her head, with his fingers in her hair and the other at her waist pressing her into his body, kissing her with a passion she hasn't felt in weeks. And she gives back in return. Ending the kiss, they break apart and continue the ride up in silence. Lea fiddles with her necklace, wondering what to say. Zion reaches to wipe the lipstick off his mouth, not realizing there's nothing there because Lea is wearing a lip stain again.

Exiting the elevator, Lea is relieved when Zion breaks the silence, "Damn that was some kind of meeting."

"Fuck the meeting. That was some kind of kiss. Damn."

They laugh.

"Lea, I don't know why Wendy said all that."

How should Lea bring up her past about loving a man and not getting that man as Wendy loves and wants Zion?

'Cause damn, I see Jake and I all over again and can't believe this shit.

Upon entering his apartment, Lea stands in the foyer looking at the pictures. She turns toward Zion with a smirk on her face. "C'mon Zion seriously? You know why."

"Okay, I know but I wasn't expecting it. At least not in front of you."

"She's in love with you. So much so that she can't think straight. She's waited and pined for you, hoping someday you would want her for your wife. Getting artificially inseminated may have been her way to have kids, but it was also her way to get you to see her, to love her. Her one last ditch effort to have you be hers, forever, and she's succeeded. In a way. She's blinded by the love she has for you to see that part of it."

They walk into his living room and plop down on the couch. "No, she hasn't. I'm not hers. I'm yours, forever. How do you know all this? You've never even met her until today."

"Zion, there was a time I was Wendy." He's about to hear a part of Lea's past she's not proud of, but it did help get her to where she's at now, so she continues.

"Loving someone, waiting for them to see me, to want me, to desire me the way I wanted and desired them, that was me three years ago. You've been seeing Wendy for, what, two maybe three years? I was her for six years. The only difference is I didn't get pregnant. But I waited and held on for six long years, hoping for any scrap of attention, of a date, of inclusion. The little droplets I got, I was willing to say were perfect and I was happy. Man, the excuses I made up for his behavior. I had justification for every reason why I wasn't being treated well or getting what I needed from him. You could not tell me any different.

"I saw all the red flags and I still held on, hoping he would see me. He never did. He's happy with someone else now. Even after he told me he was seeing her, I kept hope alive, explaining away why he chose her instead of me. I made one last ditch effort to be his temporary anything. See, even I was willing to be a temporary like Wendy. I know all about temporary."

Lea gets up and walks over to his bar, pouring them drinks. He follows, taking a glass from her, gulping it down. It's hard for Zion to imagine Lea, his Lea waiting for a man to see her when he saw and wanted her before he even knew her name. He listens.

"My light bulb moment was when I realized I couldn't pick up the phone, call him, or go see him when I was having a bad day. I was having a hard time and there was no him to call and talk it over with, to get comfort from. He even stopped responding to all my calls, texts, and emails. I would see them out somewhere, and he would speak, but it was cold and unfeeling. I finally had to cut off all communication with him.

"I stopped going to places where I knew I would run into him. People would tell me about them not knowing how I felt about him. No one even knew we were talking, let alone fucking. It's humiliating to look back on it. He had moved on and here I was alone, completely, still wanting to be with him. I had no one because I wanted nothing but him. I'm not telling you this to make you feel sorry for Wendy or to consider what she's asked, because I'll be damned if I'm going to let you play house and home with her while I am waiting on the side lines for her to die. You can fucking forget that shit right now. I'm telling you this so you can see behind my offer to her if she wants to meet me again." Lea has a strange feeling that will never happen, but the offer is out there and she'll stick to it no matter what.

"Just understand you ARE mine and she's not getting you, so don't even think you're going to consider what she said. I don't know if that man got away because of my lack of standing up and saying what I wanted and needed, letting things slide, hoping he would see me. I don't even care. I know with you I'm not going to let this go. You keep saying how you love me and how happy you are as a part of my life. With that encouragement, I'll hold on for dear life and fight anyone and everyone to be with you. But I'm not stupid or masochistic. I will and can walk away heartbroken if I need to. If you at any point decide to walk away from me and marry her, don't think you can come back after she's dead. She's not getting you away from me without a fight."

He turns Lea to face him. "Lea, I would never consider what she asked. And no offense, but I'm so fucking happy that jackass walked away from you and is with someone else. He didn't deserve what you had to offer him and I do. If I ever run into him, I'll buy him and his new love drinks because what he did was the best thing ever for your life and mine. I'm here now and I'm not going away. God, Lea. Six years! We men can be some really fucked-up human beings in the way we treat women."

"It's not just you men. I accepted what he wasn't offering. I take as much blame in it as he may have thought he had blame in it, which I'm sure he doesn't think that way. That's why I wouldn't let anything get started with you unless I knew it was more than temporary."

"I'll talk to Wendy about her attitude this evening. She was wrong."

"Don't. Don't bring it up again. Get back to calling them our boys and our sons with her."

"What?"

"When you were berating her, you said 'your sons'."

"I hadn't noticed it."

"I didn't think so. Look, she'll probably never bring me up again. Focus on your sons."

"Okay, I will. How about we de-stress and have some dinner?"

"You don't have any more questions about my past? About what I just told you?"

"Hell no. Kitten, I'm sure there are many women who can tell you how much of an ass I was to them. I'd like to know more about how you got the strength to move on. I still don't see the introvert in you."

Walking over to the kitchen, they prepare dinner. A salad, grilled shank steak, buttered potato medallions and fried apple pies with ice cream for dessert.

While they are fixing dinner, Lea explains, "I moved on by focusing on work. I removed all other men from my life, deleted numbers, thinking I would finally give myself to someone. When that didn't happen, I had no one to fall back on. Even the women I was hanging out with I cut off, thinking I would go into a relationship, and I would focus on him and us. Turns out they didn't miss me so no love lost there.

"The new me drove Gordon mad. I went from talk of our teenage love to BDSM, going to sex toy parties, and cutting men off without a second chance. He thought I was becoming mean and bitchy. I wanted more and knew any man who wasn't meeting my basic standards was a waste of my time. Then you come along."

"Yes, tell me about me coming along. I wanna hear this."

"Zion, when I saw you in the boardroom, I couldn't stop thinking sex and how I had no chance. But it was fun to flirt. I had a difficult time staying the course and no temporary or reverting back to whatever it takes for him to see me ima do that."

"Would you have become a temporary with me?" he asks.

"No, but I knew I wanted to fuck you," Lea admits. "What about you? What where your thoughts of me when you first saw me?"

"In the lobby when you were walking away before I could say anything, I was thinking about how I was going to find you. Then, when you walked into the boardroom, I wanted to lean you over the table and take you. It wasn't until the night of the charity ball I knew I wanted more. I became territorial, watching other men approach you. I've never been that way with other women. Hell, I pushed them toward other men as fast as I could. A number of them can thank me for marriages and divorces over the years.

"I'd been thinking about growing old and whether it would be alone, happy, miserable, or plain boring. Meeting you gave me hope. Still gives me hope."

"Hope? I thought you were the decisive one and I was the one with the doubts."

"Lea, I'm becoming a father at fifty. Marrying for the first time at fifty. Of course, I have doubts. But no regrets. We're doing this. All of this. Understand? Together."

"Understood," Lea says. Zion yawns, then stretches. Lea loves seeing him stretch. Like a bear waking up from a winter's sleep. Her phone buzzes. A quick look at the screen tells her Gordon is calling.

"Answer it," Zion says. Lea puts him on speaker phone.

"Where in the hell have you been and why haven't you called me and given me any kind of updates on your life. Woman, I could beat you, but I guess you have a man for that!!" He yells at her.

"Hi, Gordon. How are you tonight? And the family?" Lea asks sweetly.

"Yes, she has a man for that," Zion says in the background. Lea giggles.

"Lea, I done told you don't put me on speaker phone without warning first. What up Zion?"

"It's all good, man. It's all good. I'll let you two talk." Zion leaves Lea to her phone call with Gordon, going to his office.

Lea takes the phone off speaker. "Sorry about that. Well not really. I get into a relationship and do things other folks do and I get berated. Geez. The stalker is still out there somewhere but hasn't given Zion any grief. Today, I got to meet Wendy. She hates me."

"Well of course she would. Did you expect differently?"

"No. Gordon, she's me the way I was with Jake. Only she giving Zion kids."

"Whoa, that's gotta hurt. You, okay?"

"I guess. I gotta be nice, but man I wanna be so bratty."

"Don't be bratty. Your future depends on it. Remember you gotta live with all the decisions you make now. And you wanna be clear of guilt. Why don't we get together soon? Are you still being shadowed? Can you go out and party? Everyone's been missing you and asking me what the hell Lea is up to. I keep telling people you got a new man, and he's wearing that ass out every night and you haven't come up for air yet. Hope that's okay. And accurate."

Lea looks up into Zion's eyes. He's leaning against his office door staring at her, smiling.

"Yes, wearing my ass out is pretty accurate, keep up with that. I can hang out this weekend. If Zion's in town, maybe he'll join us. Or I'll have my shadow. Just let me know."

"Will do. I'm sure you're on your way to having more sex, so bye. Nympho."

"Later, Gordon." Lea ensures the call is disconnected.

"I'm not wearing that ass out. We're wearing each other's ass out and we like it." Zion says taking his clothes off as he walks toward her.

"The thought of some other man getting what I'm about to get into right now angers me."

"Well sir, the thought of you having sex with Wendy angers me."

"Kitten, the thought never crossed my mind. The idea of some other woman riding me, stroking me, begging me to take her, does not compute in my brain."

Lea stands and strips out of her clothes. She walks into Zion's arms for her bear hug and kiss. Gladly obliging, he presses her into him, ensuring they are touching from chest, to stomach, to pelvis, to thighs. Zion squeezes her ass, lifting and kneading it, loving the feel of her mounds in his hands. Sliding his hand around, Zion slips it between them, moving to Lea's pussy. She grants him access by slightly spreading her thighs. Zion smiles, kissing her neck, and sticking two fingers inside her, finding her g-spot teasing it over and over. He presses his thumb on her clit, and she jumps.

Lea strokes Zion's engorged manhood up and down, scraping her nails against the veins. He groans.

Zion bends down and sucks Lea's hardened nipples, continually finger fucking her. Lea backs up to the dining room table and leans back on it.

Zion lifts her up onto the table, slowly kissing his way down. Lea caresses his head, pressing it into her stomach, excited for the first flick of his tongue on her clit.

He goes lower and licks the folds of her pussy. *Shit she tastes so damn good.* He slowly licks up and down nibbling and biting her inner thighs still stroking her clit and g-spot. *My baby can't sit still. Yes, I know how to make her cum over and over.* "Oh, baby you like that? Ready for me to suck on your clit?"

"Yes. Zion, please suck it. Please, suck it hard."

Zion lowers his head and latches onto Lea's clit and lightly sucks on it 'til she gets comfortable with the pressure. As she grinds into his face fucking him, he picks up speed and pressure flicking her clit and adding another finger to caress her g-spot. She's moving so fast and hard he can barely keep up. He pins her to the table by pressing her waist with his other hand and keeps licking and sucking. Her moans of pleasure are driving him to cum. He groans into her pussy, eating like there's no tomorrow. She's bucking getting close to orgasm. He's thinking *cum for me baby, yes shoot, hard.* It's as if she can read his thoughts and she shoots, screaming, cumming hard, wrapping her legs around his head, pressing him into her pussy.

"Oh yes, baby yes," she screams.

She releases his head, and he lifts up to kiss her. She grabs his dick and caresses him. "Oh, baby don't do that, I'm about ready to cum. I want to be inside you."

"Sit down on the couch. I want to ride you."

Zion sits on the couch, and she straddles him. He slides in smoothly. "Oh yes, I've missed this."

"It's only been a couple of days, and it'll be a couple more. Will you ever be sated sexually? And if you say yes, I'll stop and leave you hard and wanting," she says to him.

"Never. I can never get enough of you, never. Shit never, oh fuck Lea, your pussy is so damn good. Ride me. Ride your dick."

She glides up and down on his dick with her hot tight ass pussy. He slaps her ass. *Shit it's so damn soft and plump.* "Damn baby that's it. Oh yes. Fuck me."

He grabs her tits sucking them alternating between them, squeezing them together, licking her nipples. She's grinding her pussy into his dick pushing him deep into her. He moves to the end of the couch so he can get a better grip on her ass pumping in harder. She matches him thrust for thrust. One more thrust into her and he shoots, holding her in place. She tenses and cums, holding onto him, squeezing him hard. "Oh baby, girl damn," he groans with pleasure finishing off, jerking everything out of him.

Lea gets up from Zion's lap and sits on the couch next to him putting his underwear in between her legs to catch his sperm. She leans against him and turns his head toward her giving him a kiss.

This right here, him at this moment is the best.

"You're insatiable, and I love being on the receiving end of it," he tells her. "Let's clean up and have another serving of fried apple pies and ice cream. Mrs. Vance outdid herself on those today."

While sitting at the dining room table eating, they discuss the nursery. "All the clothes I bought the boys have been delivered. They're still in boxes in the second bedroom," he tells Lea.

"You haven't unboxed or unpacked anything? Mrs. Vance either? Why?"

"I want you to do it. I want you to help me finish the nursery. It's been painted."

"Really, oh come on show me, let's go see," she says getting up.

"Wait, can't we finish this first?"

"Ugh. You eat, I'm going upstairs." She goes to the nursery. Lea opens the door and sees that the room has been painted in the same muted earth tones as his bedroom. There's no furniture but the room has two closets and the bathroom has been re-done with everything that a baby will need. Deeper sinks for bathing, a shower for adults to bathe with them. The room is waiting for furniture and wall decorations. He's standing in the door watching her. Her excitement is infectious.

"So, when are you going to buy the furniture?" She asks him walking into his arms.

"When I get back. So be thinking of ideas."

"I'll come by the apartment to unpack the clothes. That will get me started at least. And once we look at furniture, we can decide on how to store diapers, bibs, everything. I'm making them receiving blankets. You'll love them."

"I wish you would move in before they're born. Please consider moving in soon. Come by anytime to do anything you want. Do the unpacking, hanging, making lists, whatever. Mrs. Vance has been wanting to get to it, but I told her this is yours to do and I want you to handle it with her assistance. By the time I get back, I want to see a dent made in the unpacking and organizing, Miss Adams," he says.

"You will, Mr. Landon, you will. You get into bed and I'll go clean up the kitchen. You have a flight tomorrow. Go ahead."

"Lea, I want you with me. That can wait 'til morning. Come on baby," he says kissing her neck.

"Zion, go to bed."

Downstairs, Lea makes a late-night call to Bobbie about the visit with Wendy. "Bobbie, woman to woman, how do I handle this chick?"

Bobbie halts her player in the video game she and Ferguson are playing, "Lea, you want the politically correct answer or the 'sister girl' answer?"

"I want your opinion?"

"Okay 'sister girl' answer it is. She's dying. No way to ignore it. When home girl is gone, you become mom and wife. Ain't shit Wendy can do about that. She got Zion's attention for, what, the next two months or less. I know I sound harsh, but from what you said, half the time she not always in the moment to know what's going on. Don't you let Wendy's anger get to you."

"It's difficult. You know my mind. I can come up with some scenarios that puts them in love and together forever."

"Lea, don't go there. You got enough to get through. Your emotions are outta whack because of the extra hormones you taking right now. When are you stopping those by the way?"

"Doctor is weaning me off of them. This week is the last dosage. They didn't work like we expected."

"They got you freaking out about the smallest things. I'm surprised Gordon hasn't noticed."

"I've been avoiding him."

Bobbie laughs. Gordon will point out the changes in Lea's body in such a way, that even Lily will knock him upside his head.

"I hear ya. Well, back to Wendy. Let her have her moments. It's you that will win in the end."

"Ok. Thanks for the bending of the ear. Whose winning tonight?"

"Ferguson is, but I just stripped out of my clothes and am about to walk into the room naked. I'll catch up tomorrow when he's at work. Bye girl." Bobbie disconnects the call before Lea could hear Ferguson's "oh hell yeah" reaction.

-26-

Upon waking the next morning, Lea and Zion haven't moved from the bed. Lea is lightly caressing his shoulders, trailing her nails in the hairs on his arms. Zion shudders from each stroke.

"I'll miss you", he says lazily, while laying on her stomach. "You can still come with me."

"No. I can't. I have to work. But I'll be thinking about you."

"Good. I can't wait to get back and see everything."

Zion starts caressing Lea's breasts. The underside, slowly around to her stomach. "I've been thinking about the things you said about me last night."

"Which things?" Lea's nipples are hardening at his caress. "And when did you become a boob man? You can't leave my tits alone." She laughs at him staring at her breasts.

"Hell, I don't know. I'm obsessed with them. Don't take this the wrong way because I don't want her."

"Can't wait to hear this."

"Wendy's tits have increased in size, and I almost swear yours have, too. I'm noticing some of the weirdest stuff now-a-days."

"Are you often comparing us."

Looking at her he says, "Truthfully, yes. Only because I wish you were pregnant. Back to last night. I was flattered at how you presented me to Wendy. And staked your claim. Continue to do that."

Lea caresses his furrowed brow. "Bear, knowing you want me, don't worry. I will. Now, do we have time for this?"

"Lea, we always have time for sex. Slow drawn-out love making. Fast in the shower quickie. A send away before a flight and a drought of seventy-two hours. Baby always." He looks up at her and opens his mouth and latches onto a tit.

"Hmmm. Nice. Perfect size. Slightly swollen. Are you about to start your cycle?"

"Yes, in a few days."

"Well, we both know what that means don't we?"

"Bear, yes, we do. That I'm swollen, moist, aroused, horny and ready to give you a great send off."

"Kitten, that's what I'm talking about."

Zion throws back the covers and slides down in between Lea's legs. He spreads them open, kissing her thighs, trailing his tongue down each side. He looks up at her as he bends down to tongue her pussy lips.

"Kiss me baby. French kiss my clit."

"Oh baby." Zion says and presses Lea's clit in between his lips. He sticks out his tongue and starts licking it left and right and in circles.

"Oh, shit baby yes. Yes." Lea says pleading with him to lick her more.

Zion hums on her clit, encouraging her to shoot for him. Lea wraps her legs around his shoulders, pressing his face into her pussy.

"Oh Zion. Shit. Yes."

Zion picks up speed and licks Lea's pussy faster, sliding up and down her pussy lips. She starts bouncing up and down and cums, screaming.

"Oh damn."

Zion lifts up and places his dick on her slick pussy, gliding it up and down. "Baby, I love it when you about to start your period. Shit, you be so damn hot and wet. I can slide in so easily."

He places the tip of his dick at the opening of her vagina. Throwing one leg over his shoulder and stretching her other leg out, to avoid a cramp, he slides in.

"Oh Lea. Fuck. Baby yes."

Zion fucks Lea, pounding into her. With her leg on his shoulder, he licks and kisses her calf. He pulls her closer to him gripping her by the waist with one hand and playing with her tits with the other.

"Lea, play with your clit. Baby let me see you finger yourself off."

Zion watches as Lea squeezes and pats her clit.

"Oh, fuck yes baby. Nice."

He throws his head back, enjoying the feel of her tits in his hand, the tightness of her wet, soaking pussy, the feel of his nuts hitting her ass and the sound of their bodies slapping against each other.

"Oh shit. Yes. Yes. Yes." Lea pleads.

"Baby." Zion picks up speed feeling his orgasm about to explode. He bends over for a deeper penetration into Lea. He puts a tit in his mouth and fucks her feverishly.

"Shit Zion. I'm cumming."

Zion explodes a few seconds later, growling into her chest. He pumps long deep thrusts, draining himself inside of her. Lea throws her head back on the pillow riding the waves of her orgasm. Zion slowly strokes inside of her until he goes limp. He pulls out and lays next to her. They are breathing hard, drenched in sweat.

Lea looks down at her calf. "Bear, you left a hickey on my leg."

"You taste good. Can't help myself."

Lea is sitting in her office thinking about what happened with Wendy. Lea admits to herself, she was hoping for a mother-to-mother bonding moment with Wendy, an inclusion of this entire situation. But with her being so in love with Zion there is no place for Lea until after Wendy is dead.

Lea calls Gordon to update him on everything that has happened since the last time they talked.

"Lea, you're a lot better than any woman I know," he comforts her.

"Gordon, I have a mean girl confession."

"Ooo mean girl, tell me, tell me."

"I didn't feel any guilt in pointing out to Wendy what she lost and what I will get when she's gone. I savored the moment when Zion was telling her he loved me, and was going to marry me and that sex was never going to happen between them. I even have visions of never acknowledging her while raising the boys. I mean I am not going to ever put her down. But I'm not going to be bringing her up and reminding them of her. And I don't feel bad about that."

"Lawd, Lea, who is this woman you have become?" He laughs to ease the tension. "I expected to be dealing with the wimpy Lea, not this fighting spirit. Zion has had a good effect on you."

"But I'm being mean though, right?"

"Well, yes, a little. Remember you don't wanna do anything you may have to explain to your sons later in life."

"I won't."

"So, will you and Zion be able to hang or just you?"

"It'll probably be just me."

"Keep in touch then, give me more updates. I don't want to have to track your ass down. Be careful, let him keep you safe."

"All right. I'll be staying at my house tonight but will be back at his tomorrow night."

After work, Ryan takes Lea home and does his full pre-check before allowing her to go in. She thanks him and locks up. Getting out her computer, she looks at nursery room ideas for the boys. She finds three she likes and sends them to Zion.

He calls her after the third text. "Hey, I like these ideas. I think I like the ones with the beds pushed together so they can connect. Not too crazy about the ones with the bed split up or across the room from each other."

"And hello to you handsome. I like the ones with the beds together also."

"Sorry sweetheart, I was in business mode and stayed there."

"That's okay. Sounds like you're really busy. Is everything going, okay?"

"Yes, the usual, high-end clients wanting everything and more. Now tell me where are you and what you're wearing? Give me a visual so I can really dream about you tonight."

"Currently naked, just got of the shower, putting on lotion and then I'll climb up under the covers listening to some Marvin Gaye until I fall asleep."

"Uhhhmmm. Nice, real nice. Did you shave all over?" His voice lowers to his deep seductive drawl.

"Yes, shaved all over. I want to be smooth for you when you get home."

"Now don't get upset if you happen to see me on some tabloid or gossip website. I have to go to a party with lots of celebs and I'm sure to get photographed. I tried to get out of it and back to you, but I have to go."

"Thanks for the warning. I should Google you again, see if there's anything new."

"Hell, I hope not. I'm trying to keep on the low until after the babies are here. I'm going into a dinner meeting. You get some rest; I'll call you tomorrow. Be at my place Saturday when I get home. I don't want to have to send out a search party and drag you back."

"I'll be there. Talk to you tomorrow."

They disconnect. Friday is a repeat of Thursday at work but when Lea gets off, she goes straight to Zion's apartment. She's invited Mrs. Vance to have an unpacking and organizing party.

"Mrs. Vance this has been great. I've enjoyed myself."

"It's been my pleasure, Miss Adams. It's nice seeing Mr. Landon and you together. And how you've handled Ms. Noelin and the baby situation is amazing. You're a strong, loving and caring woman. He's lucky to have you."

"I think I'm lucky to have him in my life. Sometimes I'm unsure about the baby issue but it's what he wants and I don't want to mess it up for him in case we don't end up together."

"Oh, that's not going to be a problem. You two will end up together. Be assured of that."

"Thank you, Mrs. Vance. It's comforting hearing that from you. Considering the closeness you have with him. Are you sure you won't get into trouble by doing that? I don't want to cause any problems."

"No worries. He freely speaks of your relationship with him, so I know I'm not saying anything he wouldn't want you to hear. Trust me. I wouldn't share anything without Mr. Landon's approval. So, what are we planning for dinner tomorrow night?"

"How about something to grill? Or maybe pasta and a salad? That's different. Wait, does he even eat pasta? We're always eating healthy and have yet to have pasta or Italian."

"I have the perfect dish. I'll have it ready to go for you guys to eat at any time."

"Thanks, Mrs. Vance, for everything. Especially tonight."

"You are welcome my dear. Have a good rest of the evening."

Lea putters around Zion's apartment feeling lonely and bored. He calls her on his way to his celeb party. "Hey Bear, are you dressed and ready to be seen tonight?"

"Hi Kitten. I would rather be undressed and ready to be inside you. But yes, I'm ready to be seen and socialize with the beautiful people. How's your night going? What are you up to?"

"Nothing much. Mrs. Vance and I have finished unpacking all the clothes and hung them in the closets. I've laid out paper on the floor for ideas in the nursery. So what time are you due in tomorrow?"

"I should be landing around three, home by four. I have a client that lives in St. Louis. He's flying in with me, so we'll be dropping him off before I head home. I like the maxi dress pic. Without underwear. Nice. But you did put on underwear before anyone saw you in it right?"

"Yes, the non-underwear picture was for you."

Zion gets comfortable in the limo leaning back. Before he can hide it, a yawn/growl escape.

"Was that just a yawn? Babe, have you had any kind of sleep at all?" Lea asks him with worry in her voice.

"No, not this trip, maybe four hours max each night. It's cool. I don't have to do any driving so I cat nap during the drives and I'll sleep on the plane. Go out tonight. Call Gordon and have some drinks. I don't want you sitting at home alone. Ryan is already on standby waiting for your call. I'll see you tomorrow. Love you."

"Okay. Love you too. Bye."

She checks her phone. She has two texts from Gordon suggesting two outings for the weekend. One with him and Lily going to the movies, the other is at Club Déjà Vu for a group hangout. She texts back.

Lea:	*I want the group hangout. I want to be around people for a while.*
Gordon:	*Group hangout it is. I'll let you know what time I'll be picking you up.*
Lea:	*I got transportation covered. My shadow will be driving us. So, no worries.*
Gordon:	*Excellent, I can chill and not worry about being the designated driver. Pick me up at my house around nine. Be ready to dance.*

Saturday night Lea is dressed in a shimmery gray, off-the-shoulder jumpsuit. She's wearing a pair of four-inch clear pumps. Lea insisted on Ryan driving the Caddy tonight with Gordon in the front seat with Ryan and she and Lily in the back.

At his hesitation she explains, "Ryan, I don't wanna draw attention to us arriving in a limo. I'd like to be as low key as possible. Don't you think that would be a good idea?"

"No ma'am. But I'll be going in with you and watching closely."

"That's fine. Even sit with us if you like. I'll tell anyone who asks, you're my cousins, great aunt nephews, brother, whatever."

"Well, at least you've given me relative status."

"Heck, you feel like family by now as much as we hang out."

As they pull up to the club, Ryan surveys the parking lot, attempting to decide where to park, and how quickly they could get out if needed. He doesn't want to be blocked in. As he is about to park, a couple comes out of the club arguing. Ryan watches them, on alert. They get into a car parked two cars away from the main door. Ryan takes the spot feeling the couple won't be back anytime soon. They exit the car, with Ryan following behind. Gordon opens the door of the club for Lily and Lea to walk in first.

The lady in the car looks back at the club, hating they just lost their prime parking space. She zeroes in on the group of people walking to the door. The woman in the gray jump suit walks under the light and the lady in the car recognizes her.

She screams, "Oh my fucking god, that's her. Stop the damn car we gotta go back." She alternately punches the driver in the arm and pulls on his sleeve.

"What do you mean we gotta go back. They ain't letting us back in after what you did to the photographer."

"Dammit, I don't care about going back in. That's that bitch Zion's dating. Go back. If I have to sit out here all night and wait for her I will. Now turn this fucking car around and go back."

"But we have to get back to—."

"Fuck him. I want me a piece of that bitch. Turn the fucking car around now!"

"Shit, fine. But I swear if we out here for more than a half hour, you gone be sucking dick, nuts, and ass while we wait."

"Oh baby, whatever you want. Just get back to the fucking club."

-27-

As Lea, Lily, and Gordon enter, Lily waves to a table of about ten people and maneuvers toward them. Lea hangs back talking with Ryan. "You gonna sit with us, or do I need to stay over here?"

Looking around where he can snag a seat and be able to watch the table he says, "No. I'll sit here." Ryan points to a tall table against the wall with seating for one. It gives him a clear view of the door and Lea. "I only ask that you sit facing me. Unless a seven-foot giant stands in front of me, we'll at least be able to make eye contact."

"Thanks Ryan. And I promise not to start any trouble."

"Miss Adams, is that something I need to worry about? I can call for backup."

"No. I'm just kidding. I forget I'm talking to on-duty Ryan."

"Yes ma'am. On-duty."

Lea walks away and takes a seat at the table. Everyone gives her shit for not hanging out and ask for details about her new man. With them grilling her, Lea realizes she isn't as comfortable telling people about Zion as she thought she would be. She wants to brag about him but a part of her feels as if she will be judged negatively about the relationship, how she attracted Zion, and how she could possibly be his love interest. Without him here proving he loves her, she decides to say only basic information, "Uh well he's in finance, work keeps him busy, he's sexy, has his own place and car, smart, highly educated, and we've been seeing each other for about six months now. We spend as much time together as our schedules allow."

"So, when do we get to meet him? Or is this just one of your imaginary friends? It's been what five years since you've been in a relationship. Is this guy even real?"

A catty female friend is so annoying. "Yes, Vicky, he exists. Of all people, you know how new relationships are. You disappear for about six months once a year."

"Yes, well, at least I bring mine around the group and we have yet to meet yours. Does he even have a name or are you trying to think of one?"

"Yes, his name is Zion. He's a business associate. We got to know each other from working on his project my company was hired for and things took off from there."

"So, you dating on the job now?" Vicky asks. "About damn time. What, you designing and setting up his small home office? A desk and a computer? How does that work by the way? You take them to the local computer store when a sale is going on and help them spend their money for the cheapest computer? Hey maybe I can hire you to do the same for me."

"Vicky you are in true form tonight. What's the matter? You haven't been royally fucked lately? Or does your latest and greatest even know how to fuck? I would ask you what his mouth do but 'cause you constantly complain online how you not getting ate out, that mouth not doing much. Right?"

I can rise to the catty occasion when needed, and this one is pushing me tonight. I refuse to run off and let her get the best of me. I got anger in me and can let it flow toward her like her jealousy is flowing toward me.

"Well, I guess your new lil boyfriend is teaching you how to be rude?" Vicky snaps back.

"Oh, baby there's nothing little about him, and I've always known how to be rude. I just never had the need to. Until now."

"Okay, y'all. You two need to stop and give it a rest," Gordon says. "I've met the guy, he exists. And like you said Vicky, the newness hasn't worn off. What does she need to share it with everyone for? When does your next newness kick in?"

"Whatever, I'm going to find some lucky man to buy me a drink. One that exists, flesh and blood." Vicky struts off, ass jiggling in her body suit, in search of her latest dick.

Gordon turns to Lea, "Hey, let's go get some drinks. And you can update me away from this group about what's happening. Lily has placed the order for food. Wings and fries as usual."

Lea and Gordon are standing at the bar and Lea has taken steps to make sure she's in full view of Ryan. She tells Gordon about the visit with Wendy.

Gordon compliments Lea on the jumpsuit remarking how her trainer is focusing on Lea's curves.

Not wanting to admit to him about the hormones she's been taking, she agrees with him. "Yep, that's the focus."

"So, baby mama showed the claws. Were you expecting anything less?" Gordon asks her.

"Nope. I was expecting a lot more and it would've been if Zion hadn't been there. I won't be her punching bag, but I won't add to any stress either. Zion staked his claim and let her know what's up. What else am I supposed to do?"

"Nothing, keep planning your future. Can I just say one thing?"

"Go ahead."

"I really hope you guys do end up together after this is all over with. I know that sounds mean but if after all of this you guys' breakup, I'll wring his neck myself."

"Gee thanks. I think. He asked me the question of how do I feel about her, and I was honest," Lea tells him.

"Wow, how did that go?"

"He listened, he heard, he understood, and he didn't judge. I think it strengthened our bond even more."

"Good. I'm glad you're learning that relationships aren't all roses and butterflies. It's nice seeing how happy you are."

Walking back to their table, Lea places a glass of water next to Ryan on the way. He nods. The night flies by. Lea has worn out her feet dancing and is almost hoarse having to yell over the music to talk and catch up with everyone. Before the crowd in the club starts winding down and leaving, Lea suggests to Gordon they head out. They stand up saying their goodbyes.

Ryan has them wait at the door for a small crowd to disperse. When it does, they walk outside. As Lea steps away from the door, a woman walks across her path bumping into her. Lea drops her clutch. Before she can bend down to pick it up, Lea hears the woman say, "Bitch, Zion is mine. Fuck off."

Gordon and Lily step toward the woman. Gordon pushes Lily back toward Lea.

Before Lea could think, she went into fighting mode. As with Vicky, taking the opportunity to release some anger and frustration is an opportunity Lea won't pass up. "Tramp. You wanna come back and say that?"

The woman comes back, side-steps Gordon before he could reach out for her and pushes Lea. As Ryan takes a step to move Lily out of the way to get to Lea, Lea takes the opportunity to haul off and back slap, 'Addison' leaving a fresh scar down the side of her cheek from Lea's class ring. Lea's knuckles made contact with Addison's front teeth with a small crack, scraping across them, as Addison turned her head to deflect Lea's hand. Lea's knuckles are left bleeding, bruised, with the skin broken. Lea put all of her anger and frustration into that slap.

If Lea hadn't heard Zion's name, she woulda thought this was some typical late night drunk and woulda walked away. But hearing his name, she knew exactly who the woman was. Without a doubt. The idea of this woman showing her face, threatening her of being locked away, sets off Lea's anger. Whooping someone's ass is exactly what she needs. Lea walks out of her shoes moving toward 'Addison'.

Gordon and Ryan move into protection mode and get in between them pushing Lily toward the car.

"You fucking bitch. Don't worry. When Zion and I end up together we'll, make sure your ass pays for this. You fucking bitch!" Addison screams. She's rubbing her cheek trying to stem the flow of blood from the slap which caused her to bite the inside of her jaw and tongue.

"Why wait? ADDISON. Bring your ass back over here and I'll finish you off right now. Are you getting aroused ADDISON? You want your ass kicked ADDISON? You gonna go find a dick and get fucked ADDISON?" Before Lea can get to Addison, a car drives up and she hops in, and it speeds off. This took place in the span of fewer than five minutes without any witnesses. Talk about luck. Lily managed to grab Lea's shoes and clutch before she got into the car. Ryan pushes Lea in the car and gets them out of there before anyone comes out of the door.

"Lea, are you okay?" Lily asks.

"No, but I will be. Ryan, you don't report this to Zion. I promise I'll tell him tomorrow. Don't call him with this right now. Just pick me up first and I'll tell him everything," Lea instructs him. She wraps her hand in a scarf Lily handed her. Lea slowly slides her ring off her finger staring at the skin left in it. She puts it in her purse.

"Okay Miss Adams. But I'll need to tell the detective about this incident. It's too late tonight, but I'll write up what happened and get it to him, after you've talked with Mr. Landon," he says looking at her in the rear-view mirror.

"Thank you," she says. "Sorry guys, but you've just saw the crazy crack bitch Addison. I hope she wasn't paying attention to you and was fixated on me. If you start getting any threats, let me know."

"It's okay. Who was driving the car?" Gordon asks.

Ryan doesn't say anything, but he recognized the car from the one whose parking space he took. He thinks back to a few hours ago, recalling all the details about the car and the couple who were arguing earlier.

Lea says, "I don't know, but I'm sure we'll know something by Sunday. Fuck, now I'll never get to go anywhere. Dammit my hand hurts. I can't hide this from Zion. He's going to be pissed. Fuccccckkk."

"Maybe a little. Gangsta Lea. I'm too damn old to be fighting. You gotta hold that shit down woman." Gordon tries to lighten the mood.

"I'll try. I'll try." Lea says.

"You see what that bitch did to me. Now my beautiful face is scarred for my Zion to see. I hate the both of you. You punny ass motherfuckers. Can't do shit right. Ima get my Zion back," she's pacing the room cursing the others out. They know to let her blow off steam.

One walks over to her and grabs her by the neck choking her into silence.

"Don't ever refer to her as a bitch. You the bitch in all this, remember that," he pushes her back onto the bed, strips down and fucks her in the ass hard. The other stands in the shadows watching, jacking off. Within minutes they all cum. He pulls out wiping his dick on the sheets. The other approaches her, flips her over and slams into her pussy.

"Yeah, fuck that bitch real hard and good. I need this for later," he takes out his camera recording the action. "Yes, my baby and I'll be enjoying these."

-28-

After dropping off Gordon and Lily, Ryan drove Lea to her house. They decided it would be easier for Ryan to bring the extended stretch limo there instead of maneuvering it into Zion's apartment garage or having it pull up to the outside attracting unwanted attention.

Upon his arrival back at her house, Lea walks outside, meeting him in her driveway. She's chosen the sexiest Maxi Dress she has, wearing her ultimate push-up bra, showing off as much cleavage as possible with a jacket over it, wearing her best strappy sandals, and smelling like Allure by Chanel. She's put on her best red lip stain with a smoky brown eye. Hopefully, she can distract Zion enough before she tells him about the Addison run in.

Biting her lower lip and taking a deep breath she says, "Okay, Ryan, I promise to take all the blame for the delay in telling Zion about this morning. I promise. Don't worry. Just let me tell him," she implores.

"Okay, Miss Adams, if you say so, but it truly is no problem. You don't have to do that."

"Yes, I do. My instincts for some reason are screaming at me to tell Zion what happened, and I'm going to listen."

"Well, he's arriving with a client we have to drop off in Lake St. Louis, so that may help. I got a low-down on the car. It was reported stolen about a month ago from the riverfront. It was found this morning parked at the O'Fallon Family Arena. I've reported this to the detective and informed him Mr. Landon was traveling and will be updated as soon as he lands."

"Wait, a client? Someone else will be in the car? Shit, I forgot about that. Zion did mention it earlier. Let me go change jackets." Lea goes back in the house. Instead of grabbing a different jacket, she pulls out two of the scarves Zion purchased for her when they went to Charleston. She ties them together and wraps them around her neck in a way her upper chest isn't on full display.

Walking back to the car, she's confident she's presenting a dignified woman to Zion's client and Zion's sexy Kitten to him. "Okay let's get this over with." Lea gets in the limo. She stares at her hand with the missing ring. During the drive, she practices different sitting positions, attempting to find the right one that keeps her hand hidden.

"Ryan, can you ensure Zion and his client are getting in on the passenger side. That way I can sorta hide my hand."

"Will do, Miss Adams." Ryan smiles thinking, *Mr. Landon will absolutely be distracted by Miss Adams when he gets in the car.*

They arrive at the airport with a thirty-minute wait for Zion's plane to land. Lea's stomach is in knots.

He's going to be pissed that he wasn't told about this earlier.

Zion, Sam, Morgan, and the client exit the airplane. Sam gets the luggage, and the others walk toward the limo. Morgan's car was left at the airport. Zion stands outside of the limo, talking to Ryan and looking at his phone, texting. He sends Lea a message telling her he's home and to be ready, because they're going out to dinner tonight.

Lea looks at her phone, sees his text come in, and responds, okay. Grinning at the idea of how ready she is.

Ryan opens the door from the passenger side as requested by Lea. Zion's client peaks in, noticing Lea, then steps back out. Grinning and about to enjoy some good-natured ribbing with Zion, he says in his most southern St. Louis drawl, "Yo, Zion, man. Uh, I hope this lovely goddess is for me. If not, can I have her? Please?" he says bending back into the limo looking at Lea mouthing, 'I'm just playing with him'.

She grins.

The client makes a motion to hop in, but Zion pulls him out and looks in.

"Welcome home, Bear," Lea says, staring at him, loving on him, reacting to the heat in his eyes.

"Hello, Kitten. Nice surprise." Zion eyes zero in on the scarves. He mumbles 'Shit', under his breath then steps back, outside the car. Looking at his client laughing at him, knowing he's joking, Zion says, "Man, hell naw you can't have her; she belongs to me. Get in and don't sit next to her and don't touch her and don't look at her. Hell, why don't I just call you a cab?" Zion bends down looking into the car again. "Shit, what's the number to the nearest taxi service? Or why don't you just walk?"

"Zion, are you getting in or not?"

Zion looks back into the car and growls, "Vixen."

Lea caresses the scarves lightly. Before Zion can do or say anything more, his client slides into the car, moving to the longer seat to the right of Lea. Zion gets in, sitting next to Lea, with his leg blocking hers from his client. Ryan and Sam get in the front, with Ryan driving.

"Man, don't I get an introduction? Hi, I'm Bradley Williamson. It's so wonderful to meet you. Finally. I heard he was off the market but couldn't believe it. I see why he's been keeping you to himself."

"It's nice to meet you. I hope you two don't mind me joining you for the ride from the airport. I missed Zion and wanted to see him as soon as I could." Lea made sure Zion is on her right so he can't play with the missing class ring on her left hand. He grabs her hand and kisses it.

"No, I don't mind. And my man Zion here really doesn't mind," he says looking, at Zion who hasn't taken his eyes off her.

They make small talk during the drive to Mr. Williamson's house. Lea has managed to dominate the conversation, discussing her job. Zion sits back, admiring the business Lea in action. Her confidence always shines when she's in business mode. By the time they get to Bradley's house, he has taken her name, number and company information and has scheduled an appointment with Lea to discuss setting up his home office once he's finished remodeling his basement. From the conversation, Lea has just negotiated a six-figure contract in the span of about forty-five minutes.

Arriving at Bradley's house, Zion steps out of the limo to say his goodbyes in the drive way, refusing the offer of drinks and dinner.

Ryan stares at Lea in the rear-view mirror.

"I am, geez calm down will ya," she tells him. Sam goes on alert.

Zion gets in the car and is about to raise the privacy window, but she stops him. Ryan and Sam switch places in case he has to turn around and chime in.

"Baby, we need some privacy. Now. Right now," he says trying to raise the window again.

"Zion wait, I have something to tell you and well, I need witnesses." Lea smiles trying to make a joke, but he's turned serious.

"What, is Wendy okay?" he asks.

"Really, your first thought is of her? Geez! I see what you been thinking about!"

"Miss Adams," Ryan says.

"What? Shit. Okay, okay!"

"Zion, first please stay calm and let me say everything I need to say before you hit the roof. Sam, you may as well start driving. We can't sit in Mr. Williamson's driveway the entire time. He may come back out." Lea turns to Zion.

"Last night, Gordon, Lily and I went out and we had a good time. A wonderful time. We went to a club to have drinks and hang out. Well, as we were leaving the club, a lady crossed in front of me, trying to trip me, and called me a bitch. When I realized it was Addison, well, my anger and frustration took over and I called her a tramp. She came back and pushed me, and I back slapped her with my left hand slashing her jaw.

"She threatened me about how you and she were going to have me locked up for attacking her, then she hopped in a car and drove off. Ryan managed to get information on the car, called Detective Greg, and they found the car this morning, abandoned in O'Fallon."

Lea pauses attempting to gauge Zion's reaction before she continues. She's expecting him to interrupt her, anticipating a blow-up. She continues when he says nothing. "Yes, I antagonized her about needing her ass kicked and how she was getting aroused and stuff. Ryan got us all out of there, and there were no witnesses. It all happened in less than five minutes. I asked Ryan not to tell you because it was like three-fifteen this morning, and I figured you would be sleeping so I could explain all this today. I went home and haven't left until we came to pick you up. Ryan has written up a report and given it to Greg. Don't yell at Ryan or tell me I can't go out anywhere again. We did everything right. Well, except for the part about not telling you and Sam right away, but that was my idea. I asked him not to. Please don't fire him." Lea rushes all this out so fast she isn't sure if Zion heard all of it. Biting her lip, she sits waiting for the blow up, twisting the scarves into knots.

Zion sits staring at Lea, listening. He's alternating from scared, to angry, to proud, to scared and back to angry.

"Well, say something. Please," she begs.

Unraveling her hand from the scarves and placing it on his thigh, Zion looks at the front seat of the car. "Sam, take us to Interludes Intimate Steakhouse. Ryan can then take you home, and I'll see you Monday morning. Ryan, I'll call when we're ready to be picked up in the Cadillac. Thank you for all you did in protecting Lea and reporting things to Greg," he says making eye contact with him. Then he raises the privacy window.

"May I see your ring please?" he asks, reaching for her left hand.

"I'm not wearing it. My hand was bruised and swollen after I slapped, slashed the bitch," Lea shows him her hand. It doesn't look bruised, but she feels tenderness.

Zion removes the scarves, wanting to see all of Lea. The memories of South Carolina keep flooding his mind.

SHE TIED ME UP. THE ICE. WHIP CREAM. ZION, FOCUS. DINNER THEN MAYBE...

HEY ADONIS? I CONTROL THE SEX THOUGHTS HERE. *DOESN'T HURT TO HAVE A LITTLE EXTRA HELP.*

Once revealed, Lea's cleavage is on display and he can't take his eyes off her. *Oops, them. God-damn my mouth watering. That's some fucking bra.*

"Tell me. How in the hell are your tits sitting up like that? Did you get a boob job in twenty-four hours? Don't get me wrong, they're looking nice, and I want to bury my face in them, but tell me, how are they looking so damn fucking luscious?" he asks, caressing her hand while staring at her tits.

"Extreme push-up bra. You aren't mad? You won't fire Ryan, will you? Talk to me, Zion? And stop staring at my tits. They're just tits. Or in this case, it's just cleavage." Lea attempts to put the scarves back over her chest, but Zion takes them and tosses them on the window ledge behind them.

"Kitten, don't ever cover up for me. Never. No one gets fired. Tonight. I'll punish you later for having my staff hide this from me." Then with his knee-weakening voice he adds, "You've been a bad girl. You need a tongue lashing." He kisses her neck, nibbling and biting, giving Lea a sample of the punishment, she'll be getting.

Lea takes in a deep breath trying to concentrate on speaking. "He didn't hide it. There was just a small delay in informing you of it. That's all."

"Why, so you could distract me with your sexiness. Shit, Lea, your tits." He lowers his head into her cleavage and breathes deeply, moving her hand to his dick, covering it with his and squeezing. Lea presses his head into her cleavage moaning from him licking it.

"Mr. Landon, we've arrived," Sam announces via the car's speaker in the rear. Ryan gets out to open their door.

The restaurant is located on Lindell Boulevard in walking distance of Grand Center, St. Louis University and Chaifetz Arena. From the amount of traffic and crowd, the area is popping tonight with excitement. It was a good thing Zion made reservations.

"We'll pick this up after dinner," he says getting out staring at her. Lea steps out of the car looking up at him. He considers reaching back in and grabbing the scarves or taking off his suit jacket to cover her up but vetoes both ideas. Wiping his hand across his face, smiling, he says, "Lady, you're up to something. I know it."

"I don't know what you're talking about. Bear," Lea says, standing next to him grabbing his hand and holding on.

Zion squeezes it and turns to Ryan, "Ryan, thanks again for taking care of her. I really appreciate it. Have a copy of the report in the car for me to read."

"Yes sir." Ryan looks at Lea, smirking, then gets in the car and he and Sam leave.

Zion notices the look. "A conspirator. Lady, you've tamed another of my security team. I don't like that," Zion says as they walk into the restaurant. They are escorted to a private dining room.

When they're settled and he has placed the food order, he turns to her, addressing what she told him. "My first thought was of Wendy because it never crossed my mind that you could be in any danger or trouble. My heart dropped into my gut when you were telling me about what happened. Did either of you see who was driving the car?" he asks.

"No. Like I said it happened fast."

"So, you slapped her. Never knew you could be so violent. I'm glad there were no cops or witnesses around. That you know of. We still need to figure out if she followed you there or if she was there by accident and saw you there. We need to find out who was driving the car, who's helping her. Personally, I don't believe what happened was by accident. By the way, I missed you, so thank you for my surprise. Being in the car," he tells her.

"Welcome home. I surprised you? I figured you would have known by looking at your phone for my location," she tells him, leaning over to kiss him, but he leans away.

"Zion, no you do not back off from a kiss. What the hell," she says staring at him.

"Lea, I can't kiss you when you wear that damn red lipstick. I prefer your lips on my dick right now. Licking it. Sucking it. Watching those red lips wrapped around it, feeling your tongue sliding up and down the sides of it. Shit baby, that red lipstick does all kinds of things to me. Kissing it off is the last thing I ever want to do. Wipe it off first," he says, handing her a napkin, not taking his eyes off her.

"I can't wipe it off. It's lip stain. I can eat, kiss, lick and suck a dick and balls and it won't come off. Until I use the remover. I barely have to freshen it up. But the lip gloss makes them glisten. For later."

"Oh, really." Zion kisses her. When he pulls back her lips are just as red as they were before. Wiping the napkin across his lips, there's no trace of the kiss. "Vixen."

They're served their food and finish enjoying the night and him being home. "Are you having dinner with Wendy tomorrow?"

"Yes. These Sunday dinners seem to calm her for the coming week. I've been talking with her every day I was gone. She was upbeat, ignoring the visit. I'm going to address that with her."

"Zion, don't. She had her say."

"Kitten, I can't leave it. I don't want Wendy upset or stressed. But I need her to understand what she and I have together. That's all.

By letting that slide, to me it's like denying you, and I won't deny you to her or anyone for any reason. Understand?"

"Sure, I guess." Lea whispers. *This is my take-charge business man Zion again.* Lea has gone from impressed to aroused.

SO, CAN WE GET THE HELL OUT OF HERE? NOW? Sex Diva is ready for some action.

"Now, I want to talk to you about our living arrangements. When will you be moving in? I would like this to happen before the boys are born."

"It's overwhelming. I have a whole house to pack up. A lot of stuff to deal with," she tells him, avoiding his gaze.

"You know I can have that taken care of. Hire all the help you need. Why are you hesitating? Talk to me," he prods.

"I'm scared. Never lived with someone, never been married. You're too clean. I have lots of stuff. Being a mom. Having you get tired of having me around every day. Not being enough for you. Not being able to do it all. We have only dated for a few months, then it's move in and become a mom. Am I simply a check-mark item in your life? Will I ever be a priority? Am I to give up my life and career to become the stay-at-home mom? We have a huge learning curve. Are you ready for that?"

"Yes and no. Never lived with someone, and never been married either. We won't have enough alone time before we get the boys, but I want to make the best of what we have. I know one reason you haven't is because you hate the thought of me leaving you to go down and spend time with Wendy. I can't change that. I do know I want to come home to you every day, fall asleep with you every night, and wake up next to you every morning. Your questions give me a lot to think about that I hadn't considered. Or maybe took for granted. When we get home, we'll talk about them. All of them. Please think about moving in with me."

"Okay. I will."

"Wonderful. Now let's get the hell out of here. Every time you breathe or laugh your tits just, oh lord they call for my mouth. What is going on with them today?"

"I need to stop off at the bathroom first." Lea takes out the tube of red lipstick, showing him. Distracting him. Tonight, she has to fess up to why her boobs are larger than usual. But first, distraction.

He grins, knowing what's to come. He lifts his hand up for the waiter. "Check please. I'll meet you in front. Kitten."

Zion checks the location of the car. With the large crowds outside he would like to avoid standing around waiting. Ryan has been sitting a block away for about thirty minutes. Zion lets him know he and Lea are on their way out.

"Where are you? Where's the fucking crack head?" male one asks.

"Out looking for some phones to snatch like you ordered. My darling is safely tucked away."

Male one snorts, "Your darling. Man, you fucking stupid. I need the bitch back here to call on her Zion. Stoke some fucking fires. I don't know where the fuck Lea is. and I need to find her."

"Well, you can just wait." Male two stops talking, dodging a group of college students barreling down the sidewalk. "Oh fuck. Man, I see the car. I see the fucking caddy from the club. It's parked outside of Interludes Intimate Steakhouse."

"Shit, that means they're in there. Park your fucking ass outside and don't fucking move."

"Man, it could be hours before they come out."

"Jackass, think. With everything going on down there tonight, the car isn't waiting for hours. It's there to pick they ass up. It can't sit there for fucking hours."

"Oh yeah, right. So, what the hell am I supposed to do?"

"Get pictures. Of them all. The driver, Lea, fucking Zion, car, just get fucking pictures. Shit, my wife picked a really dumb ass one in you."

"I'm the dumb ass helping you, so you need to fucking chill."

"I'll show you my fucking chill when you get that bitch back here."

-29-

While sitting in the car, Ryan has been scrutinizing the crowd looking for Addison. He notices an individual standing across the street watching the door of the restaurant. The man caught Ryan's inquisitive stare because of his posture and the way he snapped to attention whenever he saw a black couple step out the door. He attempts to snap clear pictures of the guy. Looking at the images, he was only able to get a couple of side views and a blurred frontal view. He sends a message to Zion.

"Noticed an individual standing outside of restaurant. Images sent to Sam and Saul for face check. Exit quickly into car."

Zion is standing in the lobby of the restaurant waiting on Lea when he gets the text from Ryan. Reading it, he frowns, murmuring 'fuck' under his breath. Looking up, he puts a smile on his face, hiding his concerns about the message, watching Lea walk toward him.

When they come out the restaurant's door, the guy perks up and starts snapping pictures. Zion keeps his head down and attempts to block views of Lea, ushering her along. She notices nothing.

Once in the car, Zion turns Lea toward him. He looks past her to across the street. There's no one there. Zion makes eye contact with Ryan, both nodding heads. At this point, Ryan knows to drive, making sure they're not being followed and if so to alert him. He keeps the privacy window down. When they get to the garage, Zion sees Sam is sitting across the street from the entrance in a car Lea has never seen him in, waiting to see if any other cars drive past.

By the time they pull up to the elevators, Sam reports there's no one following them, but he'll sit for a while. Zion can now relax and allow Lea to welcome him home. They exit the car, Zion staring at Lea's ass. Vixen has taken off her underwear. As they enter the elevator and the doors close, he slaps her ass. "And where is your underwear young lady."

"In my purse. Sir." She takes them out, twirling them in the air. He reaches for them as she puts them behind her back, forcing him to press her against the elevator wall.

"Uhm, now that feels nice." She slides her leg in between his, pressing it against his dick. "You ready to christen the elevator baby or should we wait until we get to the apartment?" Lea licks her red lips.

He leans back and un-zips his pants. After pulling out his penis, he stops the elevator with his personal key card. Lea stares at his engorged manhood, then up at him. His eyes are glazed with passion, awaiting her first lick. She strokes him up and down, milking pre-cum to the tip.

"Hmmmmmm, yessssss," he groans. Now knowing the lipstick will not rub off, he kisses her.

FINALLY, OUR KINDA KISS.

After Zion releases her from the kiss, Lea looks down at him, stroking and squeezing. She forms an 'o' with her mouth and bends over, swallowing him.

"Oh Fuck." Zion whispers. He reaches over and presses the material of the sundress between her ass cheeks, stroking up and down. Reaching a little further, he slides his fingers between her thighs, slipping them between her wet lips.

Lea lifts up from sucking him, grinning.

"Nope, no you don't. Not yet," she tells him. "I got other plans for you."

He grins, asking, "What?" like a two-year old caught doing something he could get in trouble for.

Lea unbuttons his shirt, moving it back so it isn't in his line of view from watching her suck him off. She kneels in between his legs. Holding his delicious looking manhood.

GIRL DID YOU JUST CALL IT DELICIOUS LOOKING?

Fuck yeah, 'cause it is.

Lea licks him up and down, paying special attention to under the hood of the tip. Once Zion starts jerking with every lick and suck, Lea knows she has him at her mercy. She slides him into her mouth. As Lea rubs the tip of his penis against the skin of her jaw and lightly scrapes the veins of his penis with her teeth, Zion starts begging for release. He attempts to fuck her in her mouth, but she forces him back against the wall and takes control, holding his hands on the rail. In this position, he can only move his hips and not grip her head.

Shit he tastes so good. Dick so smooth and hard.

Lea hums on his dick, finding her rhythm.

"OOOOOO," he moans. She pulls down the top of her dress, opening the front closure of her bra. He looks down at her and grabs her tits, playing with them. "Oh, baby, they feel so good."

Lea pulls back and asks him if he wants to fuck them.

"What?" he responds, stunned.

"Zion, do you wanna fuck my tits? Rub your dick in between them, cumming on them, all over them?"

He stands there staring.

She puts his dick back into her mouth, lubing it up with her saliva, then places it between her tits. She moves up and down on his dick. He finally catches on and grips her shoulders, going up and down. This allows her to concentrate on squeezing her breasts together around his penis, creating friction.

"See baby, it feels good, don't it?" she asks him.

"Oh yes. Yes, it does. Shit," Zion picks up speed and Lea keeps squeezing his penis between her tits. Every time he gets closer to her mouth, she sticks out her tongue to touch the slit. On one movement up he pauses, and she rolls her tongue around the tip of his penis, licking his pre-cum.

"Oh, Lea, baby, I'm about to cum." Lea presses in to him squeezing him as hard as she can, keeping up with his movements.

"Yes baby, cum for me. Shoot it all on my tits. Tell me when you getting ready to shoot so I can lean back and catch it on them."

"Oh, Lea, yes, baby. Nowwwwww." She pulls back and he shoots all over her breasts, squeezing his penis, milking it.

"Oh fuck, damn!" He stops cumming and drops to his knees, unable to stand anymore. Zion opens his eyes and stares at Lea. She rubs his sperm into her breasts then sticks a finger in her mouth, sucking on it. His dick hardens again.

"Turn around and stand up." He orders her. She stands up raising her dress. She's soaking wet and he slips in easily.

"Oh yes, Zion fuck, me." She begs him.

"Dammit Lea." He's pounding into her hard, slamming into her pussy. She groans, moving his fingers to her clit. Lea covers his hand with her's, making sure he doesn't pull away. With every thrust he squeezes her nub, making her whole-body jerk and tremble.

"Zion, yes, yes." With one final plunge, Zion grips Lea, not letting her pull away, she cums and he follows behind her. They groan in ecstasy, cumming hard.

Lea lifts up and presses Zion against the elevator wall. Gripping her skirt, she rubs her ass against him, trying to keep his dick inside her. She covers his hand over her clit, having him play with it some more. She's still aroused and needs to get off again. She's so close. Zion can tell baby needs another orgasm.

"Lea, you need to cum again, don't you? Yes, baby, you need me to bring you off again, don't you?"

"Yes, Zion, please. Again, please. Finger fuck me," Zion slips two fingers along the sides of Lea's pussy and presses her ass into his pelvis, moving in circular movements on her clit. He's kissing her neck, telling her how good she feels, how sexy she is, how he loves seeing her when she wants to fuck.

"Baby, squeeze your nice tits. Damn, baby, they look so fucking good. Cum for me. I know you close. Yes, that's it. Yes, baby cum. Fuck, yes Lea. Shit, you sound so good. Fuck yeeesssss. Baby yes," Zion watches as Lea cums, riding through her orgasm, loving the feel of her ass stroking against his dick.

He holds her pressed against him, not wanting to break the contact. "Dammit, can we just sleep in this elevator tonight? Baby, I'm going to get a hard-on every time I get on here," he says, kissing the back of her neck.

After a few minutes, they assist each other with straightening their clothes. Zion turns the elevator back on. They ascend to the top and exit, going straight to the bathroom to shower.

"I love making memories with you. Promise me we never stop." she coaxes, kissing him while standing under the shower spray.

"Never, baby, never."

They are lying in bed and Zion questions Lea about the size of her chest again. "I know there's something different about your chest. What's going on? They're bigger by at least a cup size."

Lea sits up and stares at him. "I contacted my doctor about being able to breast feed the boys using my own milk. I've been poked, prodded, smooshed, and even put on medication that would hopefully get me to lactate. It didn't work. Even if I were to get pregnant the doctors said I may not produce milk. Made my tits increase as you've noticed. They'll probably go back to their normal size. My emotions will be off kilter until the meds are out of my system."

"When have you been going to the doctor? I have all your appointments in my calendar," he asks sitting up, reaching for his phone. "Have you been lying to me, sneaking away from Ryan?"

"No, I haven't on either point. I made sure every appointment I had was and is in your calendar. My last one was Thursday. They're entered in your calendar as the address. If you would've asked about them, I would've explained further. Ryan took me to each appointment. He wasn't hiding anything from you nor were we conspiring against you. Well, he kinda was. My doctors' appointments technically are my business. You can ask him about anything, and he will give you a full report. I have stuck to all your rules."

"I can't believe you've been going to the doctors without telling me. Lea, don't do that. We're in this together," he tells her, leaning on the headboard. "Geez, I can't believe this."

"Zion, it's over now. No more testing, no more drugs, no milk from my tits. I didn't want you having to go to any more doctors' appointments than you had to with Wendy. That could get tiring and draining. I've looked into one more option."

"Option, but you just said no more testing and drugs. What does it involve? We're not going to some other country to get you operated on. It's not that serious about you being able to breast-feed," he tells her.

"No. It's called supplemental breast-feeding. One of the main ideas behind breast-feeding is bonding with the child and helping them to learn to suckle. I can wear a bag containing formula. A tube will come around my neck and attach to my breast next to the nipple. The baby latches onto the end of the tube and the nipple and suckles. It's just a thought and something to try. If it doesn't work, I'll bond with them in other ways," she says, hoping to reassure him.

"You did all that? I didn't think you were into the idea of becoming a mother to them yet. To hear you have been getting tested to do this, well, it blows my mind," he admits.

"I'm confused about it. One minute I'm happy and look at the future and then the real world sets in, and I think about how you can decide you don't want me to be a part of this equation. I guess I'm trying to protect my heart and emotions. You can clear me out of your life quickly, but it would take me years to clear you out of my soul."

"Lea, I can never clear you out of my life, and I don't want to. Baby, you're here forever. It's not because of the sex, it's not because of our future with the boys, it's because of you and how you have encroached on what I thought was my normal day-to-day existence."

Lea lays her head on his chest, listening to his heart and breathing. "You haven't seen the nursery yet."

"I'll see it later. Right now, I want to continue seeing you cumming over and over. What can I say, we have lots of time to make up for." They make love, make out, and cuddle the remainder of the night.

After breakfast on Sunday, they go shopping for nursery furniture and other big-ticket items. They stop off at Ikea and Pottery Barn Kids. After looking at many options, Zion again goes overboard with purchases. Usually this would be gifts a mother would get at a baby shower. Zion has purchased everything so, at this point, Lea won't be having any kind of celebration in recognition of becoming a mom. He selects cribs, car seats, highchairs, strollers, baby linens, and manly baby bags as he describes them because he has to carry them, too. Everything he could get his hands on and that was recommended. Lea talks to the sales lady, asking what can be returned in case everything isn't needed. She tells her any of it and to give her a call. She can send someone over to pick up whatever they don't use. Everything is scheduled to be delivered in a couple of weeks.

After the shopping excursion, Zion drops Lea off at home. Lea sits down at her computer, logging into the baby shower registry's she created. Slowly, she deletes everything and closes the accounts.

YOU KNOW YOU COULDA SPOKE UP AND TOLD HIM ABOUT THESE.

No Sex Diva. I would've looked stupid. Only a few people know about this, and they could never afford to buy me any of the stuff Zion has purchased. Hell, out of all of them I probably would've gotten a couple of bags and a few boxes of diapers and wipes. This is the way to do this.

Lea tells herself, hating to admit it. Again, she's back to thinking how she doesn't belong in this equation and questioning why she's sticking around.

-30-

Zion meets with Ryan, Sam and Saul and Detective Greg to discuss the guy they saw Saturday and the fight Lea had with Addison.

"So, what now, Greg? We all know this could be connected some way with Lea and Addison's fight. Did you get any prints off the car?"

"Yeah, we ran them. This is the guy they matched." He shows Zion the pictures. They match the picture of the guy on his phone. "So, this Drake is connected to Addison and is following us around instead of her. She's hiding out I take it?"

"Probably. The police department can't have Drake followed. Yet. Don't do anything illegal and keep me informed of any new information. Regarding your girl's gate being opened, we couldn't find out anything. It could have been opened by anyone. Put a lock on it," Greg says.

"She's moving in with me. Or we're working on that. Combining two households is gonna be crazy. Thanks, Greg, for coming by on a Sunday. Off the record, of course."

"Hey, man, I'm sitting at home watching a game right now." Greg gets up and leaves.

"We have to find Addison and now this Drake."

"Gentlemen, hire whom you need to, but find Addison. Maybe it's time I draw her out a little."

"Zion, do you really want to draw out 'crazy'?" Sam asks him. "Let me do some things first. Don't ask."

Saul speaks up. "We've received some emails from Addison this weekend. They're on the server and ready for your review. They're coming from different IP addresses from a phone. Different phones. It would seem she's purchasing those pay-as-you-go phones, uses them, then trashes them."

"I doubt she's purchasing anything, but whatever." Zion reviews the emails and sees they're escalating again. Addison hates that Lea attacked her after she started the altercation and how, after she and Zion are together, they'll have her arrested. The emails go into apologizing for taking so long, to them getting back together and how she's looking forward to living in Zion's apartment building. Zion runs his hands over his face and head. He can't believe she now knows where he lives and this 'we' and 'us' crap. He can't have this.

Don't draw out 'crazy', Sam told him. Ugh.

"Do what you need to do and let me know later what's going on and what you find. I need to get back to the apartment."

After Sam drives Zion home and drops him off in the garage, Zion goes directly to Wendy's apartment for dinner, letting himself in. His sister, brother-in-law, and their girls are there. "Hey, what the heck is going on here?" His nieces run toward him greeting him boisterously. He reaches down and easily grabs them up, carrying them back into the apartment. Wendy lights up at seeing Zion. Watching him carrying the girls, in her mind, it's Zion coming home from work to her and their boys, who greeted him at the door.

"Wendy wanted to see the girls and how twins interact and play together." Star offers. "She had some questions, so we decided to stop by today. How you doing, big bro? How was your trip?" Star asks keeping upbeat, making eye contact with him over Wendy's head.

Star shakes her head conveying to Zion things are a little off with Wendy. He catches on, sitting down next to Wendy, responding to Star but, giving Wendy his full attention.

"Same ole same ole. Business as usual. Wendy, how are you feeling and tell me the truth?" he presses.

"I'm tiring out faster and for longer periods of time. I'm wanting more pain meds but don't take them so I don't harm the boys. I like feeling them move. My temperature is normal. Everything's normal.

Becky keeps a close eye on me and reports any changes she may notice. I'm so glad you're back. I've missed you. Our boys have missed you. They moved frantically when they heard your voice. See, feel them."

She takes his hand and places it on her stomach. "Oh, Zion, we're so lucky to have them. I can't wait 'til they're born. Our boys, our family. Just like Star and Garett and the girls."

"Hey, are you sure you're, okay?" Wendy turns her head away from Zion. She places her hand on the back of her neck, massaging a spot at the base of her skull. Zion brings his hand up, placing it over Wendy's rubbing the same location. She lays her head on his chest, relaxing into the massage. "Becky, call her doctor and see how soon we can get in, hopefully tomorrow," he tells her.

"Mr. Landon, she has these moments infrequently then goes back to normal. But I'll call him right now." Becky leaves the room and calls Wendy's doctor to get her into the office. Returning, Becky informs Zion, "The doctor is on his way over now, sir."

Wendy says, "You guys are worrying too much. I'm fine," With her head on Zion's shoulder, she keeps his hand on her stomach. She brings her feet up onto the couch and leans further into Zion's embrace.

Star and Garrett watches them in silence. Garrett turns to Star, gaining her attention. He mouths, "What the hell?"

Star responds back with a shrug of her shoulders and shakes her head back and forth, mouthing, "Later."

When the doctor arrives, he moves Wendy to the bedroom and takes her vital signs, checking on the babies. He allows her to have pain medication, sits with her to see how it takes effect, and checks the boys while she's using it. Their hearts are beating strong, but they aren't moving as much. He has Becky sit with her, watching for any changes.

"I would like to see her in the office tomorrow. I want to do an MRI and check on the tumor. Make sure it hasn't grown and isn't pressing on anything. Ten tomorrow. I'll see you then." He leaves.

"Becky, call me if you need anything or anything changes. Anything. You understand me?" Zion emphasizes the importance of her calling him.

"Yes sir, I will."

The rest of them leave the apartment, going up to his. "What do you think is wrong Zion?" Garrett asks.

"We were told once the tumor starts affecting her it would mess with her mind and escalate her pain. When she met with Lea, she wanted Lea to step out of the picture so she and I could marry and be a family and when she died Lea could have me back. Even though this could be a cause of the tumor, I really think she's believing we are a family now." Zion is playing with the girls and telling Star and Garrett about Wendy and Lea meeting. He can't wait until he's playing with his boys like this.

"Are you going to correct her or go with it?" Star asks him, giving the girls a glass of milk to calm them down.

"Please don't repeat any of this to anyone. I was gonna speak with Wendy tonight about the visit we had with Lea, but maybe I should let Wendy have her fantasy. I would feel kind of heartless correcting her. I'll stick with the truth, meaning they're our boys. We're kind of a family. Beyond that as soon as she's sleeping our visits are over and I'll leave. It looks like I'll be working from my home office more to stay close. I can work from the apartment with Wendy downstairs but it's back up here every night. Some setup, huh," he says to them.

"No, you're making it work. Don't worry, we're not going to say anything to anyone. Especially Mom or Dad. She'll take this to another level where it doesn't need to be. Well, 'cause we didn't eat downstairs, we gotta get these two some dinner. Wanna join us?"

"No. Crazy is out there and knows where I live. Why don't you guys get out of the neighborhood? Good night, you two." He hugs and kisses the girls, saying goodbye to Star and Garrett.

After his sister and her family leave, Zion spends the night prowling the apartment. Wandering from room to room, he thinks about life before he met Lea. So much of it was about making money, traveling the world, and not being committed. Now it's about becoming a father, getting married, having a future he never thought of having.

Kids. I'm going to be a father. Okay, yeah at the age of fifty it's pretty damn ridiculous. At seventy I'll be taking my kids to college. Along with the love of his life, Lea. After only six months, she's the love of my life.

Each room, there's an imprint of her. His bedroom with her phone charger on her side of the bed. *Yes, the woman has a side of my bed.* The bathroom. She's tried not to take it over, but he enjoys seeing her hair and shower products on the shelves. The closet is the biggest change. Her tops are mixed in with his shirts, her pants and jeans are mixed in with his pants and jeans. Hell, even her dresses are mixed in with his suits. With all the underwear he purchased, they have a supply on hand when he gets itchy fingers to rip them off; have their own two drawers.

Zion calls Lea, needing to hear her voice. "Hello, my sexy Adonis, how are you this wonderful evening?" she says as a greeting.

"I'm just wonderful, my Nubian queen. I'm missing you so much right now," he tells her.

"I miss you, too. But you need some rest. Your welcome home wore us both out. How was dinner?"

"It went okay. Wendy enjoyed watching the girls interact. I've been walking around the apartment. I like the changes in my life, Lea. All of them. You, the boys. I can skip out on the crazy stalker part, but other than that, my life is fantastic."

"My life is pretty amazing also," Lea says, agreeing with him.

"Glad to hear that," Zion yawns and stretches. "Lea, I don't want to hang up and go to sleep, but I'm tired."

"Zion, sleep, dream of me. We'll talk tomorrow. I love you," she says.

"I love you too, sweetheart. Talk to you tomorrow." He's even loving these simple, quick calls as a part of his life. Life is wonderful.

-31-

Zion has been thinking about getting Lea moved into his apartment sooner rather than later. Especially after the doctor's appointment with Wendy. Sunday's visit has been bothering him. He's realizing Wendy's time is running short, and he needs Lea's strength.

He's cleared his evening schedule of all appointments and heads to Lea's house. This sticking to business and keeping their relationship to themselves is getting old. He wants to track down Addison and have her either locked up in jail or a mental hospital. But Sam has convinced him to not go looking for 'crazy'. It could set off a world of issues they don't need right now, considering how things are. So, he's decided he isn't going out to look for 'crazy', but he isn't going to let 'crazy' continue to control his every move.

The hell with it all, Lea and I are sleeping together under the same roof tonight. And just maybe I can convince her to move in permanently.

Lea has been going to her house after work because of his schedule. She told him there wouldn't be any point to have Ryan up waiting to get her back to his apartment at all hours of the night, so she's been staying at her house more. Zion accepted the logic of the situation, but still hated that Lea wasn't next to him in bed.

Letting himself into her house, the eerie silence un-nerves him. The TV is off, her computer is on the table with the screen saver running, so she hasn't been on it for some time. He walks around looking for her, calling her name.

"Down in the basement." She's standing at the bottom of the steps looking up at him. "Hey you. Everything okay? No meetings tonight?"

He sits down at the top of the steps, staring at Lea, wondering how to say what he needs to tell her. "Wendy wasn't feeling well Sunday during our visit, saying strange things." He doesn't glance away from Lea. He wants her to ask questions on how much she wants to know.

"Strange things like what?"

Zion hesitates. How does he tell the woman he loves that another woman fantasizes about him as her husband? And he doesn't correct her.

Lea presses him. "Strange things like what Zion? Like you, her husband. Your future together? The happiness you two will enjoy as a family?"

Thanks babe. "Lea, how did you know?" He was hoping to keep some of how he treats Wendy a secret between him and Wendy. But wanted to talk to Lea about it also.

"Today, when I was at your apartment, I had to pick up my tablet from your home office. Your computer was on. I could hear voices. Your voice is very distinctive. Rolls up and down my spine."

Zion smiles at how he affects her. Hearing her say things like this gives him a rush.

"Then I heard Wendy and Star and Garrett and the girls. So, I knew I was hearing a recording. From down in the apartment. You're recording what happens. And looking at the recordings later." At his engaging stare, she presses on. "Don't worry. I didn't look. I'd heard enough."

"Lea, I can say let me explain, but would anything make a difference?" No one was supposed to know about those recordings outside of Sam and Saul.

"You should practice closing your computer. I know you do it at work. No reason not to do it at home. Private business and all."

He steps fully into the basement as she backs up and walks away from him. "No. I can't remote into the computer from work if it's closed. You know that. I'll write down the passwords if you want them. You can see anything you like."

"No worries, Zion. I wanted to know if you were going to answer me truthfully. It's obvious you were never going to share them with me." Lea picks through a pile of clothes, separating them. When she heard the voices on Zion's computer she was so fucking tempted to go over and look at the screen. Hearing the clip repeating was enough to make her sick. It kept stopping and starting. From the sounds, she could tell someone had to be remoted into the system. Confronting Zion about it was another sick moment. Would he lie or would he tell her the truth? Should she even waste her time asking about it? Well, she asked and here they are. Now she wants to move on.

"Kitten, I'll share every recording with you. No hiding, no lying. Lea, look at me."

She looks up at him with a fake smile. "Zion, I have no desire to watch movies of you and Wendy. You know my limits. Cross them and we're done."

"Never will I cross your limits and never will we be done." He takes a seat on a chair at the table in her finished basement. "What you didn't see was the part of the video showing the doctor. I had him come examine her. These ramblings or the rambling you heard was something the doctor told me to look out for. The next day at our appointment, she had an MRI and ultrasound to check on the boys. Anything else you would like to know? Sweetheart, ask me."

"How is she? Everything okay? Anything we need to worry about? Anything I can do to help?"

"Baby, no. Nothing to worry about. There may be something you can do to help. But we'll discuss it later. What are you doing?" he asks, surveying what he can only describe as utter chaos. He sees what he assumes are bags of clothes in one corner of the basement and at the other end, on the table, felt material is spread out.

"Multi-tasking. Purging clothes and finishing the receiving blankets for the boys," she explains walking over to them and showing him. She found the idea on the Internet. "You lay out two different kinds of felt material on top of each other the same size. You cut the edges into strips and tie them together, working your way around the blanket until done."

"These are nice. I can't wait to see the finished product. Warm, soft, and cuddly," he tells her.

"Thanks. You hungry? I can make you a sandwich and salad," she says walking toward the steps.

"Sure, I would like that." Before she can get away from his grasp, he stops her, forcing her to look at him. "Lea, are we okay? The cameras in the apartment are, well, were meant to provide proof if I was being scammed. It's gotten to the point now I save recordings for the boys to have something in the future to review about the woman who brought them into this world. That's all. I promise."

"Bear, we good." Lea kisses him.

Zion eats while Lea continues to work in the basement closet, choosing what to get rid of. She makes it into a fashion show, trying on clothes, shoes, and boots.

"You know you don't have to get rid of so much stuff. I understand how women have way more clothes than men."

"I needed to do this anyway. I can't bring all of this with me. It's either too big, old, out-of-fashion or I don't wear any of it. Except for the shoes. I promise to keep them under one hundred and fifty pair. Well maybe."

"A hundred and fifty per pair, I can afford that."

"Uhm no, I mean no more than one hundred and fifty pairs of shoes, boots, flats, casual, and workout shoes combined."

"You have a hundred and fifty pairs of shoes? Where at?" he gets up and goes to look into the closet and does not see a hundred and fifty pairs of shoes.

"Actually, I have two hundred plus pairs of shoes, maybe three. I do have four closets you know," she says laughing.

"Two, three hundred pairs of shoes? I'm speechless. I have maybe twenty and you have two hundred?"

"Zion, get out of my basement. Go to bed. I'm not discussing this with you anymore." She grabs the empty plate and glass and walks up the steps, turning off the basement light.

"Baby wait. This is great. How many pairs of black shoes you have?" he laughs teasing her.

"Twenty-five. Shut up," she tells him, enjoying the moment, wanting it to last.

"Geez, okay. How many brown pairs of shoes do you have?"

"Twenty. They're multiple-hues of brown, with designs and various heights. Ugh. Shut up! You're going to bust a gut laughing so hard. Just you wait 'til you see me in a pair that shows off my ass and legs. You're gonna go out and buy me every color you can find."

"You're probably right. But, hey, if you really need help purging, I'm here to help. I betcha we can get it down to fifty total."

"Are you nuts? Fifty. That's blasphemy. No self-respecting woman has as few as fifty pairs of shoes."

"Baby, you know I'm just teasing you. You can have a thousand pairs of shoes, and I'll love you and every pair." Zion walks over to Lea and kisses her then steps back staring into her face. She's life, she's home, she's his future.

HHHMM, I THINK ITS TIME FOR SOME TOY BOX ACTION.

HEY, HOW YOU KNOW ABOUT THE TOY BOX? Sex Diva questions Adonis.

I'VE BEEN WATCHING AND LISTENING FROM DAY ONE. AND I GET STRONGER AND STRONGER EACH TIME WE'RE

TOGETHER. I KNOW THINGS. Adonis informs Sex Diva. *SO, YOU GONNA LET ME LEAD FINALLY.*

Sex Diva nods and shakes her head at the same time. GO AHEAD. IT'S ALL YOURS. LEAD AWAY.

"Where's your toy box?" he asks her.

"Closet like always."

"Take it out. Please."

She doesn't even ask why. She goes to her bedroom closet and takes out the box, handing it to him. He takes it and guides her to the second bedroom. He opens the box and takes out the blindfold, the feather, and a vibrator, putting the batteries in, laying them on the bed and putting the box on the dresser. She hasn't said a word, watching him.

He takes a box out of his pocket. A long jewelry box. He lays it on the bed. He stands Lea in front of the dresser mirror and undresses her. After she's fully naked, he kisses her shoulder, then he undresses and stands behind her, staring at her in the mirror.

He picks up the jewelry box, taking out the necklace, putting it on her. It's a pendant, deep sea blue topaz in strawberry gold with white and chocolate diamonds. Lea touches it lying between her breasts. "It's gorgeous. Thank you, Zion."

"My pleasure." He walks around and stands in front of her, grabbing her hands.

He uses his favorite scarf of hers to bind her wrists together, then picks her up and lays her on the bed, pulling her arms above her head and tying them to the headboard. He places the blindfold on her and goes to turn down the air conditioning. He wants them sweating.

Zion adjusts the necklace so that it's lying on her chest. When he saw it in a catalog, he knew Lea had to have it.

He spreads her legs open and runs the feather up and down her body from her feet, around her toes, caressing her knees, across her womanhood, up and down the sides of her hips, over her navel, up to her breasts, across the under sides of them, across her nipples, watching them grow hard and perky, over her neck, across her lips, touching her ear lobes, across her eyes, under her arms, up to her wrists, over the palms of her hands, touching her fingertips lightly.

Her giggles and laughter warm his soul. "Baby, you're so ticklish; your giggles are musical." He kisses her then breaks the kiss, causing her to moan from the release.

Zion crawls between her legs, up to her chest, leaning over her, kissing and licking her neck and shoulders. She lifts her pelvis, attempting to feel him, but he backs off and pins her to the bed. He moves down, sucking on her nipples. Since she told him about what she went through to produce milk for the boys he's been unable to get her tits out of his mind. As sick and selfish as it may sound, he's glad she can't produce. *These tits are my tits. All mine to enjoy.* He grins. *Get a grip man, it's a mother and child bonding experience.*

He moves down to her stomach, licking and even blowing a raspberry or two, making her laugh again, grinning. He licks and nibbles her waist where her hip and pelvis meet, making her whole body quiver. Her breathing has increased and she tastes salty from her sweat.

He moves over to her pussy and licks the 'v' area right above her clit, sticking his tongue in and rolling it around. Lea is moaning and groaning, pleading with him to lick her clit. He prods her pussy lips open with his mouth and latches onto her clit, that bud peeking out, engorged, waiting, wanting to be touched. She yelps and bucks upward when he suckles.

Zion sucks and licks on her for a while, stopping when he can tell she's close to cumming. He sits up and lifts her, placing a pillow under her back, bracing her ass on his thighs, lifting her up for better penetration, so he can pin her in place. He slowly slides inside her, pausing, allowing her to adjust and relax. They haven't said much of anything. They know how and what pleases each other without any direction.

Zion grabs the vibrator. This one is her mini handheld wand. It has a knob at the end with small protruding bumps. According to Lea it's actually made to stimulate her g-spot, but she's never inserted it. Turning it on, he presses it around her pussy, avoiding touching her clit. He moves the vibrator to the 'v' above her clit making sure it's on the lowest setting. He then slowly gyrates inside of her. After she adjusts to the lower vibration and him being inside of her, he starts moving in and out while moving the tip of the vibrator to her clit. The vibration and the contractions of her pussy walls makes him almost lose control, but he forces himself to concentrate.

"Oh! Fuck! Zion! Please! Too! Much! Too! Much!"

Zion slides the vibrator up and down the shaft of his penis when he pulls out of Lea only leaving the tip in each time. Growling he says, "Say your safe word, baby. Oh shit, this feels so good."

Lea doesn't say the safe word but keeps quietly chanting, "too much", loving the combination feel of his dick in her pussy, the vibrator on her clit, being tied up and pinned in place with Zion moving slowly in and out. She's hot and sweaty.

She feels the buildup of tension. It's rising from the balls of her feet, gliding up her legs. Her fingertips feel tingly, her tits feel swollen, and there's a swirling sensation in her stomach. Zion has her hips raised in such a way that with each thrust in, the tip of his penis rubs her g-spot. Lea lifts up to get more of him inside her. She digs her feet into the bed and lifts her ass off the pillow. This causes the vibrator to hit her clit at the right angle and moment.

"Fuck yes!" Lea screams. She cums, squirting. Zion pumps faster on the brink of shooting. He pulls out and shoots all over Lea's pelvis, watching his sperm mix with her sweat.

"Oh shit, Lea." He leans over and unties her hands and takes off the blindfold. She grabs him and pulls him close, grinding against him, kissing him. He slides back inside, gets into rhythm with her and they cum again, moaning into each other's mouth. So much sperm, cum, and sweat mixed together with tears of ecstasy.

"Oh damn, Zion. That was fucking hot and not because of the A/C being off," she sighs.

"Hhhhhmmmm good." He lays next to her, not wanting to crush her. He feels lethargic. Touching each other's legs and fingertips, they lay in silence.

After a few more minutes, they get up together, wrapping themselves in the sheets from the bed as they go to the shower. Lea hesitates after a couple steps. Her legs feel rubbery. "And how are your legs?" she asks him.

Zion bursts out laughing. "Oh, about the same as yours."

"Good idea using the bed in the second bedroom. I don't think I have the energy to make it right now," she says to him.

"It did turn out to be a good idea, didn't it?" he laughs.

After they get out of the shower, Zion takes a deep breath and asks, "Baby, can we sit down and talk about something?"

Lea panics. After admitting to what she knows about the cameras, she doesn't look forward to a serious conversation right now. "Sure," she says, grabbing the bottle of baby oil for something to keep her hands busy.

"Lea, I think Wendy's getting worse," Zion can't get the doctor's appointment out of his mind.

"The doctor told us she will begin having good and bad days. It will get to where she'll have good hours and bad hours. The good days and hours may last but the reality is, she's not getting any better. The doctor does not want to administer heavy pain meds and Wendy won't let him. I see tiredness and defeat in her. I know she's going to hold on as long as possible for the boys, but I don't think her body will allow her to.

"Wendy asked the doctor how much longer before they can perform the C-section. He stated at least two weeks. God, Lea, two weeks, and I could be a father, but their mother may be dead," Zion keeps talking not realizing some of what he's saying. Lea listens, taking daggers into her heart and mind.

"Wendy told the doctor 'I'm dead anyway. Two days, two months, two hours, if my babies need two weeks, I'm going to stay alive for two more weeks'. She's determined to do this. I'm so proud of her," he says.

"I'm sorry to hear that. Truly sorry." Lea says nothing else, waiting for him to get to the point. If this is some kind of breakup or putting something on hold, she's not going to help him get there. This is all on him.

"I may have to break one of the promises I made. I want you to move in with me as soon as you can. I want to come home to you and have you to talk to about what I'm feeling and going through. In having you live there I know I'll be leaving you to go to Wendy if I get any calls at any time of the day and night. I have to, Lea. I can't go have dinner and leave. I feel I need to do more."

"You won't be breaking a promise to me by leaving me to go see her. I agreed I would move in and I am. It's taking more time for me to pack up than I anticipated. I asked you to promise not to marry her, not to deny me to her, and not to move in with her. There was never any promise about you leaving me to go see her because we never discussed me moving into your place before her death," Lea says to him.

"But I could be doing something else that may hurt you. I may be falling asleep at the apartment and that would leave you upstairs, alone, waiting for me, with me downstairs. I can't promise you I'll come back up to our place and crawl into bed with you. I can't promise you I'll never fall asleep downstairs. I can't promise you I won't miss dinner with you to stay with Wendy if she's having a bad time and my presence comforts her. I just know I want you there when I do come back up to our apartment, our home."

"That's not our home. That's your home."

"Kitten, to me it's our home. You're my home. Your presence is home for me."

"Zion, do you understand what you're asking of me?"

"Yes, I know. I know I'm a selfish bastard with no right to ask this, but I am."

"Is this what tonight was about? To soften me up with jewelry and sex to do your bidding. God, please don't tell me that it was, 'cause that's sick, real sick?" she says moving to get up and get dressed. Being naked at this moment is no longer sexy. She feels vulnerable.

Before she gets away, Zion grabs her hand and holds her in place. He has to get this out. He needs her now more than ever.

When he got Wendy home from the doctor's appointment and settled in, he met with his family to inform them what's going on and how he would be working from home until further notice. Now he needed to convince Lea to move in, today, this very second.

"Lea, no, tonight wasn't about that. Baby I love you and I wanted you. You moving in with me didn't come to my mind until I had the scare today with Wendy and it hit me, I'll need to be around more than I have been. I've had the necklace for about a week, I just didn't know when I was going to give it to you. Lea, I would never bribe you. Believe me, please."

"Then why?"

"Lea, you're home for me. When I'm with you after visiting Wendy, I get re-energized to go and see her without anger, rejection, or sadness. Every time she talks about 'our' boys, I want to scream and say, "no, these are Lea and Zion's boys not Zion and Wendy's boy's." Sometimes, I regret having agreed to this, but then I feel them moving in her stomach and I think of us raising them. Then I come see you after seeing her and, God, Lea, it gets me through the next visit, doctor's appointment, the next phone call.

"Baby I know what I'm asking of you is crazy and selfish, but I don't know how to get through the coming weeks without you by my side. Please, Lea, baby, please don't change your mind about moving in with me. Okay? I want you to know what could be happening once you're there.

"And even if you say no, my love for you won't change, my giving you the necklace has nothing to do with it, and the amazing sex was because I can't keep my damn hands off you. If you say no, I'll just have to drive over here when I leave Wendy. Or drive to wherever you're at so I can make it through another day."

"Zion, I would never have you out like that at all hours of the night. In my mind, it is easier for me to come to you. Sneak into your bed when you're tired. Surprising you." Lea is playing with the necklace on her neck wanting to rip it off. It doesn't feel as special a gift as it did before his bombshell.

He places his hand over hers on the necklace. "Lea, the necklace has nothing to do with this. It's not a bribe. I saw it, I liked it, and I wanted you to have it. I can take it back and I'll still need you, still want you and will still make this request of you," he says caressing her. "You can still surprise me. Daily. Every minute of the day. I promise you won't regret this. Or us."

Lea puts her head down and gently hits herself in the forehead with the palm of her hand, thinking, *why, is it always me helping others and not getting what I need in return? Because that is what you do, Lea. Always have and always will.*

"Kitten stop." Zion grabs her hand, turning the palm up, kisses it, then kisses her forehead.

When he looks back at her, Lea knows she'll agree to anything he asks of her. To see that look in his eyes, that vulnerable loving look, for her, she knows she'll say yes.

"Sure, Zion." Lea says nothing more, avoiding making any promises she knows she isn't going to fully keep or adhere to. She'll move in. She'll be his peace. She'll assist him with getting through this.

But I be damned if I allow myself to lose who I am. Lea Adams not giving up more of her existence to his baby mama.

Zion decides not to question her simple acquiescence. "Sweetheart, thank you. I know this is going to be hard, and I have no business asking this of you other than I love and need you right now. I don't know where else to turn. My family can be there for me, but I want you and I need you. This is not some joke. My love for you is real and my need for you is strong. We're not breaking up, nor am I choosing another woman to love over you. I want to do this right so when we're raising the boys, we can honestly say we made Wendy's time in bringing them into this world the best we could. Me supporting her and you supporting me." He holds her tightly.

Zion knows what he's asking of Lea is completely outrageous of him, but he can't help it. He's never admitted to needing a woman the way he needs Lea. He now knows how emotionless and closed off to feeling for a woman he was before meeting her. Fucking and getting up and going home, he thought was working for him. He figured in his old age he would maybe settle down just for companionship. Now, he's found love and is becoming a father. And it's all because of Lea. Meeting her has changed him into a more loving and caring man.

-32-

The next morning Lea awakes early thinking about what Zion asked of her. She'll be moving in with him. Spending her days, waiting for him to acknowledge her after he's given all his time and energy to his dying baby mama. Or so he thinks she will.

I finally get what people mean when they say you gotta work for the love you want. If Zion loves me, he would do everything he can to keep me. And is that what Zion is doing? Yes. He's doing everything to keep me in addition to extracting plenty out of me to help him to get through this. What am I getting in return? Not a damn thing right now.

Lea looks over at Zion, sound asleep. He must've been exhausted because he usually awakes when she moves, reaching for her. *When this is over with, when Wendy is dead, I get to be Mrs. Zion Landon, mother to his kids, the wife of a billionaire. I'm being superficial. But it's all I got to hold on to. It's what will help me to get through the next few weeks.*

She gets up to prepare a light breakfast. Zion emerges showered and dressed for work. Upon awakening, he felt relief knowing Lea would be moving in with him. They discuss how they would handle getting all her things to his apartment and their schedules for the day.

"Zion, considering how busy a week I have, I'll have Ryan drop me at your apartment starting tomorrow night. I won't have any time to pack up any of my things today."

"Lea, I can have someone pack up anything you need." Zion has switched to business mode and is making lists in his mind as to what he needs to do to help Lea.

"There's no need to. I can handle this myself."

"Babe what do you need here that I don't and can't have delivered to our home?"

Lea takes in a shaky breath before answering him, "Stop calling it our home. It's your home. It's your apartment. This is my home." She waves her arms around, "You don't have my name on anything. You have stuff for me that you purchased. Why is it so damned difficult for you to let me decide what I want to make about me and my stuff and how I want to handle things?"

Zion folds his hands and places them on the table. Listening to Lea's frustration, he adjusts his attitude. He was about to snap back but thinks about the blowup in her office when she found out about Martin and Addison. Now is not the time for heavy-handed take-charge Zion.

"Lea, if you discover that at any time you need assistance with moving to the apartment that will become our home, please let me know. Is that okay with you?"

Lea looks away from his penetrating stare. The calmness in his voice tempered her anger. "Yes."

"I think I hear Ryan. Are you ready to go? If not, we can take more time to discuss whatever is bothering you. Even if it's how angry you are with me."

"I'm not angry. I'm—. Oh, who the hell am I kidding. Let's get out of here." She stands gathering her things.

Zion carries their dishes and places them in the sink. He grabs his phone and keys and walks out the door after setting Lea's alarm. Ryan is standing at the car with the door open, waiting for Lea to get in. Zion catches up to her and embraces her. "I'll see you later tonight. Be it at our home or here at your home. Kitten, I love you."

When Zion leaves after visiting with Wendy that night, he calls Lea to see where she's at. He could have checked the location on his phone but nixed that idea wanting her to tell him. "Hi sweetheart, where are you?"

"Hi Zion. Upstairs. At our place," Lea whispers.

With a smile in his voice and relief coursing through his body, he says, "I'm on my way home. To you." He takes the steps two at a time.

Lea and Zion slowly adjust to their new living arrangements with them both walking on egg shells. They comment about how strange it feels. It's not as if there haven't been times Lea has spent multiple days straight at the apartment before or Zion at her place.

Zion asks her wanting to get to the bottom of their uneasiness, "Why are we acting this way? I love it when you're here."

"Zion, neither of us have lived with anyone. No matter how many days I have stayed overnight here or you at my place, we still had the buffer of me having my house and you having your home. I have no clue how to act or what to do. You have a whole staff loyal to you. They take their direction from you."

Lea watches Mrs. Vance preparing dinner, setting the table for them. Sam walks out of Zion's office going to Mrs. Vance whispering something, then he says good night to her and Zion and leaves. If Lea was at home, she would be preparing her dinner, washing clothes, getting ready for the next day's appointments. Turning back to Zion she says, "I'm the outsider. I had so many different visions of when I moved in or when we started living together. This wasn't it. What is my place other than your peace and sex doll?"

He wipes his hands across his face and head, gathering his thoughts and words, wanting to come up with something to get her to understand. "Lea, my closest staff understand what you mean to me. Mrs. Vance, Sam, Ryan, Morgan, they have been told that whatever you ask of them, need from them, they are to react as if it's coming from me. I'll have my home office redecorated to include a setup specifically for you. Whatever you want. You—. No—. We will work this arrangement out so that it benefits us. Don't ever relegate your existence to simply my peace or sex doll."

Before Lea could respond to Zion, Mrs. Vance interrupts, "Mr. Landon, Miss Adams, dinner is in the oven, it should be ready in about thirty minutes. Miss Adams, whenever you are ready to sit down and discuss how I run Mr. Landon's home for any changes you would like to make, just let me know. I've written down what I do on a daily basis. I'm more than happy to add anything you need. Or even delete some things. Sam's here to pick me up. I'll see you both tomorrow."

"Thanks Mrs. Vance," Zion says.

"Mrs. Vance, please call me Lea. My mom is the reigning Ms. Adams. And thank you. I will look over what you left."

"My working relationship with Mr. Landon and my manners preclude me to at least address you as Miss Lea. Good night you two. Have a good evening."

"Welcome home Lea." Zion says to her, smiling.

"Yes, welcome home indeed Zion. Welcome home indeed."

Over the next few days, Zion does anything he can think of to ensure Lea adjusts to their new life. He makes sure she has selected the desk setup she wanted for "their" home office. Together, they spend an evening rearranging his bathroom and closet to make it their bathroom and closet with Lea's input, instead of Mrs. Vance putting Lea's things where Mrs. Vance thought they should go. Lea changed the setup for Zion to have one side and she has the other side. Downstairs, they setup the credenza Zion had added for Lea's camera equipment, to be the dropping area for Lea's purse, keys, phone, and bag. They sit down with Mrs. Vance to discuss her duties and incorporate changes Lea wants.

Zion stops off at the third-floor apartment to see Wendy before he goes to work as he and Morgan are hammering out the arrangements of him working from home. He splits his time with her during the day between mornings after seeing Lea off to work and evenings to avoid getting back up to Lea too late if Wendy is having a good day.

It's worked so well that Wendy has been having a number of good days in a row. She's feeling energized with the added attention she's getting from Zion, unaware of his living arrangements with Lea that helps him to see her as much as he does. Wendy broaches the subject of wanting to have a day out with him.

"Zion, can you take the day off and we go somewhere and do something? This apartment is getting on my nerves."

Zion thinks over her request and how would Lea react to him taking a day off work to spend it with Wendy. *I'm definitely not ready to deal with that argument.* "Wendy, I can't take the day off right now. With the office relocation and me working on arrangements to work from home, to be here for you, I need this time in the office. How about I pick you up for lunch today. I can make time for that."

"Oh Zion, that would be wonderful. I would love to." The excitement in Wendy's voice is contagious."

"Good. When would you like to go and you pick the place." Zion says with a smile in his voice.

"Can we go to Maggiano's? I would love their Steamed Mussels and Rigatoni Arrabbiata. Remember when we would go there? It was the best time."

In Zion's mind, he remembers it as a quick way to get laid. She liked it, it kept her happy, he got sex. Now it's about her health and keeping her upbeat. "Yes, Wendy, we can do Maggiano's. I'll return around eleven-thirty to pick you up."

"Wonderful," she says.

At the office, Zion checks Lea's calendar to see where she'll be at around the time, he and Wendy will be having lunch. She is scheduled with a client in South County. Zion calls Wendy an hour before their agreed-upon pickup to ensure she's still up for it. Wendy says she can't wait to see him.

After the call, Wendy gets up to put on her best romantic maternity dress with Becky assisting with her hair and makeup. The results are again angelic, the same image she presented when she first met Lea. When Zion arrives, even he has to admit the sight of Wendy takes his breath away. He has another "if only" moment about them.

He gives her a genuine smile. "Hi there. Ready?"

"Absolutely ready and I'm feeling great," she says.

Lea has appointments all day to deliver contracts. She knows she can have G-TEE's regular courier service do this, but she snaps up the chance to keep busy.

Ryan has driven her to three different clients this morning. All the visits have lasted longer than the in-and-out pickups because her clients wanted to chat. Back in the Caddy, Lea reviews the materials for her next appointment. She sees that she's missing a few contracts, including Landon Enterprises. Thinking about how much time she would have to go back and pick them up and get to her other clients after lunch would create a time crunch.

"Ryan, I forgot to grab three of the client contracts from work. I hate to ask this of you, but could you go back to my office and grab them from Crystal?" Lea then changes her mind, feeling guilty for asking Ryan to do her job. "I'm sorry. Never mind. I can get Crystal to have them delivered."

Thinking she can grab a quick snack; Lea receives a call from her mother to meet for lunch. "Mom, that would be great. Where you wanna meet?"

"Maggiano's. Be there at eleven forty-five."

"See you then." Turning to Ryan, she says, "Okay, change in plans. After this appointment, drop me off at Maggiano's. I can have the contracts delivered there and then we can finish out the day."

Ryan gets Lea to the restaurant fifteen minutes early. "Miss Adams, while you're eating, I'll go grab the packets and some lunch.

It's no problem at all. I'll be back here in about an hour to pick you up. We can leave Landon Enterprises for last."

"Thanks, Ryan. You're a savior. Appreciate it." As Lea walks into the restaurant, she sees her mother walking down the stairs, coming from the bathroom. After they hug, a hostess approaches and escorts them to a table.

As Ryan is driving off in the Cadillac, the SUV is pulling up outside the restaurant and stopping to drop off Zion and Wendy.

-33-

After Lea and her mother are seated and have placed their orders, the elder Ms. Adams looks toward the entrance of the restaurant and sees Zion walking in with a woman.

Zion and Wendy are escorted to their table receiving appreciative looks, Wendy as the beaming pregnant mother and Zion as the sexy man following her.

"Lea, sweetheart, where's Zion today? Why aren't you guys having lunch together?" her mother asks gently. From the looks of the lady, Lea's mother figures this has to be Wendy.

"Working. He's been doing a lot of Skype and Zoom calls with clients, so he doesn't have to travel as much. I have to take contracts over to his office later today. I guess I'll see him then or when he gets home after he sees Wendy."

"How's Wendy doing?"

"Zion says she has good days and bad days. Why are you asking?"

"Well, I think Wendy's having a good day. Zion just walked into the restaurant with a pregnant woman. I'm going to assume it's Wendy. Now don't you turn around too fast. Breathe and calm down."

"Where are they?"

"They're about five tables over to your right being seated."

Lea slowly looks over and sees that they have been seated off toward a corner of the restaurant. If Lea was a stranger, she would say Zion and Wendy make a happy loving couple. But she isn't a stranger. This is her man having lunch with another woman. *Who gives a fuck that it's his baby mama?*

"Lea Adams, take the death grip off that fork right now. You hear me young lady?" her mother whispers.

Lea says, "Yes, ma'am," as she puts her hands in her lap, turning away from the scene.

"How have the living arrangements been going?" Her mother asks, hoping to distract Lea just a little.

"Ok. I wish they were under different circumstances. I try to be bubbly and happy. But when he mentions doing anything for or with Wendy, I get an inner rage. I wanna do something to turn his attention back to me. I do what Gordon suggests, whatever it takes to relieve Zion of stress and not trouble him, I keep what I'm feeling to myself."

"Baby girl, that's a bad idea. Hiding your feelings from Zion. You need to talk with him."

"No mom I can't. The things that bother me are stupid. Baby shower, gifts, big belly attention."

"Lea, this is why I wanted you to walk away from this."

"And not have him loving on me at all? Couldn't do that. It's a few more weeks. I can do this for a few more weeks."

"Or you gonna explode."

Lea, glances at them once more. She makes eye contact with Wendy then looks away. Lea takes in deep breaths and imagines how the lunch will play out. Knowing Zion, he has placed the order for their food, so they are quickly served. They'll talk about the pregnancy, babies, past history. He'll be attentive, loving, and caring, showing her a good time.

Then he'll take her home and fuck her.

FUCK HER. WHERE THE HELL YOU GET THAT BULLSHIT. HE WILL FUCK HER? AIN'T NO FUCKING HER GONNA HAPPEN.

Sex Diva, he would with me.

YOU THE WOMAN HE LOVES, HE NOT FUCKING HER. UGH GET YOUR ASS OVER THERE N—

Before the Sex Diva could finish that thought, Zion is standing at their table.

When Zion and Wendy arrived at the restaurant, they were quickly seated and the order for their meal was confirmed. Zion was about to pull out his phone and check his emails when Wendy shocked him by saying in a sarcastic voice that gave him pause, "Oh look, your girlfriend is here." Wendy couldn't wait to get that dig in after she made eye contact with Lea. Watching her sit toying with her eating utensils makes Wendy feel superior.

He looked up at her and asked, "What?"

"Your girlfriend. She's here. Behind you, sitting with another woman. Did you plan this? Are we supposed to all eat together?"

At Wendy's attitude, Zion squares his shoulders. The change in him makes Wendy fall in love with him even more. This is the Zion she remembers. The strong virile man that takes command.

"Wendy, check your attitude. How the hell would I plan this if you chose the restaurant? And no. We will not be eating together. Why would I subject Lea to your obvious attitude? Excuse me." Zion gets up from the table going to Lea and her mom to speak.

Holy fucking shit. Can I be in anymore of an awkward position right now? Zion thinks.

He plasters a smile on his face, ready for Lea's displeasure. "Lea, Ms. Adams. How are you beautiful ladies today?"

Ms. Adams decides to speak for both of them, easily recognizing her daughter's barely controlled irritation. It's best she gets him away from their table.

"Hello, Zion. We're wonderful, thank you. I'm assuming that's Wendy. Why don't you take me over and introduce me to her? My daughter needs a moment to—" Ms. Adams pauses for affect staring directly at Lea with her 'mom' look, "—gather herself and a few minutes alone would help."

"Mom!" Lea rushes out in a low hiss. She puts her hands up in front of her mouth, linking her fingers and biting her lip to keep from crying.

"I would love to introduce you to Wendy." Zion bends over Lea, whispering in her ear, reaching for her hand to caress it. "Kitten, it's just lunch, that's all. Nothing more. I love you."

"Love you too, Zion," she whispers back.

Wendy watches the exchange between Zion and Lea with mounting jealousy. This was supposed to be her day, her date with Zion. And he kisses his girlfriend. In front of her. In public. As he walks back to their table with the elderly woman, Wendy readies herself to strike out at both of them.

Zion and Ms. Adams reach his table and he makes the introductions, "Wendy, this is Ms. Adams. Lea's mom. Ms. Adams, this is Wendy Noelin."

Neither woman stretches out a hand to shake. Making eye contact with Zion, Wendy changes her ready attack demeanor. The look on Zion's face says she better not make any kind of scene. Instead, Wendy makes it a point to be nice, not showing attitude. Ms. Adams does the same.

Ms. Adams politely says, "Wendy, it's so wonderful having this opportunity to meet you. I'm glad I get this chance to say, you're a special woman and mother. I'm lucky to have met you. Please take care. You two have a great lunch. Zion sit. No need to escort me back to my table." Ms. Adams turns and leaves.

Zion and Wendy stare, speechless at her. In their minds both were expecting a negative experience for different reasons. Wendy feels a mother's warm embrace from Ms. Adams words. Zion understands the source of Lea's strong qualities. The elder Ms. Adams was the epitome of grandeur in meeting the mother of his kids. The mother of her daughter's kids.

Lawd, I'm a lucky man to have met Lea.

Zion sits down to finish his lunch with Wendy.

Wendy's excitement of being with Zion has waned a bit. For weeks all she has been thinking about is getting Zion to love her and be with her, ignoring what life would be like after she's gone. She never gave thought to the many people who will have a hand in raising her sons. She formulates a plan to meet with Lea once again. Not as the woman whose taking away the love of her life but as the woman who will be her son's mother.

Upon returning to the table, Lea's mother sits down to finish lunch. "Mom what did you say to her?" Lea's leg is shaking so much her mother can feel it.

"Young lady, calm down." She watches her daughter take a sip of water and get control of her emotions. "You not going to like it."

"I don't care. I want to know what you said."

"I told Wendy she was a special woman and mother, and I was lucky to have met her. Lea, don't give me that look." Her mother pauses as Lea bites into her bottom lip. "Look, I know this is hard for you, but you chose to stay with that man. Right now, you can't see straight and you only thinking about your man in the presence of another woman. That woman is dying. That woman is staying alive as long as she can to give those kids a chance. And when you're raising them, you'll understand because you will give your life to ensure they live. It's what mothers do."

"It's just—. I hate being an afterthought." Lea uses both her hands to massage the back of her neck, lowering her eyes, staring at the congealed mess of fettuccine. She pushes it away. Her mother lifts her daughters chin to look at her.

Ms. Adams smiles. "It'll change baby. It'll change. Now let's get out of here. You barely ate. Guess I'll have some nice dinner tonight."

Covertly glancing at their table across the restaurant, Wendy feels gratified at the display of Lea in pain. Then jealously at her mother comforting her. Wendy re-focuses her mind on Zion and enjoys her food.

Lea responds to her mother, "Loss of appetite." When the waiter approaches, Lea asks for the check and to-go boxes.

"Oh, ma'am, everything has been paid for. The gentlemen over there," she points towards Zion, "has insisted your bill be added to his."

Lea says thank you and takes out money for a tip, leaving it on the table. She gets up and walks toward Zion's table to thank him.

"That's my daughter, I taught you well." Ms. Adams hangs back to collect the boxes of leftover food.

As Lea approaches, Zion stands. "I'm sorry to interrupt. Zion, I wanted to thank you for paying for our lunch. Wendy, hello."

"Hello, Lea."

"Well, I won't keep you from enjoying your meal. Take care, Wendy."

"Lea, my pleasure. I'll see you at home later."

"Sure Zion. Later." Lea turns to leaves, making sure she's not slouching.

I'll fall apart later.

"Home? Zion, what does that mean? Home." Wendy asks.

"Wherever Lea is at is home for me. That's what I mean," he says calmly to Wendy.

"Oh. I thought you meant like you guys were living together or something."

"We are. Lea and I are living together." Zion doesn't offer up any more details, waiting to see what Wendy will say or do.

She decides to end lunch. "I guess it was a good thing we didn't do a whole day together. I'm getting sleepy."

"Are you okay?" Zion asks with concern, motioning to the waitress for the check.

"I'm good. Honestly. Just tired. No pain. Please, calm down." She reaches for his hand. She beams at him linking their fingers. It puts her in one of her out of mind moments. "Honey this has been a wonderful lunch, but you gotta get back to work. Me and the boys will see you later when you get home."

Zion responds with a simple, "Okay."

When Lea and her mother get outside, Ryan, Sam, and her mom's driver are standing huddled talking.

"Oooo, my driver has arrived," Ms. Adams quips, "I so love being escorted around town. Do you know that young man driving me around considers Sam his father figure? Yep, Sam kept him out of jail and set his ass straight and on the righteous path. He's wealthy in his own right but got some mad street smarts. He takes on extra driving gigs when Sam needs a man he can fully trust without question."

"You know that much about him? How is that?"

"We talk. You know dang well I'm not about to be around someone I don't grill. Again, I'm proud of you, my child. Go back to work. Call me tomorrow. I needs me a nap." Lea walks her mother over to the Audi she's being driven, assisting her with getting in.

Returning to the Caddy, Lea walks past the SUV, speaking to Sam, then gets in her car. As she and Ryan are driving off, she sees Wendy and Zion coming out of the restaurant. He has his hand in the middle of her back. Zion watches the Caddy turn the corner.

Lea shakes off her feeling of depression and focuses on her afternoon meetings.

-34-

After dropping Wendy off, Zion returns to the office. He calls Lea, but it goes to voicemail. Checking the calendar, he sees she's scheduled for back-to-back meetings. He busies himself overseeing the packing of his office. He could've left this all up to Morgan, but Zion needed the distraction. While walking around Landon Enterprises, he runs into, Royal.

"Son, how are you doing? As you can see, the packing is going great. Lea and I finished up some training sessions with our least tech savvy employees," he says to his son. Zion looks tired. Royal hates to even think this, but just a few more weeks and all this stress will be over with.

"Progress is great. Lea's here?" Zion says, confused. "She was scheduled to drop off contracts with legal but that was before lunch."

"I saw her coming out of Carter's office and I roped her into the training session."

"Where is she, has she left?" Zion asks.

"She's behind you, approaching the front desk," his father says, watching his son's expression change from tired and distracted to love and happiness.

Lea stands in the front office of Landon Enterprises finishing a conversation with Saul. She hasn't asked if Zion is around. After running into him and Wendy at lunch, she could use a break from him.

OR GET SOME DICK.

Shut up.

NOPE. YOU WAS AROUSED WHEN YOU SAID GOODBYE TO HIM. I MADE SURE OF THAT.

Again, shut up.

Stepping off the elevator, a flower delivery guy walks toward the doors, carrying a large gift basket filled with baby items and decorated in blue. Lea and Saul step back quickly, giving him room. The basket is so huge the delivery guy can barely get it onto the desk. Scrutinizing it closely, Lea spots two money bouquets made with hundred-dollar bills and a banner that says, "Welcome Landon Brothers". The card is addressed to Zion Landon. Lea clutches the strap on her purse, knuckles turning white. Lately a lot of gifts have been arriving for Zion Landon, and the boys of Zion Landon.

Not a goddamn thing for Lea Adams and Zion Landon, soon to be future parents.

Before she can make her getaway with Ryan, Zion comes up behind her, kissing her on the neck.

"Hi beautiful. You were scheduled for this morning not this afternoon. What a nice surprise."

"Hi. Look, you got another delivery. Let's see who from." She snatches the card before Zion does. Reading out loud:

'Zion, congratulations on becoming a father. We'll have to ensure they carry on the BOMs Legacy. Can't wait to me your sons. L and B.'

"L and B huh? Shall I take this home for you?" Lea asks him.

"No, Kitten. Morgan, take this to my office please. Thanks. It's from two dear friends of mine. You haven't had the chance to meet them, but you will. I guarantee it. Actually, I can't wait for you to meet them."

"I need to get paperwork back to G-TEE. You need to get back to work." She tells him, grabbing her things.

"Lea, what I need is time with you," he whispers in her ear.

Lea turns around, looking up at him. Staring at his lips. Her mind switches from anger, to sadness, to arousal.

Shit, I wanna kiss him so much. I want him to fuck me. To claim me. To take me. To remind him of me and forget about her. But using sex is wrong.

NO, IT'S NOT, HE'S OURS. A LIL QUICKIE WON'T HURT NO ONE.

But why are we wanting this? Now? Because of the lunch he had with her?

WHY YOU GOTTA BE ALL MORAL AND SHIT. YOU THINK SHE GIVES A SHIT ABOUT YOU?

I can't say out loud or do anything in front of all these people. Let's just leave it for later.

CHICKEN SHIT. I GOT THIS. FUCK THE PEOPLE.

Fine.

Lea looks up at Zion and takes a deep breath, licking her lips, knowing he will react just as she needs him to.

"Lea."

"What?"

"Ryan, I'll call you when Lea is ready. You, young lady, we need to talk."

He recognizes the arousal in Lea and as much as he knows it's wrong, he marches her to his office. As Morgan exits, Zion closes and locks the door.

Lea stands in the middle of his office, staring at the basket. Turning away from it, she faces Zion, waiting for his next move. She's not left disappointed. He approaches her, takes her in his arms, kissing her. Without saying a word, he raises her skirt, caressing her thighs above the thigh highs she has on. They've never had sex in his office before. Made out, yes. Teased each other, yes. Full-on fuck session. No.

WELL, WE DOING A FUCK SESSION TODAY.

Without saying a word, Lea takes off her underwear. Pulling Zion over to the edge of his desk, they unbuckle his belt and his pants drop to the floor. Zion shoves his underwear down. Opening Lea's legs, he positions himself to slide into her. She accepts him without hesitation.

Kissing to muffle their sounds of passion, Zion fucks Lea hard. This is not one of their slow drawn-out sex sessions. Even though Zion told Lea to never use sex as a tool, she knows this sex session is exactly that. Lea buries her face in his neck, groaning. Her orgasm explodes from the tip of her toes, moving up to the top of her head. Zion grasps her ass, pressing into her, shooting. He wants to scream in ecstasy. Lea kisses him, keeping him quiet.

Their lips are bruised and both have shaky legs. Zion pulls out of her leaning his head on her shoulder. "Dammit woman, you're fucking amazing."

"Fastest quickie we've ever had."

"We need more of them."

They get dressed, properly adjusting their clothes. Lea freshens her makeup, attempting to look presentable before exiting Zion's office. He smiles at her attempts. "Lea, you look beautiful. No one will know."

Reaching for his phone, Zion calls Ryan, telling him to be downstairs, Lea's on her way, and escorts her to the car, "Kitten, I'll see you at home later. We must do more of these."

"Maybe."

Zion goes in search of his father, finding him in his old office. His father ends the call he's on and looks up, grinning at his son.

"How was the make-out session?"

"None of your business." Zion says. "And what makes you think we were making out?"

"Zion, you're your father's son. And I ain't blind."

"I really didn't need to hear that."

"I enjoy shocking my kids. Especially when they tend to think Mom and Dad are dead below the waist."

"Look, we not gonna go there." Zion laughs. "Dad, did you ever think I was moving too fast with Lea?"

"Yes. Would it have mattered if I said that in the beginning?"

"No. I don't want her to have any regrets. We won't get much time living alone, just us. Am I shortchanging her?"

"Yes. Zion, do you love her?"

"Yes."

"Do you want her in your life?"

"Yes."

"Can you see yourself living without her?"

"No."

"Then spend the rest of your lives knowing that and make her happy." His father changes the subject back to business.

Leaving the office later than he planned, Zion decides to stop off and visit with Wendy before going upstairs to Lea. When he arrives, she's lying on the couch dozing. He gently lifts the pillow under her head and lays it on his lap, holding her hand, watching the boys move. Becky brings him a drink and props his feet on a stool. He watches Wendy sleep. She wakes up looking up at him.

"How was your nap?" he asks her.

"Wonderful. What time is it?" she asks.

"Eight-thirty. You looked peaceful sleeping. I watched the boys move across your stomach. It's hypnotizing. Becky has dinner ready. How about it? Hungry?"

"After such a filling lunch, you wouldn't think so, but yes. Thanks," Zion helps her to sit up and Becky brings over a tray of food for them. They spend time talking and watching TV.

Since meeting Lea's mother, Wendy has been thinking about Lea. Wendy would like to have another visit with her, alone. "Zion, I would like to meet with Lea again."

"Say what? Why? After the last meeting, you don't think I'm going to allow you to hurt her."

"Always the protective one. I'm not going to hurt her. I just want to know her. To know the headspace of the woman you're going to have help you raise our boys."

That "our boys" again irks Zion, but he doesn't show it in his response to Wendy. He does want them to talk more. This should be a time of all three of them getting through this, not just him. Maybe this is their chance. "I'll talk to Lea and see what she wants."

"Can't you order her to meet with me?"

"No. I won't order her to meet with you. I'll let you know if she agrees and when."

Wendy takes what she can get. "Thank you, Zion."

"You're welcome, Wendy."

Around ten, Zion puts Wendy to bed and says goodnight to Becky, making sure they're okay. He wonders how in the world is he gonna broach this subject with Lea.

Damn women.

When he gets upstairs, he opens the door to an eerily silent home. He searches the entire apartment looking for Lea, calling her name. There's no response. He's in a panic.

Where the hell is she?

-35-

Lea has been feeling cut off. She hates being in that apartment waiting for her turn to be with her man. He's become all about that damn third floor. Lea has managed to get away a few times, just for an hour or so, and it's been great.

Tonight, she's really taking a chance. She was ready to blow a gasket after seeing the gift basket. *It's all about Zion. Zion and his boys. The Landon brothers. Well, what the fuck about Lea? Oh, that's right, I'm just a fucking footnote.*

Lea realizes she can't take waiting around any longer. She calls Gordon. "Lady, it's about time I've heard from you. How you doing?" he asks her.

"Gordon, I'm going nuts. Zion got a gift basket for the boys today. Addressed to him. I'm so sick of not being recognized. But whose gonna acknowledge me when I can't tell anyone about this?"

"Why don't you meet me at Ballpark Village for dinner? Can you get away? I have some acknowledgment for you."

"Yeah, I can get away. It's no big deal. Ryan's gone home for the night, and Zion's with Wendy."

"Wonderful. I'll see you in thirty."

Lea thought about sending Zion and Ryan a message stating where she was going. Then she thought, *fuck it, she was going out with her friend and have some fun at Ballpark Village. It's just across the damn street. Okay that's guilt and defiance talking.*

She had planned on being back at the apartment before ten, but the wings were good and the conversation was fun and distracting. At ten-ten her phone blows up. Zion of course.

"Hi, Zion," she says, answering upbeat.

"Stay your ass there and don't you move."

"You got it Dude," she says, then disconnects the call. "Ooops, I'm in deep shit now. Another glass of water please."

"Lea, did you tell him you were meeting with me tonight?" Gordon asks.

"No. He was down at Wendy's. I figured I had time to get back before he did. Sorry to put you in the middle of this," she tells Gordon.

"My pleasure. It's nice to see some of the old backbone coming back. Oh, and here he is. How did he know your exact location?" he asks her.

"Phone is tracked. Or maybe I'm bugged some other way. Who fucking knows." Lea watches Zion and another one of his security detail approach them.

These fools don't know how easy it is to sneak away from they ass. It just takes planning.

"Gordon," Zion says to Gordon as a greeting.

"Zion," Gordon mimics back.

"Lea, do I even need to ask why you're out in the open like this?" he asks her.

"Zion, if you need to ask her, then you don't know her," Gordon speaks up first. "Man, don't give me that look. I get what you're dealing with, but I also get who you're ignoring. You got all your family and friends looking out for you and your well-being and helping you. Guess what? Lea has no one but me and her mother. She has no friends she can tell about this. She gets no celebrations. You get baskets and cards, delivered to you."

Zion's eyebrows go up, and he silently thinks, *who the fuck this man thinks he is?* But before he can snap back, Gordon rushes on.

"Yes, I know about those. What does Lea get? Nothing. It's all about her supporting you. Frankly, I'm fed up with this entire situation. You supposed to love her, but all you doing is focus on you and Wendy and them kids. Remember, I'm here for her. Always. Hell, half the time I don't know if I should be celebrating her motherhood or tell her to run. She deserves better than what she's going through with you. I'll let you two get to your argument. By the way, congratulations. My wife sent this for Lea, thinking it would cheer her up. You can toss them in the trash on the way out for all I care. As always, Lea, when you need to break out of the tower, call me." Gordon takes out money, paying for the check as a small dig to Zion. He drops the gift bag in front of Zion on the table. He hugs and kisses Lea, then walks out.

Lea grabs the bag, putting her head down, trying not to cry. Opening it she pulls out four pairs of baby booties. Hand knitted with the letters L on the bottom of the feet. The card reads: *We're so excited for you becoming a mom. Can't wait to meet your boys. Love Gordon and Lily.*

She hands the card to Zion. "The first and only gift I'll probably ever get. How sweet of Lily."

He reads it, then looks at her. Gordon has left him feeling like shit, and the tear Lea wipes away humbles him.

"Lea, baby, let's go home," Zion says, caressing her cheek, needing to touch her.

"No. I wanna go for a drive. Give me the keys to your car. You go home, go to bed. I'll only be an hour. Shadow number four can go with me." Now that she's out, she's not going back.

Zion doesn't say anything. He remembers what her mother said. about him not allowing her to take a drive without him. "Shadow number four can call it a night and we can go for a drive. You drive and I'll be the passenger."

"Say what?" she asks him astounded.

"Let's go for a drive. As long as you haven't been drinking," he says looking at her.

"Oh yeah right, Zion. Stop bullshitting. Obviously, you're too tired to do anything. Forget it. Let's just go home." Lea grabs her phone, keys, and stuffs the booties and card back into the bag, and stands, uncompromisingly. She did consider tossing it, but they're hand knitted. Even if she never sees the boys wearing them, they should get them.

They walk back over to the lofts. Zion has a feeling it's about to be an epic fight.

"Are you hungry? Can I get you anything to eat or drink?" Lea asks him as they walk into the living room.

"No, I ate downstairs," he says.

"Of course, you did," she says plopping down on the couch.

"Lea, how many times have you disappeared alone without security?"

"Four?"

"Where did you go?" *Four fucking times she was out, and no one knew. I'm firing someone tomorrow.*

"Walking downtown with Crystal to City Garden, sitting in the building's garden, Soulard Market, and tonight."

"If I had never caught you tonight—."

"You were going to catch me. I wanted you to come after me," she says trailing off. "It's immature and childish. I know that. But it's what I wanted," Lea sits staring at him. He looks worn out. "Zion, I'm sorry. It won't happen again. I promise. Let's go to bed. You look like you're about to pass out."

She stands up. He grabs her and pulls her into his lap. "Baby, I was so scared. I thought Addison had got you. Here we are in walking distance of so much night-life and all you do is sit here in this apartment. Lea, I told you things would get like this. I don't know what to say, other than I'm sorry. Please don't ever leave like that again. I'll find the time to take you anywhere you wanna go. Talk to me, yell at me, but don't play these childish, bullshit games with me. I don't like them, and I don't need them right now. I need you and your strength. I need you and your calming nature. Lea, I need you. Okay baby. Please."

"Zion, I won't take off again. I promise. I'm here for you. No more games. Let's get you to bed."

"No, we're not going to bed. Not until we've discussed what Gordon said. Everything that comes with being a mother you're missing out on. I keep saying I'm sorry because I am."

"I don't want to talk about what Gordon said. You can't change or do anything about it. Talking about it will make us feel like shit."

"Lea—. Come on. Talk to me."

"No. Leave it alone. There's nothing you can do about what's going on, Zion. Nothing."

"I can't—."

"Fine then." *Maybe I've been waiting for this opportunity to get this out.*

"You wanna talk? It's really fucked up that your family and friends heap praise and happiness on YOU. Everybody is worried about you, making sure you get what you need. Everybody drops what they doing to assist Zion. And me! I! Don't! Get! Shit!

"I know what I said. I'll help you get through this, but again, I don't get shit. I can't celebrate. I can't smile. I can't enjoy any of this. Wendy looks at you like she has won the fricking mother lode of love because she's giving you something I can never give you, and it pisses me the fuck off. You get gift after gift. They're all addressed to Zion Landon. This is the only acknowledgement," she grabs the baby booties and throws them across the room, "—I'll get regarding these babies. And it's still all about you because they're engraved with the letter 'L'. If we get married, oh don't give me that fucking look because it's still an iffy situation. If we get married, as far as everyone else will know, I'll be walking into a ready-made family. Here Lea, here's your spot. Stand here. Smile. Support Zion. Are you gonna make me the stay-at-home mom? Will I be expected to accept you as the head of the household, and my job will be to parent your kids alone with you popping in every now and then?

"Sometimes I get so sick of watching how people fawn over you. I wanna scream, 'Hey fuckers, what about me? He loves me. He wants me to be the woman to help him raise them. Don't I get any kind of props?' But no. I can't say anything to anyone. Gordon doesn't even know half of what I'm feeling. There. You have it. Now what? You gonna tell people how to fake treat me? You gonna instruct your family and friends on how to fake acknowledge me? Don't do me any favors. They can keep their fake props and accolades to themselves. I'll get through this just fuckin' fine."

She has run out of steam, still sitting, now emotionally exhausted, on Zion's lap. He has taken all of what she said, letting her scream, cry, and attempt to get away from him but not letting her go. He wraps his arms around her, allowing her to cry it out. He says nothing. He holds her, even doing a little crying himself.

After Lea has cried herself out, Zion moves them to the couch, stretching out, holding her. Neither of them saying anything, falling asleep.

Hours later, they awaken to Zion's phone vibrating on the floor. Lea moves so he can reach for it, but he stops her.

"Leave it. I'll get it later."

"Zion, you can't. It could be something with Wendy. You don't have the luxury of not answering your phone when you're not with her. That luxury is saved for me."

"Lea, I don't care about the damn phone right now. All I care about is you."

"If that's true, respond to the call."

"Fuck." He reaches for the phone, checking to see who called. It was Wendy. This late or early or whatever. He curses again.

"Call her back. I'm going to go take a shower. I'm not in the mood to hear this right now." Lea gets up from the couch and walks upstairs to the bathroom. She surveys her appearance. Wrinkled clothes, dried tears, and depression.

Zion returns Wendy's call. "Hello, Wendy, or shall I say good morning? Why are you up so early?" he asks her, watching Lea walk away from him, needing to follow her.

"The boys were moving around and woke me. I wanted to see if you were interested in coming down to see?" *And interrupt anything that could be going on with you and that girlfriend of yours.*

"Are you feeling, okay? No pain, stress, or issues?"

"No, nothing like that. Just the kicking."

"No, I can't make it there right now. I have something going on I need to address. Are you sure you're all, right?" No way in hell is he walking out of this apartment until he has talked with Lea.

"Zion, I'm fine. Didn't mean to worry you. Stop by later. Maybe for lunch?"

"Maybe. If not lunch, I'll be by later. Is that okay?"

"Sure. That's perfect."

"Okay, see you later."

"Sure, Zion. Later it is."

Zion races up the steps to the bedroom. Lea is coming out of the bathroom, freshly showered, in her underwear. Zion forces himself to ignore his arousal and desire to make love to her. Right now, he wants to talk.

"Everything okay?" Lea asks.

"Yeah, fine."

"I'm sorry for sneaking out and my outburst. It won't happen again. You don't need to worry about me."

"Lea, we need to talk."

He sits down on the bed and Lea joins him.

Zion says, "I need to answer your question of what the fuck do you get? We aren't leaving here until I've done so. We're in an unconventional situation. Haven't dated long, barely know each other. And yet we know each other well. We talk, but I think we have been doing a lot of surface talking and not deep down talking as of late. Don't interrupt me, it's my turn," he says at her attempt to speak.

"I love you, Lea. I have no doubts about that. I want to marry you. And I want to give you a family. Biologically I can't. Thinking about it before Wendy came along, I thought about adoption and surrogacy. I even considered talking to my doctor, praying and hoping there was some kind of way I could give you a child, ignoring what I've been told for years.

"This chance fell into my lap and I couldn't pass it up. I don't regret saying yes to adopting these boys. Every day I think about raising them I feel so much pride. The thought of you by my side brings me tears of joy. I can't fricking believe my luck at times. I'm not going to regret any of the decisions I made in doing this. With them or you. I know you love me because if you didn't, you would've ended this long ago. You've hidden your frustration well. Stop doing that. I'm frustrated too.

"If we're going to make it as a family knowing the background dynamics of how this came about, we have to communicate with each other. The good and the bad. Between you and me. No one, and I mean no one, is invited to know about what we're dealing with before we discuss it with each other.

"I don't want any kind of flack or humiliating talk from family, friends, or strangers about how we chose to become a family. I'll fight any and every one about this. For you and the boys. I need to know you feel that way.

"There're going to be plenty of feelings and emotions we're going to have and have had. We need to come to each other first with these. I know you love Gordon and he's your best friend. Best friends talk and share. But Gordon becomes your secondary best friend. From this point on, I am your first best friend and we discuss everything. I'm never gonna tell you not to talk with Gordon or come between that relationship. He was there before me and knows you. I hope to someday to talk with him on a different level than what's happening now about the woman I love so much.

"Of course, you'll tell your mother what's going on. It's been the two of you for your whole lives. You and your mother don't strike me as two petty women. Y'all are the most amazing common-sense individuals who keep each other on their toes without the childish crap, I've ever met. But don't ever feel like you can't come to me with anything and everything, good or bad, that's bothering you. Is that clear, Lea?"

"Clear." Thinking back on how she's been behaving, Lea can admit her role in not communicating as she should with Zion about all of this.

"And I will be more open with you about what I'm thinking. I see now that's bugging you and is probably part of why you've been sneaking out and being rebellious. Lea, I don't want you to allow me to get into a habit of ignoring you and putting you on the back burner. I can do that easily because I've never had a woman who demanded of me more than what I was willing to give her.

"From day one, you told me what you wanted. Don't backslide on that just because of what we're going through. Keep on my ass. I'm in this to make it work and I expect the same from you. You'll fight for us, you, me and the boys, the same way I will fight for you. Nothing less will be accepted. If any of what I just said you're not agreeable to, say it now. Negative or positive."

Lea wipes away tears.

This man has just laid claim to me like no man has ever. To think the one thing I've wanted, I'm now getting and I was about to blow it by acting like a fricking child. Talk about a fucking reality check.

"I don't disagree with any of what you've said. I'm stunned and shocked. I never expected in my life to be with a man who would think, let alone say, what you've said. I loved hearing every word of it. I look forward to becoming a mom. I look forward to our future."

He takes the towel, wiping away her tears. "Wonderful. Today we start fresh. And from this point on, there will be a camera outside the apartment door and the one inside the elevator will be turned back on."

"Say what?"

"It's your own damn fault. No discussion. Decision made."

"Zion, that's bullshit."

"Bullshit, my ass. I call it keeping you safe. Deal with it. No more leaving and disappearing."

"This some bullshit. Now you saying you not trusting me when I say I won't disappear anymore."

"You either go out with me or an escort. I won't keep you locked up, but I will have you protected."

"Again, this some bullshit."

"Well, sweetheart, I got more bullshit for you. Wendy wants to meet with you again."

"Why? I thought she hated me and wants to keep the image of you and her as a family."

"After meeting your mother, Wendy would like to talk with you about your headspace in raising another woman's kids. I can't say I disagree with her at this point."

"You taking her side against me? How fucked up is that?"

"How fucked up is it that you went out alone four times without my knowledge? No, I'm not siding with Wendy against you. But I want to know your headspace about the boys as much as she does."

"I went out because I don't want to become dependent on a fricking escort. You're used to it. You know nothing else. How the hell am I supposed to be a mom, taking care of twin boys, without a shadow when they're no longer needed? I'm afraid to get dependent on that crutch. I need to keep my independence. I don't know how I'm supposed to do this." Lea waves her hands around, gesturing broadly.

"Lea, I don't know either. First things first, 'cause it's not just you. It's we. I'm not about to take on this adoption and let you do all the work. Stop thinking that. See how us not talking to each other has us thinking differently? Baby, we gotta get on the same page. We gotta communicate more."

Lea flops back on the bed. "You're right. Us not talking is making things worse."

Zion lays down, caressing her stomach. Lea places his hand over hers. "Kitten, I wish my child was in here kicking away. As shitty and wrong as what I'm about to say is, in a few weeks, it will be you, me, and our boys. Keep focusing on that. Every time, I'm with Wendy, it's what I do. I focus on our future."

Turning to him Lea says, "Thank you for saying that. 'Cause, baby, I say that to myself constantly. We may end up in hell for thinking those thoughts."

"At least we're honest and will be in hell together. I'll setup a time for us to meet with Wendy again."

"No. Not 'we'."

"I'm not letting you do this alone."

"Zion, yes you are. Wendy wants to meet and talk. I'll go meet and talk. And you have to agree to turn off the cameras in her apartment."

"They haven't been on since the one you saw. But I agree, no cameras. And no me. I don't like it, but I agree to it."

He gets up, walking to the bathroom to shower. "I love you, Lea," he says not turning around to look at her.

Lea gets up and embraces him from behind around the waist. "I love you, Bear."

-36-

After Zion and Lea's blowout, they both feel a much stronger connection. Lea attempted to convince Zion she didn't need a second shadow but he held strong. He agreed to turn off the cameras inside the elevators but leave them on outside to monitor who gets on and off. The nursery furniture is being delivered and setup. Ryan along with four other of Zion's security detail are around to 'assist' with deliveries. Paying close attention, Lea discovers they're in place to ensure the delivery people are who they say they are, here to do what they're supposed to do and then leave, making sure they are not of any Addison's plants.

Could she really be that smart? No Way.

After the furniture is setup and everyone has left, Lea decides it's time to meet with Wendy again. She calls down to the apartment to see if she's up for this "talk" she wants to have. Wendy tells her to come down any time she likes saying, "It's not like I'm going anywhere since Zion is at the office."

Yes, Wendy, I know my man is at the office, because we know his schedule. Lea mouths silently into the phone. "Great, I'll be down shortly," Lea says.

She informs her shadow where she's going. He escorts her there. "You do know it's just to the third floor. Geez, Zion even has the door man watching me."

"Ma'am, I'm taking my orders from Mr. Landon," Shadow Two says.

They arrive outside the apartment. Turning to her shadow, Lea tells him she promises not to go anywhere and will call when she's ready to leave. He stands outside the door ensuring she walks in.

Jackass.

What Lea doesn't know is there is a camera hidden outside the apartment. Security will know exactly when the apartment door opens.

As much as Wendy wants to talk, Lea wants it also. Lea knocks and the nurse answers the door.

"Hello Miss Adams. How are you today?"

Lea steps over the threshold and Becky closes the door behind her. "I'm good Becky. Wendy said I could stop by anytime to talk. If now is not a good time," *Lord please say it's not a good time*, "I can come back later."

Wendy comes into the living room. "Hello, Lea. Now is perfect. I was just getting a snack. Wanna join me? It's a Dilly bar from Dairy Queen."

"No, not right now. Thanks."

"Well, let's sit," Wendy says wobbling over to the couch. Becky puts a pillow behind her back.

"Wendy, how are you feeling?" Lea asks.

"I'm tired. My head hurts more. Lots of body aches. But the boys are thriving. Even if I'm not."

Lea stays silent, unsure of what to say. Wendy presses on.

"Lea, I know you're well aware of my love for Zion."

Get straight to the point why don't you? Lea thinks.

"I'm no longer going to hide it from you. The man is everything for me. He was supposed to be my future with our sons. But my future is being taken away and given to you."

"What do you mean given to me?"

"You get to be the wife, the mother, his future. And it makes me hate you."

"Look if you want me here to direct your hatred and anger, I'm leaving. I don't need this." Lea stands to leave.

"No wait. I want to be honest about how I'm feeling. I want you to be honest. And I want us to move beyond it."

"I'm supposed to be honest with you? Are you kidding me?"

"Yes, I want your honesty, and you'll get mine. We love the same man and we want the same thing."

"We don't quite want the same thing." Lea looks at her warily. "Go ahead."

"I wanted to be the one to give Zion children. To be the one in his eyes that gave him this miracle. But you came along and plopped it in his lap."

Lea hesitates. Wendy says nothing.

Lea continues, "Yes, I love Zion as much as you do, but I want you to know I would never hurt or take out any anger or jealousy towards these babies. I'm not some evil stepmother. I want kids. Selfishly, me not carrying them is good and bad. I wish I was going through everything you're experiencing. Then I'm happy all this is being taken care of."

"Taken care of. That's one way of putting it. When I approached Zion with the idea of adopting them, he was supposed to ask me to marry him. To make us a family. I had it all planned out. I would die as Mrs. Zion Landon. Then, I find out you exist. He's in love with another woman. I knew that all I had to do was to spend time with Zion and get him to make love to me and he would make me his wife."

"I'm sorry. Make love to you? You planned on sexing him to win him? You really don't know Zion as well as you think you do."

"All I needed was time and I could have made it happen. But he tells me about his love for you. And I hated you for taking him from me. Oh, let me stop lying. It wasn't hatred. It was pure envy. I envied you so much having the love of the man I wanted."

"Well, I guess we're even. I envy you for being able to give Zion kids and the experience of pregnancy and you envy me for having his love. So now what?"

"I didn't expect to have to deal with anyone outside of Becky and Zion during this pregnancy. Meeting his family—."

"That was my idea by the way. You meeting and spending time with his family. I figured you would want to know more about who your kids would be growing up around." Lea slides in that smug upper handed dig.

Wendy registers the look on Lea's face but doesn't say anything about it. "You have that much pull with him? I never had that. Another thing to envy. Anyway, getting to know his family has been great. When your mom came over to introduce herself, all I could think about is this lovely woman is going to be my children's grandmother. Therefore, I should know their mother."

"Did my mom tell you to have this talk with me?"

"Oh no. Heck no. This was my idea. I don't think I have much time left. I'm writing letters to the boys. I wanted to include my opinion about you. And I didn't want it to be a negative opinion, one based on me being angry 'cause I'm not here to raise them. I can see now, without you, Zion probably would not have taken on the task of adopting the boys. Or if he did, he would have been all business. Cold and distant. See? I do know something about him. He's been warm, caring, and attentive. We talk, we plan, and it doesn't feel morbid. Without you in his life, I don't think my time remaining on this earth would be so pleasant."

"You give me way too much credit."

"Lea, you don't take enough credit."

"From our last meeting, I figured you didn't want to mess up the family idea you have in your head with Zion."

"I didn't. A part of me still doesn't. I'll die with that idea. And no one's going to take that away from me. But I'll also die knowing my sons will have a woman who loves them as much as their father does. No blood relation necessary."

"I'm glad you feel that way, Wendy."

"It's been a lot of reflection and honest discussion with Becky." Wendy looks over at Becky with a thoughtful look and Becky smiles. "She's helped me to see beyond my love for Zion and accept what I'm doing is a wonderful thing and my boys will be well taken care of."

"So now what? I go back upstairs, and you go back to having your dream of a family with Zion?"

"No. I would like you to assist me with planning my funeral and burial. I know things with me are progressing faster than expected. No matter what the doctors say, no matter what Zion says, I can feel it. I don't know how much time I have. I'm determined to stay alive by whatever means necessary to ensure these babies are born healthy. But I don't want Zion worrying about my funeral. I know it may sound wrong of me to put this on you—."

"Please don't give it a second thought. If that is what you want, I'll do it."

"Thank you, Lea."

"You're welcome, Wendy."

"I guess we can consider this a mom-to-mom of the women who love Zion truce."

"You called me mom. I'm flattered you now think of me that way."

"It's what you'll be. Lea, would you like to feel the babies move? They're awake."

She smiled. "I would love that very much."

Lea moves to the couch sitting next to Wendy. She places her hands on her stomach and feels the baby's kick. She and Wendy laugh.

"Lea, meet your sons."

Lea lets her hands rest, feeling and watching them move. She and Wendy spend the rest of their visit planning her funeral.

-37-

After her meeting with Wendy, Lea is sitting in Zion's office reviewing Wendy's instructions for her funeral. They're simple: Collect body. Ideas for burial and service.

"Eeeeek. So unfeeling," Lea says out loud to the room. Looking over at Zion's desk she sees a folder labeled, 'Wendy's Funeral'. Picking it up she looks through it. "Geez more cold and unfeeling plans."

Walking past the door, Mrs. Vance asks if she's okay or was there anything Lea needed.

"No, Mrs. Vance. Just looking over some paperwork," Lea responds. She gives Zion a call.

"Hi, Kitten. How are you?" he asks.

"Good. I met with Wendy."

"Okay."

"We had a nice come-to-Jesus conversation."

"Really? Anything you want to share." Zion hopes she tells him but understands if she doesn't.

"The only part I will share with you is that she wants me to plan her funeral. I don't know if that is a good or bad thing. But I said yes anyway."

"Lea, that isn't necessary. I'm working on the plans."

"I have your plans in front of me. You and Wendy are very cold about this. I'll take over from here."

"Why would you do that?"

"Call it my good deed to get into heaven. This way you can focus on other things."

"I know what you mean when you say other things. And it's not like that."

"Zion, I know. Wendy deserves a woman's touch, so I'm going to do this."

"Thank you, Lea. I can't say that enough."

"You're welcome. I'll let you get back to work. See you later tonight."

"Love you, Kitten." Zion sits staring at the phone. He was tempted to turn on the cameras when Lea's Shadow informed him he had escorted her to Wendy's. He rose, walked through the office, turning his frustration of not knowing what was going on toward everyone else.

Maybe Wendy will offer up what happened when I stop by tonight.

Later that afternoon, Lea gets a call from Zion's mother stating she and Star will be stopping by for a visit. *Geez can you ask first?* Lea mumbles to herself but says cheerfully, "See you later."

Star is uneasy about this spur of the moment visit to Zion's apartment. She's well aware Zion is at the office working. When he barked at her about the announcements for the new office when it opens, changing all the plans he signed off on two days ago, she knew it was time to leave. Her mom's suggestion to stop by and visit with Lea makes her nervous. Patty Landon can be the sweetest adoring mom. Then she can take a trip off the deep end into overthinking land.

"Mom, why do you want to go see Lea?" she asks her, driving them to Zion's place. Star and her mom are still allowed to drive themselves, but they are using one of Zion's cars with GPS tracking. In addition to the new phones, he gave them, the entire family is electronically being tracked in some form.

"Why can't I want to visit with the woman who may be my future daughter-in-law?"

"Wait, what may be? Why do you say it like that? Zion has moved her into his apartment. He's drawn up paperwork to have her adopt the boys. There's no question about may be."

"I simply wanna talk to Lea about some things, and we can make a girls night of it." Patty says.

"Mom, what could you possibly have to talk to Lea about?"

"Why you need to keep questioning me? I'm an adult. I'm the mother here."

"You're also the mother that tends to speak without consideration of the topic."

"I simply have a few questions of Lea. It's no big deal. If things are so great between her and Zion, she can answer them and we can all move on."

"We can move on? Oh no, don't go saying 'we'. This all you. I'm not hopping on this bandwagon. I'm going to sit back and watch."

Star and Patty arrive at the apartment exchanging hugs and kisses with Lea. She takes them upstairs to see the nursery. They 'ooooooo' and 'aaaaaaah' over all the changes. Paint, clothes, furniture, and the hand-me-downs from Star.

Patty questions Lea about clothing choices, the placement of the beds, why the boys are setup in the bedroom farthest from Zion's bedroom. She asks about plans for babysitting, daycare, and Lea's working schedule after the boys arrive.

Lea's responses go from elaborate details to short word answers. *Why the fuck is this woman questioning me about this random shit that has nothing to do with her?*

Star recognizes Lea's tone and gives her mother a 'cut-it-out look'. Patty catches on and changes the direction.

"So, where is that son of mine?" Patty asks.

Looking at the clock on the wall, Lea says, "He's down at Wendy's. He may be back up for dinner, or you guys can stop by if you like," Lea tells them. At this point she's had enough of Patty Landon.

"Nope, we came to hang out with you. That's if you don't mind," Patty says. She has one more question she must ask Lea and she's not leaving until she does.

They eat and talk about the girls. Lea tells them, Zion have decided on names for the boys, giving them first and middle names. Caden Royal and Isaac Tanner. Zion felt he couldn't name them "Junior" or "Second," but he was determined they have the family men names in their somehow. The ladies get excited constantly referring to them as Caden and Isaac now instead of the boys.

"Guys please don't do that in front of Wendy. I don't know what Zion has told her yet about names, and this should be his news to tell not anyone else's."

"Lea how can you be so calm and understanding about all this?" Star asks.

"I've had my moments. Zion and I communicate. As much as there are parts I don't really want to hear about, I'm not going to stop him from talking. Communication is what we have going for us."

As they're sitting in the living room Zion arrives home. "Well hello ladies." He gives his mother and sister a kiss and sits down next to Lea on the couch hugging her. This is the first time in days he's been back upstairs before eight.

He comes back to their bed every night but it's been late, long after she's fallen asleep. Lea makes sure he releases any pent-up emotions of what he experiences with Wendy. She's having more pain, lays in bed more and is having more fantasies about them as a family.

Lea lays awake with him talking until he drifts off to sleep. It's their routine. When they wake up the next day, he's rejuvenated and Lea's on automatic pilot. Their sex life has slowed. Instead of long, sexual and passionate hours of love making and multiple orgasms, they're now sustaining themselves with shower quickies or early morning or late-night fast fucks. It's nothing like the passion for slow love making like they had before.

"How are you? Can I get you anything to eat or drink?" she asks him.

"I ate downstairs. Wendy was tired, so I figured I would come home a bit early tonight." He grabs Lea's glass drinking, staring at her. "This is perfect." He turns to his mother and sister asking them how they're doing.

When Lea turns back to Patty and Star, his mother is frowning at her. *Shit now what.* Star is looking at her grinning.

"We're doing great. We wanted to see the nursery. How you been bro?" Star asks.

"Worried about Wendy. As expected, the doctors aren't seeing any improvement." Zion gets quiet and drifts off. Lea touches his leg, and he comes back instantly talking again.

Recognizing Zion needs some rest, Star gets up announcing it was time for she and Patty to leave. She wants to get her mother out of there, hoping she has asked all the questions she needs to ask Lea.

"Before we go, I did want to talk with Lea. Privately. If that's okay?" Zion's mother asks.

"Mom. What's up? You have something to say to Lea, you can say it in front of me." Zion's not liking where a private talk could go with his mother and Lea.

"Mom. Whatever you think you want to say. Please don't." Star says.

"Look. I've been thinking about this for some time, and I need to know. Well. I'll say it. Lea, I need to know are you with my son for his money? Or an easy ready-made family? Why are you sticking around? What are you getting out of this? Is my son paying you to stay?" Patty rattles off her questions over Zion's and Star's objections.

Star is screaming, "Mom how the hell can you ask that? What is wrong with you? Do you have any idea how that sounds? This is none of your business."

Zion is sitting on the edge of the couch, confronting his mother, "Mom. Of all the crazy stuff I've put up with you doing in my life over the years, this is too far. This is why I keep you out of my personal life. I'm not going to allow you to disrespect Lea or treat her like this."

Lea screams, "EVERYBODY! SHUT THE FUCK UP! NOW!" Lea is sitting on the couch rubbing her shaking legs trying not to cry so she can get out what she wants to say. Zion reaches to touch her, but she waves him away.

"Lea, you don't have to answer any of my mother's questions," Zion says.

"Yeah, I do. She's been giving me the third degree since she arrived. Anyway, it's what a lot of people are going to be thinking. And saying. That I'm the lil gold digger waiting to get paid. Mrs. Landon, understand this. I have my own life, my own career, my own mind, and my choices are none of your goddamn business. I don't need Zion's or your money. If I have to walk the fucking streets to survive, I will never need you or your son's money. To put it quite simply, I'm with your son because I love him. I'm in love with him. And I'm happy for him. Whether he and I end up married or I legally become the mother to HIS SONS is HIS choice. From this day forward I will NEVER explain myself to you. EVER." The last word comes out shaky with Lea taking a deep breath. She has her hands balled into fists at her sides. "Goodbye to you both." Lea stands and walks to the office, slamming the door. The sound reverberates throughout the apartment.

Lea sits at her desk, taking deep breaths, trying to calm down. She calls her mom telling her what just happened.

"I'll be there in a few," her mother says.

Lea paces the office.

Zion is in the living room arguing with his mother. "Mom, what the hell?"

Star confronts her, "Seriously Mom. There are times when you need to shut up. God, how can you say those things to Lea?"

"I'm just worried about Zion. And I can't believe no one has questioned Lea about this. Why would she stick around if it's not the money?" Patty says.

"Mom, how about because Lea loves Zion? What's the matter, you don't believe anyone can love us for us and not our money. You accused Garrett of wanting me for my money, and I had nothing at the time."

"I will always look out for this family. You two will understand when your kids are our ages."

Before Zion can respond he gets a call from security announcing that Lea's mother has arrived.

"I be goddamn." He yells. "Show her up. Mom, don't you say another word. Do you understand me?"

"Watch whom you're talking to."

"No, Mom. At this point, you need to respect my household," Zion says while walking to the door opening it for Ms. Adams.

Without a hello, Lea's mother tells Zion, "Take me to my daughter. NOW!"

"Hello, Ms. Adams. Sure. She's in our office." Zion says walking her over there. He knocks. "Lea your mom is here." He opens the door and see's Lea sitting at her desk. She keeps her eyes on him as her mother walks in. "I'll leave you two alone," he says backing out and closing the door.

Turning to his mother and sister he takes a step toward them then stops. Zion roars. "UGGGGGGHHHHHHH!!!!!!" He actually roars.

He wants to comfort Lea. He wants to verbally throttle his mother. He wants to go back to the carefree times of the beginning of his relationship with Lea. "UUUGGGGGGHHHHHHH!!!!!!!!!!"

Ms. Adams goes to her daughter and holds her while she cries. "I'm here sweetheart. Cry it all out." She jumps at Zion's roar but continues holding Lea, rocking her against her chest.

Star and Patty jump at Zion's roar.

"Mom! Look, I don't know what the hell this is all about, and at this point, I don't even care. You have no right to say that to Lea. None. Seriously!"

"Maybe it's time Star and I leave," she says to Zion as he comes back into the room.

"Mom, ya think?" Star says. She knows Zion is angry and is barely holding back going off on their mother.

"Son, I—. Sorry seems rather trite at this time. I can explain to Lea—."

"Are you kidding me? I don't want you near Lea or me right now." Zion picks up his phone. "Ryan, I need you to meet me in the garage. I need you to follow my mother and sister home. Then come back here. I may need you to get Lea's mother home safely. She's here and I don't know if she came alone or not." Ending the call and turning to his mother and sister, Zion speaks to Patty, "Mom, I love you, but don't ever do this again. Let's go." Zion escorts them to Star's car. "Shit mom. What happened to my boy is in love. Let me meet my daughter-in-law. You were so happy for me at the birthday party and now this. I don't even wanna know why. Take it to your grave."

"Zion, there's so much going on that little things can be missed. I thought if I could have a talk with Lea, maybe head off some issues," Patty says.

Star speaks before Zion does, "Mom, head off what? And why is it any of your business to head off anything? You really think after all these years, Zion doesn't think of the tiniest details with anything that goes on with him and Landon Enterprises?" Star has always been amazed and her brother's thought process. Becoming so rich at a young age the way he did has always left her in awe. She's learned a lot of business acumen from her big brother.

"Okay. Maybe I went a little too far."

"Oh, you think?" Zion asks sarcastically.

"Hey, I'm still the parent here."

Zion ignores what Patty says, "Mom, come to me with your concerns. Lord, I never imagined I would need to protect Lea from you. I get it now Star."

"Oh, so you two be having secret discussions about me."

"Yes, we do. Especially when it comes to our relationships," Star admits.

Patty clams up, hurt. *My kids have secret conversations about handling me.*

Down in the garage, Ryan meets them. "Sir, Ms. Adams arrived alone. It would seem she didn't have time to call her shadow. I can call him or get back here as soon as I can to escort her home."

"Thank you, Ryan. I appreciate that. When I get back upstairs, I'll let you know what's up. Good night, everyone." Zion turns and walks away not even looking at his mother.

When he gets upstairs the office door is open. Lea and her mother are standing in the kitchen. Ms. Adams turns to Zion. "Zion, I'm not gonna discuss what happened tonight. My daughter needed me, and I came. Whenever she needs me, I will ALWAYS come. Do we understand."

"Yes ma'am. Perfectly. Whatever she told you, I can assure you, I will never allow her to be treated like that again. Not even by my mother."

"That's for you to handle. Well, I guess I'll get myself home."

"Mom, it's late. You can stay. Zion has another bedroom." Lea offers up his home without even asking, daring him to object.

"Ma'am, Lea is right. You're more than welcome to stay. Or we can drive you home. Whatever you prefer." No way is Zion gonna disagree, but he really wants to be alone with Lea.

"Y'all can drive me home. Lord knows I'll only come out driving at night to get to my daughter." Ms. Adams responds back, ensuring Zion understands. Nothing will keep Ms. Adams from getting to Lea when she's needed.

In the elevator, Lea stands close to her mother. She has yet to look at or speak to Zion. He's standing across from them. Exiting the elevator, they walk outside to Sam standing at the car waiting.

"Sam. How did you know?" Zion asks him.

"Sir, it's my job. I'll get Ms. Adams home safely. You two can go back up. I got this."

"Well dang. The head Shadow in charge driving me home. I feel so special."

"Mom, why you being such a smart ass?" Lea asks her, smiling at the way she's acting. She loves it when her mother gets this way. The change between her and Zion's mother lightens the mood.

"Because before the two of you get into a fight, I want to see you smile." Ms. Adams takes Lea into her arms. Lea is a foot taller than her mom, so she has to lean over a bit. "My child I'm so proud of you. Every day. Remember that."

"Thanks mom. Text me when you get to the house." Lea says.

"I will."

Sam and Ms. Adams drive off.

"So, are we going to fight? I'd like to get back upstairs to do so in private," he says.

"Okay." Lea walks back into the building with Zion following closely behind her. This time he stands close to her on the ride up.

"Baby, I thought you would leave me tonight," he says.

"Zion, do you believe I'm with you for your money? I need to know if you have ever believed that. Even a little."

Back in the apartment he sits her down on the couch and forces her to look at him. "Kitten, I've never once ever believed you're with me for my money."

"Prove it."

"What. How am I supposed to prove that."

"Pre-nup. With your resources, you have lawyers on retainer. You can't tell me you haven't been working on the legalities already. I want my own lawyer, independent of yours. If you believe I'm not after you for your money, I wanna know about all the legal stuff you have setup regarding me, Caden, Isaac, and us as a family. Especially if things happen to fail between us."

"Okay first off, this failing between us ain't gonna happen. I've said it before. Us finding each other so late in life, connecting the way we have, growing together, we're not getting this close to nirvana and it fails."

"How can you be so confident?"

"Dammit Lea stop it. Stop questioning what we have. I know my mother has made your doubts resurface but understand, I love and trust you."

"Your family doesn't. I wanna know legally what are my rights marrying you and being the mother of your sons. Legally, right now they're your sons. And Wendy's."

"I wanna scream again. Okay. I'll prove it. I'll get the documents for you and your lawyer to review."

"Thank you."

"You're welcome. Now forget about what my mother has said and remember we're in this together fighting for us."

"Oh, trust me. I'm fighting even harder now." Lea has resolved that Mrs. Landon will always remain Mrs. Landon.

-38-

Zion and Lea's days go on about the same. They get up, she goes to work for a few hours, to her house to do some packing, then home to the apartment ensuring she's there before Zion gets home. Zion goes down to be with Wendy or take her to doctors' appointments. He returns sometimes for dinner or late at night to sleep. Lea does everything she can to keep him focused and not drowning in misery.

Lea doesn't know what he said to his mother and Star the night they left. Royal called to discuss it with him that Friday. Zion apologized for the way things were said but not for what he said, and his mother apologized to him and to Lea. She even sent Lea two dozen yellow roses. Before Lea could trash them, Mrs. Vance moved them to the dining room table.

Every day, Lea talks with her mom, Bobbie, and Gordon about what's going on, keeping them updated. Gordon and Bobbie get the full details, and Lea gives her mom the edited version making sure not to worry her.

Gordon comes by on Monday to see the nursery. "Whoa, this is some fucking building and this apartment. The guy really is wealthy, isn't he?"

"Will you stop that?"

"Man, I told you your time would come and it really came."

"You know I'm not with him for the money. The man is sexy. He wants me."

"Anything from cray-cray lately?"

"I haven't gotten any emails or texts but Zion has. They mention Caden and Isaac, not by name of course. The say when Addison and Zion get together, they'll find me and have me locked away. I don't get the find me part."

"Really, what's he doing about it?"

"Increased security detail. Cameras turned back on."

"Well look I'm going to take off. All this richness is making me feel nervous. I mean look at this view. Just amazing. Hey, have you ever done the Green Acres dance up here? You know just for the heck of it. Wait let me go do it." Gordon goes out onto the balcony and does the Green Acres opening credits re-enactment.

"You're sick you know that?" Lea tells him.

"Yes, he really is. If you gonna do the Green Acres move, get it right man. Put some heart into it. Like this? You gotta get the turn in there and fling the doors wide open," Zion says.

Lea turns around and watches Zion walk to the balcony and do the same move in an overly dramatic display. He and Gordon stand there comparing their moves.

"Thanks man, I needed that laugh." They come back into the apartment and have a seat. Lea gets them all drinks.

"How you been?" Gordon asks Zion.

"I'm good as can be expected. Glad you finally stopped by. You're welcome to come by anytime Lea wants you to. I want her family and friends to feel welcome here. And to not help her with anymore disappearing acts without telling me," he tells him.

"Thanks man. I'll remember that. I like the nursery. Not overly frou-frou, more manly. You two will make great parents. Just keep the laughter flowing. And the sex hot," Gordon says.

"Uh yeah, I don't think we have an issue with that part," Lea says.

"We can't keep our hands off each other. I don't even think having two screaming boys in the house will diminish that. And this is a topic I don't want to discuss with the first guy the woman I love had sex with. Man, you deflowered her," Zion says.

"I may have deflowered her, but you're defiling her. She doesn't tell me about anything but every time she looks at you, she gets flushed and keeps looking at your crotch. Yes, Lea keeps staring at your crotch. Man, I'm going home to sex my wife. Now I'm horny." Gordon gets up to leave, calling Lily on the way out telling her how much he misses her and wants her. Zion walks him out making sure he gets to his car okay.

"So, you not pissed at Gordon any longer for the dinner at Ballpark Village?" she asks him when he returns.

"No. I wasn't pissed at him then. I was angry at you. At the immaturity you displayed. It reminded me of the games played in relationships. You're not that type of person. I don't ever want you stooping that low and doing that shit ever again. We're not teenagers Lea. This is a serious situation we're going through," Zion says staring at her. She doesn't look away. He's right. Everything he said he's 100% correct. She has no come back.

"How's Wendy doing?" she asks him.

"She's worse. I'm going to call the doctor tomorrow about having her admitted. She says she's doing okay and managing the pain but I don't trust her judgement. I know admitting her is essentially signing her death certificate, but I don't know what else to do. I can't continue to watch her suffer like this."

"Bear, you're doing the right thing. Tell you what, I have to go into the office tomorrow to drop some stuff off. After that, I'll come back here. I shouldn't be gone more than an hour. Make the call to the doctor's office as soon as you wake up and get her there. I'll be right behind you."

"I'll do that. Let's get some sleep. I'm kinda tired and I'd like to hold you right now."

They go to bed and Lea has Zion lay in her arms. He drifts off to sleep about an hour later. "Sweetheart I'm here for you," she whispers to him.

-39-

Instead of calling the doctors about Wendy, Zion decides to go down to see her. He wants to be sure having her admitted is the right thing to do. He's started letting himself into the apartment rather than interrupting Becky's care of Wendy. When he gets in, he sees that Wendy is crying and holding her head.

"Zion, make the pain go away!" Wendy moans, holding her head rocking back and forth on the couch. "I can't do this anymore. Please. It hurts."

Becky is sitting next to Wendy, taking her vitals. The phone is on Becky's lap. Zion can hear the dial tone as he walks in. "Mr. Landon. Thank God you're here, I was just about to call you. Ms. Wendy, sir, isn't doing well. We need to get her to the hospital. I've called for an ambulance." Becky turns off the phone and tosses it onto the other couch. She moves to Wendy's other side, making room for Zion.

"Wendy, I'm here," Zion says. He sits down and holds Wendy. Her breathing is labored and she's hot. He asks Becky nervously, "How long has this been going on?"

"It just started, sir, about five minutes ago," Becky tells him.

He takes out his phone and calls Wendy's doctors, informing them the ambulance was about to arrive to take Wendy to the hospital. Zion doesn't know what's going on, but he sure as hell isn't going to risk anything.

The ambulance arrives and Wendy is loaded onto the gurney and out of the building into the waiting vehicle parked at the curb. Zion and Becky hop in and they are driven to the hospital.

Upon arrival, Wendy is whisked into the emergency department to a room with equipment and nurses waiting. Zion is left standing in the hallway with Becky. Wendy's doctor comes out to speak to Zion.

"Mr. Landon. We've stabilized Wendy. At this time, she's awake and alert. Her ob-gyn has recommended a C-section."

"Why would you need to do a C-section if she's alert?" Zion asks.

"Sir, there's a good chance we'll have to administer heavy drugs to Wendy. These medications can affect the babies. According to the ultrasound, they're alert and moving. We would like to keep it that way. Wendy, on the other hand, is not doing well. She doesn't have the energy for a vaginal birth. Her breathing is labored and her heartbeat is irregular. She's fighting all medications. We have you on record as legal proxy for medical decision. In this capacity, you can legally decide what to do medically for her and the boys. I wanted to make you aware of what's going on."

"Make me aware? Doctor, I'm not stupid. You can lay it out for me." Zion's frustration and fear with the situation is causing him to be short and direct.

Realizing now is not the time to be gentle, the doctor explains, "Wendy could slip into a coma at any moment. A blood vessel in her brain can erupt, and she'll be left brain dead. We want to deliver the boys as soon as we can."

"Then do it. What do you want from me?"

"If you'll step over here to the nurse's station," the doctor says, pointing across the hall, "they'll get your signature agreeing to the delivery of the boys and to do whatever is medically necessary for Wendy."

Zion moves over to the nurse's station and signs the documents.

"Well, now what?" he asks the doctor.

"Wendy has been asking for you." The doctor gestures, "This way."

The doctor escorts Zion to Wendy's room. All around him, there are beeping noises, medical personnel running around. Checking Wendy. Checking the boys. Zion gets a glimpse of an image on a monitor of what he can only assume are the boys in Wendy's stomach. Hearing Wendy say his name, he goes to her and sits down on the bed.

"Zion. Boys," she gets out between breaths. "Don't. Die." She breathes in quickly again. "Safe."

"Wendy, the doctors are doing everything they can."

"Good. Sleep. Tired. Pain," Wendy says.

Zion watches the nurse give Wendy a dose of what he thinks is pain meds because she instantly quiets, and the blips on the monitor stop moving so fast.

"Wait? What just happened? They aren't moving."

"Sir, it's the pain meds. It's affecting the boys. We have to get Wendy to the operating room," her ob-gyn says.

Zion moves aside, watching as they prepare to wheel Wendy out of the room.

"Mr. Landon, I can escort you back to the waiting room. The doctors will meet you there to give you updates," a nurse says.

Zion turns to her with a blank look. "Yeah, okay fine."

As Zion turns to go into the waiting room, he sees Lea approaching. He instantly calms down. "Where? How?" he starts to ask her. "I was about to call you and let you know what was happening."

Arriving back at the apartment after her morning errands, Lea and Ryan watched the activity taking place inside the ambulance. She caught a glimpse of Zion and Becky in the back.

Without instruction, Ryan knows to follow behind, keeping up as best as he can without causing an accident or getting pulled over. Lea sends out the agreed-upon text to everyone, letting them know to get to the hospital.

Ryan pulls up to the emergency room entrance and drops Lea off. Upon entering, she sees a nurse leading Zion toward the waiting room. She rushes to catch up with them.

"I saw the ambulance leave the apartment building as Ryan and I were returning. We followed you here," she says looking into his eyes.

"Lea, I was so scared. Something told me to go see her. She was complaining of a headache," he tries to explain, but trails off, going silent.

"Sweetheart, you did the right thing. Let's sit down." She puts her hand in his, and they walk to the back of the room for seats. His family's arrived, and they are following behind them.

Zion is pacing, he's so scared. Lea guides him to a chair because he looks as if he's about to wander off. "Bear, sit down," she tells him.

When he's settled, he finally notices his family has gathered around him. His support system. Everyone's there, even Sam, Mrs. Vance, Tom and Crystal. Lea starts to stand to greet everyone, but Zion keeps her pinned to her seat next to him.

She holds onto his hand while his mother is bending down in front of him, kissing him, reassuring him as only a mother can. "Sweetheart, we're here for you. We all are. Look around. Everyone's here for you. Whatever you need, we got you. Okay?"

He looks at her, shaking his head. "Thanks, Mom."

"What happened?" his father asks Becky.

"Ms. Wendy started having a headache, much worse than before. She started begging for pain medication. I called for an ambulance and was about to call Mr. Landon when he walked in. Her vitals were dropping rapidly. I knew we had to get her to the hospital," Becky explains.

Zion clasps Lea's hand between his, needing her strength, her warmth, her love. She hugs him. "Bear, I'm here," she whispers, wrapping her arm around him, caressing his shoulders.

The doctor comes into the waiting room informing Zion they will be performing the C-section as the boys are displaying signs of distress. "We'll keep you abreast of what's going on."

Zion nods. The doctor leaves and a nurse approaches him.

"Mr. Landon, you can't be directly in the room with Ms. Noelin, but we're taking her to an operating room that has a viewing window. You can see your sons being born. Would you like to go?"

"No, I, I can't do that," he says.

Lea urges, "Bear, yes you can. Go see your sons being born."

He stares at Lea, not understanding. She stands up and holds out her hand, forcing him to stand. "Zion, come on."

He stands up, pulling her with him as he walks behind the nurse. They get to a door and he hesitates.

Lea prods him on, "Zion, I'll be waiting for you right here. Love you."

He turns to Lea mouthing, "I love you."

As the door closes, Lea feels left out. She wants to go watch but understands only Zion can.

Gordon goes to Lea's side. "You did great. I'm here for you. Remember that," he says.

"Thanks, Gordon." Lea turns back to everyone. They say nothing, instead taking seats in small groups, bracing for the news.

Zion is led into an observation operating room. He assumes Wendy is sedated because she hasn't moved. There's a barrier hiding the view of her lower body. All the commotion is taking place beyond what Zion can see. Within minutes of standing there, he watches a pair of hands lift a baby above the barrier. Zion smiles and tears up. He mouths "Hello, Isaac."

Isaac is quickly moved to a side table. Zion watches him get cleaned up and then put into a glass covered miniature bed. He turns back to Wendy and sees Caden is being lifted above the barrier. Zion wipes tears from his face while grinning from ear to ear. He looks around, wanting to scream, shout, and jump for joy, hating that Lea isn't there to hug and experience this with him. Caden is placed in his own glass-covered miniature bed and they're both rolled out of the operating room.

Behind the barrier, the ob-gyn closes up Wendy's abdomen. As Zion is thinking all went well, a doctor moves quickly to Wendy. From what Zion can tell, he's speaking to her but not getting a response. Shutters on the window slowly move to block Zion's view. A nurse comes into the room to escort him back to his waiting family. "What's going on?" he asks.

"Sir, I'm not sure. But the doctor will be with you as soon as he can." She walks away quickly, leaving Zion at the waiting room entrance.

Before Lea can reach him or Zion can reach her, his family hops up, going to him, bombarding him with questions.

"Zion, what happened? Is everything okay?"

"How are the boys?"

"We've been going nuts waiting. Is Wendy, okay?"

"Everyone, please shut up. To answer your questions. The C-section went smoothly. The boys are tiny but breathing on their own. I got a quick glimpse of them. They were taken away to the NICU. It looked like Wendy made it through the birth, but I was rushed out of there so fast. Something's wrong." He rushes out, moving closer and closer to Lea, trying to get to her. He needs to feel her arms around him. Before he gets to her, Wendy's doctor comes to the waiting room. Zion turns to him.

"Mr. Landon, Wendy's vitals are dropping. She's going in and out of consciousness. I don't know how much longer she has," he says.

"What? No. She can't. She hasn't seen the boys yet," he says.

This hurts Lea's feelings, but she understands.

"Please, I need her to see them. Can't you do something."

"Sir, we can bring the incubators to her room. It's not something we usually do but they are stabilized. Because of the situation we can do this."

"Can I come? I don't want Wendy to be alone." Zion says.

"Of course, Sir. As Ms. Noelin's POA and the father of the boys, you have every right to be present."

"Great." Zion breaks away from his family and goes over to Lea. "Baby, I'll be right back. I need to do this. I love you so much."

"Zion, go. Go be with Wendy, Isaac, and Caden."

Zion is taken to Wendy's room. He rushes to the side of her bed. They have her sitting up.

She watches him walking toward her. Her hands are gripping the sheet. When he sits down, he can barely hear her mumble, "Babies."

"They've arrived and have been stabilized."

"See," she mumbles.

As Wendy says this, two nurses are pushing incubators into the room. They place them next to her bed. Zion moves to the side and helps her lean in to get a look. Tears run down her cheeks. The nurses take them back out of the room. Zion sits back down on the bed, getting as close to Wendy as he can. She places her head on his shoulder, closing her eyes.

The doctor checks her vitals. "Sir, she's slipped into a coma. I don't know how much time she has. Brain activity is diminishing."

"Can I hold her a little longer?" he asks.

"Of course. Talk to her."

"Wendy, you're a wonderful human being. Don't think that you're not. You've done a wonderful job giving these boys life. You made the ultimate sacrifice, and they'll always love you for that. No matter what, I'll make sure of that." Zion keeps talking, encouraging words, caressing Wendy's head and shoulders, kissing her temple and pressing his skin against hers.

"I know you're tired. Tired of the pain. You just gave birth to two wonderful healthy baby boys. It's okay to go now, sweetheart. It really is. I'll raise them, and they'll know you. Everything you went through to give them life they'll know. I promise you."

Her breathing has slowed and her heart rate has weakened. The doctors are aware of the DNR directive. There's nothing they can do to save her. The nurses turn off the sounds of the machine to avoid disturbing this final heartbreaking goodbye.

"Wendy, thank you. Thank you so much." Zion, crying, hugs her tighter. "Thank you. I can't say it enough. I love you for giving me this opportunity." She slips away with one last breath, cradled in Zion's arms.

Recalling Lea's dream, the night they were first together of not dying alone, he feels privileged being here with Wendy. No one should die alone, feeling unloved. He'll do everything within his power to make sure Lea never feels that way. Never feel unloved, unwanted. After Wendy's final breath, he gives her a kiss on the forehead and a nurse escorts him out. He turns around in time to see another nurse covering her body and calling the date and time of death. September 15, 2016, 11:05 pm.

-40-

Experiencing Wendy die in his arms has drained Zion. He stands outside of her hospital room, attempting to gather his emotions. Staring out a window overlooking the hospital parking lot, he lets the tears flow silently.

Dammit, I need Lea right now.

Taking a deep breath and squaring his shoulders, he wipes his face on the sleeve of his shirt. He senses someone behind him. He turns and look into a nurse's eyes. She asks, "Mr. Landon, would you like to see your sons?"

"Yes, I would, more than you can imagine. But my family, they would like to see them also."

"At this time, I'm afraid you're the only one allowed to see them in the NICU. If you follow me, I'll take you there. Zion is escorted to a room where he puts on sterile clothing and a nurse takes him to the NICU to see his boys. They were placed in incubators as a precaution as they were born two months premature. Zion approaches them, staring at their little bodies hooked up to wires.

My small, adorable sons.

"Congratulations, Mr. Landon, on the birth of your sons Caden and Isaac," another nurse says.

Zion looks down on them, crying, wanting to hold them, smell them, touch them, needing to bond with them. He doesn't know how long he stood there; he knew he couldn't walk away.

"When can I hold them?" he asks the nurse.

The pediatrician walks in and responds for her.

"Twenty-four hours, Mr. Landon. We can have a cot made up for you tonight and you can stay here. Tomorrow you'll get to hold them. They're some strong preemies. All their vitals are strong, no issues with lungs, and they're breathing well. I have plans to release them once they have started feeding, suckling and gaining some weight.

I'm so sorry about their mother. But she did a wonderful job bringing these two guys into the world. Take care and try to get a couple hours of sleep tonight." The doctor looks over the charts, makes some notations and leaves.

"My family. They're out in the waiting room. Do they know anything and is Lea Adams on the approved list to see Caden and Isaac. She's their adopted mom," he says to the nurse.

"The doctor has informed them about Ms. Noelin. Yes, a Miss Lea Adams has been added to the visitors list. But no one in your family can visit at this time. The hospital has cameras set up in certain areas of the NICU." The nurse points out cameras in different areas of the room. "They allow us to maneuver the babies over and family and friends can view from a monitor outside of this room. Your sons are pointed toward one of the cameras and your family is waiting to see," she says smiling.

Zion looks up and waves and points to the boys. The monitor shows a split view of him and the babies and of his family waving, grinning, laughing, and taking pictures, trying to get a good look. He doesn't see Lea.

Where the hell is she?

"Thank you for pointing that out. I need to go get their mom. Would it be okay to come back with her?"

"Of course."

Zion exits the NICU and goes to the waiting room for hugs and greetings and congratulations.

"Where's Lea?" he asks.

"She went to go to talk with the doctors about Wendy's body, getting it released and sent to the funeral home. She insisted," his sister says.

Lea has confirmed with the doctors the date of when Wendy's body will be released. This entire experience has been nerve-racking for her. With a hell of a lot of confusion.

It's supposed to be her and Zion going through this. She's supposed to be by his side. At the forefront with them comforting one another. But every time she went to get close to him, his family was right there with Lea being pushed to the side. To the back.

You would think I don't fucking exist any longer.

If it wasn't for Gordon, she would've probably left. He's stayed at Lea's side. He hates that Zion's family has not given HER the respect that she deserves after all this time.

"Gordon, why are you so angry?" she asks him. He's been giving her his "this shit you doing is getting on my nerves" look a lot tonight.

"It bugs the hell out of me how all his family is so focused on him and not giving you any kind of acknowledgement. It's pissing me off. If I hadn't been here, you would be going through this alone. I mean, seriously, you're up here taking care of the woman's remains making sure they get to the funeral home to be cremated. Shit, Lea, how much more of this will you continue to put up with?" he asks her.

"Gordon, remember my dreams. Dying alone and unloved. I'm going to make sure her wishes are carried out, and she's not left in some damn pauper's grave to be forgotten. Don't be so damn small-minded about this right now. Please. I'll fall apart later and you can do I told you so's all you want to. Not now. I wanted you here to allow me to vent, not for you to give me your looks of pity. Lay the fuck off me," she tells him.

"Some way to spend your birthday. His sons are born and their mother dies the day before. Do you even think Zion has remembered?" he asks. "Happy forty-fifth birthday."

"Thanks. It's after midnight, isn't it? My birthday is his phone lock code. Unless he has unlocked it for any reason, I don't think he's remembered yet. Even then, he may be so out of it that he hasn't connected the dots. Now I'll never want to celebrate it."

"Oh, don't you fucking dare say that. I'll beat your ass myself. Your birthday is your day, don't let them take that away from you, too. So, what will happen to Wendy now?"

"I've identified the body. She'll be moved to the funeral home. They'll cremate her. She requested her burial be over as soon as possible and for Zion to get on with raising the boys. Am I wrong for looking forward to that? If all goes as planned the service will be held September twenty-second, and the happiness will begin. Selfish of me or not?" she asks him.

"No, not at all selfish. It's about time you start being selfish. Have you guys decided anything about the wedding? Have you moved everything into his place yet?"

"Wedding no. Moved in, about fifty percent. It's my house. I'll get through it. Are you coming to the service? After all this I'll understand if you don't want to."

"I'll be there. Count on me. Always there for you, Lea. Let's go see those babies and give congrats to the new daddy and mommy. I want to see this family's reactions anyway. What? Don't look at me like that. I'll be good. Enough."

They get on the elevators, pushing the button for the Neonatal floor. As the doors open, Zion is standing there about to get on. He pulls Lea off and into his arms.

"Hi Zion, how are you doing?" she asks him.

He pulls back, looking at her intently and starts crying. "I'm a grown man, and I can't stop crying."

"It's okay and expected. There are a lot of emotions going on with you right now. The boys are here. Your sons are here," she says to him.

"Lea, our boys. *Our* sons are here. You have to see them. Come on."

They go in to see Caden and Isaac, and Gordon walks to the waiting room. It's time he confronts the family.

Gordon stares at the monitor watching Zion and Lea looking at the boys. *She finally gets to be a mom. Not in the conventional way, but she is and she has a man who loves her almost as much as I do. That family of Zion's is on my shit list though.* From behind him someone addresses him.

"Young man, who are you?" Gordon turns around and looks directly into the spitting image of an older Zion. His father, Royal Landon. Gordon offers up silent apologies to Lea.

"I'm Lea's best friend. Gordon," he doesn't offer his hand in a shake. He ain't got that kinda respect for him. Not yet. "I'm the only one in this group who has supported Lea through these last few weeks."

"We've all supported Lea," Zion's mother says.

"Gordon, stop. Now you know I've been there for Lea," Crystal interjects.

"Well, okay, let me clarify my statement. Mrs. Landon, I know all about the money questions."

Zion's mother looks like she's about to say something, but Royal halts her by putting his hand on her arm. "Young man, my wife has apologized for that unfortunate occurrence."

"Unfortunate occurrence? Yeah, okay? Well, back to my questions? How many times have any of you visited her? How many of you have asked her did she need anything? A hug, a shoulder to cry on, an ear to vent to? How many times have any of you made sure she was fully welcomed into your tight-knit group? Oh yeah, that one dinner. You happened to ask about her when you happened to see her? Is that it? All night I've watched you all huddle and whisper. Every time Lea looked at any of you, you would look away. Is there something she doesn't know about or is she the butt of all your jokes, someone to pity, to feel sorry for? I know Zion loves her and this was her choice, but dammit, I just wish you people could have shown her the same kind of love and support you lavished, yes, I said lavished, on Wendy. Did you guys really need to be told to reach out to Lea to include her? That's just ridiculous," Gordon says in frustration.

They stand there stunned.

Zion's father was about to get into Gordon's ass along with Garrett but was stopped by Star.

"Well, we've been put in our places," Zion's mother says. "And we, or at least I have no rebuttal. I don't know about anyone else, but young man, Gordon, is it? You're right. I have treated Lea horribly lately. I hope she and you give me the opportunity to fix that. As you stated, our son loves her very much. She makes him, has made him, a very happy man."

"Look, my goal and presence here is to make sure Lea is okay and being looked after. I don't care what any of you think about me or what I said. I'm not going to allow any of you to continue to disrespect her or devalue her place in Zion's life or as those boys' mother."

Gordon walks away from them and stands at the door of the waiting room. *I've had my say, I don't need to be huddled with them.* He calls Lily and gives her a full update on what happened, ending any chance any one could to talk to him about what he just said.

Zion and Lea return, looking at everyone.

"Do I even want to know?" she asks, looking at Gordon.

"Probably not, but I'm sure the 'family' will inform you. Anyway, you know me. It's what I do. I'm going to take off now. Lily sends her love and congrats. Zion, man, it's been a hard road for you. I don't think I could have done this. Lea, I love you. You know I'm always here ready to fight any battles. Even those you ignore or don't see coming." He hugs and kisses her on the cheek. "Call me when you need me. Anytime. Happy birthday," he whispers in her ear.

"Goodbye everyone," he says, without even looking at the others.

"What was that all about? Will someone clue me the fuck in?" Zion asks.

"We were set straight, and we deserved it. Let's give these other parents and family the opportunity to look at their babies and go for coffee or something," Royal says.

When they all, or those that elected to stay, settle into the cafeteria, Royal tells them about what Gordon said. Lea has nothing to say. Gordon only repeated what she's told him and what he has or has not witnessed. They apologize profusely and promise to do better. As long as Lea had Zion's love and reassurance, what his family gave or feel about Wendy is on them.

"Baby, why didn't you say anything to me," he asks.

"You had enough to worry about. And before you go there, this wasn't about hiding anything from you. Zion, you were being pulled in so many directions. That was a battle not worth bringing up. Now it's about the future, so let's focus on that. Wendy's body is on its way to the funeral home once the hospital has released it. We can discuss the service when we get home. I've made some changes you'll like. Wendy's last wish was to keep it simple. Whatever you decide on, I'll take care of it."

"Lea, why don't Mom and I handle things for Wendy from this point on?" Star says. "You and Zion need to be with the boys. Please, let us do this. For you guys. You've been doing so much and, well, it's time something was done for you."

Lea looks at her. "Thanks Star." She takes out the paperwork and hands it to her. Then her phone starts buzzing. Looking at it, she sees it's her mom, calling with birthday greetings. "Excuse me, I need to take this in private."

Lea gets up walking away from Zion and everyone answering the call.

Zion watches her, the weariness in her movements. She smiles at the call, probably her mom wishing her a happy birthday. He has major plans in their future to make this up to her and to never ignore her on her day. Lea's date of birth is as important to him as his sons' date of birth, maybe even more. Never will he allow her day to be diminished in any way. He stands up, following her, needing to give her a birthday hug and kiss.

She listens to her mom singing her annual birthday song. She thanks her and gives her the update on the boys being born and Wendy's death. Her mom tells Lea to give Zion her congratulations and tells her how proud she is that Lea has supported him in this and she can't wait to meet her grandsons. If that is still the case. "I hope so mom, I really hope so. I'll talk to you later. Get some sleep it's late or early."

Lea ends the call and turns to see Zion standing close, listening and watching her.

"She's up early. Everything okay?" he asks.

"Yes. Fine. She's a night owl. She sends her congratulations and says she can't wait to meet the boys. How are you holding up?" she asks him wanting to deflect any questions about why she walked away to take the call.

He walks over to her and takes her face into his hands, making her look at him. "Happy birthday Lea. I love you. I know things are crazy right now. We'll celebrate as soon as we can. I haven't forgotten," he kisses her.

"Thanks, Zion. Can we not say anything to anyone else? I'm not in the mood right now. It's not about me."

"For now. Come on, let's get back up to the nursery, the others have left."

As Zion's family were leaving, none of them noticed the guy snapping pictures of them on his phone.

*"I fucking cannot understand why all this shit is needed. Just kill the bitch and get it over with. As soon as she's dead, he can get his big payoff and move the fuck on. It's time he go beat her ass so he can get his dick sucked tonight. It's nice being with a woman who understands her fucking place and when she steps out of line, she accepts, no, **demands**, her punishments brutally. Fucking yes. Time for some fighting sex. And I got a free phone out of this tonight. Dumb-ass woman, just walked away from it. Finally, I can stop stealing phones from stores."*

-41-

Every day since Isaac and Caden's birth Zion and Lea have been at the hospital. They've been allowed to change them, feed them, and rock them to sleep. Most of the time they sit near them, talking to them and waiting for the opportunity to hold them.

Several days after the boys' birth, the service for Wendy is held. Earlier that day, Zion and Lea stopped by the hospital for the boy's morning feedings and baths. Their suckling has improved with each feeding and they're gaining weight.

Lea and Zion arrive at Hotchkiss Chapel, greeting everyone and thanking them for attending. The mourners attending are Zion's family, Sam and Mrs. Vance, Lea and her mother, Gordon and Lily, and a few of Wendy's close friends from the smoking club.

Zion stands to read his prepared eulogy.

"Thank you all for coming today. Wendy would have appreciated this. When she first contacted me about adopting the boys, Caden and Isaac, and about her fatal illness, it truly threw me for a loop. I'll forever be grateful to her for giving me this opportunity to be a father."

Staring directly at Lea he says, "Wendy giving me the opportunity to become a father at my age has become my second greatest life challenge. I'm proud of you, Wendy, proud of your sacrifice, proud of the strength you showed, proud of the determination you displayed. Your boys will always be proud of you. Rest in heaven. I know you'll be looking down upon them.

"In Wendy's own words 'Don't mourn my death, don't feel sorry for me not being on this earth to raise my sons. Don't feel sad for me. Feel happy for me. I have given you two wonderful precious human beings to nurture, to raise, to make you happy. You have a wonderful future ahead of you.' Thank you."

Zion goes to Lea's side and they watch while the funeral director places Wendy's ashes into the columbarium of the Chapel and seals it shut. There is a temporary vase in place for everyone to put in a single rose. This is the only memorial Wendy has requested. She didn't want a permanent vase and to avoid treating her resting place as a shrine to visit every year. That was one of the items Zion changed. Not only is there a permanent bronze vase, he had it engraved with the boys' names.

Everyone goes back to Zion's parents' house for dinner. This is Lea's first time being here. His mother gives her a tour of Zion's childhood home. Lea shakes her head at the remodel of Zion's old bedroom. Here it's done in baby boy blues, and Star's old bedroom is remodeled in baby girl pinks. Ready to go for overnights with the grandparents.

In the kitchen, they are talking and chatting and getting to know each other. Zion's family has made Lea's mother feel extremely welcomed in their home. Surprised the hell outta Lea. They even make Gordon and Lily feel welcome. *Okay, what alternate world have I walked into?* Zion's mood has improved with each passing moment. He's showing off pictures of the boys, bragging like the proud father he is.

They still haven't signed the paperwork making Lea their legal adoptive mother. Tonight, Lea plans to bring that up when they're alone. If he's serious about marrying her and doing this, she wants to get it done quickly.

"Zion, will you tell us about the birth of the boys? What happened with Wendy?" Patty asks him.

Lea, standing at the kitchen sink, speaks up before anyone else does, "Oh hell no. I don't want to hear that. Put it in a letter, address it to Caden and Isaac and let them read about it when they're old enough. Better yet Zion, discuss it between the three of you when they are old enough to understand. I better not ever hear you told anyone about what was said or done other than them. Got it Zion?"

"Got it," he says. As much as Lea has been through since this started, at this point he can't see himself denying her anything. She gives him that look once again that pins him in place, telling him not to fuck with her on this point. He catches it loud and clear.

"Lea, I'm sorry, I didn't think. Again," his mother says.

"Yeah, sure, whatever. Can we leave now? I'm ready to go home." Lea walks out of the kitchen. Her mother gets up and follows her.

"Thank you for dinner. Until next time," her mother says, remembering her manners even if her daughter can't muster up hers right now.

Lea holds her purse out to her mother and they go out the front door, getting into the limo waiting for someone to drive them home. Lily and Gordon get in and sit. Out comes Zion and Sam, with Sam getting into the driver's seat. Lea has made sure she's holding her hand in her lap instead of closer to Zion so he can't reach for it and start playing with it like he usually does. There's silence in the car.

First, they drop Lily and Gordon off, Zion thanking them for attending.

"See you, Lea," Lily says.

"Goodnight, Lily, and thanks for coming," she says looking at them. They can tell she's pissed.

Next, they drive to Lea's mother's house. When they arrive, Ms. Adams tells Lea to get out and come with her and tells Zion to sit.

"Ms. Adams, I can—." Zion starts.

"Son, you sit there in your seat. I need to talk to my daughter," she tells him.

Still the gentlemen, he gets out and helps her out of the car. Lea gets out on the other side, ensuring she wouldn't be touching Zion.

He notices the move but says nothing. He closes the door of the car, leaning on it. Sam steps out the driver's door and turns to him.

"Can you blame her for being hurt and pissed?" he asks Zion. They know what he's referring to. "It's been about you, the boys, and Wendy. Not even her birthday was acknowledged. Then to hear that from your mother. How you gonna handle this Zion?"

Zion looks away from Sam, staring down the street. Some part of him did want to share what happened during the birth. His mother blurting out the question like that wasn't a part of the plan. For now, maybe this is something he needs to put away and think about later.

"I'm going to make Lea a priority. Tonight, we celebrate her birthday. It's all about her and no one else. I can worry about my thoughts later."

"If you want to talk about what happened, I'm sure she'll listen to you. Just not with your mother. We've all experienced her 'helpful' gestures over the years."

"You're right about my mother. With Lea I have my doubts."

"Zion, you doubting Lea at this stage in the game. Come on son."

"I'm human. I want to tell her about what happened but I don't want to filter it. How can I share with Lea what I said, how I felt, and what I did and not hurt her?"

"Very carefully. Or put it in a letter. For your sons. You can always leave the letter on your desk for Lea to happen to read it."

"That's a cop-out."

"That's talking without talking," Sam says.

They get back in the car, waiting for Lea.

Zion calls his mother. "Mom, before you start with the apologies, hear me out. I'm in love with Lea. She and the boys are my priority. I won't let anyone hurt her, including you. I love you dearly, but what you said tonight was completely out of line. I won't be discussing what happened. So please don't bring it up again."

"Son. We have butted heads so much since you've fallen in love. This is new territory for me. My son with his own family. In love. And not being the jet set playboy. I'm proud of you. And Lea. It's about raising our grandsons now. Let's focus on that. And I'll never bring up the subject of the birth again."

"Thanks, mom. Talk to you tomorrow."

In the house, Lea's mother says what they are thinking, "That mother of his sure can ask some really dumb-ass questions at the wrong time. I'm not putting her down but, really, she's a nut case. I'm glad you set her straight. Well, happy forty-fifth birthday. Don't punish him too much." Ms. Adams hands Lea her birthday gift. She's ensured it will bring a smile and laugh to her daughter's face at this moment.

"Thanks, mom," she grabs an iridescent blue bag and leaves, making sure to lock up.

Fuck, now I have to hear about how sorry his mother is and how I shouldn't have said that. Well, fuck him.

Sam steps out of the car and holds the door open for her while she gets in. Once they're settled, Lea speaks up.

"I'm not apologizing for what I said and how I said it."

"I don't want you to. It was an inappropriate question. I like the suggestion you had of putting it in a letter addressed to the boys and locking it away for them to read when they're older. It gets it out of my head and allows me to move on and not having to rehash it verbally. I want to someday discuss it with you. Full disclosure. But I can understand how raw for the both of us it would be right now."

"Zion, I'm not ready to hear about how you told another woman how much and in what way you loved her. And don't bother saying you never said it to her. I can only imagine emotions on high. Who wouldn't say it in your position. And with the way your mother lets every thought flow out of her mouth, I don't want to be discussing something with her one day and hear her say, 'You know Zion really loved your mother, he told me what he said to her on her death bed'," she tells him. "We can talk and share anything with each other. Even what happened in the delivery room. But it's just between us and please, not yet. I beg of you, not yet. Give me some time. Please?"

"I get it. Baby, I do get it," he says, absentmindedly playing with the ring on her finger. Tonight, that will be his ring. It's time to retire all the others.

"What's in the bag?" he asks.

Lea reaches down and opens the bag. It's a movie and a gift card to her favorite purse store. She bursts out laughing. "Thanks, mom."

"Can I be let in on the joke?"

"Mom and I went to see this movie years ago. She hated it and I loved it. One year, I bought it on DVD and gave it to her as part of another gift. We started the tradition of giving it back and forth. No matter what we give each other, we continue to incorporate this into the gift every year. Now I have to come up with a way to get it back to her. She got me this year; she really got me." Lea can't stop smiling.

"Well, can you hold onto that feeling for a while longer? I have a surprise for you," he says. They get home and drive into the underground garage toward the elevators. She notices her car is missing. She panics.

"Zion, my car's gone."

"It's okay baby, I sent it out to be detailed." He holds onto her as they ride the elevator up, caressing her behind. As they enter the apartment, Lea sees vases of Calla lilies placed throughout the foyer. Zion follows her in, slowly walking behind her.

"Zion, what's going on?"

"Keep walking and find out."

She walks further into the apartment and sees there are more vases of flowers spread throughout in addition to balloons everywhere. Hidden within the balloons are cameras Lea can't see. On the dining room table are boxes, and envelopes, waiting to be opened. Lea is overly giddy with excitement.

"Happy birthday, Kitten. Better late than never. This is your night. Just the two of us, celebrating you. Let's have some fun, shall we?" He walks her over to the biggest box.

Lea tears off the paper. It's a new camera with lenses, camera bag, and memory cards, lighting equipment, backdrops, everything she needed or was looking at to upgrade and create her own studio. He places the next box in her hands. When she opens it, there are two sets of car keys and pictures. One is of a Nissan Maxima, Platinum Edition and the other is of the Range Rover SV.

"You can choose either one or both. Personally, I say go with both. You'll need a vehicle for when you're not shuffling our sons around. Yes, you'll be back to driving as soon as all this crap with Addison is over with."

She runs into his arms hugging him. "Thanks. I love you. I like the sound 'of our boys'."

"I love you, too, but you're not finished." He hands her the first envelope. These next gifts have him nervous as hell.

She opens it and starts to read it. It's the papers for officially adopting Caden and Isaac.

"Once you sign these, Lea, you legally become their mother. Please tell me you still want that?"

Lea looks at him with tears in her eyes. "Of course, I do. I was going to bring that up when we got here. I'm so glad you're ahead of me. Give me your pen."

He takes the pen he had hidden behind the biggest box and hands it to her. She signs it where noted and hands them back to him.

He takes them with shaky hands. Now for the next envelope. He hands it to her and she opens it. It's the pre-nuptial agreement. They've been discussing all the issues and going back and forth with lawyers for quite some time now. Zion initially wanted Lea to have everything of his should anything happen to him and vice versa. This agreement breaks down what she gets and adds provisions of providing for her mother, and counseling for martial issues should either want a divorce. Lea signs without hesitation. She hands the folded papers back to him. He looks for uncertainty in her eyes but sees none. Okay, now for the last and big one.

He walks over to the credenza and flicks on a monitor. He logs in to his laptop, opening a zoom window. Images of Gordon and Lily, Ms. Adams, Sam and Mrs. Vance, Star, Garrett and the girls and Zions parents pop up. They're all grinning and waving. Her mom is teary eyed.

Zion walks back to Lea and has her stand in the middle of the living room. With a remote in his hand, Zion touches a button that changes the lighting in the room. He and Lea are now standing in a circle of beaming light in the middle of an emblem on the floor, displaying their names.

Lea knows this is her engagement question. What she doesn't know is Zion is streaming it to their loved ones so they can experience the moment. He'll cut the feed after Lea says yes. There are cameras pointed at them as a couple, pointed at him for when he kneels with the ring and her hand, and pointed at Lea for her reaction.

"What the heck." She whispers. She was expecting a simple pop the question. Not all this.

"Kitten, wave. You're on candid camera." Zion turns her so she can see the monitor. Everyone waves at her. They're yelling and cheering. She waves, unable to determine where the cameras are at.

Zion turns her back to him. He takes the ring out of this pocket and gets down on one knee.

"Lea Grace Adams. Will you marry me? Will you complete our family?" he asks her, opening the box and displaying the ring he designed for her. She stares at it, then looks at him. All she said was blue, infinity, and not too big. The ring has two diamonds in the middle of the opening of the infinity symbols. The scrawling designs of the infinity are an electric blue topaz and diamonds. The uniqueness of the ring is the intricate details and not the size of diamonds. It's perfect.

"Yes, Zion Isaac Landon, I'll marry you and complete our family!"

Zion slides the ring on her finger. In the background they hear the cheers and the popping of corks. He stands and embraces Lea giving her a kiss. Turning to the monitors, he points the remote to the ceiling and says, "Good night y'all." And kills the feed to the cameras.

-42-

The next day after the proposal and birthday celebration, Lea couldn't get to her mother's house fast enough to show off her ring.

Turning Lea's finger left and right so she could examine it, Lea's mother says, "Geez, Lea, it's gorgeous. He didn't spare any expense. But what about the boys and the adoption?" Ms. Adams asks.

Lea takes out her signed and notarized copies. "All signed. These are mine to take to my safe deposit box along with the pre-nup."

"My baby is a mom. I can now officially say I have grand-babies. They need to hurry and get fat so I can see them."

"Mom, you will soon. Zion and I are going to see them today and hound the doctor on when he will release them." Lea gets up to leave, giving her mom a hug. Hugging her even harder than usual.

Ms. Adams smiles. She knows that hug well. It's Lea's I'm-so-excited-I-can-scream hug.

For days, Lea walks around flashing her ring. Her wrist started hurting, she was talking with her hand so much. Anytime someone would comment on it, she would say she was newly engaged but never mentioning to whom. She even claimed to a few people she was engaged to herself just to piss them off and have some fun.

Lea and Zion have been spending every moment they can at the hospital with Caden and Isaac. Born at seven months, they weighed five pounds, two ounces and five pounds, three ounces respectively. Each has gained two pounds in two weeks. Meeting with the doctor, Lea and Zion are told they will be released in another week's time.

Lea is changing Isaac and Zion is holding Caden pressed against his cheek, swaying him to sleep when Zion gets a call from Detective Greg. He takes the call, listening through his earpiece and softly talking, "Hey man what's up?"

"What's with the voice? Oh, never mind. Can you come to the station? I have some updates for you regarding Addison."

Zion makes eye contact with Lea, responding back to the detective, "Sure. We'll be there in about thirty minutes."

"What's going on?" Lea whispers as he disconnects the call. She puts Isaac back into his crib.

"Thank you," she says to the nurse.

Caden is sound asleep and Zion lays him next to Isaac. They're now sharing the same bed.

"I don't know. Come on, let's go see." Zion strokes the boys' cheeks and says goodnight to the nurse.

They arrive at the station and ask to speak to Detective Greg. He comes out and shows them to a conference room. "Thanks for stopping by. We've found Addison. Or she's turned up. For some reason, she returned to the mental hospital. They have her locked away in seclusion but sent me these pictures of her. Zion, I need to know if you recognize her."

Zion looks at the pictures, "Yes that's Addison." She looks worn out, tired, and doped up. "What do you mean she just showed up? What the hell is wrong with her, she didn't look that bad when I saw her, but that was months ago. Lea, did she look like this when you had the run in with her?"

"No, not this bad."

"Well, we got a call from the facility saying she was there. I went over to talk to her. All she kept saying is 'Zion told me to come here. I'm supposed to meet Zion and our boys. Zion loves me, wants me, and adores me. Zion wants to fuck me. He needs me. Zion is here, bring me Zion. I want my Zion'," the Detective reads from a note pad. "I gotta say the woman is totally out of it. She'll be in seclusion for detoxing. Until she's coherent, we can't do much. At least now you know she's locked away. We don't have any idea where she was or if she was still with the Drake guy. He hasn't been located."

"Are you saying we can ease up on the security, or should I keep everything in place?" Zion asks. He really doesn't want to let it slack off unless he can absolutely sure Lea and the boys are safe.

"Tell you what, whatever you have in place, keep. Once you get moved into the new office and there isn't a plethora of strangers around and the boys are home safe and sound, then decide. Hopefully, by then Addison will be lucid and we can find out what's been going on," Greg says.

"We start moving into the office this weekend. The boys may come home October seventh. So that weekend we'll have a lot to celebrate. We'll have our lives back," Zion says, looking at Lea.

She smiles. "And focus on planning our wedding."

"You mean you haven't started yet?"

"Only mentally."

Zion hugs her as they leave the police station both smiling from ear to ear. "We're getting our lives back. Yay."

"So, when can we snatch her ass? I want my baby. When can I get her?"

"Give it time, give it time. We're getting close. The phone will help us. You can get her Sunday. Then we send the message, and we get mine."

"Do I still get to fuck yours? That was the deal. I get to fuck them both."

"Look, once you've finished with yours and if you still have the life force to get it on with mine, you're more than welcome to have a go at it."

-43-

The final move into Landon Enterprises proceeds without incident. G-TEE's contract services ended September thirtieth so there's no need for Lea to be there. She decides to stay at the hospital with the boys while Zion and everyone is completing the move. Ryan is still her shadow. The second one has been relieved of duty.

Zion calls Lea to check in. "Hey babe. How are our boys?" His office is all setup and ready to go for him on Monday morning. Now he needs his Lea here to break open the bottle of Champagne to celebrate.

"They're sound asleep, I'm about to leave. I miss you," Lea tells him. They know exactly what's about to happen. They get to christen the office today.

"Good baby. You know I miss you, too. Get over here. I need to be inside you. Deep inside you. Throbbing inside you. Feeling you squeeze me tight. I need my tongue on your clit. I can't wait to have you on my desk. Cumming, moaning my name. Oh, Lea baby my dick is already hard for you. Has been all day since I been here, thinking about what I'm going to do to you in my office. Baby get here fast."

"I'll be there in fifteen minutes. Keep stroking it for me." *Shit I love that man.*

Exiting the hospital garage, Ryan makes sure no one is following them as usual. Lea gets to the new headquarters and sees the parking lot is full. All the employees are moving in and setting up their desks. The building is only accessible via security badge and the Executive floor is off limits to everyone today except for Zion, his family and his security team. As Lea exits the elevator, she sees Morgan packing up getting ready to leave.

"Hi Morgan, how you like the new digs?"

"Hello, Miss Adams. It's wonderful. I'm like a kid in a candy store. I hope Mr. Landon understands there's still a learning curve to figuring everything out again. He's in his office, you can go right in. Take care."

"You, too, Morgan." Lea walks down to Zion's office with excitement trying not to run. Today, she has on a miniskirt, a t-shirt, and blazer. She opens his office door and he's sitting at his desk finishing up a phone call. Closing the door behind her, Zion locks it and sets the glass window walls so no one can see them. Lea walks toward him taking off her blazer and top and unsnapping her bra. By the time she reaches his desk, she has taken off her skirt and stands before him nude.

"Hey man, I gotta go. There's some kinda commotion down on one of the floors. I'll call you back later," Zion ends the call and leans back in his chair looking her up and down. "You know I coulda been on a video conference call. You coulda been walking into a wall full of old men giving them a strip show." He smiles.

"Now Zion, do you think I believe you would allow a screen full of men to see what you get to enjoy?" She bends down and kisses him.

"Hell, fuck naw. Ain't nobody ever seeing what I get. Shit baby, you looking damn good. Hop up here so I can feast on your pussy. I'm starving."

Zion rolls his chair back and Lea stands in front of him. He's laid out a red and white checkered picnic blanket on top of his desk. He lifts her up and sits her on it.

"My oh my, you do have a meal planned out don't you baby," she says to him.

"You better believe it," he rolls his chair close to the desk and pulls her ass to the edge. "Baby feed me my titties. I need to feel them nipples on my tongue."

Lea leans toward him and places her hands behind his head pulling his face toward her chest, watching him lick and suck on her tits. *Shit, that feeling goes straight to my clit every time.* "Oh, baby yes, suck them hard. Bite them," Zion scrapes his teeth across her nipples then opens his mouth wide and takes one in whole.

Pulling back, he looks up at her devilishly. He glides his hands up her legs caressing her thighs.

"Oh, baby you ready for lunch," Lea asks him.

Zion stands up and takes off his clothes. Pulling her further to the edge with her ass now hanging off the desk he positions himself to slide his dick inside her. "I need my dick inside of you first baby. Shit, your pussy so hot. Oh, yes," Zion slides in and out of her, squeezing her ass and kissing her at the same time. "Don't cum Lea. Keep yourself from cumming baby. Do it for me." He slowly fucks her watching her concentrate on not cumming. *Shit, I can't almost take it I want to shoot.* She pulls back and Zion slips out.

"Eat me Zion. I need your tongue on my clit. Suck me hard."

He bends down and attacks her pussy licking and sucking. She leans back onto the desk fucking his face. She's so wound up from keeping herself from cumming, she can't take it. After only a few licks, she cums squirting in his mouth. He catches it all.

Zion stands back up and slips inside her again. She kisses him licking her pussy juices off his face. He shoots cumming hard, moaning into the kiss.

Oh fuck, what a way to break in my new office.

"Shit Lea. Oh baby you're so damn good."

"You're not so bad yourself handsome. Now, why don't we break in your private bathroom and get cleaned up and really eat. Or did you even bring any food?"

"Uh food, yeah, food. Hmmmm. Let's go out to dinner." They laugh, and get dressed, and go out to dinner.

The remainder of the week goes smoothly. The new headquarters has been a wonderful and welcome change. Zion can relax better knowing he has more control of his surroundings. His staff is making great use of the new digs. All the technology G-TEE suggested is working out better than expected.

Things are falling into place so well, Zion finally agreed to relax some of the security detail on Lea and his family. Lea is now allowed to drive her new Nissan, with its GPS and tracking device. She's promised no disappearing acts or long drives alone until Zion's nerves can handle it. She's been driving from home to her mom's and to Landon Enterprises. Ryan is still driving her to the hospital for now. It's only her third day of driving without her shadow and she's due at Landon Enterprises to check out the day care center.

Zion is pleased with this new program. "So, what do you think? I'm allowing the employees to volunteer days or hours in exchange for lower fees. That way they can be closer to their children and pay a fraction of what they would pay if they had to use an outside childcare service. I didn't think about that as another option to save on money but we could make it work."

"Zion, it's wonderful. I can't wait until the boys get strong enough so they can come to work with their father. I'll be so jealous," she says leaning into his arms.

"Anytime you want to come work with me is okay. I'll still keep trying to convince you. Let's go upstairs."

Zion and Lea go up to his office to hang out. He doesn't have any appointments, and they're to have lunch before Lea has to get back to the boys. Her phone starts vibrating.

"It's a text from your mom. Suggesting we meet for lunch. Just the two of us. Okay. What have you done or said to her now?"

"Baby, I haven't done or said anything. Go on, have lunch with her. I'll see you back at home and you can tell me all about it. I can't wait to hear how it goes."

"I guess," Lea texts his mother back, letting her know she's open for lunch and she's on her way. "Okay Zion, I'm going to go have lunch with your mother. This should be interesting."

"Baby it'll be fine. Have fun." He walks her to her car and sees her off.

Back up in his office an hour later, Zion is working when he hears his father outside the door. He looks up and sees both his parents.

Okay what the fuck is going on? Mom is supposed to be having lunch with Lea right now. Shit Zion don't panic. Maybe they canceled.

-44-

"Mom, Dad, what are you doing here? Especially you Mom, you're supposed to be having lunch with Lea right now." His mother looks at him oddly.

"No, I'm not. I'm going to have lunch with your father. We've been spending the morning together," she tells him.

"Mom, Lea got a text from you this morning saying to meet you for lunch. I saw the text. It was from your number. She left over an hour ago, going to meet you. Are you telling me you haven't texted her today?" Zion feels a rising panic in his gut, of fear, helplessness, and anger.

"No Zion. I did not text Lea today. I haven't called and or texted anyone in weeks. I can't find my phone. It's lost somewhere in the house. Maybe in one of my purses. I've changed them a number of times," she says, unconcerned.

"Sweetheart, something's up," his father says to Patty, looking at Zion.

"Sam, get in here, now! Morgan, call Detective Greg," Zion yells.

"Mom, exactly how long has your phone been missing?" Zion asks her.

"I don't know. Since the night the boys were born, I guess. Zion, it's just in the house," she says softly.

"Mom, it's not in your house. Lea got a text from you this morning. I saw it. You're standing here and telling me you didn't send it because you haven't seen your phone in who knows how long. Lea went off to have lunch with you based on a text she received from your damn lost cell phone. God no," he utters, in frustration.

"Mom, with everything that's been going on, you've lost your phone and haven't said anything to anyone? Why?" Zion growls while walking to his office phone and calling for Saul.

"Get to my office now!" he tells him. Zion tries calling Lea's phone, but it just keeps ringing and ringing and ringing.

She's not answering. Shit! God no, not my Lea, please good God no.

"Mr. Landon, I have Detective Greg on the line for you," Morgan says. Now Sam, Star, Garrett, and Morgan, along with Zion's parents are in his office waiting, trying to figure out what's going on.

"Greg, man, please tell me that Addison is still locked up, please tell me you haven't heard any changes with her?" Zion asks him. He has him on speaker phone.

"I wish I could. I was just about to call you. Someone has broken her out of the hospital. It happened Sunday. Late Sunday night. They didn't realize it until this morning. I just got the call. I hope you haven't cancelled any of your security detail on your family."

"Greg, Lea's missing. She got a text from what we thought was my mother, but my mother's standing here in my office. She told me her phone's been missing since September fifteenth. Greg, we have to find her, it's been over two hours, and I can't reach her by phone, she isn't answering," Zion tells him.

"Okay, man. I'll get on it and keep you posted," Detective Greg tells him and ends the call.

Saul arrived in Zion's office while he was talking with Detective Greg. "What's up boss?"

"My mother lost her cell phone the day my sons were born. My fiancée left, going to have lunch with my mother based on a text she received from my mother's phone and is not answering her phone. The woman we thought was locked away is out AGAIN, and the police can't find her, AGAIN. Do you get what the hell I'm saying here!!!?" he yells at Saul.

"Yes Sir. May I?" Saul walks over to Zion's computer and pulls up a screen on his wall monitor. On the screen, he accesses the locations of phones and cars. They start populating on a map as different colored dots. Because all of Zion's family and security detail are in the room with him, those are clustered in one location. Three dots are outside of the others. Lea's and his mother's phone and Lea's car. The car is parked someplace on the south side of St. Louis, but the phones, those two are together, speeding down highway three-seventy toward St. Charles, Missouri.

Zion grabs his car keys and phone. "Sam, car, now! Saul, stay with these two and don't let them out of your sight! Ryan, get to my house and stay with Mrs. Vance! Star and Garrett, get to the hospital and make sure the boys are okay! Talk to the nurses, doctors, whoever and explain to them about a possible kidnapping of their mother. Saul, when I get in the car and I call, you keep me posted! Don't listen to my parents' directions, understand me! If they start trying to talk you into doing anything other than what I tell you, go lock yourself downstairs!"

"Zion, wait, can't you let the authorities handle this?" his mother pleads.

Zion looks at her and calmly says, "No." Then turns and leaves, running down the stairs with Sam behind him. They head to the garage, getting into the SUV to drive to the location Saul indicates. Zion grabs his gun from the hidden location in the truck. "Sam, do what you have to do, understand me," Zion tells him.

"Yes, Sir," Sam responds.

Saul is watching the dots on the screen down in his office. After the boss had left, senior Mr. Landon attempted to instruct Saul to only tell him everything that is going on and not to let Zion know. Zion's mother is unable to control her emotions and is alternating between crying and pleading with him to keep her son safe.

"Sir, Ma'am, I've been instructed by your son to provide him with the information he needs. I'm sorry, but I'm going to have to leave you here and go downstairs to do this," Saul tells them. He turned off Zion's computer, making sure they cannot log back on.

When he got downstairs, he informed Zion where the dots stopped and provided him with the exact address location.

Royal is able to get Patty to calm down and they go in search of Saul's office. Royal promises Saul he and Patty would sit and be quiet, but they need to watch the screen he is watching to know something. They know where everyone was at per the dots on the screen. Star and Garrett at the hospital with the boys. Zion is moving on the highway toward Patty's and Lea's dots. Then they saw Zion's dot stop moving. When Lea's dot blinks off but Zion's keeps moving, Patty takes it to mean that Lea is dead. It took the longest of time to explain to her it only meant something happened to the phone and not Lea. It is damaged somehow and they can't track it any longer.

Detective Greg has been given all the information Zion has regarding the location and he and his offices are on their way. Even if Zion manages not to get there first and the police handle the situation, there's no way in hell he's going to allow himself to be far away from Lea. Not. At. All.

-45-

Lea arrived at the Gallery Pond Wine and Cheese Bar ten minutes early. She drove around for about five minutes looking for a parking space, one well-populated, close to the entrance of the bar, on the corner, making sure her car could not be blocked in. Sam has taught her well.

As she walks toward the bar, she notices a man standing to the side. Lea puts distance between them by walking closer to the curb. While paying attention to him, she's bumped. Before she can turn and say excuse you, she's pushed toward another man and is forced away from the restaurant. She feels a stinging sensation on her side, like she just got stung by a bee. Her legs have that running in the ocean sensation and she feels loopy. She turns to walk to her car but finds her arms are linked in the arms of two men. They walk her toward a white van.

When they get to the van, Lea can feel the strength returning to her legs. She twists around and kicks one of the men in the ankle, attempting to break the grip he has on her. She's punched in the shoulder and pushed into the back of the van, landing on the floor, on the opposite side of her hip from her phone, hoping to keep it on and safe for as long as possible. The guy hops into the back of the van with her and slaps her across the face. Lea couldn't duck fast enough to miss it. It got her square on the jaw causing a split lip.

She lands a kick toward his crotch. One to the side of his penis and with the other she feels the heel of her foot grazing the tip of his dick. This causes him to double over in pain and dry heave. With him bent over, Lea lands a kick onto his shoulder just missing his ear. The guy grabs Lea's foot and twists it away from his body. She screams.

"Man, chill! I told you not across the fucking face. Never where it can be seen," the driver says. "Tie her down before she gets away."

Lea thinks she recognizes the voice but can't be sure above the loud muffler sound. Her mind is racing.

Fuck, what the hell is this? Addison is locked up in the looney bin. Has been for over two weeks. Everything was going fine. We were getting into raising the boys, planning the wedding, the grand opening event for the new office and here I am being kidnapped. What the fucking hell?

Lea looks around, trying to figure out how to escape or to grab something to do some more damage. Before she can get her true bearings, she gets shocked with a taser and goes limp. She doesn't pass out but she can't move. By some miracle, she doesn't land on her phone.

About an hour's drive later, the van comes to a stop and drives into a building. Lea can tell because they went from sun to dark and she heard the difference in the sound as the engine's roar bounces off the concrete floor. The grinding noise of doors closing leaves her in fear. The driver hops out the front of the van. The second man slides to the back of the van, pushing open the double doors. Lea is dragged out of the van and over to a wall of chains and cuffs.

Oh, fuck no!!

The shock from the taser has worn off, she struggles, attempting to run. The second guy, the driver, hits her in the thigh with the butt of a long gun and she stumbles to the ground landing on all fours, scraping her knees on the concrete through her pants on shards of glass. The palms of her hands scrape the ragged concrete.

She's yanked upright and dragged to a concrete post and tied to it with ropes. With her hands tied above her head, she's turned to face the open space. Though her legs are, surprisingly, left untied, she can barely move them from the pain. She can tell they're in some kind of warehouse. If not for the sun shining into the building from the glass in the ceiling, Lea wouldn't be able to make out the location of the doors. There's a set of double doors across the room from her, which the van drove through. Another is to the left, too far away to run for if she could. There's a single door behind her. A thirty-foot-wide circle is lit by bright beaming lights. There's a bed in the middle of the circle with a woman lying on it.

Shit, that's Addison.

Passed out and naked from the waist down, it looks like someone has her laid out on a plastic mattress and has dumped water on her. Her arms are chained to the bed-post above her head in a similar position to Lea's. Addison's legs are spread wide open, displaying her crouch.

Lea stares at her dumbfounded. There's no way that woman can possibly be the person that's been stalking and harassing her and Zion. She even looked better when Lea saw her at the club that night. Just barely. This woman here is doped up and looks as if she can't even lift her head. Lea stares at her, knowing there's no way Addison could have possibly managed to do all this.

A pair of shiny clean shoes come into view. Lea slowly looks up, scrutinizing the style and cut of the suit. As she gets to the face of the person, she jerks back, bumping her head against the brick pillar, realizing whose face she's staring into. It's Martin. Martin Jones, the former electrician on the Landon Enterprises project.

-46-

"What the holy fucking hell!!?" Lea exclaims, looking up at Martin.

This is not the Martin Jones she fired. He shied away from Lea that day. When she ran into him at the mall, he was hesitant in his mannerisms when speaking to her. This man is in command. This is a Martin, who from the looks of him could be running a board of directors in any company he tried.

What the hell is going on? And who is the dipshit standing next to the bed with Addison in it, stroking himself?

"Well, hello there to the Miss Lovely Lea Adams. And how are we this fine wonderful day?" Martin greets her. He bends down, squatting, putting himself face to face with her.

"Just peachy," Lea says, adding, "considering I can barely move and am trussed up against a pole. And yourself?"

"Oh, I'm fantastic now that you've joined us."

Lea goes on, "What the hell do I have to do with this? And if it's such a wonderful day, why don't you untie me?"

"Sweetheart, I can't do that yet. Not until we come to a clear understanding." He stands up. Martin prefers Lea looking up to him. *This bitch will never be on my level of looking me in my eye.*

"Let me introduce you to everyone. On the bed is Addison Jones, my wife and former college sweetheart of Zion Landon. Standing next to her waiting to fuck her is Drake. No last name, which is really none of your concern. God, woman! It's truly wonderful to see you," he says to her jovially.

"Martin, why am I here? Like this?" she calmly asks him.

Why am I so calm? 'Cause you wanna get out of here. Alive. Stay calm and think.

He walks over to Lea, standing next to her, forcing her to look up at him again. "That's my girl. Get used to this position. You'll be looking up at me like that for the rest of our lives. That's the way I enjoy seeing you. You're here because I love you, and we're finally going to be together. Sweetheart."

That's the second time Martin has called Lea "sweetheart," and it sounds like fingernails on a chalkboard. She focuses on what he's saying.

"You're here like this because I need to train you and this is how I'll make sure you learn to obey me. As of tonight, you and I'll ride off into the sunset and live happily ever after where no one can find us," he bends down and whispers closer to her ear. "After I get rid of the old ball and chain over there. She's so doped up and out of it waiting to be fucked, she has no clue what's going on or about to happen."

"Martin, what the hell makes you think I'll be going anywhere with you, let alone obey you, you dumb sorry ass fucking excuse for a man," Lea spits at him.

Martin turns his hand towards Lea's shoulder with a closed fist ready to strike her. At the same time, Lea leans away from him, unaware the punch is coming and it lands on the side of her jaw hard, causing her to bite the inside of her mouth. This angers Martin because he knows it will leave a bruise on her face. Snatching the rifle from the floor, he walks to her left side and hits her in the thigh with the butt of the gun. "Look, Lea, I'm trying not to get upset here. I want you to understand you're going to love me, and you're going to obey me because you won't have any choice if you want to live. If you want your mother to live and especially if you want those precious boys to live. Yes, I know about the boys. Now close your fucking mouth and get ready to enjoy the show."

Martin then walks over to Addison. "Addison, baby, your Zion is here. Finally, we're together. I forgive you for everything. You were so right. Lea and I would've never been happy together. I'm so glad you came back into my life."

"Oh, Zion. Yes, so am I," Addison says drunkenly.

Martin walks back to Lea giving her an explanation, "Well Lea, sweetheart, let me bring you up to date. I met Addison years ago when she would come home from college. One of many college whores. We fucked some, but there was always something lacking. I couldn't figure the bitch out. But I loved her to no end. When she dropped out of college, we got married."

Martin speaks while pacing back and forth between Lea tied up at the pole and Addison on the bed. He's in his on world, reciting the story of his life, "It was the best few years of my life. I had a beautiful woman; the sex was off the chain, and my business was taking off. Then she started with the crazy acting shit. Fighting and fucking. We would fight for months on end, fuck like crazy. Then shit would get boring. How she managed to hide her crazy from me I still don't know to this fucking day. Bitch," he slaps Addison across the face, and she smiles.

"Even her damn family didn't tell me about the crazy. They were thrilled for us to get married. And as soon as she was my responsibility, they fucking asses practically disappeared. They never gave a shit whether they saw us or not. Never asked for kids. Avoided any talk of it. Then she gets locked up in a mental hold in jail one night from driving drunk. I get the diagnosis. Bipolar with a touch, a touch mind you, of sex addiction. Touch my ass. I couldn't keep up with the whore. As long as she was on drugs, she was good, we were good. Then when she got off the drugs she would vanish and be fucking up a storm."

"Ain't that right, whorish Addison? Answer me, you nasty ass fucker," Martin goes to her and slaps her until she wakes up. Drake grabs him to stop him, but steps back when Martin looks at him. "You ever wanna fuck her again and get your drugs, you'll back the hell off me now. Got it," Martin tells Drake.

Drake retreats into the background and stands waiting.

Lea gets Martin's attention. "But Addison met with Zion. She wasn't like that at the restaurant, like she is on that bed. All those emails. Martin, what the fuck is going on and what the hell makes you think I'm going off anywhere with you?" she asks him, all calmness gone.

Screw being scared.

"Darling, that is the best part. Lea, honey, don't you know I have loved you from the first contract we worked on together. Why the hell would I under-bid everyone? I did everything to be around you, to work with you, for you to see me. But I had that bitch to hide. Turns out it was easy because, you sweetheart, didn't care about her. You never asked me about her. You just wanted to work with me. That's why you picked me all those times. I know that now. At first, people kept telling me it was because I was cheap and you were getting a good price, but I knew you wanted me as much as I wanted you, but we were both too scared to say anything." Martin points the rifle toward Addison. "Then she got lucid and stayed lucid and started hounding that fucking ex of hers."

Lea stares at Martin dumbfounded. "Loved you? Wanted to work with you? Fool! It sounds like you on the same doped ass drugs as your wife. Like you said, I was getting good work for cheap," Lea says.

Martin walks back over to Lea with quick agitated steps. Lea braces herself for the pain to come from whatever he might do. Instead, he stops, pulls a pistol from his waist and fires at the door behind Lea. It strikes the flimsy wall, leaving a hole at eye level.

"Lea, I know you're trying to anger me so I can punish you. Don't worry, sweetheart. I will. Later. Now back to my wife. God, I hate calling her that in front of you. But don't worry. You'll get that title and you'll love it. Anyway, Addison showing back up lucid and contacting Zion, what kinda fucking name is that anyway? She pushed you two together. I had it all planned. We were about to make our love announcement when I asked you out. She was gone, stuck in some fucking crack house, it would have been a little more time, then I could have killed her off and made it look like a drug overdose while having sex. NOOOOOOO, she came back into the picture and contacted ZION!

"Do you know how much I hate that man? He's not the one for you. I am and you know it, but you have been blinded by his damn money. I've kept all men away from you for years. Every one that showed interest in your life, I scared them away. Me. They were not good enough for you and I made sure of it. But this damn Zion. I couldn't get to the bastard and you kept getting closer. So, I had to use that stupid bitch. I had to get her lucid for periods of time and control her to do my bidding by stalking the two of you long enough to keep you unhappy, scared, insecure." Martin is pacing back and forth, shouting about how he has been controlling Addison and Drake and having them stalk Lea and Zion when all along it was him. Him keeping Lea single by scaring away men.

"Martin, if your punk ass was able to scare away men from my life, I really need to thank you. They were as weak and pathetic as your bitch ass. The man that gets me can't be scared away by a puny lil wanna be fucker like you. Where did you get the suit? Goodwill or your uncle's closet from the '70s?"

Martin goes over to Lea and slaps her across the face twice, kicking her in her side and legs.

"Don't say that, Lea. That's Zion talking. Stop it. I don't want to beat you and I can't dope you up yet. We have time darling." He then bends down next to her ear again. "See, I have to kill these two and get rid of the bodies. I plan on burning this place down. With those two inside of it. Locked in a sexual position. With a bullet through them. Oh, I'm so excited. It gives one helluva major fucking orgasm. This one will be good. I've been practicing. Look around at all the bullet holes in the walls. I've become a fucking topnotch bullseye shot."

Lea looks around at all the bullet holes in the wall. She thinks, *Shit, the walls have holes as big as peep holes that you can stick the barrel of other guns out of them and get off clean shots at intruders. Some are fucking erratic or going up and down the walls in straight lines. This asshole is crazy.* Looking at the wall above Addison's head, there are multiple holes directly in the center of the links of chains hanging down from a board that is screwed into the wall.

Drake is standing next to the bed, caressing Addison's hair. She keeps mumbling Zion's name.

Martin goes over to Lea and twists her head up, forcing her to look at them, talking in her ear. "I want you to watch them closely. See how they keep moving. They're in heat. They wanna fuck. He can't stop grabbing his dick and she can't stop humping air. Nasty ass bitch. Only she not thinking about Drake. She thinking about your Zion. God, it's sick watching them get going, but damn it's a good show to jack off, too. You'll like the videos baby. I have plenty of footage."

"I'm not watching these two dumbasses in heat fuck."

"Oh yes you will. Watch them, Lea. Watch it all," he tells her, forcing her to look at Drake and Addison.

Martin then stands up and walks over to Drake. "Yo, man, look at Addison. She ready. She ready to fuck. You ready man. Let's do this."

Drake responds, "Naw, man, I ain't ready to fuck her yet. I want a piece of yours first," Drake walks over to Lea and grabs one of her tits, squeezing. She turns away from him and Martin walks up and punches him in the face.

"I fucking told you, if you got any life force left over, you'll be more than welcomed to fuck her, but don't you ever touch her unless I say so."

Drake is rubbing his jaw, backing away from Lea and walking back over to the bed and Addison.

While Martin is bragging and focusing on Drake and Addison, Lea has worked herself free.

Thank you, Drake, for being so doped up you couldn't tie a damn knot.

Lea keeps her hands out of sight of the bright lights so Martin can't see them. It took everything in her to fake being tied up while Drake was groping her, but she managed it.

Martin tells Drake that he can fuck Addison now and tells Addison that Zion is here to fuck her. She gets into place, breathing hard, getting excited for what's about to come. Martin props her up so she's at a position where her middle is lifted up and propped against the back wall. He tells Drake to get in front of her and lift her legs and to slide in. "Don't you fucking move until I tell you to. My Lea and I must get into position so we can watch and have this memory when we're away enjoying our lives together."

If Lea wasn't trying to make sure that when she ran from Martin while he was focused on Drake and Addison in the bed, she would run now. Instead, she sits there and waits for him to come back. He sits down next to her. "Okay, Lea, get ready. This will be quick, I promise. We can leave after." Martin turns toward Drake and says, "Drake start fucking her. Now."

Drake starts fucking Addison. They quickly get into action. As they get closer to really getting it on, Martin picks up the military-style assault rifle he keeps in the building, clicking the safety off and aims it at them. Lea jerks away from him, thinking she waited too long and he's going to shoot her. He looks at her and smiles broadly, then turns back to the two fucking and starts playing with his dick. As they start grunting and moaning loudly, Martin raises the gun, aims it at Drake's back and fires. He shoots at Drake's back multiple times. The bullets leaving the gun slice through Drake and into Addison's chest, exiting her back into the wall. Drake slumps on Addison, dead. Addison's body is holding up both of theirs because she's still strapped into the chains and handcuffs, dead, her face frozen in sexual ecstasy.

Martin jumps up and down screaming and cheering. "Yes, yes, yes. Lea honey, did you see that shit. Yes, yes, yes." When he turns around to look at Lea, he sees that she's gone.

-47-

Following Saul's directions, Sam and Zion arrive at a warehouse off route three-seventy. "Saul, are you sure this is where you found the phone's locations?" Zion asks quietly, looking around.

"Yes, sir. They disappeared right before I called you. So, it's either that exact location or someplace close to it."

Before Zion can respond, they hear gun shots and loud cheering. Laughter is coming from a building toward the back. He and Sam hop out of the SUV and run toward it. When they round the corner, Detective Greg halts them in their tracks. "Stay here and stay down," he whispers. The police are there with vehicles, hidden out of sight.

Scrutinizing the location, Sam takes in everything quickly. Police have surrounded the building. The building has wide double doors at each end, regular doors on sides, glass windows on roof. Walls of the building has rotten boards and holes. Zion silently waits, then asks, "Well, what do you think?"

"If we can get close enough to a door or any of the rotted planks with holes, I can take a look. I'll do what I can."

"I'll get you close. Do it, Sam. Don't hesitate. I want a full end to this. Whatever it takes." Zion states calmly, understanding what he's asking, no demanding of Sam is dangerous. He turns to look at him.

"Sir, it will end today."

Inside the building, Lea is hiding in the shadows from Martin. She slips around some concrete pillars, picks up an iron pipe that was lying there and walks toward Martin's blind side. He's shouts for her. "Lea, honey, don't be scared. Come out. It's okay. The bad people are gone. I'm here to protect you from everyone now!" Martin yells into the empty space.

Just as he's about to turn toward her, she hits him in the shoulder with the pipe. "Fuck you, Martin, you weak dumb punk pussy ass son of a bitch. I would never be with you. EVER!" she yells at him, backing away.

He screams, dropping to his knees. The gun points up toward the ceiling of glass, firing bullets. Glass fragments rain down on both her and Martin, bathing them in bright sunlight. Lea screams, falling back into a darkened area of the building.

"You bitch. How the hell am I supposed to set this place on fire now? Dammit, Lea, I should kill you. Where the fuck are you, you bitch? Don't you understand I'm doing this for you? For us? Shit, woman!" Martin gets up, his arm dangling to its side. Lea hit him in his weak right arm. As much as he's been practicing, he can fire off a shot and hit a target with his left arm without feeling any recoil.

Lea has glass shards cutting into the back of her hand and arm. She pulls them out while trying to get away from Martin, but she trips onto a wood plank, falling to the concrete.

He reaches her and kicks her in the hip, stomping her multiple times, finally pinning her in place. She screams in agony.

"Now keep your ass still. Don't you fucking move you bitch! Understand me?"

He bends down and places his face close to hers. "Don't move again, Lea." He slaps her.

Lea's hip is in extreme pain, and she can feel the stickiness of the blood on her blouse. "Fuck you, jackass," she tells him. He backhands her again, kicking her in her arms and back. Lea lifts her leg and gives him two swift kicks in his dick. He doubles over and falls across her legs.

"Oooooo shit, bitch, I'll kill you, I'm going to fucking kill you," he tells her, grabbing his crotch.

He's so immobilized that Lea is able to roll him off her legs and scoots away as fast as she can. She can hear Martin moving behind her, but she doesn't look around. Now that there's more light shining in the building from the damaged skylights, she can see more doors and crawls to the closest one. Before she can reach it, there's another gun shot. Martin is standing up and pointing at the door. Or standing as best as he can with a cracked shoulder and his dick throbbing in pain.

"Bitch, touch that fucking door and you're dead," Martin tells her. She stops moving. "Now be a good lil lady and move away from it. Go on, move away from the door."

Lea crawls away from the door trying to grab something on the floor she can use as a weapon. As soon as she's far enough away, another door bursts open. Martin turns toward it and starts shooting. Shots are fired back into the building, all hitting Martin. He drops to the ground at Lea's feet a few inches away, dead. A pool of blood gathering under his head, slowly running toward her. One wound is directly in the middle of his forehead, while all the other shots are body shots.

Lea lays on the floor in pain, staring at Martin's dead body. People are running in with guns drawn. She can't take her eyes off Martin, his un-seeing gaze watching her.

She's in so much pain at this point she doesn't know who's talking to her or what they're saying. She just keeps pushing them away, not allowing anyone to touch her. As another pair of hands reaches for her, she screams, "LEAVE ME THE FUCK ALONE!"

A face bends down, entering her field of vision and forces her to focus on it. "Lea, look at me. It's Bear. Baby, see me."

Lea adjusts her gaze on Zion and away from Martin. She raises her hand, wanting to touch him.

Zion lays his face in her hand and kisses her palm. "I'm here baby. It's your Bear, here to take you home. See, feel my tears. That's it, baby, I'm here. Let me pick you up and get you out of here, okay?"

"NOOOOO, it hurts. It all hurts," she tells him.

"Okay sweetheart."

"DON'T CALL ME THAT. DON'T CALL ME SWEETHEART, HE CALLED ME THAT. THAT WEAK ASS BASTARD CALLED ME HIS SWEETHEART DON'T EVER CALL ME THAT AGAIN!" Lea screams at him.

"Okay baby, but we have to get you out of here so we can get you to the hospital. Okay? I'm right here every step of the way. I won't leave you." Zion moves in closer to Lea. "This lady is going to help so we can get you up on this bed okay. I'll pick you up. It's just me, Zion."

Zion bends down and Lea puts her arms around his shoulders. She winces out in pain and starts crying. She buries her face in his shoulder and squeezes hard digging her nails in him, because her side hurts so much. He lays her down and they wheel her out to an ambulance. She's pushed inside and Zion climbs in beside her.

-48-

Sam makes phone calls to the office to inform them of events. "Miss Adams has been found and is on her way to the hospital with Mr. Landon. We'll call when we arrive."

He then calls Gordon to inform him of what's going on and to pick up Lea's mother to bring her to the hospital if he can or Sam can go pick her up. "Naw man, I got this," Gordon tells him.

Gordon sits down dropping the phone.

"What? What is it?" Lily asks.

"Lea was taken. Somebody snatched her. They got her back, but she's been hurt. They're taking her to the hospital. I've to go pick up her mother. What am I going to say to this woman? Fucking bastard. He said he loved her; he would protect her, and he let them get her. I coulda did a better job of protecting her, and I don't even know what the fuck is going on. I wanna kill the bastard."

"Gordon, come on. Let's go. We gotta get to Ms. Adams. I'll drive. You get ahold of yourself. You're not going to jail. You can cuss out Zion later. Punch him if you like."

On the drive to Ms. Adams house, Gordon checks the news on his phone. "There's nothing about a kidnapping. Nothing about Landon Enterprises."

"Well, that's a good thing, right?" Lily asks, "What are you going to say to Ms. Adams?"

They arrive at Ms. Adams house. Gordon looks over at Lily before hopping out the truck saying, "The truth. Lea's been hurt and has been taken to the hospital, and we're here to take her to her child."

"Like, that's all you gonna say?"

"Yes. Until she grills me."

Lea's mother is coming out of the backyard when he gets to her door.

"Gordon, I thought that was your truck. What are you doing here?"

Gordon inhales and fidgets a little. Ms. Adams knows he's hiding something when he does that. "Gordon. Where's my daughter?" she asks, knowing this has to be about Lea.

"Ms. Adams, Lea's in the hospital. Zion wanted me to pick you up and get you there."

"Gordon. Why is my daughter in the hospital? Gordon. What's going on?"

"Ma'am, someone took her. But the police and Zion rescued her."

"Why is she going to a hospital, Gordon?" Lea's mother slowly walks toward Gordon. "Tell me."

"Ms. Adams, all I know is she was hurt, and I'm to get you there. Please can we leave now? We're wasting time."

"Fine." Ms. Adams locks up her house. She stands in the middle of her driveway placing a hand on her chest. "Lord, please, don't take my baby away from me," she pleads. Then she gets into the truck and is silent during the ride to the hospital.

The ambulance arrives at SSM Health Care's emergency room in St. Charles with Lea and Zion in record time. Lea's rushed from the ambulance and into an exam room. Zion stays with her, not leaving and threatening anyone who tries to make him.

Rehashing in his mind what happened at the warehouse brings back the harrowing details.

At the sound of the gunfire, coming from the direction of the warehouse, and hearing glass break, Zion took off running, not caring what would happen. He was halted midway by two police officers.

Sam pulled Zion to the side, stealthily moving them close to the building, but steering them out of the way. "Zion, if you want this to end correctly, let the authorities do their jobs," he says to Zion loud enough for others to hear.

Hearing Sam use his first name in years brought Zion back to the reason they were there and kept him from doing something irrational. Zion moved to the side of the building. The officers kept a close eye on him, watching him pace a few feet away, ignoring Sam.

Gunshots went off inside the building. The officers ran toward the doors, bursting them open. As they did this, shots from inside the building rang out. As Zion moved to rush toward the building, Sam placed himself close to an entrance that was going unnoticed.

When the gunfire finally stopped and the police secured the area, Zion ran in looking for Lea. He saw one dead body on the dirty floor of the warehouse, unaware it was Martin Jones. Detective Greg had picked up the gun lying next to it. He bent down and checked for a pulse. "One down," he barked into a radio.

Where the hell is Lea? Was all Zion could think over and over. He didn't see Lea anywhere. He almost thought one of the dead bodies on the bed was her, but it didn't have Lea's spiral curls.

His attention was drawn to the left, hearing a woman scream. It was Lea. He rushed over.

His kitten. Her face was bloodied and bruised, blood on her hands and arms and she was laying on one hip grabbing her side.

He focused on her attempting to get her to calm down. When she focused on him, he was able to pick her up and get her on the gurney and out of the building. As they were leaving Zion turned back to see Detective Greg standing over the other bodies. From his angle, he saw Addison and Drake. Dead with gunshot wounds through Drake and into Addison, lying in a sexual position.

What the hell kinda sick shit was that.

Zion turned back to Lea and he saw that she was looking at them also. He leaned to block her view. "Baby, no, don't look. It's over, we're going home," he said to her.

The nurse speaks to Zion, bringing him back to the present moment. "Sir, if you could stand outside, we need to get Miss Adams cleaned up and have a doctor look at her. Please, Sir."

"Lady, I'm not going anywhere. I've seen her naked, hell, I'll clean her up my damn self, but I'm not leaving this spot. Do what you need to do. I'm standing right in this spot," Zion tells her.

They're in an emergency room stall with the sliding door partially closed because of the magnitude of the situation. Per police orders, no one is to get to Zion and Lea and discuss anything with them until Detective Greg arrives.

At every touch Lea winces, bites her lip, cries out, answers questions and points them to the pain. She may have cracked ribs. They clean and stitch up her arm and hand. The nurses move to lift the sides of the bed up to take her to get x-rays to check for internal injuries. Zion moves to follow, but this time is firmly told to stay where he's at. Before Lea gets back his family arrives.

Star asks him. "Is she okay? Is Lea, okay?" They've been scared shitless since this started. Being stuck at the office, the hospital and his apartment without any word or updates, did not help.

"Yes, they're taking x-rays to be sure there are no internal injuries. Addison and Martin are dead. I saw their bodies. This time it's really over," Zion tells them.

"Do you have any idea what happened?" Garrett asks.

"No. The police haven't come and talked to us yet. Actually, we've been told not to talk about any of it until Detective Greg gets here. Because of the severity of the situation, the detective has instructed the hospital to move Lea to a closed off section of the emergency department away from other patients," Zion says. He's pacing back and forth in front of the empty room. His parents, Star, and Garrett are standing in the room, leaning against the walls. Royal goes and grabs chairs for the ladies and has them sit.

Zion sees Lea being wheeled toward the room. "Here, here comes Lea."

Her bed is pushed into the room. She's sleeping. The nurses get her settled and leave, giving them privacy. Zion moves to her side and lets down the side of her bed. He caresses the bruises on her face, her swollen eye and jaw. He gingerly sits next to her, slowly laying her head into the crook of his arm, holding her hand. He looks at her left hand and sees that her engagement ring is missing. He checks her neck and there's no necklace.

Hell, fuck it, I'll buy out the damned jewelry store.

About fifteen minutes later he heard a commotion outside of Lea's room. "Where the hell is my daughter? Listen, lady, I understand you're doing your job, but my daughters in this hospital somewhere. I've been directed down here."

"Ma'am, we've been instructed to not let anyone near her. If you'll just let me make a call to confirm—," the nurse tries to explain.

"I've nicely told you who I am. Now I can look into every room to find her, I got all night. But I ain't leaving here UNTIL I SEE MY DAUGHTER!"

"Ms. Adams, please—." Gordon starts.

"Shut up and go start looking for her, Gordon," she tells him.

Zion gets up from Lea's side. He exits her room and walks up to Ms. Adams, "Ms. Adams."

Ms. Adams turns and looks up at Zion, singeing him to the spot.

"Lea's over here. Please come with me. She's sleeping," he says, backing away toward the room.

"Fine," Ms. Adams says, walking behind Zion, with Lily and Gordon following her.

Zion steps aside allowing them to enter. Ms. Adams walks in and sees Lea laying in the bed and hesitates. *My baby. So helpless.* She walks straight to her. Everyone moves as if they are parting the Red

Sea. Ms. Adams leans over, embracing Lea and kisses her on the forehead and whispers in her ear. No one can hear what she's saying.

Lea wakes up laughing. "Ma stop, shut up. My sides hurt. You know you liked that scene too," Lea fully opens her eyes and looks at her, smiling. "We're going to sit down and watch it from beginning to end, remember that. I wasn't that deep in sleep."

"Crap, I take it back," her mother says crying. "Glad granny sent you back to me."

"She said I had more hell to raise down here with you." Lea kisses her mother on the cheek, wiping away her tears.

Zion leans over the edge of the bed and gives Lea a nudge on her shoulder with his nose. "Hey, Kitten, welcome back."

She turns and smiles at him. "Hi, Bear."

"The best two words I've heard all day."

"How are Caden and Isaac?" she asks.

"They're fine. They're safe and sound at the hospital. Baby I thought—," he trails off.

"Shhhhh don't. Not now. Later," she tells him.

Ms. Adams orders, "Bullshit, not now. I need to know what the hell happened that he got you. Son, lean back over there. I need to check my child out." Lea's mother starts examining every inch of her body. It's embarrassing with everyone standing there watching. At least she leaves her covered up. Lea winces when she hits her ribs, unable to hide the pain. The stitches on her arm and hand will probably leave a nasty scar. Lea stares at her bruises. Everything will heal. Well almost everything. Her mother caresses her bruised face. Tears run down her cheeks.

Seeing this, Lea asks for a mirror. "I must be really ugly if you crying," she says to her mother.

"No. No mirror. Not yet. And you are my beautiful baby Punkin."

Lea touches her face and feels the swelling. She avoids looking at the others.

"And what damage did you cause?" her mother asks her.

"Attempted castration, but I didn't have on shoes that were able to do the kind of damage I wanted to. I think I broke his shoulder with an iron pipe."

"Well, as long as you got in a few nice kicks."

All the men in the room adjust the fronts of their pants. Detective Greg enters the room with a stack of papers and a small plastic bag. "Hello, Miss Adams. I have something that you would want back. Hello everyone." The detective hands Lea a plastic bag. It has her engagement ring and necklace in it. When Martin took them off and threw them across the room, she figured they were lost forever. The chain is broken so she can't put the necklace back on. Zion takes the ring out of the bag and slips it back on. It glitters better than ever. Lea looks up at him, wanting to cry.

He bends down whispering, "The swelling will leave, bruises heel. You're still and always will be my sexy kitten."

-49-

The detective clears his throat. "Well, it seems we can clear up everything tonight and close out this case. Miss Adams, I wanted to get some information from you. I tell you this is the strangest case setup ever."

"It was Addison, right?" Zion asks.

"No, it wasn't. It was Martin," Lea speaks up. "I was the target. Everything about this is because of me," Lea says gripping the bed sheets. "Zion, if you and I had never met, I might have been dead or missing," Lea says feeling the panic in her mother. Mr. Landon brings over a chair for her to sit down. She looks as if she could pass out.

"Here, Ms. Adams. Please sit," he tells her.

"What?" Zion asks sitting back in the bed, grabbing Lea's hand and squeezing it so hard she winces. "Oh, baby, sorry."

"Miss Adams, this is where I need you to fill in the blanks for me. Tell me what all you can," the detective asks.

"Martin and I really did meet at a Home and Garden show at the convention center. We had one official date. All the others were business meetings. He never told me about being married, never mentioned being in a relationship. I kept things as business. He stated he fell in love with me on our first date. I didn't feel any connection. He never showed any inkling about his feelings for me or maybe I wasn't paying attention. Well, he figured if he could work with me, I would fall in love with him." On this Lea squeezes Zion's hand, giving him a sly look about that waiting for someone to see you. *Back at this again.*

"Long before he met me, Martin had met Addison one of those summers she had come home from college when she and Zion where dating. When she dropped out, she married Martin. He didn't get the warning from her family that Zion did. They were glad to give her up to Martin. She became his problem. He got the Addison with the bipolar issues, on and off drug use, screwing around, and the disappearing and re-appearing. Martin put up with all of it because he figured she would be dead, and he could be the grieving widower. She went missing right around the time Martin and I met.

"By the time she came back, he believed he had fallen in love with me. He started working on getting Addison out of the picture. He would push her toward her exes suggesting she should reach out to them. Martin even pushed her into hard drug use and sex, thinking she would get killed. Or die of an overdose."

"How did Martin find out about Zion and Addison?" Lea's mother asks.

"By accident. After I fired Martin from Zion's project, Martin was looking at the St. Louis Business Journal. Martin would read those magazines, looking for contracts G-TEE would be working on, then submit bids for those projects, under bidding everyone else. It didn't matter if he was losing money." Lea adjusts her body on the bed, flexing her feet.

Her mother notices. Using her childhood name she says, "Punkin, don't you want to rest?"

Lea turned to her mom, said, "Thanks, Mom. I'll be fine," and continued. "Martin saw a picture of Zion and me talking at Tom's wine tasting. Addison saw the picture also and told Martin about their past relationship. After seeing that photo, Addison did at first reach out to Zion on her own. When Zion sent her home in the taxi the night he met up with her at the Moonrise Hotel, Addison was done with Zion. Martin wasn't. If Martin discovered a man had an interest in me, he would work to divert it. I have no clue what Martin thought was interest. I've barely dated in the last decade.

"Martin didn't even know Zion and I were dating until the night of his birthday party. That was our first official outing when anyone saw us together. We were kissing out in the parking lot.

"Martin said he tried to get to Zion but was blocked by Morgan at every turn. So, he pushed Addison to contact Zion. The emails to Zion and me where from Martin and not from Addison. Or after those first ones you received where, the rest were from Martin. He kept Addison around when he needed to stoke the fires. It only pushed Zion and me together with me either being glued to his hip or multiple people watching me."

A nurse comes in and checks Lea's vitals. She asks if Lea wanted any pain killers. Lea accepts a couple of Tylenol, refusing anything stronger and ice packs for her face. She's determined to finish what Martin told her during the time he had her and to hear what the detective has to say.

"Mrs. Landon losing her phone was the break Martin got. He couldn't figure out how to get me away. After the boys were born, he ensured Addison got caught or found and locked back up. I don't know how Drake comes into the picture.

"When Addison was found, Zion relaxed the security detail, I got the text to meet Mrs. Landon, and he abducted me. If your mother would have said anything about her phone missing, it would have only delayed Martin getting me."

Zion's mother exhales loudly on a sob. His father embraces her, comforting her.

Lea continues, "If Zion and I had never met, I really would have been dead, missing, or in an abusive relationship. When I first met Martin, I didn't think he was a bad guy. I could've ended up with him just as much as I ended up with Zion. I was interested in someone else then. After that man was no longer in the picture, I decided to reevaluate my life. Martin would never have gotten any play. But according to Martin, I was meant for him. He got to the point that he didn't care what happened to him. He wanted me and he wanted Addison dead.

"It's rather a catch twenty-two situation. I'm here. Alive, bruised up, but alive. Zion is a father. I'm not claiming that's because of me—."

Zion interrupts her, "Lea Adams, you know damn well me becoming a father is largely due to you being a part of my life."

"Bear, you could still have become a father, a widower, you have resources to do it alone," Lea attempts to convince him.

"There is no way—."

Ms. Adams yells, "Will you two hush? NOW!!"

Lea and Zion look at her stunned. And close their mouths.

Detective Greg speaks into the silence and fills in the remainder of the story. "That does explain the remainder of the case. Drake came into the picture from being one of Addison's fuck buddies. He was able to obtain the drugs and was a sex addict and extremely abusive. He worked in the medical field and was a functioning drug addict. When he and Addison met in a sex addiction group, they latched onto each other and never let go. She would always go back to him when her hubby wouldn't cooperate. When Martin decided he wanted Lea and found out Zion was the love of Addison's life, he decided to use that to break you guys apart, but Zion had more resources to keep everyone safe."

The detective continues, "I can't be sure how Drake got your mother's phone. I only know it was at the hospital the night of the boys' birth. We tracked the phone from tower pings. Martin allowed Addison to get caught by having Drake find her walking outside the hospital so she could get locked up, and Zion would relax the security detail. When Martin was sure Lea was no longer being tailed, he sent the text that got her away. Without that phone and text, he would have been still trying to get Lea, but it would have been difficult again because, as soon as Zion would have found out Addison was missing, he would have re-instated the security thinking it was about him and not Lea.

"And it was all about Lea. We discovered Martin had passports, drugs, cash, rental car and cabin setups. He had plans to go off the fucking grid with Lea in the back woods of Alaska. He would have gotten her away, brainwashed her into accepting him and no one would have heard from her again. So, Zion meeting you has been a plus in this situation. All of you remember and believe that. Yes, people made mistakes, but Lea's still here. In pain and bruised up, but here. We've confirmed that all the parties are now deceased. I'm not going to even go into that part of the story. Y'all discuss that if you want." Standing up, the detective says, "I'm taking off now. If I have any more questions, I'll be in touch."

"Wait. So, because of a missing phone, that sick bastard got my daughter," Lea's mother starts.

"Mom."

"Lea."

"Mom."

"Lea."

"MOM!"

"Lea don't Mom me!"

"Would you excuse us so my daughter and I can talk please?" Ms. Adams says to everyone, pinning Lea with a stern look.

She mumbles under her breath, "shit", knowing she's about to get a tongue lashing from her mother.

"Please wait." Zion's mother Patty steps forward. "Lea, your mother is right to be upset about the phone. I can never apologize enough for my part in this, and you've done your best to try and deflect your mother's anger."

"Anger? Lady, I'm pissed," Lea's mom jumps in. "People with money don't value jack shit. Yes, to you it was a simple phone you lost, and your son could easily replace. I don't know about you, but I've appreciated everything he's put into keeping me and my daughter safe. I was finally able to breathe when I was told Addison was locked up. Then I get a visit telling me my only child, my daughter, is in the hospital after being kidnapped. Again, don't get me wrong. I'm so grateful your son has played a major part in her life that she's still alive and here with me, but come on. Your phone was missing for weeks and you didn't mention it?"

"I know, I know. Again, I'm so sorry. Please, please forgive me. I do care about all that's happened. I'm devastated knowing I could've been the reason she would've disappeared," Patty sobs and Royal, Zion, Star and Garrett envelop her in an embrace holding her.

Lea stares at her mother finally whispering, "Mom."

"No, Lea, don't 'Mom' me. Patty had you labeled as a gold digger. I've sat back and watched you fall in love with this man against my better judgement. Look at them. The family group over there. I'm still scared and you're here. They need to understand." Ms. Adams turns away from Lea, focusing on Zion and his family comforting his mother. It angers her even more. "All of you over there, you have each other. It's just been Lea and me. I don't have her, I can't exist. To think that something so simple could have been one of the causes to something that could've ended so badly for Lea and me is hard to take. When you all leave here, you go home with your family unit intact. Probably stronger than ever. I could be without my daughter. That scares me. I could be sitting in a police station filling out a missing person's report, looking for my daughter. You have no idea how scared I am right now," Lea's mother says. "Look at my baby. Her face, her body, she's laying here hurting, and I can do nothing to take away her pain and fear. But y'all. Over there. Again, the family unit intact. Pissing me the fuck off right now."

Lea reaches for her mother's hand, squeezing it hard. Ms. Adams returns the grip.

Lily and Gordon move to also comfort Ms. Adams.

"Ms. Adams, you're a part of our family as much as Lea is." Royal says. "You come with the package. Don't ever believe you'll be left out. We've been put together by divine intervention with these two meeting." Zion's father walks over to stand at the foot of Lea's bed. "These two have only been together eight months. We're still getting to know each other, and yes, we made mistakes. But we're a family now. We're staying that way, and we're supporting one another fully. No apologies needed. If the situation was reversed, we'd be wanting to scream, yell, lash out and blame. And we'd be scared as hell."

Lea and her mother look at each other and say, "Divine intervention. Adelle. Jinx."

"Thank you, Mr. Landon. I appreciate your words of comfort," Lea's mother tells him. "Now I need a comfy bed so I can rest. When we busting out of here?"

The doctor comes in. "We're moving Miss Adams to a private room and are holding her for the night. I can't allow all of you to stay."

"Her mother and I will be staying," Zion says. "Star, can you go check on the boys once more, I—."

"It's okay bro, I'll send pictures." Star and Garrett give Lea and her mother hugs telling them they love them and they'll see them tomorrow.

Patty stands and approaches Lea and her mother. "Lea, I apologize for thinking you were a gold digger. I hope to someday prove to you how happy I am that you're with my son and the mother to my grandsons." She then turns to Lea's mother. "Ms. Adams, I hope to be close with you as a fellow mother-in-law. Good night to you both and if there's anything you need, call my husband. He can reach me." This last line eases some of the tension in the room.

"Gordon, you've been pretty quiet," Lea says to him.

Lea's mother moves to the side so Gordon and Lily can get closer to Lea's side. Gordon looks at Zion with a look of disdain, staking a position and claim knowing it's a dig to Zion's ego. *Well, Fuck Zion's ego.*

Zion glances at Lea but steps aside. He understands their closeness, but it doesn't mean he has to like it.

"Dammit sis. I can't lose my best friend. Who am I gonna rehash the eighties and nineties with? Our clubbing days? You're the only one that understands my love of catfish nuggets and syrup. Lily won't let me indulge like that. Rainbow unicorn sis." He leans over kissing her and giving her a hug.

"Rainbow unicorn forever bro."

Lily speaks up. "Nasty ass nuggets and syrup. Eeeeeek. Lea, I love it when you bring my hubby's soft side out. He's so adorable." She smiles at him. "Call us. You need anything, anything at all, call on us."

"Thank you both. And yes, he's so cute." Lea says grinning, relishing in all the love.

Gordon kisses Lily then looks back at Lea. "Look, you know I'm overwhelmed that you're okay. Loving you for years is darn easy to do. I'm going on about thirty right now. As of tonight, this is no more of a discussion okay. Focus on the future. Only the future." Turning to Lea's mother, Gordon gives her a hug. "Ms. Adams, take care and call me if you need anything."

As he and Lily move to leave, Gordon pauses and addresses Zion's family. "Mr. and Mrs. Landon and Mr. and Mrs. Leon take care. Maybe we'll someday get together in happier times," Gordon says with one last dig at them even if they don't know it.

"You know you can call us all by our first names," Star tells him.

"Maybe you and your husband. I can't with your parents. My mother would disown me showing that level of disrespect. Just can't do it." Gordon then walks over to Zion and stands toe to toe with him looking eye to eye. They bro hug saying nothing. Gordon turns to the door saying, "Goodnight, everyone." He turns back looking at Lea one last time, winking, then he and Lily are gone.

Next, Zion's family takes their leave giving hugs all around. Mrs. Landon apologizes in Lea's ear once more. "Lea, I'm so sorry for ever thinking you were with Zion for his money. Please forgive me? I will make this up to you. And re-earn your trust. I promise."

"Thank you, Mrs. Landon."

They leave and Lea is moved to a larger room, thanks to the pockets of Zion. Her mom climbs into the bed next to her and Zion climbs into the bed with Lea. The nurses stop protesting when Zion starts taking off his pants to get really comfortable.

"Young man, don't you dare, I don't want to see all that. Nurse, we'll be okay, let him crawl up in there," her mom says shooing her out of the room.

As Lea drifts off to sleep, Sam comes with toiletries and a change of clothes and food for Zion and Ms. Adams. He looks down on Lea sleeping in Zion's arms. To think what could have happened. He's glad that she's okay.

"Thanks Sam. For everything tonight," Zion tells him quietly.

"My pleasure Mr. Landon. Really my pleasure."

-50-

Lea lays in Zion's arms in a fretful sleep. She jerks, moans, and clenches her fists against his chest. Zion mumbles to her, telling her she's okay, he's with her, and she's safe. He feels her tears soaking his shirt and he wipes them away. He caresses her brow gently, keeping her accustomed to his comforting touch. *Oh, my Lea, I won't let these memories haunt you,* he says to himself. He can't believe how close he came to losing her, hell, never meeting her.

Upon waking the next morning, Lea sits up in the hospital bed, in the room alone. She stares at the flowers on the window's ledge. *Man, overnight news travels fast, or they're all from Zion.* She re-hashes in her mind what happened. Lea's life could be so different from the direction it took by telling one man she did not want temporary, that she needed more.

She looks under the sheets at the bruises on her body. *I'm so ugly right now. So very ugly.* Glancing in the wall mirror, she turns her face left and right to inspect the bruises. *Yep, ugly as ever.*

Zion and her mother come walking back into the hospital room with Crystal and Tom, along with their spouses. Lea jumps at the noise, pulling the sheet up to cover herself. Zion notices but can't get to her before Crystal runs to her bawling, with her husband trailing behind trying to comfort her. Tom's wife is equally in tears with Tom attempting to comfort her.

"Crystal, I'm okay, calm down. I'm fine," Lea tells her, hugging her, trying not to cringe away from her touch.

Crystal keeps mumbling over and over, "It's all our fault. This is all our fault. We did this to you. Lea I'm so sorry."

"Crystal, how is this your fault? What are you talking about? This is Martin's fault."

"No, you don't understand," Tom speaks up. "Look, Zion and Lea, Crystal and I, well, all of us. We played cupid to get you and Zion together."

"What?" Lea asks.

I know all about the cupids and their hookups. But Zion and I weren't a Cupid match. We met as business associates, that's all.

"We, all four of us, worked to get you two together. At first, it was keeping you apart because we knew Zion wasn't ready for a relationship. That's why you guys never met before that day in the office," Linda says.

"Carl did not have to go out on leave as soon as he did. Zion never had to come into the office to meet as he did. Once we all decided to play matchmaker, we did all in our efforts to get you guys together," Tom says.

Lea's mother offers up, "Well, I guess it wasn't Adelle." She watches her daughter gradually getting more agitated, bunching the bed sheets.

"Wait, you guys did what? How long did you keep us from meeting each other?" Lea asks staring at everyone.

Tom responds, "Right around the time Zion moved back to St. Louis."

"You mean Zion and I coulda met over a year ago. Fucking geez." Lea whispers under her breath. *All these people. Directing her life. What kinda puppet strings am I wearing?* She can feel a panic attack coming on. She grips the bed sheets and looks away from everyone.

Zion hasn't taken his eyes off her after Crystal's confession.

Lea is about to freak the fuck out.

"Uh, could everyone give me some time, I just need to think, to breathe," Lea says, moving to get out of the bed. Crystal reaches for her, but Lea pulls away. "Crystal, not now please. I just need a minute." Lea's breathing becomes labored. Zion and her mother move to her side to calm her.

"Lea, look at me, breathe, deep breaths, come on, it's over with now, breathe," her mother says.

"Mom, no it's not." Lea's voice rises and tears start streaming down her cheeks. "Everyone has been running my life, treating me like a fucking puppet. Playing Cupid? I've been locked away, kidnapped, told who to love and when to love, having had men kept away from me. Everything is a lie."

She's backed herself into a corner and knocked over one of the bouquets of flowers. The water is flowing across her feet. She tries not to step on broken glass. "Zion, do you even care about me, do you even love me, are you pulling strings, am I a puppet to you? I've been pushed along while everyone else got to live. Has any of what I thought and felt meant anything to any of you? What the hell, this is or was my life?" Lea screams, bawling, shaking, and bawling.

Zion reaches her. The nurses come in wondering what the commotion is. "Crystal, Tom, you guys leave. Now!" he tells them. The nurses escort them out of the room. One comes back with a shot ready to calm Lea down with drugs, but Zion holds them off. Another stands at the door waiting to clean up the flower mess.

Watching Lea step on the glass and flowers, Zion winces. He wants to grab her and pick her up. But instead, continues to talk to her calmly. "Lea, look at me. I love you. They may have set us up to be introduced, but this is our relationship. You told me what you wanted and needed. You did. We learned about each other. This is **our** relationship. I'm not working any puppet strings. I haven't been controlling your life other than the security to keep you safe and you knew about that." He inches closer to her with every sentence.

"Kitten, you're free to make any decision you want. You can tell me to get the hell out of your life. Your decision. I pray that you don't because the boys and I need you. I need you. I don't agree with what the Cupids have done but, baby, we took it this far ourselves. Beyond Addison, Martin, and Wendy, we're here with each other. For each other. Think about it, Lea." Zion keeps his eyes on her. He needs to hold her, and she'll be okay. She's terrified and angry, but he can get her over this. He finally gets within a hair's breadth of her face, and she reaches for him, holding him. "See, this is us, this is ours, our relationship. No strings attached. I love you, and I pray you love me and still want me. Do you love and want me, Lea?"

"Yes. I want you. I love you. I need you. But Zion—."

"No buts. You said you want, love and need me. You said it. That's all I need to hear. I don't give a flying fuck how we got together or who introduced us. What about you?" he asks, slightly lifting her so her feet are touching his instead of the floor. He keeps calming her. She's shaking like a leaf.

"No, I don't care."

"Good. Now I'm going to put you back in bed," he tells her, picking her up and placing her back in bed.

The nurse works to clean up Lea's feet. She has a couple of scratches from stepping on the glass. Her mother covers her with the sheets after the nurse gives her a sedative to relax her. Lea drifts off to sleep holding her mother's hand and Zion's hand, squeezing his hard, digging her nails into his flesh. Zion doesn't wince at the pain. *Squeeze all you want, baby, all you want.* After a few minutes, Zion kisses her and dislodges his hand, allowing her mother to comfort her in her drugged sleep. "Ms. Adams, I'll be right back, I need a word with our Cupids."

She looks up at him with gratitude. "Better you than me. Thanks Zion, for everything just now. I'm glad she fell in love with you."

"So am I, so am I." Zion leaves the room going in search of Crystal and Tom and their spouses. He finds them in the hall looking lost.

"Guys, you know she loves you all but, she's overwhelmed right now. With everything she knows about Martin and what he was planning, it's a bit much to hear what you Cupids were doing," he tells them.

"Man, Zion, we're done with the matchmaking, never again," Tom says.

"No, you guys aren't. It's what you do. Lea, Zion, Caden and Isaac are a family and are staying that way," Zion says. "Ladies, please, stop your crying, and let's move on. Lea's sleeping, she'll be okay," Zion says, making a promise to himself he'll be doing all in his power to make sure of that.

"Okay, we'll go. Tell Lea to take all the time she needs off. Don't worry about anything at the office, her job, nothing. It'll all be there for her when she returns. Whenever that is," Tom says hoping he hasn't lost a working colleague as well as a friend and daughter.

Lea had to stay in the hospital for two days. Her mother did not leave her side. She pampered Lea, was in on every discussion with doctors and nurses regarding her daughter's care and health. Even arguing with them when they mentioned how soon Lea would be released.

Before Zion returned to pick them up, Ms. Adams broached the topic of where Lea was going when released. "So, you going back to your house or coming home with me?" her mother asks.

"I'm not ready to go back to my house. And I need you to get some rest. Mom, you haven't slept much in the last three days. I know every time I moved, you jumped."

"It's what a mother does. Gotta make sure my Punkin is okay."

"Mom, I love you for it. But I want you to go home and get some rest. Please. Do this for me. Zion and I'll take you home, make sure you're safely inside and you can rest."

"Lea, I don't want to leave your side."

Lea gives her mom a hug. "Rest in your own bed tonight. Tomorrow Zion will send the car back to get you. Do this for me."

Ms. Adams hugs her daughter tightly. "Okay. Tonight, I'll go home. And tomorrow, I'll bring your favorite dessert and we can watch that damn movie. I keeps my promise."

Zion walks into the hospital room with Sam following him. Watching Lea and her mother hugging, the men halt and smile at the scene. Zion clears his throat announcing their presence.

"Ms. Adams, we're going to see your grandsons, would you like to join us?" Zion asks her mother.

Ms. Adams, dabs her eyes, after releasing Lea. "Zion, I would so much enjoy that," she says smiling.

After Lea is released from SSM Healthcare in St. Charles, they drive to see Isaac and Caden. While visiting the boys, Zion stands off to the side talking with the doctor about their release date.

While holding Caden, Lea's mother watches her daughter smiling, holding Isaac. "That man really loves you, Lea. Yes, indeed he really does," her mother says.

"Do you think he still wants me after all of this? Wants to still marry me?" she asks her mother.

Zion comes over answering the question. "Yes, Zion still wants you, Zion still loves you, and Zion is going to marry you. Especially after all this. You never have to doubt my love for you Lea. We may have unconventionally gotten to this point, but we're here," he says. Zion then informs them the boys are being released in two days' time. They're in heaven.

They drive Lea's mother home and Zion walks her in to get her settled. "Zion, please call me if she can't sleep or has a night terror or another panic attack. Her mind is racing and is still on overload. I hate that I won't be with her tonight. But as my daughter told me, I need to get some rest. And let you take care of her tonight," she tells him.

"I promise. If I have to send a car back here for you, I will. Don't worry. I'll continue to protect her, sleeping and awake," Zion kisses her on her cheek and leaves her, anxious to get Lea home.

-51-

Lea watches Zion lock Ms. Adams door. As he walks toward the car, she looks around for suspicious activity, unable to stop thinking about Martin hopping out of a dark corner to attack. Even knowing he's dead doesn't help. As Sam steps out to open the door for Zion, Lea looks toward Sam's waist wanting to see the bulge of his gun. When she sees it, she relaxes.

During the drive back to Zion's apartment, he notices Lea is intently focused on the drive and the cars around them instead of him. He and Sam make eye contact in the mirror, silently acknowledging how skittish she is. Driving into the underground garage of the building, this would be the first time she understands how secure Zion's cars and the elevator are to his apartment. Until now, she has never paid close attention. She steps out of the car, waiting for Zion, not moving far away from the door. Instead of walking ahead of him toward the elevator, she walks as close to him as she can without causing them to trip. On the ride up all three are silent.

When they step into the apartment, Sam takes Lea's things from the hospital up to their bedroom and says goodnight. Lea watches him swipe his security card for the elevator. Once it closes, she goes to set it to lock. Returning, she stands in the middle of the living room not knowing which way to go or what to do.

"Lea, you okay? Can I get you anything?" Zion asks her. She jumps at the sound of his voice. Zion feels kinda awkward and hesitant. He doesn't know how to approach her right now. She looks as if she wants to run.

She turns and look at him. "I want to take a shower. I can still feel and smell that on me."

"Okay, come on. I'll run a shower for you, and you can get into bed and get some rest." They walk upstairs into the bedroom and straight to the bathroom. When her mother examined her, he was watching closely and saw how Lea would wince and jerk away. He even saw some of the bruises on her thighs when she was getting dressed. When she saw him looking, she quickly covered up and turned away. He couldn't go to her because her mother was helping her to get dress. He plans on addressing that tonight.

In the bathroom, Zion turns on the water in the shower and takes out one of his t-shirts for her to sleep in. Lea undresses revealing each bruise and staring at it. On her shoulder from when she was shoved in the van by Drake. On her arm, the stitches from the glass cutting her, on her hand another cut from the glass. On her chest when Martin would hit her, on her hip and buttocks from the many kicks and falls, on her thighs from the butt of the gun. Tears stream down her face.

Lea talks to her reflection in the mirror, not looking at Zion. "I tried to stop him. With words. I cussed him out, I fought back. I kicked him and told him how weak he was. I fought. I got away. Out of the ropes. When I did, I picked up a pipe and broke his shoulder. But he was still able to shoot the gun. He was still able to hit me, kick me, punch me. He told Drake and Addison to have sex. So, he could shoot them. He was excited jumping up and down screaming yes when they slumped over dead. He walked over to them and was laughing in their dead faces."

The words flow from her mouth, leaving Zion stunned. He never expected her to discuss any of this. Especially not so soon and not so freely. She hasn't looked at him once since she started speaking. He goes to her and envelopes her in his embrace. She keeps speaking into his chest, not looking up at him.

"I wanted to kill him. He made me sick to my stomach. I wanted to get back to you. I kept thinking how you would feel I was playing a game when you couldn't reach me. How you would think it was a repeat of me being childish. It was my fault he got me. All this is my fault. Zion I'm so sorry he got me. How did he know about the boys? They could have gotten Caden and Isaac. Why did you talk to me, why didn't you just say no to me? Your life would be so much easier. All this hell I've brought you. I'm so sorry Zion. You would be so much better off without me. I'm so sorry."

Lea collapses onto the floor bringing Zion with her. He scoops her up and holds her, rocking her. "Baby, shhhh. This wasn't your fault, don't ever believe that." He holds her letting her cry it out. Now he understands why she didn't want her mother here tonight. Lea needed this emotional release without scaring her mother. "Go on cry it out. Scream it out. I'm here. Always."

As her tears dry up, Zion confesses, "Kitten, I was so scared when you came up missing. I knew from the moment I saw my mother at the office, something didn't feel right. I rushed to you as fast as I could. I'm so glad I didn't walk away from you. We are alive in so many different ways because of each other. Lea, when I saw you laying there I wanted to die. When you screamed, that was the best sound I heard next to hearing the boys scream when they were born. You recognized me. You wanted me. All you wanted was me."

For the second time in his life he can remember, he's crying, "Lea, baby, I love you so much."

They hold onto each other, rocking and crying. Lea grips him harder attempting to crawl into his embrace further. The tighter he squeezes her, the safer she feels.

He stands up, bringing her with him.

"Zion, no. I don't want you to see my body. All the bruises."

"It's okay sweetheart. I want to see you. Never hide your body from me. Every bump and bruise, you're still my beautiful Lea, my sexy Kitten." He tells her kneeling in front of her.

Zion kisses each and every scar, bump, and bruise. He doesn't miss a one. Lea keeps covering herself and closing her eyes, turning away from the mirror hating looking at herself. She doesn't want to see any rejection from him.

He stands up and guides her hand down to his crotch. "See, you still arouse me. Your body, everything about you still arouses me. Nothing about you turns me off and nothing ever will. Understand, I love you. All of you, I want all of you. The good, the bad, the sexy, the bumps and the bruises."

He adjusts the temperature of the water. After he takes off his clothes, he pulls her into the shower behind him. Zion changes the jet sprays to spray onto Lea's back and legs. Soaping a washcloth with her favorite soap, he cleanses her body. Starting from top to bottom, Zion gently caresses each bruise. He takes special care with bandage coverings. If any fall off, so be it. Tonight, he is Lea's nurse. He'll replace whatever needs to be replaced.

After their shower, they go to the bedroom, climbing into bed. But Lea is unable to sleep. She watches Zion watching TV. "Kitten, talk to me. What's in that pretty head of yours?"

"Safety." She sits up opening the nightstand drawer in search of pen and paper.

"Lea what are you doing?"

"Looking for your pen and pad. I have all these items going through my head. I need to write them down."

Zion hands her the pen and pad from his side of the bed, sitting up beside her. She takes them.

"Thanks."

He watches her scribbling away, reading over her shoulder not saying anything.

Purse

Garage key card

House and car keys

Change locks

Check house

Car

Buy gun

Conceal and carry permit and class
Get new keys for locks
Where are clothes, have destroyed
Look for easy entries, fix them
Change patterns

Lea is writing away and Zion hasn't said a word. Finally, she runs out of things to write and starts doodling on the page.

Her name. His name. The boys names. Scribble lines.

"Kitten, may I see that?" he asks with his hand out.

"Why? No. It's nothing. Just stuff in my head." She's feeling kinda silly now.

"Lea. Please."

She hands him the pad. He also takes the pen. Looking it over, he sees the fear in her words.

"Okay. Your purse is in the office. Let's go get it."

They get out of bed going downstairs. On their way, Lea is looking at the balcony doors, walking over to make sure they're locked. Zion slows his pace, watching her. She checks the door of the apartment that leads to the buildings hallway, making sure it's locked. Turning, she follows him into the office.

Zion takes out two plastic bags he got from Detective Greg from the bottom draw of his desk. Handing one to Lea, he places the other back in the draw.

Lea dumps the bag. It contains her purse, broken phone, and her necklace. Dumping out her purse, checking the contents she sees she's missing from her wallet, her debit cards, driver's license, health and dental cards. It still has her cash. She's also missing her mini tablet.

"Greg found the remains of anything that had your name one it, burned in a pile in the warehouse."

"My iPad mini is missing. Any ideas on what happened to that?"

Zion takes out another bag. The iPad and its case have been snapped in two, both containing bullet holes.

"Martin destroyed everything?"

"Yes. It's not anything that can't be replaced. They're things Kitten. You're here." Zion picks up the pad looking at the list again.

"The garage key card was never found. I've had all the others destroyed and re-calibrated my security system. I've had all new cards made. House and car keys. Not found. Your car is with the dealer having the security system reset and new keys made. I've had a security detail at your house. I can have them change the locks, just say the word."

"Thank you, Zion. What about the rest of the list?"

"We'll work on it together."

"What's in the other bag?"

"We'll discuss that when you're stronger. When you feel safe. Don't look at me like that. I'm not hiding anything from you. I'm not pulling puppet strings. I'm asking you to trust me. Please, Lea. What's in this bag is something we'll discuss. Later. Please trust me."

"Okay."

"Good. Now about the gun. I'll talk with Sam about getting you trained and getting a conceal and carry permit. If you're serious about getting one after you have had some time to recover. I'm not going to allow you to make major decisions with us still terrified and dealing with what's happened. Fair enough?"

"Yes."

"Fix points of entry. Well, you discover them, whatever you think they are, and I'll get them fixed. To your satisfaction."

"You must think I'm crazy?"

"No. I think we are scared as hell. This is not only about you. I've added the security detail back on us. It won't be relaxed until, well, I don't know when."

"Thank you."

"Lea, stop saying thank you. I love you. Your safety is a priority."

"You've done so much."

"Sweetheart. Can I still call you sweetheart?"

"Yes. Please. I love the way it rolls off your tongue."

"Hhhhmmmm Sweetheart. He got you away from me. I thought I had done everything I needed to do and he got you. He touched you. He hurt you. I can never do enough to make what happened not have happened. We can sit here and say I'm sorry or thank you over and over and it won't change anything. We're not going to let it rule our future. Is that clear?"

"Yes, clear. Can I have a bear hug?"

"Always every day." They stand and he brings her into his arms holding her.

"Lea, I don't know about you, but I am wide awake. How about I make us breakfast, and we lay on the couch and stuff ourselves?"

"Zion, breakfast would be great."

-52-

The following day, Ms. Adams arrives with Lea's favorite dessert, homemade Banana Pudding Cake with shaved Ghirardelli chocolate and whip cream. Lea and her mother spend the morning setting up the nursery, with Zion moving the heavy stuff. They drive to the hospital to visit the boys again and get all the information needed for their release.

Arriving back at the apartment, Zion, leaves the ladies alone to enjoy their movie while he takes care of the items on Lea's list, making arrangements to transition the apartment back to its corporate status and get all of Wendy's things put into storage or sold.

Dinner is refreshing. Mrs. Vance prepares them a dinner of Italian spiral meatloaf, Caesar salad, mashed red potatoes, and homemade popover rolls. Watching Lea and her mother interact with each other has Zion gushing over them.

In front of her mother, Lea does everything she can to act normal, not letting on how much pain she's in or how tired she is. When she drifts off to sleep during a second movie, Ms. Adams makes her comfortable on the couch, goes in search of Zion and finds him in his office. She wants to question him about how Lea coped her first night home.

"Zion, I know my daughter. There's no way she calmly went to sleep. Tell me all that happened."

Without breaking Lea's confidence, he only says, "She talked a lot and made lists. Ms. Adams," he starts wanting to explain why he didn't call her, "I needed Lea to believe she can trust me. And selfishly, I wanted to comfort her. I wanted to feel her needing me. I know that's wrong, but, well there you go."

"Zion, I kinda understand. It was hard for me to go home. It was my way of forcing my baby to put trust into you 'cause I know someday I won't be here. I need to know she'll be loved and taken care of. But don't get used to me stepping back too much. I'm still the mom and I ain't going nowhere fast young man."

"I don't expect you to," he gives her a hug.

Two days later, Zion and Lea bring Caden and Isaac home with little fanfare. Nothing about what happened the last few days has ended up in the media. When Zion told Lea keeps his personal life private, he wasn't kidding. There wasn't one story about any of what went down.

The first night with the boys was an all-nighter. The boys slept perfectly, only waking up and wanting to be fed. On the other hand, Lea and Zion, jumped at every little noise coming from their bassinets. After the third time of jumping up with the boy's sound asleep, they sat up and watched them while whispering. Waiting. Staying on alert. The next day everyone close to them was in and out of the apartment, visiting and getting a good look at the new additions.

After Wendy's death, all of her final instructions were followed to the exact letter. Her treasure box is now in the boy's closet. The letters she wrote to them to be given to them on their eighteenth birthdays are safely locked in Zion's safety deposit box along with his letter to them talking about the day of their birth. Lea decided she didn't need to write them a letter because she was going to spend every day showing them how much they mean to her and how she feels about being given the opportunity to be their mother.

Zion and Lea have taken the remainder of the year off from their jobs. Zion couldn't take three months off from work, but he's elected not to do any traveling until after the first of the year and will be going to every doctor's appointment for Lea and the boys and enjoying every bonding moment in between. He works from home four days a week, going into the office for meetings.

During one of Zion's work-from-home days, he and Sam are in his home office discussing the status of the security detail.

"I guess now we can get back to normal, or as normal as can be," Zion says to Sam. "It's been over a month since all this has happened. Do you think the threats are over and done with?"

"I'm confident they are. We even managed to keep it out of the papers. I agree with keeping the tracking on the phones and cars, though. That's good common sense," Sam says.

"I agree, we'll do that. Especially with Lea and the boys. God, three months, they're three months old and thriving. And I so love being a father more than I could have ever imagined," Zion says smiling.

"How is Miss Lea doing?" Sam asks.

"She's Miss Lea now? She's come to mean a lot to you and Mrs. Vance just as much as she means to me, huh?"

"Yes, she has. You take chances for people who mean something to you," Sam admits.

"Have you looked into getting her a gun and some training?"

"Yes. Is that what you really want? For her to be armed?"

"We discussed it. She needs some control. She needs to feel safe. We agreed when she's no longer on edge and is thinking clearly and not from being haunted by memories, you'll train her properly and not before then. I'm hoping, she'll agree to the training only and not the purchase. I want her confidence back before I put a firearm in her reach."

"Makes a lot of sense. How is she holding up?"

"I'm in a catch twenty-two situation. She won't go anywhere without me or security. I love that she's around me so much, that I know where she is and what she's doing. But I want her to feel free to go places and do things. I don't want this dictating how she exists."

"It hasn't been long enough, Sir. Give her 'til after the wedding. With her strong personality, she'll start taking back her independence."

Before Zion can respond, Lea knocks on door and enters. Following her is Greg. "Detective, thanks again for everything you've done. I appreciate it," Lea tells him. "I'll leave you all alone," Lea winks at Zion and he winks back.

"Greg, man, what's up? Or is this an official visit?" Zion asks him, standing to shake hands.

"Hell no, on a Sunday and I'm in sweats. I'm just stopping by to return something of your head security man," he says.

Greg pulls out a small plastic bag wrapped in a handkerchief and hands it to Sam. "I figured you would want to have these destroyed along with what they came from. Considering they don't match up to any of the other officers that were there that night, it was to my advantage to return them to the owner and to keep this out of my report," Greg looks between Zion and Sam. Sam takes the bag and pockets it without saying a word, gliding the bag across his leg, wiping it as clean as he can get it, considering.

"Well, back to the gym for me. Take care. And your boys are precious." Greg leaves without a backward glance.

Upon his exit, Lea enters the room, staring at Zion and Sam. They say nothing. Sam stands up, saying to Zion, "If you'll excuse me, Sir, I need to go run an errand. If you need me for anything else just call."

As Sam moves to leave the office, Lea stands in front of him and stops him in his tracks. "Yes, Miss Lea," he says to her.

"Sam, bend down please." He bends down and Lea kisses him on the cheek. "Thank you. I don't have any idea what it's like to have a father in my life. You've made me wish I had one like you. I'll never be able to convey my gratitude to you, ever. Thank you."

"Don't mention it, Miss Lea," he says and walks out of the room. Blushing.

Zion gets up from behind his desk. "Where are the boys at?" he asks before they get into what can be a heated discussion.

"Mrs. Vance is watching them," Lea stands not moving. Waiting for him to ask the all-important question.

"Lea, how much or what all do you know or think you know?"

"Know about what, Zion?"

"Woman, don't play with me. You just made a grown man I've known for years blush. And you kissed him on the cheek. I think I'm jealous. What do you know?"

"At first, I could not understand why this did not end up in the media. There's not one single thing about what happened. Three people dying and there was nothing. I told you, I'm a watcher. I read the police report from that night. There was only one shot to Martin's head. All the others were body shots. The shot to the head is what could have killed him. I know you didn't make it into the building until after Martin was killed. One cop is not going to shoot toward the head while all the others shoot toward the body. But a bodyguard, ex-military man, who has worked closely with his employer, will do pretty much anything he needs to when it comes to protecting him and those he loves. So, I'm thinking, two people who are not on the police force, get to the place to save someone they care about deeply. One has a gun and is ready and on alert to take the shot. The other one is going to ensure he does what he can gets that person into place to get that shot off. How close am I?" she asks him.

"Too damn fucking close," he admits. "I love you, Lea. Just know that okay? All I do, I do for us. Lea, I pray you don't regret us. Not ever. We met in March and now here it's November and we're parents. We haven't had enough Lea and Zion time before we became Lea, Zion, Caden, and Isaac. I promise to do all I can to make sure you're forever as important to me as the boys are and we'll get our time."

"I know, Bear, I know. It's taken me time to understand, but I know. I love you too. More and more with each passing moment."

ARE YOU GONNA DO THIS OR NOT? Sex Diva asks.

Hell fucking yes, I am.

Lea looks Zion in the eye and steps into dom/sub persona, "Z."

Zion slowly straightens up and looks down at Lea asking, "Yes? My Kitten."

"We haven't, well we—." Lea trails off, unsure of what to say.

"My Kitten. Are we being coy? What is it you would like?"

"I want you. Z. I've missed you inside of me."

Zion and Lea haven't had sex since she came home from the hospital. They've masturbated with each other. They've performed oral sex on each other. Their Naughty Sassy Journal is getting full with ideas of what more they want to include in their BDSM world.

"My Kitten. I'm not strong enough to resist you. How are your injuries?"

"Z. I don't want you to resist. I need you. Please."

Lea has asked Mrs. Vance to watch the boys for a few hours. She's taken them down to the corporate apartment to visit with his family and her mother. Lea has provided a catered dinner for them.

"How long do we have?" he asks her.

"About four hours. We're alone."

Zion holds out his hand and Lea excitedly places hers in it.

"Okay. Let's go." They run upstairs to their bedroom closing the door.

HEY, AREN'T WE SUPPOSED TO SLOWLY WALK.

BEAUTIFUL, WE DON'T HAVE TIME TO WALK, YOU WANNA GET IT IN DON'T YOU? Adonis asks.

WELL, YES, I DO, she replies back loving that Adonis is just as horny, freaky and controlling as she is.

Laid out on their bed is an extra-long cobalt blue scarf, a medium sized gold hoop and an adjustable leg spreader.

Zion picks up the leg spreader, gripping it by the ends and pull them apart. Staring at Lea, he licks his lips, grinning seductively.

"Z. Your shower awaits you." Lea, steps to the open door of the bathroom.

He walks over and caresses her cheek, "I'll be back in five minutes. Assume the wait pose."

"Yes. Sir."

While Zion is showering, Lea strips out of her clothes. She takes the scarf and puts it around her neck. She loops the ends between the gold hoop making sure it lays in the middle of her chest. She pulls both ends of the scarf under her arms, criss-crossing them behind her back, bringing them to the front. She ties it across her stomach, leaving the long ends to cover her womanhood.

Lea places the leg spreader on the bed. She takes a deep breath, shakes out her hands, twists her neck left and right and does a couple of squats and leg stretches.

WHY THE HELL YOU GOTTA DO ALL THAT? Sex Diva asks.

Did you see how far that contraption spreads?

YEAH, BUT ITS NOT LIKE HE GONNA SPREAD US THAT WIDE.

DIVA, HAVE YOU FORGOTTEN HOW LONG IT'S BEEN SINCE WE'VE BODILY CONNECTED? Adonis questions her.

YOU GOT A POINT. OKAY, KEEP STRETCHING. OH SHIT, SHOWER HAS STOPPED. POSITION, POSITION, POSITION.

Lea stops stretching and stands waiting. When Zion comes out of the bathroom, he stops in his tracks and stares with his mouth open.

How in the fuck did she get herself tied up like that. My Kitten been doing some practicing without me.

He approaches her, circling her without touching. He tests out the knots of the scarf around her waist and pulls on the gold hoop sitting in the middle of her chest. The scarf is pulled tightly enough to lift up her breasts and won't come loose from her waist.

Unable to hold back any longer, he stands in front of her, places his hands on both sides of her face and lifts her head up for a bruising erotic opened mouth kiss. Lea gives back the same, stepping forward to press her body against his. Any other time, Zion would step back and punish her for breaking formation but he's so excited, he forgets.

He breaks the kiss and has her lie on the bed.

"Scoot back to the headboard," he tells her.

Lea scoots back with excitement.

Zion picks up the leg spreader. He has Lea open her legs and he places the spreader at her ankles. He buckles them in. Spreading it slightly open, he bends her knees and crawls up the bed between her legs.

Lea bites her lips watching him. Zion, buries his face into her vagina, moving the ends of the scarf around her pussy with his face. He breathes in her scent, loving it. Lea tries to lift her feet.

"No," Zion says.

He lifts his knees up and places them on the leg spreader keeping Lea from moving. He moves the ends of the scarf to display her womanhood. He uses his right hand to spread her pussy lips open and uses his left hand to caress himself.

"Watch me," he tells her.

Lea stares at him caressing his penis, playing with his pre-cum.

"Let me taste it," she pleads.

He obliges her request by placing his fingers in her mouth. Lea licks them clean. He grins. Pulling back, he bends down in between her legs and French kisses her vagina. Opened mouth, tongue flicking, licking, lips pressing and sucking. Her clit is engorged with blood, and it's hot, and hard.

Lea bucks up and down enjoying the pleasure. Zion stops. He sits up and grips the gold loop on Lea's chest, lifting her up. She's staring directly at his dick. Licking her lips she takes in a deep breath, smelling his sweat and body wash.

"Suck me," he tells her.

Without hesitation Lea opens her mouth and swallows him. Using her hands, she strokes his balls and caresses his dick each time she pulls back to swirl her tongue around the tip.

"Oh, fucking hell yes." Zion roars.

Before Lea can bring him off, he pulls out and pushes her back onto the bed. Stepping off the bed, he pulls Lea to the end, grips the leg spreaders and opens them.

"Are you comfortable? Are you in any pain?" he asks Lea.

"Comfortable yes, pain no."

Zion grips the knot of the scarf at her waist with both hands. With Lea's knees bent, he mounts the bed and lifts her. He slides in slowly and sits allowing Lea to adjust to him.

"You, okay?" he asks her.

"Yes."

"Grip my arms, Lea." Zion steps out of persona. He needs to fuck Lea, and he's going to fuck Lea. Hard.

Lea grips his arms by the wrist.

"Ready."

"Zion, fuck yes. I'm ready."

Zion, gripping the scarf and Lea gripping his wrists, he starts to fuck her slowly. As they get into their rhythm, they speed up. For every thrust, push, and slide one gets, the other gives. Zion is loving the feeling of being inside of Lea and she's relishing the feel of his dick hitting every crevice inside of her.

Zion lifts her up a fraction of an inch. The adjustment causes him to caress Lea's g-spot.

"Oh, shit." She screams.

"Yes baby. That's it. Fuck yes." Zion encourages them both.

They're moving so hard and fast all you hear is their bodies slapping against each other. Lea digs her nails into Zion's wrists, trying to hold on. They're sweaty. Zion can tell she's about to cum.

"Cum baby, cum for me."

Lea lifts her bottom up as much as she can and cums, her body shaking. Zion grips her by the waist, releasing the ends of the scarf, burying himself deep in her and releases.

"Oh. Shit. Dammit," he yells.

He jerks, trying to keep the feeling of the orgasm going.

"Yes," they both scream.

Zion slowly rocks them back and forth, getting every feeling of the orgasm out, not wanting to stop. He finally pulls out and steps off the bed. Unlatching Lea's ankles, he tosses the leg spreader across the room.

It lands with a clink and thud. Lea laughs at the sound. Staring at Zion, he laughs too. He crawls into bed, bringing her into his arms.

"Lea, you've awakened my soul. In only nine months, you've fully changed everything about me with just a few words," he tells her.

She looks up at him asking, "What words, Bear? I love you?"

"No Kitten. By telling me you would not be a temporary fuck. Lea Grace Adams, my awakened soul is yours. Forever."

Tears run down Lea's cheeks. "Zion Isaac Landon, I'll carry your love with me forever, never feeling alone, never feeling unwanted."

Adonis and Sex Diva are hugged up, crying tears of ecstasy.

Epilogue

On December sixteenth, four months after Caden Royal and Isaac Turner came into the world, their father and mother makes their family official. Zion Isaac Landon marries Lea Grace Adams in an elaborate private ceremony at the Chase Park Plaza Hotel on the top-level overlooking Forest Park. There's an expected snowstorm on its way. It's St. Louis in December after all. By the time of the wedding, it's snowing heavily. For the guests, it doesn't matter. They checked into their rooms before the storm was due to arrive. It's a family and friends multi-day event.

At first, Lea was planning a simple justice of the peace ceremony. Nothing flashy or over the top, something quick to seal the deal. After the kidnapping, she needed to have a party, a welcome into the future and a big fuck you to the strife they experienced. When she approached Zion about it, he told her the skies the limit and she could do whatever she wanted. He wanted her to have the celebrity wedding of her dreams. She indulged and planned herself that and more not compromising on any detail without the celebrities.

Lea has chosen a form-fitting wedding gown with pure sex appeal. When she consulted Zion on the style he wanted to see her in, his request was, 'I want to see my babes' figure, and I don't want anything hampering me from standing close to her'. Zion is in a white tux tailored made for his muscle-bound body. Lea went with decorating colors of cobalt blue, her favorite, wine red, and silver.

The decorations created their own indoor winter wonderland. Flowing materials, sprinkling lights and idyllic throughout.

The ceremony is attended by everyone they're close to. Zion's parents Royal and Patty. His sister Star and her husband Garrett along with their twin daughters Denise and Cam. The Cupids are in attendance; Tom with his wife Linda and Crystal with her husband

Stanley, along with their children and grandchildren, fully forgiven and probably planning their next Cupid match.

Gordon and Lily are overjoyed for Lea. He even sheds a tear watching Ms. Adams escort Lea down the aisle. Sam along with his wife Mrs. Vance and their children and grandchildren are in attendance along with Saul, Ryan and Morgan with their significant others.

And to round off the guest list, the stars of the night Caden and Isaac steal the show from their mom and dad at every chance they could.

This ceremony is for those who are close to them, in their hearts, mind and souls, those that have touched them in many aspects of their lives whom they will forever treasure.

Thank you for taking this journey with me, Zion and Lea. Love, romance and happiness can happen at any age. You gotta know what you want, be willing to wait for it and be determined to work for it. Something the other BOMs, Bryson Mackey and Larson Davies, are having trouble with.